A TASTE OF PASSION

Closing her eyes, Drew twisted around to face Adam, then clasped her hands behind his neck and returned his kiss with three years worth of frustrated passion. If he didn't know how much she loved him now, he never would.

This time he did not back away. Groaning, he covered her face with kisses, then returned again to her mouth, parting her lips with the tip of his tongue. "Oh Jesus, Drew," he murmured. "What am I doing?"

"Don't you mean *we?*" she whispered. She wanted to tell him that she loved him but was afraid to say more. Twice before, Adam had controlled his ardor, then pretended that nothing had happened. She couldn't stand for that tonight. Her lips still tasting his and her arms still twined around his neck, she backed up until her legs touched the bed. She sank onto it, pulling him with her. She wasn't really sure what would happen next, but as long as he kept kissing her as if he couldn't get enough, that was all that mattered.

TODAY'S HOTTEST READS
ARE TOMORROW'S SUPERSTARS

VICTORY'S WOMAN   (4484, $4.50)
by Gretchen Genet
Andrew—the carefree soldier who sought glory on the battlefield, and returned a shattered man . . . Niall—the legendary frontiersman and a former Shawnee captive, tormented by his past . . . Roger—the troubled youth, who would rise up to claim a shocking legacy . . . and Clarice—the passionate beauty bound by one man, and hopelessly in love with another. Set against the backdrop of the American revolution, three men fight for their heritage—and one woman is destined to change all their lives forever!

FORBIDDEN   (4488, $4.99)
by Jo Beverley
While fleeing from her brothers, who are attempting to sell her into a loveless marriage, Serena Riverton accepts a carriage ride from a stranger—who is the handsomest man she has ever seen. Lord Middlethorpe, himself, is actually contemplating marriage to a dull daughter of the aristocracy, when he encounters the breathtaking Serena. She arouses him as no woman ever has. And after a night of thrilling intimacy—a forbidden liaison—Serena must choose between a lady's place and a woman's passion!

WINDS OF DESTINY   (4489, $4.99)
by Victoria Thompson
Becky Tate is a half-breed outcast—branded by her Comanche heritage. Then she meets a rugged stranger who awakens her heart to the magic and mystery of passion. Hiding a desperate past, Texas Ranger Clint Masterson has ridden into cattle country to bring peace to a divided land. But a greater battle rages inside him when he dares to desire the beautiful Becky!

WILDEST HEART   (4456, $4.99)
by Virginia Brown
Maggie Malone had come to cattle country to forge her future as a healer. Now she was faced by Devon Conrad, an outlaw wounded body and soul by his shadowy past . . . whose eyes blazed with fury even as his burning caress sent her spiraling with desire. They came together in a Texas town about to explode in sin and scandal. Danger was their destiny—and there was nothing they wouldn't dare for love!

Available wherever paperbacks are sold, or order direct from the Publisher. Send cover price plus 50¢ per copy for mailing and handling to Penguin USA, P.O. Box 999, c/o Dept. 17109, Bergenfield, NJ 07621. Residents of New York and Tennessee must include sales tax. DO NOT SEND CASH.

BLUEGRASS
and
ROSES

LEE
HAYWARD

ZEBRA BOOKS
KENSINGTON PUBLISHING CORP.

ZEBRA BOOKS are published by

Kensington Publishing Corp.
850 Third Avenue
New York, NY 10022

First Printing: December, 1995

Printed in the United States of America

For Curtis, Alex,
Catherine, and Juliet

Special thanks to Stephanie Bartlett and Curtis Hayden for reading every page of every book I've written; Tracy Gantz White, Managing Editor of *The Thoroughbred of California,* who answered innumerable questions and researched horse-racing data from the 1920s and 1930s for me; Jim Bolus, author of *Kentucky Derby* and many other books, who sent a copy of the 1926 Derby program as well as information about starting barriers; Joan Combs, Bluegrass guide extraordinaire; J. D. Andrews, who provided information on tobacco growing; my AOL Published Romance Writers Group for their encouragement and support; and John Scognamiglio, who is probably the nicest editor in New York.

One

Drew Ashworth couldn't keep herself from sprinting the last few yards to the bend in the long gravel lane leading to her house. No one could see her yet, and besides, Momma had given up on making her into a proper young lady years ago. Momma said that everything about Drew was too much of something to be correct—she was either too happy, or too sad, or too enthusiastic, or too impulsive. The list was endless.

Today she was too excited. Her best friend Trixie had slipped her a note during United States history, their only class together. It was in Drew's pocket now, but she didn't need to look at it. "Chase told me Adam's expected at Ballantrae Farm today, and there's going to be a party. Are you going?"

A sliver of doubt wedged itself into Drew's happiness. What if Adam wasn't visiting her parents when she got home? She gulped a huge breath of the sparkling April air and pushed the thought away. Adam always paid her folks a visit when he came back to Kentucky, no matter how much his father, old Hugh MacKenzie, looked down on the Ashworths.

She slowed at the turn and clasped her book bag demurely to her chest. Adam just had to be at Ashworth

Farm, and if there was going to be a party at Ballantrae, he'd invite them himself, the way he always did. Her half-brother Scott had been his best friend, and Scott had died saving Adam's life during the Great War.

That had been seven years ago, when Drew was ten. Adam had returned from France and adopted Drew as his little sister. He'd never let her down before—and there wasn't any reason to believe he would this time.

Ballantrae Farm parties were famous throughout the Bluegrass. The MacKenzies invited hundreds of people, rich friends from up north as well as local horsepeople. From the bourbon guests sipped while watching old Hugh show off his yearlings to the jazz band playing after dinner until the wee hours, the MacKenzies served up only the best and spared no expense. And whenever he was in Kentucky, Adam always made sure the Ashworths got a personal invitation. Drew sauntered around the curve, certain that he would be there.

Her shoulders slumped with disappointment. The only car parked in the semi-circular drive in front of the sagging front porch was her father's Model T, as old and worn as the house itself. Tears flooded her eyes, and she let them wash over her cheeks as she glared at the unkempt lawn and the run-down fences. The only part of Ashworth Farm that looked cared for were the tobacco fields with their neatly plowed furrows awaiting the young seedlings they'd begin transplanting soon from the seed-beds.

No wonder Mr. MacKenzie snubbed the Ashworths, and the rest of the horse people followed suit. One of the prettiest pieces of land in Bourbon County, right between two of the best studs in America, and all the Ashworths did was grow tobacco. Not a thoroughbred on the place, just draft horses and mules.

It was the tragedy of her life. She stopped short and brushed the tears away, a smile tugging at her lips. She was doing it again. Adam always teased her for being so dramatic about everything. Scott getting killed, now that was a real tragedy. So was her mother's long illness and her Uncle Andrew's mysterious death. Not having a horse was not truly a tragedy.

It was just a temporary inconvenience, one that she planned to remedy as soon as she could. And that wouldn't be long now that she was almost graduated from high school. She slung her bag over her shoulder and headed toward the white brick house.

The lace curtains at Momma's second floor window fluttered, and Drew waved. Momma must have had a good day if she was sitting in her chair instead of lying in bed. Maybe she would even come downstairs for dinner. And if Adam did show up after all, Momma would certainly make the effort for him. Everyone loved Adam.

Halfway up the steps to the front porch, Drew heard a car heading up the gravel drive. She'd recognize the sound of that engine anywhere. Her heart filled with so much happiness she could hardly breathe. She knew he'd come.

The bright yellow Stutz, its top folded back, rounded the corner and zipped up the drive. So unlike Adam, that flashy car—everything else about him was so reserved, so understated. Grinning at her, Adam waved, then pulled the car in next to her daddy's. Not bothering to smooth his wind-tousled black hair, he swung his long legs out of the sportscar, stood, and held his arms open.

Drew dropped her book bag on the porch, then raced down the steps toward him, the same way she'd been doing since she was a little girl. Which was exactly how Adam still thought of her, she knew. To him she was Scott's impish little half-sister, the child he'd rescued from the back of a runaway thoroughbred when she was only seven. He'd kept her secret, never revealing to anyone that she'd climbed on one of his father's racehorses, and she'd worshipped him from that moment on.

Her hero worship had changed to love, though, when she turned fifteen. Unfortunately, Adam hadn't seemed to notice that she'd grown up, but this was the day she planned to open his eyes. She flung herself into his arms and returned his hug, then tilted back her head and looked up into his eyes, sea green eyes framed by thick eyelashes and heavy black eyebrows. She raised herself up on her toes, then pressed her lips against his.

Suddenly, his arms tightened around her, and the friendly greeting kiss deepened into something entirely different. Finally, Adam pulled gently away from her lips. Her whole body trembling, Drew held her breath and leaned against him. It had been even more wonderful than she'd imagined. He had to know now how much she loved him—and she knew he felt the same way. How could he kiss her like that if he didn't?

He cleared his throat and stepped back, then carefully placed his hands on her shoulders. He shook his head. "As impetuous as ever, I see," he said, his eyes sparkling.

Speechless, she stared at him, embarrassment then anger flushing her cheeks. He'd turned her victory into a rout and put her firmly back into her place. Still, for one instant he hadn't thought of her as a child. She'd made him respond to her as a woman even though he chose to pretend otherwise.

"How are your parents?" he continued, lifting his hands from her shoulders and shoving them into his pockets.

She shrugged. "They're fine." She could play this game, too. "How are your folks?"

He lifted a thick black eyebrow. "The same. Mother is as serene as ever, and Father's still . . ." He sighed. "Anyway, Father has decided to get rid of Secret Wish if he doesn't do well in the Derby."

Drew sucked in her breath. "Oh, no," she said. She'd always thought of Wish as *her* horse, ever since Adam had shown her the wobbly-legged little foal with the white diamond-shaped star in the center of his forehead on the day he was born. Wish was the first offspring of First Star, Adam's favorite mare by Rock Sand, and his sire was Fair Play, the same stallion who'd sired Man O' War. Since Mr. Riddle, the owner of Man O' War, bred Big Red mainly to his own broodmares, Adam had decided to duplicate the match that had produced the best racehorse in the world; and Drew believed with her whole heart from the day of Wish's birth that Adam had succeeded. Later, Adam had even let Drew choose the colt's name when he was registered with the Jockey Club as a yearling. "It's not Wish's fault," she said. "They're working him too hard."

"I know. I tried to tell Father that Willie isn't the right trainer for Wish, but, as usual, he had no interest in anyone else's opinions." Adam's voice was bland although his eyes were narrow and hard.

Tears burned Drew's eyes. Goddamn old man MacKenzie. Willie Williams knew nothing about Wish's strengths and weaknesses; he'd raced the colt too often and at distances that were all wrong for him. He'd even run Wish when the colt was injured. She'd heard about it from Jack Nolan, Trixie and Rob's trainer at Blue Meadow Farm. "Willie's going to ruin that colt," he'd said. "Just you watch."

She blinked away the tears and forced herself to take a deep breath. "What are you going to do?"

"Father's in charge. It's his horse and his decision. He wants a Triple Crown winner. How he gets one isn't important."

"Buy Secret Wish from him."

"And then buy a farm to keep him on?" Adam smiled at her, but there was no laughter in his eyes. "I don't have the resources or the time."

"You could board him at Blue Meadow."

"Father would interpret that as an outright challenge. I'm not sure that would be the wisest course right now."

Drew clenched her teeth. Adam could be so infuriatingly calm. Nothing ever seemed to shake him up for long. Not even the prospect of losing Wish. "Don't you care?" she cried, unable to restrain herself or to keep the accusatory tone from her voice.

"Of course I do," he said quietly. "But there's nothing I can do. Especially not now." He winked at her. "Speaking of secrets, can you keep one?"

"You're trying to change the subject." She glared at him, her hands on her hips. "It's not going to work."

"All right," he grinned. "Let's go say hello to you parents, then."

Drew sputtered. "You always win. It's not fair."

"You have to promise not to tell anyone."

She tilted her head and looked up at him. Affection and amusement shone in his eyes, but that was all. Nothing had changed. She'd imagined so many times the day Adam would suddenly open his eyes and see that she was no longer a pig-tailed child. Rob didn't have any problems recognizing that she'd grown up—Trixie, giggling the whole time, had told her in strictest confidence that her big brother was crazy in love with Drew, that he thought she was the most beautiful creature he'd ever seen, that he sat in his office writing poems about her when he was supposed to be working on Blue Meadow's ledgers.

She almost laughed aloud. That sounded just like Rob, the dreamer who'd rather write poetry than run a farm. Why couldn't Adam think of her the same way?

"All right," she said. "I promise. What is this wonderful secret?"

He pulled an envelope from his pocket and handed it to her.

She ripped it open. It was an invitation to the party at

Ballantrae on Saturday. She'd known he'd bring one with him. "Is this the big secret?"

He shook his head. "It's the reason for the party that no one else knows—except for Mother and Father and Victoria, of course." The smile disappeared from his eyes, and his face became serious and older looking. "Victoria and I are planning to announce our engagement at the dinner."

A buzzing sound as loud as cicadas in July filled Drew's head. She had to say something, but her throat ached from holding back her tears. Adam smiled expectantly at her, waiting for her pleased response, oblivious to her anguish. How could he know he'd just destroyed her happiness forever?

"Congratulations," she managed to choke out. "I hope you'll—"

Momma appeared on the porch and waved at them before Drew could utter her lie. *I hope you'll both be as wretched and miserable as I am,* she finished silently as she watched Adam bound up the steps and greet her mother.

Two

Thank the Lord, Adam had finally gone home. Drew's face ached from smiling when she felt like dying instead. Hidden behind the wall of baled hay in the barn, she hugged her knees to her chest and let the tears wash over her cheeks. She'd heard about Victoria Seton from Trixie, who'd pressed Adam's younger brother Chase for information when he'd been at Ballantrae at Christmas. But Drew had never imagined Adam was truly serious about the snooty Philadelphia heiress. There'd been a lot of other women before Victoria; Drew had always imagined Adam was just playing around while he waited for her to grow up.

What a fool she was. A fresh wave of tears blurred her vision. She'd been so sure he'd see the difference in her. She'd tamed her unruly dark brown curls, rouged her cheeks and lips, even shortened her skirts to the fashionable new length. Maybe she didn't look like a flapper or a society lady, but she didn't look like a child, either. Why didn't he notice?

Because he was the fool, not she—that was why. And crying wasn't going to change that—or anything else. She leaned against a bale of hay, ignoring the prickles at her back. Gradually, her sobs gave away to deep, wrenching gasps, then to hiccups. She wiped her nose with the back of her hand and wished she'd remembered to put a handkerchief in her pocket.

The barn door creaked open, and a shaft of light lit up

the dust and little pieces of hay floating in the air. Drew stood and swiped at the back of her skirt as her father stepped into the barn.

Frowning, he paused at the entrance while his eyes adjusted to the dim lighting, and Drew noticed for the first time how much he'd aged in the last year. He was twenty-three years older than Momma, but he'd always been so healthy and vigorous compared to her that the age difference hadn't been all that noticeable.

But today his back looked stooped, and his gray hair seemed thin and lackluster. He was sixty-two, old enough to be her grandfather, and suddenly he looked it. Deep lines furrowed his forehead, and the skin at his jaw sagged wearily.

Drew shivered, pushing away the recognition of her father's mortality. Sixty-two wasn't that old. She lifted her hand and stepped forward. "Hi, Daddy."

He blinked, and his back straightened. "What are you doing out here?" A smile softened the harshness of his voice and lit up his deep brown eyes, eyes so similar to hers that people always remarked that they must be as common to Ashworths as staying blood was to the Man O' War line.

She tried to keep her tone light. "I just wanted to imagine what it would be like to have Secret Wish here."

He shook his head. "Well, just don't confuse imagination and reality. There hasn't been a thoroughbred on Ashworth Farm since before you were born. And I have no intention of changing my mind."

Fresh tears welled up in her eyes. Adam was lost to her forever, and now it looked as if Wish would be, too. If what Jack Nolan said about the colt's ankles was true, Wish would never win the Derby. "But Daddy—"

"I can't believe you're even asking again." He sighed loudly.

"This is different. It's not just any horse. It's Secret

Wish. Willie is ruining him, and you know it. We *have* to buy him." Her voice soared, then broke. "They're killing him, Daddy."

"I doubt that. What would MacKenzie want with a dead colt? All that's beside the point, anyway. We simply cannot afford a thoroughbred. Racing is for rich men or fools. I'm neither." Edward lifted her chin with a finger and looked into her eyes. He hated disappointing Drew, but he had no intention of allowing her to make the same mistakes his younger brother had. Ashworth Farm was still paying for Andrew's follies eighteen years after his death. "We've been over this road so many times, Drew. Too many times."

Her shoulders sagged, and she brushed knuckled fists across her tear-streaked cheeks. A glimmer of defiance still shone in her dark eyes, though. Edward knew what that look meant; Drew considered his refusal a temporary setback, not a defeat. She was gathering her forces for a second attack.

He held up his hand before she could speak. "No more. I have work to do." He headed toward the tool room at the far end of the old stone barn, then stopped and turned around. "I almost forgot. Your mother wants to talk to you. Probably about the MacKenzie's party." He winked at her. "A new dress or some such nonsense, I imagine."

Drew scowled at her father's retreating back. The last thing she wanted to discuss was what she was planning to wear to Adam's engagement party. She had absolutely no intention of going, anyway.

The minute she stepped into the huge marble-floored entry hall at Ballantrae, Drew knew she should never have let her mother shame her into coming. "Adam's feelings would be so hurt if you didn't go," Momma had said, "especially after he made such an effort to ask us. And your father and I couldn't possibly attend without you. I've been so looking forward to the opportunity to see some of my friends again. You know it's been three years since I last attended anything like this. I so seldom feel well enough to get out."

She'd chattered on and on, pulling one of her old dresses out of a trunk in the attic and insisting that with a few clever alterations it would be perfect for Drew to wear to the party. "It might be twenty years old, but it was the best money could buy," she said. "A Poiret, from Paris. Such attention to detail, such quality, such workmanship."

Drew had finally just given in and let Momma have her way. Now, though, she wished she'd stuck to her guns. Her mother's Poiret might have been the cat's meow in 1905, or whatever people said back then, but on her today it was a disaster. All the other women fluttered about like delicate butterflies in soft pastel day dresses with handkerchief hems and dropped waists while the navy sailor dress she wore looked exactly like what it was—some ancient horror from the attic.

Drew cringed as people glanced at the three of them, then let their eyes slide on by. No friendly welcoming smiles greeted them, but no one sneered openly, either. Everyone was too well-bred, she supposed. She didn't remember being embarrassed at the last party she'd been to at Ballantrae, but three years ago she'd been such a hoyden she'd spent most of the afternoon at the stables, then escaped to the veranda with Trixie when the music and dancing started in the ballroom upstairs. She wondered for a minute where all of Momma's good friends were, but as soon as she spotted Adam, the thought fled her mind.

He stood at the entrance to the west parlor, his arm linked with that of the beautiful young woman next to him. The girl's light brown hair, cut in a smart chin-length bob, glistened when she tilted her head back and smiled up at Adam. Her dress was a delicate powder blue trimmed with ivory satin bands, and her shiny new T-straps had never been two steps around a dance floor, let alone a country mile on a dirt lane.

Drew's heart constricted. So that was Victoria Seton, Adam's future wife. She was sophisticated and polished and so sleek Drew could almost hear her purr. No wonder Adam was besotted. No wonder he hadn't noticed how grown up Drew had become. Drew pushed a wayward curl back into the little bun at the nape of her neck and tucked her clutch more firmly under her arm. Next to Victoria she looked like a frumpy, old-fashioned hayseed.

While Adam chatted with a middle-aged couple Drew had never seen before, Victoria stared around the room, her china blue eyes glazed with boredom and her small red lips pursed in a slight pout. A shiver crawled down Drew's spine as the cold eyes passed over her, then shifted to her parents. When Victoria nudged Adam and he lowered his head so she could whisper in his ear, Drew was sure she was telling him that some hicks had trespassed on their party.

His face quizzical, Adam glanced in their direction, then grinned and held out his hand. "Welcome," he said, shaking her father's hand. He kissed her mother's cheek. "I'm so glad you could come."

Drew hung back while her parents exchanged pleasantries with Adam, but when he introduced Victoria, Momma prodded her forward.

"And this is our Drew," Adam said to Victoria. "She's been like a little sister to me ever since I first met her."

"How nice." Victoria's smile was condescending and brief. "Oh, look, isn't that Chase's friend from Harvard?" She nodded toward a handsome man with brown hair already streaked with gray even though he didn't look much older than Adam's younger brother Chase. Ignoring Drew, Victoria smiled at the tall young man.

Drew's cheeks burned and her insides tightened into a knot. She knew she didn't belong with the fancy people, the rich Yankees who came to their Kentucky farms for a month or two in the spring and fall. But she'd never be so rude to any who happened to show up in her home. Not that that was likely to happen. Except for Adam, the MacKenzies acted like the Ashworths didn't exist.

Well, that wasn't exactly true. Chase was pleasant enough, especially now that he was interested in her best friend, Trixie.

She made a point of surveying the room to hide her embarrassment. "Are Trixie and Rob here yet?" she asked Adam.

"They're out on the back terrace, I believe," Adam said, nodding toward the open French doors on the opposite side of the entry hall. He smiled warmly at Drew and lowered his voice to a conspiratorial whisper. "I think Chase has fallen pretty hard this time. I hope Trixie doesn't plan to break his heart. You know what a madcap she is." He laughed. "Actually, from what Chase's friend Neal has told me about his escapades at Harvard, I think Chase may have finally found his match."

Drew's face ached from her false smile, but she managed to keep her tone light. "Well, I guess that makes two of you." She glanced at Victoria, who continued to talk mechanically with Momma while gazing around the room, and her cheeks heated up again. "I'm going to look for Trixie," she said too loudly, almost defiantly.

Momma arched a delicate eyebrow at her, but Drew turned abruptly and scurried toward the doors. She didn't care what Momma was going to say when they got home—she couldn't stand to be in the same room with Adam and his fiancée another second.

Her face still hot and her teeth clenched, Drew slipped through the open doors. Trixie and Rob stood with Chase at the other end of the terrace.

Trixie grinned and waved at Drew. "There you are," she said. "We've been wondering when you were going to get here." Standing on tiptoe, she threw her arms around Drew and gave her a hug, then held her at arm's length. "Oh, Drew," she said, giggling. "That dress is almost as bad as you claimed. You poor old thing."

Shaking his head, Chase nudged Trixie with his elbow. "Don't listen to her. I think it's a nice dress."

Drew smiled at him. She felt better already. "Well, thank you, Chase, for the gallantry," she said, then turned to Trixie. "And thank *you* for the honesty."

"I guess that leaves the flattery to me," Rob said. He lowered himself to one knee and gazed up at Drew, self-mockery tingeing the adoration in his soft gray-blue eyes. He adjusted the steel-rimmed glasses on the bridge of his nose and cleared his throat, then caught up Drew's hand and pressed it to his lips. "Oh, divine angel, your presence lights up these dim surroundings with the warm glow of sunshine, the silvery radiance of moonbeams, the—"

Trixie hooted, and Rob clambered to his feet. "My little sister has never been one to appreciate poetry." He shrugged. "What I really want to say, Drew, is that it doesn't make any difference to me what you wear. I'm glad you're here."

"You guys are swell," Drew said. Even the yearning look in Rob's eyes, normally awkward and painful to her, was welcome after the humiliation she'd suffered a few minutes ago, and she couldn't imagine what life would be like without Trixie for her best friend.

"Anyone interested in visiting the barns?" Chase asked. "I think we have time for a tour before dinner."

"I'd love to." Drew patted her clutch. She'd wrapped a carrot in a handkerchief and stuck it in the bag right before they left. "I even brought a little present for Secret Wish."

"You spoil that colt." Smiling, Adam joined the group.

"Chase, I hate to tear you away from your friends, but Father would like to see you in the library." He turned to Rob. "You're welcome to escort the ladies to the barns, if you wish."

"I'd be delighted." Rob offered an arm to Trixie and then Drew as Chase and Adam strode across the terrace.

Staring at Adam's back, Drew ignored Rob's courtly gesture with as much kindness as she could muster. She knew exactly how Rob felt, loving a person who was in love with someone else, and she didn't want to hurt him the way Adam was hurting her. But she didn't want to give him any false hopes, either. "Let's go," she said when she saw that Rob's proffered arm hung limply by his side.

Trixie chattered on about Chase during the short walk to the stables. "Did you meet Chase's friend Neal?" she asked, then continued without a pause for Drew's response. "He's been going gray since he was sixteen. His family owned a big distillery over in Bardstown, but Prohibition almost ruined them. Chase says you'd never know it, though, by the way Neal lives. Chase says he's never seen a better handicapper. Neal's paid his way through Harvard with the money he makes betting on the horses. And Chase says that he wouldn't be surprised if Neal was a wealthy man again by the time he graduates."

Relieved that she didn't have to make conversation, Drew listened, smiling and nodding encouragement at Trixie until they reached Secret Wish's stall.

The handsome bay colt nickered and thrust his head over the top of the stall door when he heard their voices. Drew unwrapped the carrot and held it out to him. He nuzzled it from her hand, crunched it noisily, then nudged her with his nose as if to ask for another, the way he always did.

Drew laughed. That little nudge was like a joke between her and Wish. "Greedy boy." She rubbed his cheek, then laid hers against the side of Wish's neck. If Hugh MacKenzie sold Wish, she'd never be able to sneak him another carrot—Wish's groom old Ben always just winked at her and looked the other way.

The laughter left her voice. "It's a good thing you don't know what they have planned for you if you don't win the Derby." She turned back to Rob and Trixie and told them what Adam had said and then about her father's refusal to even consider having a thoroughbred on the farm.

"So, even if I could somehow raise the money, I wouldn't have a place to keep him," she finished, sighing.

His eyes shining, Rob smiled at her. "I'll buy him for you, then," he said. "And you can keep him at Blue Meadow."

Drew closed her eyes and thought about Rob's offer. It was tempting. She'd be able to see Wish whenever she wanted, and Rob's trainer Jack Nolan seemed to like and understand the colt a lot better than Willie Williams did. But there was no way she could accept that kind of a gift from Rob. It just wasn't fair to him. Or to her. Offers like that *always* had strings attached, no matter what the giver said. She shook her head. "No," she said at last. "I can't let you do that."

Rob shrugged. "Then I'll claim him for myself."

She didn't like that solution either. What she wanted was to own Secret Wish herself. Nothing less would do. The beginning of an idea poked at the edges of Drew's mind. Maybe there *was* a way for her to get the money, after all. Suddenly, it didn't seem so hopeless. "What if I got together enough money to claim him? Would you board him for me? I could help pay by working for you." Her voice lilted with her excitement.

"Now that sounds like a good compromise to me," Rob said, grinning.

A tingle ran down Drew's spine. It was risky, but the plan taking shape in her brain just might work.

Three

Drew set the lighted candle on the dusty top of the table next to her mother's old trunk. She'd loved poking about in the attic when she was a child, but the morning last week she'd spent with Momma looking through her mother's ancient things had been her first visit in years. It was the peculiar look on Momma's face when she carelessly pushed the beautifully beaded drawstring bag to the side that had jarred loose a long ago remembrance.

She and Trixie had been about eight years old when they stole candles from the kitchen and sneaked into the attic. Ignoring the cobwebs and thick layers of dust, they'd rifled through Momma's trunks, trying on her long dresses and fancy flower-covered hats. But the true treasure had been in *that* evening bag hiding at the bottom of the trunk.

Inside it was a sparkling diamond and emerald tiara. They'd taken turns setting it on their heads and pretending to be the Princess of Paris, then inventing stories to explain how Momma came to have such a thing and why she'd hidden it inside a bag in the bottom of a dirty old trunk. For months they returned to the attic regularly to play their favorite dress-up game.

Later, in one of Momma's books, Drew found an old photograph of her mother wearing the same tiara. She was dressed in an evening gown and standing next to a handsome young man with dark curly hair and dark eyes that gleamed with good humor and more than a little mischief. He looked like a younger version of Daddy, but Drew knew it had to be her uncle Andrew. She carried the picture to Momma in her bed and asked her about it.

Momma stared at the photograph for a long time before she spoke. "The dress was by Worth. Andrew and I were on our way to the coming out party of one of New York's richest debutantes."

Drew knew better than to say anything about Uncle Andrew. She pointed at the tiara. "What about that?"

Momma's voice was soft and faraway. "He gave it to me the same night. I never wore it again. My parents found it an unacceptable gift for a girl my age, and he refused to take it back. And then he died. I'm not even sure where it is. I always thought of it as bad luck."

"Was it real? Where did he get it?" Drew couldn't help herself even though she was afraid Momma might give her that sharp look she had and just stop talking.

"Oh, it was real, all right. He never said where he got it, but I suspected he won it in some game of chance. He was such a gambler. Over the years I've occasionally thought about asking your father to sell it, but I could never bring myself to go through with it. Someday it'll be yours, and you can do whatever you want with it." Momma blinked a couple of times, then lay back on the pillows. She waved her hand and mumbled, "I'm tired, child. Put the photograph back and let it be."

Drew had returned the picture, but the next time she and Trixie tried to get into the attic, the door was padlocked. In the six years since, she'd hardly thought of the tiara; other things—horses, and then Adam—interested her a lot more than some old jewelry, no matter how mysterious or expensive it was. But that funny look on Momma's face the other day had brought the tiara back to mind.

And then Trixie's casual comment about Neal Rafferty's betting had planted the seed of a plan.

Drew lifted the lid of the trunk and pawed through the folded layers of Momma's old dresses until she reached the beaded bag. Carefully, she loosened the cord and pulled apart the gathers, then peered inside. The tiara lay nestled inside a cambric handkerchief.

She extracted it gently, then held it next to the candle. The silver and green gems sparkled in the light like tiny moonbeams dappled with leaves. She was sure it was worth a lot of money, but she knew enough about pawnbrokers to realize she wouldn't be able to get nearly its value.

A little stab of guilt made her catch her breath as she slipped the tiara into her pocket. She'd never stolen anything before in her life, except maybe a few cookies from the kitchen. But this wasn't exactly stealing, was it? More like borrowing from herself, really. Momma had said the tiara would be hers someday. She just had to win enough at the Derby to claim Secret Wish and get back the tiara, and no one would ever know.

Talking her parents into letting her go to Louisville for Derby weekend wasn't a problem as soon as Drew told them she'd be accompanying Trixie and Rob. Daddy had started to object, but Momma silenced him with a glance. "Robert is a trustworthy young man," Momma had told him. "I know we can count on him to keep Drew out of trouble." She hadn't even minded that Drew would be missing a day of school. Daddy had muttered something about it making Drew even more horse crazy than she already was, but he gave in to Momma anyway.

The night before they left, Drew's excitement kept her awake so late she remembered hearing the grandfather clock in the parlor strike three. Less than two hours later

she was dressed and waiting for Trixie and Rob in the
rocking chair on the front porch, her purse, with her
mother's tiara inside it, clutched in her arms. When Rob's
ancient Oldsmobile runabout sputtered up the drive, she
grabbed her suitcase in one shaking hand and her purse
in the other and ran down the steps.

Leaving the car idling, Rob set the brake, then jumped
out and hoisted Drew's suitcase into the open box behind
the car's only seat. "We're off," he said.

Drew grinned and put her finger to her lips. "Shhh.
Don't wake Momma and Daddy. I'm afraid they'll change
their minds." She tucked her purse under the seat, then
slid across the seat next to Trixie and gave her friend a
hug. "Lordy, I'm so excited I can't stand it." She turned
to Rob, who'd squeezed in beside her. "Let's get out of
here!"

Several hours later, dusty, tired, and thirsty, they pulled
up in front of the Brown Hotel on Broadway. Drew clambered out of the car and stretched. Her body ached from
the jolting ride and the lack of sleep, but she didn't care.
Finally, she was in Louisville, and there wasn't anyone
around to tell her what to do—or not to do. If Rob
thought he was going to be the boss, he had another think
coming.

She brushed some of the dust from her dress and
laughed, pointing her finger at Trixie's dirty face. "Do I
look as awful as you do?" She grabbed her purse and
tucked it under her arm, feeling the reassuring bump of
the tissue-wrapped tiara. Her stomach quivered just thinking about it, but whether from guilt or excitement she
wasn't sure.

She'd told Trixie what she planned to do, and the two
of them had decided it was best not to tell Rob about the
temporary theft or pawning of the tiara or even that she
was going to try raising the money by betting on the
Derby. The less Rob knew, the better, they'd agreed. "He'd

probably make you give it back to your mother, then try
to lend you the money," Trixie had said. Drew had agreed
with her, and they'd plotted how to escape from Rob for
long enough to pawn the damn thing.

"I hope they'll let us in." Trixie nodded toward the marble entrance of the Brown Hotel, an impressively tall
building on the corner of 4th and Broadway. "It's a pretty
fancy place, and we look like coal miners." She put her
hands on her hips and glared at Rob. "I told you we
should have brought Mother's Cadillac."

He lifted his shoulders, then hefted the baggage from
the trunk onto the sidewalk. A porter appeared immediately and in a minute disappeared inside with their lug-
gage.

Trixie poked Drew in the ribs with her elbow. "He just
wanted to sit close to you," she whispered loudly enough
for Rob to hear. "He was afraid you'd sit in the back seat
if he brought the big car."

Rob ignored her remarks, but his cheeks flushed. "Ladies," he said. "After you."

Clutching her purse, Drew stepped inside and followed
the revolving door into the lobby. She was sure Trixie was
right about why Rob decided to drive the tiny, open
Oldsmobile. His leg had been pressed tightly against hers
during the entire trip no matter how hard she tried to scoot
next to Trixie. After a while she'd just given up because,
in truth, there was really no way to avoid touching him
when the three of them were crammed together in a seat
meant for two.

It wasn't that she *minded* touching Rob, either. She just
didn't want him to get the wrong notion. He had no idea
how she felt about Adam, so he simply didn't realize that
no matter what he did, she wasn't going to fall in love
with him. Adam was the one she loved; Rob was a dear
friend, but nothing more.

Drew smiled at Trixie and Rob as they emerged from

the revolving door, and the three of them presented themselves at the check-in desk. Rob answered the clerk's queries, and a few minutes later they followed the bellhop into the elevator, then to their rooms on the fifth floor.

Rob tipped the bellhop after he deposited the baggage in Trixie and Drew's room. "Well," Rob said, "are you ready for the MacKenzie's Derby Eve bash? Or do you want to unpack and rest for a bit?"

Trixie started to speak, but Drew cut her off before she could say the wrong thing. "Give us an hour," she said, narrowing her eyes to warn Trixie to keep her mouth shut. She knew how anxious Trixie was to see Chase, but this might be Drew's only chance before the Derby to pawn the tiara at the pawnshop she'd spotted a few blocks from the hotel. "It'll take me at least that long just to clean up."

Glancing conspiratorially at Drew, Trixie chimed in her agreement. "We'll come and get you when we're ready," she said. "You know us—it might take a while."

Rob shrugged. "I'll be waiting, then. If I'm not in my room, try the hotel coffee shop."

Drew frowned at Trixie after the door closed behind Rob. "Isn't the coffee shop right off the lobby?"

Trixie nodded. "It has windows that face the sidewalk, too."

"So, we'll just have to use a back entrance," Drew said. She unbuttoned her dress and tossed it on the bed, then rummaged through her suitcase. She shook the wrinkles out of the pink crepe dress she was planning to wear to the MacKenzie's party and held it up for Trixie to inspect. "What do you think? Momma actually let me buy two new dresses."

"I love it," Trixie said, "but don't you think you'd better wash your face before you put it on?"

Drew laughed and draped the dress over a chair before she stepped into the tiny bathroom. She took off her hat, removed her hairpins, and fluffed her dark hair over her shoulders. Not even being cooped up for several hours under a hat could tame her unruly curls. She tied her hair at the nape of her neck with a pink ribbon, then hurriedly splashed water on her face and patted it dry with a white, monogrammed towel. She inspected herself in the mirror. Compared to Victoria, she looked so . . .

Unpolished. Unsophisticated. Gawky.

"Hurry up," Trixie called from the other room. "We've got a lot to do in an hour."

Drew stuck out her tongue at her reflection in the mirror. Well, Adam could have picture-perfect Victoria. At this minute she loved Secret Wish more than she did him anyway. And Secret Wish was going to be hers.

She rouged her cheeks and lips, gave her hair a pat, and strode back into the bedroom, where she slipped quickly into her new dress and T-strap shoes while Trixie washed up and primped.

Five minutes later, Drew opened the door quietly and peeked into the hall. Neither of them had heard Rob's door open, so she was pretty sure he was in his room. Still, it was easier to be cautious at this point than to have a lot of explaining to do. "All clear," she said, and the two of them scurried to the stairway, which they'd figured was a lot safer than waiting for the elevator.

Stifling their giggles, they trotted down the stairs, then crossed the lobby as primly and unobtrusively as possible. When they reached the sidewalk, Drew laughed and patted her handbag. "We made it!" she said, mentally ticking off another obstacle on her list. Of course, there were about a dozen left, and any one of them could keep her from owning Secret Wish.

But she'd worry about that later. Right now, she only had one goal—to get as much money as possible for the tiara.

Four

Drew couldn't help gaping in astonishment at the luxury before her when she and Trixie and Rob stepped into the MacKenzies' private railroad car. Such a contrast from the dirty, crowded railroad yard! Heavy hunter green velvet drapes covered the windows, and polished cherrywood wainscoting trimmed the walls. The soft light of the small chandeliers sparkled in the china and crystal, and cast seductive shadows over the plush velvet and tapestry upholstery. Women in lovely gowns and men in black evening dress stood in clusters throughout the car.

Trixie nudged her in the side with an elbow as they threaded their way through the crowd. "Close your mouth," she whispered, then giggled. "Here comes Chase. And he's got that Neal Rafferty with him. Lord, he's good-looking."

Drew struggled to compose her face into a study of nonchalance, as if she attended Derby Eve parties all the time and there was nothing extraordinary about a railroad car that probably cost ten times as much as her house. After all, she'd been to Ballantrae, and it was far grander. And she had every right to be here; not only had Trixie and Rob invited her, but when Adam had discovered that she was coming to Louisville for the Derby, he'd also seen to it that she had an invitation of her own.

Chase wrapped his arm around Trixie's shoulders and pulled her close to him, then shook Rob's hand. "Glad you could make it," he said to Drew. "Have you met Neal?"

"Not really," Drew said, offering her hand.

Neal shook her hand. "I remember seeing you at Adam and Victoria's engagement party, though. I never forget a beautiful woman." His friendly, open grin made it clear that even though he knew his compliment sounded glib, it was sincere, and that the faint mockery in his tone was directed at himself.

Despite her own better judgment—and Trixie's warnings—Drew was intrigued. "I remember you, too," she said.

He ran his hand through his thick, gray-streaked, light brown hair and laughed. "People always remember my hair. They can't figure out if I'm an old man with a young face or a young man with old hair."

"Oh, I didn't have a hard time figuring that out," Drew said, then blushed. Why was she always so obvious? "I mean, Trixie told me you went to Harvard with Chase." Worse and worse. Now he'd know that she and Trixie had talked about him. Her cheeks grew even hotter.

Neal's smile broadened. "And she told me that you were quite a horsewoman. Is that true?"

Trixie hadn't mentioned talking to Neal about her. Drew shot a quick frown in her direction, but she and Chase had settled themselves cozily on an overstuffed burgundy velvet sofa several feet away.

"It's true," Rob said before Drew could answer. "Sometimes I think Drew was born on a horse. Best exercise boy we've ever had."

"Don't tell Daddy that." Drew laughed to cover her embarrassment. "There hasn't been a thoroughbred on the place since before I was born," she explained to Neal. "I did all my riding at Blue Meadow and Ballantrae whenever anyone would let me. I was convinced I was going to be a great jockey. It didn't matter that I was a girl. I always just imagined that I'd cut all my hair off and no one would ever know." She smiled ruefully. "What did matter was that I grew too much."

"Personally, I think you grew just fine. Hair or not, you'd never have fooled me." Neal's gaze was frankly admiring.

Drew's cheeks betrayed her again, but she refused to be daunted this time and stared right back at him. With his soft golden-brown eyes and full lips, he was even more handsome than she remembered; and his open admiration did a lot more to restore her damaged self-confidence than Rob's adoration did. Rob was so dull. Neal radiated excitement, daring. If she couldn't have Adam, she could at least have some fun. "Well, thank you," she said.

"My pleasure. And it would also be my pleasure to fetch a drink for you. I brought along a case of medicinal spirits as a gift to the MacKenzies—you know my family distilled bourbon before Prohibition?"

Ignoring Rob because she knew his mouth was pinched into that disapproving look of his, Drew nodded. "I'd love a drink."

"May I offer you one as well, Carlisle?" Neal asked Rob.

"Why not?" Rob said, but he didn't sound very happy about it to Drew. As soon as Neal disappeared into the crowd at the back of the car, Rob said, "Do you think that's wise, Drew?"

She shrugged. Wise people never seemed to have much fun. "Well, at least it's not boring. Besides, I'm sure that if I do anything stupid, you'll tell me about it."

The hurt look in his eyes immediately made her sorry for her meanness, but before she could make amends, Neal arrived with their drinks. Drew accepted hers, then clicked it against Neal's.

"To your health," he said with a wink. "It's medicine, remember."

Drew sipped the bourbon and water cautiously. Neither Daddy nor Momma ever drank, and alcohol had been illegal since she was eleven. The first—and only—time she'd ever drunk any was at a roadhouse on the Paris Pike that she and Trixie had sneaked into a couple of months ago, and the stuff had been awful. "Gin," they'd called it, but as far as she was concerned it had tasted like kerosene.

The bourbon smelled considerably better than the gin had and didn't burn her throat nearly as bad. She smiled at Neal. "This is good."

"You sound surprised," he said. "Haven't you ever drunk bourbon before?"

"I'm sure she hasn't," Rob said. "She's only seventeen, Rafferty."

"Almost eighteen," Drew muttered, narrowing her eyes at Rob. She gulped a big drink of the bourbon, then looked defiantly at Rob. Just let him try to tell her what to do! That was why it was so important to her to buy Secret Wish with her own money—if Rob tried to take over, she could just remind him that she was the owner. Her stomach tightened a little when she thought of the hundred dollars she'd gotten by pawning the tiara. She hoped it was enough.

And she hoped like hell she bet it on the right horse. She turned her face toward Neal so she didn't have to see the hang dog look on Rob's face. It was time to change the topic to something much safer—and far more interesting. "Who do you favor tomorrow?" she asked.

"Not Secret Wish," Neal said quietly, with a glance in Chase's direction. "The odds are going to be great, but that doesn't help unless the individual has a chance of winning. And Secret Wish has no chance at all. His legs are in terrible shape." He sipped his bourbon from the sparkling crystal glass. "What I always look for is an 'overlay'—a good horse with high enough odds that it makes the risk worth it. There's no point in putting your money on the favorite if you don't get something to show for it."

Rob shook his head. "I don't agree entirely," he said. "Both Bubbling Over and Pompey look good, and if I bet a hundred dollars on either, I'll surely win something. On the other hand, if I bet on a longshot, I might lose it all."

Neal lifted his shoulders in a shrug, but his face remained bland. "Favorites don't always win. You still might lose it all. Of course, if you really believe Pompey or Bubbling Over are going to do it, bet on them. Right now, though, I'm planning to put my money on Rock Man."

"Rock Man? The colt from Sagamore Stable?" Drew said. She'd read everything she could get her hands on about the nominees during the last couple of weeks, so she knew Rock Man had won four stakes races as a two-year-old, as well as the Chesapeake Stakes at Havre de Grace just three weeks ago. Still, the colt hadn't been touted as a favorite, not with Pompey and Bubbling Over in the running. "What about Colonel Bradley's entry? He has two horses running this year."

"Between the two of them, I favor Bubbling Over," Neal said. "Bagenbaggage is a fine colt, too, but I've heard that Bradley's bet $85,000 on a horse-on-horse wager—Bubbling Over against Pompey. And there's another rumor going around that Colonel Bradley's promised his jockey Albert Johnson a big bonus if Bubbling Over comes in first. Still, the odds—especially with an entry of two horses—aren't likely to be great." He rattled the ice cubes against the side of his glass before he drank. "No, I think Rock Man's the ticket. I talked to his trainer Bud Stotler yesterday, and he says the colt is in fine form." He smiled at Drew.

"Isn't he the one who likes to set the pace, but then fades?" Drew asked. She remembered reading something about that but couldn't place exactly what.

"That's true. That's what happened at the Preakness a couple of weeks ago. He ran like a pig—finished tenth. Got in a speed duel with Dress Parade and Canter and wore himself out. But I watched his workout yesterday. He breezed right through it. To be safe, though, I'm planning on a win-place-show bet."

Drew stared at Neal over the top of her glass and finished the rest of her drink. A second later a waiter with a silver tray picked up the glass and offered her another filled with a fizzy pale liquid.

"Ah, champagne," Neal said, taking the bottle from the tray and pouring it carelessly into his empty bourbon glass. The champagne frothed over the top and ran down the sides of the glass. Hanging onto the bottle, he waved away the waiter. He lifted his glass. "Bubbling Over would make a more appropriate toast, but this one's to Rock Man—and some terrific odds."

When Drew lifted her glass and met Neal's eyes, a strange shiver twitched down her back. Maybe Trixie was right—maybe Neal *was* a wild Irishman, a rake, a ladies' man who shouldn't be trusted with a girl's reputation. On the other hand, he was charming, handsome, and interesting—and, besides, she was contemplating trusting him with her money, not her heart. She smiled at him, her mind made up. She couldn't risk dividing her small stake three ways, but if the odds turned out to be as good as Neal predicted, a show bet might do the trick. "To Rock Man," she said just as Adam stepped into the railroad car with Victoria on his arm.

Instantly the warm pleasure of the liquor flowing through her veins disappeared, and Drew stiffened. Her first impulse was to hide the glass of champagne behind her back, but she restrained herself. Adam was neither her father nor her brother. It was no more his business what she did than it was Rob's. Sometimes it was just easier to pretend that Adam didn't really matter to her anymore

than it was to admit how much it hurt to see him with
Victoria. Brashly, she drained the champagne and held her
glass out to Neal for a refill.

Neal smiled into her eyes and sloshed more champagne
into her glass. "So, you have money to bet tomorrow?"

Watching Adam and Victoria's progress through the
crowded car out of the corner of her eye, Drew nodded.

"How much?"

She glanced at Rob, wishing he would just go away for
a while instead of watching her with that irritating concerned look in his eyes. She'd been purposely vague with
him about how she was planning to come up with the
money to claim Secret Wish.

Adam and Victoria reached their little circle before
Drew had to answer, and Adam enveloped her in a big
hug, carefully kissing her on the cheek. As usual, Victoria
looked cool and elegant, but somewhat annoyed, as if she
would really rather not be there. Chase had told Trixie,
who had told Drew, that Victoria wasn't particularly interested in horses, and that she considered the whole business of racing a waste of time. "If Adam listens to her,
I don't foresee him spending much time in Kentucky anymore," Chase had said. "She'll probably try to drag him
off to Europe to visit museums and art galleries and cou-
turiers."

Drew had been horrified to think that Adam would
choose a fiancée who disliked horse racing, but at this
point—especially after the bourbon and champagne she'd
drunk—she was beginning to think maybe he was getting
what he deserved. Drew greeted Victoria politely, but remained silent while Rob and Neal chatted with her about
the train trip down from Philadelphia.

Adam leaned toward Drew and whispered in her ear.
"What are you doing with that?" he said, nodding toward
her drink.

Drew's cheeks burned again, but with a flash of anger

this time rather than embarrassment. "I'm old enough." Her voice came out a little louder than she meant it to.

Rob lifted both eyebrows above his glasses this time and looked back and forth from Drew to Adam.

"She's special to me," Adam told Rob quietly, with a meaningful tilt of his head in Neal's direction. "Take care of her."

"I intend to." Neal responded before Rob could say anything.

The only reason Drew gritted her teeth and kept back the angry words was because of the smug, knowing look on Victoria's face. She'd be damned if she'd give that woman anything to gossip about. Dredging up the sugariest tone she could muster, she drawled instead, "Well, thank you, boys. I truly appreciate your concern." She rested her hand on Neal's arm. "Would you all please excuse me? I think I need some fresh air."

"May I accompany you?" Without waiting for her answer, Neal tucked Drew's hand under his arm.

Shaking his head, Adam watched as Neal and Drew wove their way through the crowd and stepped outside. He liked Rafferty well enough, but for some reason he didn't quite understand, seeing the fellow with Drew made him damned uneasy. Probably because he didn't trust the bastard. He turned to Rob. "Did she have much to drink before we got here?"

"Only two drinks," Rob said, "but the first one was pretty strong. And she isn't used to booze." He stared at the door Drew had walked out of, his face a picture of misery.

Adam couldn't stand to watch him. Poor guy had it bad. Not that he blamed him—nor Rafferty either, for that matter. Drew was definitely a beauty—lively big brown eyes, thick shiny hair, long coltish legs. It was true she knew very little about clothing, but somehow, because it was Drew, it didn't seem to matter what she wore. "I hope she's going to be all right."

Victoria frowned at him. "Why are *you* so concerned about her? She's hardly our type," she said, a slight sneer lifting one corner of her mouth.

Adam winced at her acid tone, but didn't comment on it. He knew Victoria was a snob, but she was also intelligent, well-educated and interesting, as well as beautiful. Furthermore, most of the people he knew were snobs. It wasn't a trait he admired, but he'd had a lot of practice overlooking it. "She's always been like a little sister to me," he said, only the slightest hint of irritation creeping into his voice.

"Well, it looks to me as if your *little sister* is growing up," Victoria said.

Adam sighed. He knew Victoria was right.

Five

Drew opened her eyes slowly, squinting into the piercing morning light. Her head throbbed, her stomach rolled, and her mouth was so dry she could hardly swallow. Lordy, what had she done to herself? She squeezed her eyes shut again. She couldn't imagine dragging herself out of bed when she felt this awful. Maybe if she slept a little longer it would just go away.

She turned slowly onto her side and nestled her head gently into the pillow, hoping that the softness would ease the pain. But it didn't work; in fact, moving made it even worse, and she realized she wasn't going to fall asleep again. So this was what Rob had warned her about last night. Of course, she hadn't listened to him. Or to Adam either.

Another jolt of pain invaded her entire skull, shaking loose a barrage of embarrassing memories from the night before. When Chase had announced that he and Trixie were going dancing back at the Rooftop Garden at the Brown Hotel, Drew had let Neal talk her into going with them even though Rob protested. Then a little while later, Rob had shown up at the nightclub, along with Adam and Victoria. Drew had been so sure that they were there only to spy on her that she'd decided to give them an eyeful. She'd smiled encouragingly at Neal while he spiked her Coca-Cola with bourbon from the flask he carried in his jacket pocket, then let him sweep her off her feet in a daring dip at the end of "Tea for Two." To top everything off, she'd thrown her arms around his neck and kissed him right in the middle of the dance floor.

Remembering *that* made her stomach even queasier than it had been before, and she pulled her knees up closer to her chest. If Rob went home and told Momma and Daddy, her goose would be cooked. No, it would be burned to a crisp. They'd never let her out of the house again.

Still, it *had* been fun—for a while. Just the expressions on Adam's face—first shock, then anger, then unhappiness—had made it worth it. It didn't even matter that Victoria sat smirking next to him.

That wasn't really the truth. Another sharp pain stabbed her forehead. For the life of her, she couldn't figure out what Adam saw in Victoria—except for her beauty and her wealth. Drew grimaced. If she didn't feel so much like crying, she'd laugh. Victoria was everything Drew wasn't—polished, sophisticated, cool, rich. Drew was just a hayseed, an incorrigible tomboy. No wonder Adam didn't take her seriously.

And last night certainly hadn't helped her cause. She'd proved to him that she was everything a nice girl shouldn't be. A shudder ran down her spine when she remembered the last emotion in Adam's eyes—coldness, pure and simple. He'd stared at her as if he didn't know her, and didn't care to. She'd seen him look at other people that way, but never her. His eyes had always had a smile for her, even after he'd come back from France. She'd only been ten at the time, but she had seen the black despair in his face when he didn't think she was watching. The only time it went away was when he smiled at her. She'd been special to Adam; she knew it.

But not now. Her behavior last night had ruined everything, even more than Victoria had. She had to make Adam forgive her, somehow. She couldn't bear it if he ever looked at her that way again.

She heard Trixie stirring in the bedroom and sighed. Everything had been confusing enough before last night, but now it was a real mess. Rob was angry with her; Adam didn't care about her at all; and Neal probably thought she was a slut. No matter what, though, Trixie was still her friend, and Trixie would make sure Rob carried through with their plans to claim Secret Wish even if he was mad at Drew. At least she didn't have to worry about that.

Slowly, she pushed herself up on her elbow, fighting back the nausea that swirled up from her stomach to her throat. Gritting her teeth and willing herself to ignore the way her body felt, she sat up, then swung her feet over the edge of the bed.

Trixie poked her head into the room. "Do you feel as awful as I do?"

"You mean like the Derby's already been run and your head was the racetrack?" Drew stood up and stretched carefully.

"That sounds about right," Trixie said. She giggled, then groaned. "It even hurts to laugh."

A loud thump rattled the door. "Are you two up?" Rob's voice sounded impatient. "We need to get going."

"Hold your horses," Trixie said. "We're not dressed yet."

"Well, hurry it up."

He definitely seemed cranky, Drew thought, and probably for good reason. "We'll be right there," she called. "Wait for us in the coffee shop."

"All right." The thud of his footsteps receded down the hallway.

Drew gave Trixie a wobbly grin, then covered her mouth with her hand and scurried toward the bathroom. She wished she had someone else to blame for her misery, but she knew it was her own damn fault.

* * *

A couple of hours later Drew followed Trixie into the Blue Meadow box at Churchill Downs. Breakfast had helped her touchy stomach, and time had soothed the horrible headache she'd awakened with, but she still didn't feel quite normal. And the sounds and smells of the racetrack didn't help much. She didn't mind the odors of popcorn and burgoo, but the reek of Hugh MacKenzie's cigar smoke from the neighboring box threatened to undo all the good of the big platter of scrambled eggs and toast Neal had insisted was the best thing for a hangover when he stopped by the coffee shop where she and Rob and Trixie were ordering breakfast. That, and a little "hair of the dog" would work wonders, he'd claimed.

Well, she'd taken his advice on the first and passed on the latter. "Dog hair" was about the last thing she wanted. Even the faint smell of bourbon on Neal's breath had been too much for her—and not even Rob's glare could provoke her into taking Neal up on his offer.

She settled herself next to Trixie, and Rob plopped down in the seat next to her. At least the weather was better than last year's Derby, when the skies had opened at post time and turned the track into mud soup. She had no idea whether Rock Man was much of a mudder. Thank the Lord for one thing she didn't have to worry about.

A little gust of wind played with her hair, and she tapped her lace-trimmed hat more securely onto her head. Normally she didn't much care for hats, but everyone wore one to the Derby. She grasped her handbag tightly, and a nervous spasm skittered down her spine at the thought of the hundred dollars inside. Maybe she should just leave the money there, not bet anything, and reclaim the tiara. She was already in plenty of trouble as it was—especially if Rob or Adam said anything to her parents. If she lost the tiara as well . . .

She shuddered. She didn't want to think about it. Losing the tiara meant losing Secret Wish as well. And if that happened, it didn't matter how much trouble she was in. She was going to be miserable for the rest of her life anyway.

So there really wasn't any point in worrying about it. She had one chance, and she was going to take it—the consequences be damned.

Rob touched her shoulder. "Feeling better?"

Drew shrugged. She had no intention of letting Rob know how horrid she'd felt this morning. She was tired of his condescending "I told you so" smiles. "I didn't really feel that bad," she said. "I'm just nervous about the race."

Trixie giggled, and Drew aimed a frown at her, then shook her head slightly. She needn't have worried—before Trixie could say anything to contradict Drew's claims, Chase and Neal tromped noisily into the Ballantrae box to the right, with Adam and Victoria following more sedately after them.

A hot flush spread up Drew's neck to her cheeks, but she made herself keep her chin up and smile directly at all of them. If she acted as if everything were normal, Adam would have to, also. She wouldn't give him a chance to say anything. She turned her smile on a little more brightly for Neal. "Hi, you all," she said. "I'm so excited I can hardly stand it."

Neal grinned at her. "Only three more races to go." He nudged Chase. "Come on. Let's go visiting."

The two of them ducked under the waist-high rail separating the boxes, and Trixie stood and hugged Chase.

Immediately, Neal slipped into Trixie's empty seat next to Drew. "You look swell," he said.

Drew wanted to roll her eyes, but she knew it would hurt her head too much. "And Secret Wish is going to come in first," she whispered to him, her voice thick with sarcasm.

"No, I mean it," Neal said. "Your dress is lovely, and you look radiant. Ah, the resilience of youth."

"You're not *that* much older than I am," Drew hissed. She glanced at Rob to see if he was eavesdropping on their conversation, but he was discussing the next race with Trixie and Chase.

"I've got the gray hair to prove it." Neal ran his fingers through his backswept hair.

Adam leaned over the railing. "Don't believe a word this man says, Drew," he said. "He's definitely one Irishman who's kissed the Blarney Stone."

"Come on, Mac," Neal said. "I was just starting to make some headway here."

Drew looked back and forth at the two of them while they bantered. Adam's handsome face showed not the slightest trace of disapproval for her behavior last night, but nonetheless there was a hint of strain in his jovial tone. Suddenly, Drew realized that Adam didn't really like Neal, but he was too reserved and polite to ever let it show because Neal, after all, was Chase's best friend.

How it must gall Adam that she seemed to have fallen for Neal's charm as well. Drew compressed her lips to keep them from breaking into a gleeful smile. Adam certainly didn't need to know that she wasn't taken in by Neal one bit. Sure, he was good-looking, a great dancer, and a smooth talker, but none of that really mattered to her, not when she loved Adam as much as she did.

The urge to grin faded, and Drew forced herself to exchange a tepid greeting with Victoria.

"And how is our little Drew feeling this morning?" Victoria asked.

"Swell," Drew said, forcing a cheerful tone and wondering again for the hundredth time how Adam could marry such a bitch. Was he really so unhappy with his life that it didn't matter to him that Victoria was cold and mean? Or was he so infatuated with her that he didn't see what she was really like? "How about yourself?"

Instead of answering, Victoria laid a possessive hand on Adam's arm. "The race is about to start," she said.

Drew lifted an eyebrow. Victoria didn't care about the race; for some reason, she didn't like Adam paying any attention to Drew. Maybe she sensed that Drew was in love with Adam.

Her thoughts were interrupted by the falling of the yellow flag and the swelling noise of the crowd. Everyone around who wasn't already standing jumped up, and Drew joined them. She hadn't even looked at the program yet so she didn't know who was running, but the beauty and excitement and power of the race caught her up anyway. A few seconds later the thoroughbreds thundered by, and the stands erupted into a roar right before they crossed the finish line.

"Port Star. No surprise there," Neal said when things quieted down. He sat down and leaned back in the chair, crossing his long legs in front of him.

Drew lowered herself into her seat, too. "Did you bet on him?"

"Nah," Neal said. "Look at the board. See the odds for number four?"

"Two-thirty-to-one," Drew said.

"He was one of the favorites," Rob said, as if that proved the point he'd been trying to make the night before.

"What if he'd stumbled coming out of the gate, though?" Neal said. "You'd have risked your money for damn little return."

Trixie leaned forward from the seat she'd taken next to Chase in the second row of the Blue Meadow box. "Are you still arguing about *that?*" She nudged Drew. "We're going down to place a bet on the next race. Want to come?"

Drew shook her head. "I'm saving it all up for the big one," she said.

"Now there's a girl after my own heart." Neal grinned triumphantly at Rob. "Wish I could toast you with a mint julep," he said to Drew, "but this is all I have." He patted his jacket pocket. "Care for some?"

"No, thanks." Drew shuddered at the thought.

Adam propped his elbow on the rail between the boxes and questioned Neal about the next race. Drew listened half-heartedly while the men talked; there was only one race she cared anything about this time, and she was so preoccupied with it that it was hard to muster any enthusiasm for anything else.

The next two races went by for Drew in a blur of noise and commotion, and the harder she tried to relax and pretend to be carefree, the more tense she became.

Finally, Adam stood and announced that it was time to watch the horses walk to the paddock. "Anyone else care to go with me?"

Victoria and his parents demurred, but everyone in the Blue Meadow box joined him. They made their way from the clubhouse to the brick pathway, moving ahead slowly with the mass of racetrackers heading toward the paddock. It took several minutes, but they reached the paddock just as Secret Wish was led in by the Ballantrae trainer, Willie Williams.

Adam grabbed Drew's hand and pulled her toward the paddock gate. "Come on," he said. "I'll take you inside with me." He turned to the others. "Chase, you can come along, too, if you want. It's too damn crowded in there for all of us to go."

Chase raised his hand. "I'll pass. Trixie's better company than Wish."

Still grasping Drew's hand, Adam shouldered his way through the mob and Drew followed, her heart racing crazily and her throat swelling with so much happiness it was hard for her to breathe. For a minute she could pretend that Adam loved her, and they belonged together. As they entered the paddock, Secret Wish jerked his head up and nickered at them.

Tears stinging her eyes, Drew fumbled in her handbag for the sugar cubes she'd taken from the coffee shop at breakfast. She found them and snapped the bag shut before Adam could see the stack of bills inside.

Adam winked at her. "I knew you'd have something for him." He clasped her elbow and guided her through the throng to Wish's stall just as Rock Man entered the paddock.

Drew stopped and stared at the horse for a second. He was a magnificent-looking individual, all right. But right now he only meant one thing to her.

She held her hand out to Wish, and he nuzzled it, looking for his treat. She rubbed his cheek, then laid hers against it. "Don't worry," she whispered. "See that big guy over there? Rock Man's going to take care of everything. I just know it."

Wish nickered again and nudged her hand for more, then tossed his head as if he were agreeing with her.

"Yeah," she said. "Everything." She hoped to hell she was right.

Six

After the visit to the paddock, Drew waited until her whole group was heading back in the direction of the clubhouse before she whispered, "Come on," in Trixie's ear, then announced that they were going to the ladies' room. Without waiting for a response from anyone, she tugged Trixie back down the path until they were out of view.

"Hurry," Drew said. "I want to place my bet before the post parade starts." She tightened her grip on her handbag, her resolution no longer wavering the least little bit. Seeing Secret Wish in the paddock had made her even more sure that what she was doing was right. She'd spoken quietly with Ben, Wish's groom, and he'd told her there was a lot of heat in both of Wish's hocks and that it had gotten worse over the last three months instead of better. "This here colt needs a good rest," he'd said, shaking his head.

She dragged Trixie to the shortest line she could find. All around them people chatted and gestured excitedly, and the air was filled with the smells of hotdogs, popcorn and cigarette smoke. Drew forced herself to breathe slowly, to try to isolate herself from the commotion.

But it wasn't any use. Her hands shook and her stomach quivered with nervousness this time, not a stupid hangover. She stared at the odds posted on the clicker machine, and her ears started buzzing. Secret Wish was posted in the revised line at twenty-two to one, and Rock Man was going off at forty-two to one. Was Neal crazy? Rock Man's odds were almost double Secret Wish's, and as much as she loved him, she knew Secret Wish had about as much chance of winning as a two-legged goat.

Finally, she reached the pari-mutuel machine. She opened her bag and handed the five $20 bills to the short, plump man on the left of the clicker machine, then told him, her voice quaking, "One hundred dollars on Rock Man to show, number two." She held her breath and squeezed her eyes shut for a second. Too late now.

The man counted the money and handed her a ticket while the other clerk recorded her bet on the machine.

Drew grinned with relief at Trixie. "There," she said. "It's done." Arm-in-arm and giggling like conspirators, they headed back to the Clubhouse together.

"What are you going to tell Rob about the money?" Trixie asked. "I mean, where you got it and all."

"I'll just tell him it was a graduation present from my grandparents in New York," Drew said. "They'll probably send something, anyway, though not nearly that much. He doesn't need to know that, though."

When they entered the Blue Meadow box, Neal, Rob and Chase stood. Trixie sat down in the second row next to Chase, and Drew returned to her seat between Neal and Rob.

Neal smiled at her. "Did you—"

Drew put her finger to her lips and shook her head, hoping Rob hadn't noticed. "I wonder what the final odds will be," she said.

Neal lifted an eyebrow, then smiled at her. "Well, when I put my money on Rock Man, it was fifty to one. Of course, that was the opening line. I'm sure it's changed by now."

Rob turned around to talk to Chase, and Drew whispered to Neal, "Forty-two to one a few minutes ago."

"Still not bad," Neal said. "Fifty dollars to win would bring in a little over a thousand."

"A thousand dollars?" Drew sucked in her breath. At those odds, she would win two thousand dollars if she'd made a win bet. Of course, she'd bet on Rock Man to show, so she'd have to wait and see how the betting pool divided up. Still, old Hugh could race Wish in a thousand dollar claimer, and she'd probably have more than enough.

But she was getting ahead of herself. First, Rock Man had to come in at least third. When Neal nudged her in the ribs and surreptitiously offered her his flask, she took it this time, gulping down a quick swallow while everyone's attention was turned to the beginning of the parade to the post. If she'd been a little fluttery before, now she felt like she wanted to jump out of her skin.

Secret Wish, in the number one position, entered the track first, and Drew rose when everyone in the boxes stood for a better view. His jockey, wearing the green and yellow Ballantrae silks, sat perched atop him with knees high. "Atta boy," Chase bellowed from behind Drew. She thought the colt looked washy, the sweat on his neck turning his brilliant bay coat black, and she could almost feel the pain in his hind joints. She clamped her jaws together in anger and frustration. No horse of hers would ever race in that condition.

She stole a glance at Hugh MacKenzie, whose florid but still handsome face was impassive. Only his narrowed eyes betrayed any emotion, and to Drew that emotion was greed. He didn't care a fig about Secret Wish—all he wanted was to win, and he'd do whatever it took. If Wish broke down, he'd throw him away and buy a new horse.

Rock Man came next, rearing slightly as his jockey Frank Coltiletti, in cerise silks with white blocks and a white cap, pulled back on the reins. A big bay, Rock Man looked in grand condition. He snorted and tossed his head, gazing at the crowd arrogantly, as if he knew—and didn't care—what a small chance the damn fools thought he had of winning. Drew's hands steadied a bit as she watched him. Maybe there was some hope, after all.

Two more colts pranced by, and Drew marveled, as always, at their grace and strength. Nothing was more beautiful to her than a thoroughbred at its peak. Watching them made her heart soar.

But when Bubbling Over stepped onto the track, her heart almost stopped. Instead of prancing like the others, he strode majestically, almost as if he were alone instead of in the company of thousands of bellowing humans and a dozen other horses. His arrogance was palpable; he knew he would run and he would win. That was the way Secret Wish would look if he were taken care of properly—she just knew it. Drew sucked in a deep breath, hoping to imbibe some of Bubbling Over's placid confidence.

The rest of the parade passed in a blur for Drew. The horses were beautiful and the crowd noisy, and her own nervousness made her forget all caution as she clutched Neal's arm.

"Excited?" Neal asked, patting her hand, then leaving his own on top of it.

Drew nodded, then pulled her hand away and clapped it over her mouth when Rock Man reached the gate. For two minutes that seemed like an eternity, the bay colt resisted his jockeys efforts to bring him up to the web barrier. Finally, though, he appeared to change his mind and walked calmly to his place.

Drew let out the breath she hadn't realized she'd been holding and smiled with relief at Neal. Her muscles felt as tense as those of the horses parading below her had looked. She giggled at the thought of herself as one of them, a jockey on her back, prancing around the track.

Neal looked down at her, a curious expression on his

face, and slipped the flask into her hand again. She rolled her eyes at him and took another swig, then handed it back. What the hell. If Rock Man took at least third, she'd really be in a mood to celebrate. If he lost—well, she'd have to drink a lot more than a couple of sips to forget how bad she felt.

Finally, all the horses were lined up, and the barrier shot up. They all emerged in a bunch. In a few seconds, Bubbling Over took the lead with Pompey and Rock Man close behind. Secret Wish was somewhere in the middle of the pack.

Drew jumped up and down, screaming so hard it hurt her throat. "Come on! Come on! Head for the rail!" No one needed to know whom her encouragement was for. She didn't really need to worry, though, she realized. Nobody could hear her individual cries, anyway. The entire crowd had erupted into one enormous thunder the instant the yellow flag dropped.

Seconds later, the horses were on the backstretch, and the positions stayed the same. Pompey was behind by a couple of lengths, and Wish was lagging so far behind that there wasn't a prayer.

The noise in the stands became even more deafening. Drew's throat hurt from yelling. She smacked her hands together in furious clapping, then clutched Neal's arm when Bubbling Over pulled even further ahead from Pompey at the half-mile, while Rock Man gained on the second place colt.

By the time the horses swung around the far turn, Rock Man overtook and passed up Pompey. "He's going to do it! He's going to do it!" Neal shouted, pounding Drew on the shoulder.

Then the field was on the homestretch. Bubbling Over bounded ahead, and so did his stablemate Bagenbaggage. Drew clenched her fists as Bagenbaggage blew by Rock

Man and Rhinock came almost even with him. "Go! Go!" she screamed. "Don't give up now!"

A few seconds later it was all over. Bubbling Over thundered across the finish line at least four or five lengths ahead of Bagenbaggage, and Rock Man kept his nose in front of Rhinock's to finish third. Wish crossed the line last.

Drew threw her arms around Neal. "We did it!" she shouted. Then she remembered. Everyone else in the box was pulling for Secret Wish. No one but Trixie knew that her jubilation was because she'd just saved Wish from who knew what. She dropped her arms and tried to control herself before anyone noticed.

She glanced at the MacKenzies in the adjacent box. Victoria looked blasé and Adam, serious. Hugh's thick white eyebrows were pulled into a line across his forehead, and his lips curved downward like his mustache. "That's it," he announced. "I'm through. Dead last." He spit the words out in disgust as if they had a bad taste, like rotten fish.

Drew exchanged a sneaky grin with Trixie, then turned to Chase. "Wish was in bad shape," she said, ignoring Trixie's warning glare. "He shouldn't have raced today."

Chase just shrugged. "You're probably right," he said. "It's too bad."

Rob patted Drew on the shoulder. "I'm sorry. I know how much you love that colt." Then he winked at her. "But maybe it's for the best."

Drew narrowed her eyes at Trixie. Had Trixie told Rob about the bet? Or was he simply referring to her plan to claim Wish if he lost the Derby?

Neal just looked at all of them as if they were crazy. "I'm going to collect my winnings," he said to Drew. "Want to come along?"

Drew bit back her elated smile. "Sure," she said. "I'd like that very much."

* * *

Fortunately for Drew, Rob had business that kept him in Louisville until Monday afternoon, so she had no problem redeeming her mother's tiara. Smiling smugly to herself, she patted the handbag in her lap as they drove out of town. Inside was not only the tiara, but also more than enough money to claim Wish and board him at Blue Meadow.

She stared at Rob's profile while he concentrated on maneuvering the little car through the traffic. "Did you really mean what you said?" she asked.

He glanced at her, a mystified expression on his face. "What did I say now?" he asked.

"About letting me board Wish at Blue Meadow in exchange for my labor."

"Oh, that," Rob grinned. If Drew managed to claim Wish, he'd be more than happy to let her keep the colt in his barn. He couldn't think of a better way to get to see her every day. "I sure did. You think you're going to be able to come up with money? Because if you can't, I'd be happy to loan—"

"It won't be a problem," Drew said. She smiled at Trixie as if she knew something he didn't, but that wasn't unusual. The two of them always seemed to have some kind of secret that amused them—and it made them even happier if he was left out in the cold. "Believe me."

"Do you plan to claim the colt yourself?" he asked. "Your father might get wind of it." That would give her something to think about—and it just might work out to his advantage. He glanced out of the corner of his eyes at her to gauge her reaction.

"I hadn't thought of that," Drew said. Her thick, dark brows pulled together over her lovely eyes.

Rob forced himself to look at the road when all he really wanted to do was to stare at Drew. But he knew it wasn't to his advantage for her to realize that he had a stake in the answer of his superficially innocent question.

She was silent until they reached the outskirts of Louisville. "I think you might be right," she said. "Daddy has a way of finding out everything."

"Let me act as the buyer," Rob said. "With your money, of course," he added quickly. "That way the whole arrangement makes more sense. It'd be only natural that Wish would be in our stables, trained by our trainer." Appealing to Drew's sense of logic was dangerous, he knew, but he really had no other choice. "And if I ask you to help me out, your parents might be more understanding. They know you've always had a way with Wish that no one else has ever had."

And he couldn't think of a better way to see more of Drew. A pleased smile tugged at his lips, but he kept it under control. She was as skittish as a mare at her first go with an eager young stallion. He didn't want to scare her off. He'd watched her with Neal Rafferty—she'd flirt outrageously, then retreat at the first sign of reciprocation. From now on, Rob planned to play the game a little more smartly with her.

Drew nodded slowly. "Have you heard when Mr. MacKenzie plans to race Wish again?"

Hallelujah, he had her. He kept his voice solemn even though he felt like shouting. "At Dade Park in Henderson," he said. "In late June."

"Right after graduation?" Trixie asked.

He nodded.

"Is it a claimer?" Drew's voice sounded hesitant, afraid.

"Yep." He wasn't going to volunteer anything; he wanted her to drag the information out of him.

She coughed, as if she'd swallowed the wrong way, and leaned forward, her hands clasped tightly on her lap. "How much?"

"One thousand dollars," he said.

56   *Lee Hayward*

Drew settled back against her seat and exchanged a smug glance with Trixie. "No problem," she said.

Rob frowned and jerked his eyes back to the road. He knew better than to ask where she was going to come up with that kind of money, but knowing Drew, he had no doubt that she'd find it somewhere.

Seven

June 1926

Grimacing at herself in the mirror, Drew dragged the brush through the tangles in her hair, but her efforts only made little wisps stand out in a crackling halo of static electricity. She was just about to give up when Momma, in an old but elegant frock, perfectly groomed, and with every hair in place, stepped into her bedroom.

"You aren't even dressed yet?" Momma said. "Your father is waiting in the parlor. He sent me up to see what was taking you so long."

"Look at this mess," Drew said, twisting around on the bench to face her mother and stretching out one of her curls. She turned back to the mirror and threw the brush onto the top of the vanity. "I'm about ready to cut if all off."

"Young ladies about to attend their high school graduation do not whine, dear." Momma gazed at Drew's reflection, the friendly smile in her eyes belying her stern tone. "Here. Let me help." She poured a small drop of lotion from a bottle on the vanity into her hand, then rubbed her palms vigorously together before smoothing them lightly over Drew's hair. "I have the same problem. Hair like ours should never be washed the same day as an important event."

"I know." Drew sighed and picked up the brush again.

She couldn't tell Momma that she'd had to wash it to get out the dust and tiny pieces of hay from helping out in the stables over at Blue Meadow. Momma never did anything to get her hair dirty; in fact, she hardly ever did anything at all because of her asthma. Drew ran the brush through her hair, and this time the curls cascaded obediently onto her shoulders.

Momma reached into the pocket of dress and brought out a small box wrapped in paper lace. "This is for you." She handed Drew the package. "I'm so proud of you."

Drew carefully removed the wrapping, then opened the box and pulled out a tiny bottle of perfume.

"Amour-Amour," Momma said. "From Paris. It's the latest thing."

Drew stared down at the crystal bottle so she didn't have to meet Momma's eyes. How in the world could Momma afford fancy French perfume when they hardly had enough money to buy tobacco seed? Besides, Drew never wore perfume—not only did it make her sneeze, but she wanted the horses to be able to smell *her*, not some strange scent from a bottle. "Thank you. I'm sure it's wonderful," she murmured.

Momma eased herself onto the edge of Drew's bed and leaned back on her hands. "Aren't you going to try it?"

Drew carefully pulled out the stopper and sniffed it.

"Dab a little on your wrists," her mother said, suppressing a sigh. Drew was such a beautiful girl—and her beauty meant absolutely nothing to her. It had always been horses, horses, horses with Drew. She cared nothing for fashion or scent—or for her studies, for that matter. She was happier in a pair of dungarees mucking out a stall than she was at a dinner party or dance. Margaret remembered very clearly what she'd been like at eighteen, and it was not at all like Drew.

But their differences weren't what bothered Margaret the most. If only she knew how to reach Drew, find some kind of common ground. It was only too obvious that the perfume was a failure. She should have known better about that, but she'd be damned if she'd encourage all of this horse nonsense.

Obediently, Drew touched the stopper to both wrists. "It's swell," she said. "Thanks, Momma." She set the bottle on top of the vanity.

"It's better than horse manure, anyway." Margaret smiled at the surprised look on Drew's face. "I know how little use you have for these kinds of things right now," she said. "But that may change someday." She fortified herself with a deep breath; she might as well get it over with. At least this way there wouldn't be much time to listen to Drew's arguments. "That's why your father and I have enrolled you at Smith College. We both think it's important that you be prepared to do something more with your life than grow tobacco—or tend horses."

Drew opened her mouth to respond, but Margaret raised her hand. "Let me finish. And even if you and your future husband take over the farm after we're gone, we want you to have an education first."

Drew's cheeks turned red, and her eyes glistened with unshed tears—of rage, Margaret supposed, knowing her daughter.

"You don't care a fig about my education." Drew stood up, hands on her hips, and faced her mother. "You just want me to go off to college so I can meet a husband. Isn't that what you did? You never even graduated. You married Daddy instead. What good did your priceless education do you?" Drew sputtered to a finish, her face flaming even more brightly as she impatiently brushed a tear from her cheek.

"I didn't do so badly," Margaret said softly, drawing in another deep breath to ease the telltale tightening in her chest. She tried not to let Drew's emotional upheavals upset her too much, but sometimes her body seemed to have a will of its own. "I thank the Lord every day for giving me you and your father, and I thank my parents for seeing to it that my mind was opened to possibilities I could not have imagined before I went to Smith."

Rubbing one hand lightly over the back of the other, Margaret fought the constriction in her lungs and forced herself to focus on what she saw. Her skin was like fine parchment, dry and thin and crossed with tiny wrinkles, and age spots already dotted her knuckles, even though she was only thirty-nine. Damn the poor health that had made her into a semi-invalid. She'd wanted to *live* her life, not simply exist in fear from day to day, but she couldn't tell Drew that, especially not now. It was bad enough her daughter'd had to live with a mother who was constantly indisposed, let alone feel guilt for having caused it.

Ignoring the tickling in her throat, Margaret swallowed back a cough. Where had the years gone? Scott, who'd been ten when she married his father, would have been twenty-nine next week if he'd lived, and her baby was graduating from high school tonight.

Drew clasped her hands behind her back and stared down at her bare feet, but mercifully she said nothing else.

Covering her mouth, Margaret coughed, then pushed herself up off the bed. "Hurry up, now," she said. "Don't keep your father waiting any longer." She crossed the room slowly to the door, her hand over her chest, then let herself out.

Her mother's chest might have been congested with asthma, but guilt and fury warred in Drew's. How could Momma decide her future for her this way? Because she knew it was Momma's doing. Her father thought running a farm was a fine life, even though he had a college degree in history. *He'd* never force her to go away to a fancy woman's college in the East. He'd even said once in a rare comment about his younger brother that college had been Uncle Andrew's ruination.

Drew snatched her pink dress off the hanger in the wardrobe. Maybe that was why Momma had brought the subject up when she did—so Daddy couldn't hear her. Maybe Daddy didn't know what Momma had planned. And anyway, how could they afford it? The only way was if Grandfather and Grandmother Lewis paid for it.

It would ruin everything if they made her go to college. She'd have to sell Wish to Rob because she wouldn't be able to afford the board and training fees, let alone the entry fees and transportation to races. She'd probably have to spend holidays at her grandparents' house in New York because there wouldn't be enough money for her to come back home, so she'd never get to see Trixie and Rob.

Not to mention Adam. She stepped into the dress, catching her heel on the hem as she pulled it up. "Damn it!" She inspected the rip, then shrugged. It was tiny, and her graduation gown would cover it anyway, so who cared?

But her lip trembled, and a new wave of hot tears stung her eyes. For a few seconds she almost succumbed to self-pity; if anyone deserved to feel sorry for herself, she did. It was impossible to argue with Momma. Every time Drew got upset, it brought on one of Momma's asthma attacks. Even now, Drew's guilt for her outburst almost outweighed her anger.

She sank onto her bed and cupped her chin in her hand. She was almost eighteen—there had to be some way out of this mess.

The drive to the county high school in the old Model-T was accomplished in a strained silence. Her father cleared his throat a few times; Momma coughed—that dry little hack that seemed always to presage an attack; and Drew sniffed back the tears that kept threatening to flood her cheeks against her will every time she came up with another solution she knew was crazy or stupid, or both. The Model-T bumped over the ruts, jolting Drew until her teeth ached from clenching her jaw. She would *not* cry. It would only make her eyes ugly and red and do nothing to solve anything.

As soon as they reached the high school, Drew escaped from her parents to the school library, where the girls were lining up for the ceremony. After they'd both gotten into their white graduation robes and mortarboards, Drew dragged Trixie to the back corner behind a tall bookshelf. "Momma's enrolled me in a college in Massachusetts," she hissed. "You've got to help me figure out some way to get out of it."

"You can't go!" The happy sparkle in Trixie's blue eyes instantly turned to concern. "She didn't even ask you?"

Drew shook her head, another bout of misery shuddering through her bones. "I think she thought I'd be happy. It's the same school she went to, and I'm sure Grandfather has offered to pay." She narrowed her eyes, staring for a second at the row of books behind Trixie's shoulders. "In fact, it's probably his idea, now that I think about it. Or Grandmother's. She probably doesn't think there are any suitable husbands in Kentucky—she certainly wasn't happy when Momma married Daddy. Neither was Grandfather, for that matter."

Trixie puckered her lips and drew her eyebrows together in consternation, then a mischievous gleam appeared in her eyes. "You could always run away and get married," she said. "I'm sure Rob would be only too happy to oblige if you asked him."

"Trixie!" Drew grimaced at her friend. "This is serious." Still, she couldn't help the little chuckle that escaped. "Besides, I already thought of that." In fact, it had been crazy and stupid idea number one.

"Well?" Trixie poked her in the ribs. "Then we'd be sisters—and you'd live on the same farm as Wish."

Drew rolled her eyes. "Great reason to get married," she said. "So I can live with a horse." She hesitated a moment, then giggled and affected her grandmother's snobbish Northern accent. "Of course, it's not just any horse, you understand. Secret Wish is truly special."

Trixie laughed until the tears rolled down her cheeks, then gasped out, "Wouldn't Rob die if he heard us?"

"Shhhh," Drew said. "It'll be even worse if that old bat Miss Kennedy hears us." She peeked out from behind the bookshelf. "It's all right. She's still gabbing with Lucy Claire Thompson and Nancy Wilkes. Probably telling them how she remembers the day their daddies and mommas graduated."

"Hell," Trixie said, "she's probably telling them about their grandmas and granddads."

Drew laughed. She felt better just talking to Trixie even though they'd figured out absolutely nothing to do about Momma's plans for her.

"You look a little happier now," Trixie said. "Did you have any other ideas besides marrying my brother?"

"Sure did. And all of them were just as bad." Drew ticked them off on her fingers. "First, drown myself. Second, run away from home. Third, get drunk, steal Daddy's car, and wreck it, thereby disgracing myself. Fourth, get pregnant and refuse to get married, also thereby disgracing myself. Fifth, pretend I'm really sick and refuse to get out of bed." Sighing, she lifted her shoulders up to her ears and grinned at Trixie. "See what I mean?"

Trixie tilted her head in that elfin way she had and screwed up her face again, a sure sign that she was thinking as deeply as she possibly could. "What about just telling them that you won't go? Would they lock you in a trunk or something and take you there against your will?"

Suddenly, Trixie snapped her fingers right in Drew's face. "God, we're stupid! The answer's right under our nose." She lifted her eyebrows, opened her bright blue eyes even wider, and wiggled her shoulders in excitement.

"Well, give! Don't just stand there twitching all over like a moron!" Drew snapped her fingers in Trixie's face. "Come on!"

Just then Miss Kennedy clapped her hands loudly and called out, "Girls! It's time to line up."

Trixie grabbed Drew's arm and pulled her out from behind the bookshelf. "Listen," she whispered as they joined the line. "If your parents insist that you have to go, just move in with us. My mother wouldn't mind, and we've got plenty of room. You don't have to marry Rob, and you get to be with both me and Wish. Isn't that simple?"

Drew nodded at her, but already her mind was whirring with the repercussions. It wasn't quite as simple as Trixie thought, but at least it was better than no plan at all.

"No talking, girls," Miss Kennedy said, her thin lips making a stern line across her face. "This is an occasion that calls for the utmost dignity. You have all accomplished something of which you should be very proud." She stared at Trixie and Drew, and a tiny spark of humor lit her sharp brown eyes. "Some of you more than others, since it borders on a miracle that you actually managed to pass all of your courses and hence make it to this evening's ceremony."

Drew nudged Trixie, and the two of them exchanged a triumphant grin.

Eight

Pushing his steel-rimmed glasses back up on the bridge of his nose, Rob trudged up the dirt road to the yearling barn. As much as he loved his heritage, there was damn little joy for him in running Blue Meadow Stud; during the year since his father's death had forced him to leave the university, he'd made almost no progress at all on the book of poetry he'd started as his junior year project. He sighed from deep in his gut, the grief from his father's passing and the yearning for the freedom to follow his own inclinations intertwining into an almost physical pain.

Still, he had no choice; it was his duty to manage the stud and to take care of his mother and sister. It was simply his misfortune to prefer poetry to horses and writing to running a farm. He stopped outside the barn and inhaled, mentally cataloguing the scents for use in some future poem: dust from the road, straw, the pungent aromas of horse sweat and manure, the fresh smell of new grass, all underlaid by the odor of the white paint young Thomas Clarke was applying to the paddock fences across the way. Professor Bartell advocated sensory images and concrete details in poetry rather than ungrounded metaphysical and philosophical meanderings, and Bartell's favorite modern poets—Robert Frost, A.E. Housman, E.E. Cummings—had become Rob's favorites, too. His notebooks bulged with his tributes to their genius—poems written in imitation of their styles.

A horse whinnied inside the barn, and Rob started, reluctantly forcing himself to put aside the poem taking shape in his head and pay attention to the matters at hand. A second later Joshua emerged from the barn, leading Lucy Bluestocking with Drew on her back, and the last remaining traces of what had promised to be an excellent piece of poetry fled his mind entirely.

"What are you doing on *her?*" he asked, worry for Drew tingeing his voice with irritation. Lucy was notorious among the grooms and exercise boys as a poor doer with a mean streak. She was not only finicky about her food, but seemed to enjoy biting and kicking whatever was nearby, whether human or equine.

Drew frowned at him. "We're breaking her. What does it look like?"

"You don't have to do this, you know," Rob said. "I'd be willing to board and train Wish for a percentage of his winnings." He eyed the bad-tempered Lucy, who stamped her hooves and tossed her head like a cranky toddler. A very large cranky toddler. "I really wish you'd just let Sam or one of the other exercise boys break her. I don't trust her."

"We get along just fine, don't we, Lucy?" Drew leaned slowly forward and patted Lucy's neck, and, miraculously, the filly quieted. "Besides, Wish may never win another dime, not to mention the entry fees I'm going to have to come up with. And if he doesn't run, he may never catch on as a stud. I'm set on paying our way."

"You can easily pay your way without endangering life and limb," Rob said. He ignored the stubborn thrust of Drew's chin and continued even though he knew the cause was hopeless. Perhaps that was what made him a poet, he thought—his ability to disregard the obvious and count on the impossible, in this case Drew's common sense. "I know how hard you work helping your father out in the tobacco fields and taking care of your mother. What's going to happen to them if you end up with a broken leg?"

Drew emitted an exasperated snort and crossed her eyes. "I helped break Wish and he was ten times worse than this little filly," she said. "Don't worry yourself about me, Rob. I won't thank you for it. I just get annoyed at people who fret at me." She softened the words with a smile that lit up her sparkling brown eyes, mercifully now uncrossed.

Rob stared at her, memorizing the lovely curve of her smiling eyes. He'd always been fascinated by their shape—tilted slightly up at the outer corners, slightly down at the inner, and rounded in the middle. They were long enough to be called almond shaped, but probably too wide. And the color—dark pure shiny brown with an outer ring of brown so deep it almost looked black. No speckles of gray or green or gold like so many other brown-eyed people. He could get lost in Drew's eyes, write an ode to them.

"So," Drew said.

"So?"

"Are you going to move, or do we have to walk right over the top of you?"

"Oh." Rob stepped aside and let them pass. "I want her off of that filly at the first sign of trouble," he told Joshua.

Joshua nodded solemnly at him, but Rob caught the wink and quick grin his black groom directed at Drew. "Yes, sir."

"I'll hold you personally responsible if anything happens to Drew," Rob said, his voice stern.

"Yes, sir." This time Joshua neither winked nor grinned.

Drew surprised Rob by slipping off the filly's back. "Get Sam, please," she said to Joshua. "I think Mr. Carlisle and I need to have a little talk." She glared at Rob, fury narrowing her eyes and constricting her pupils to tiny black points as she grabbed his arm and led him back down the road toward the stallion paddock.

Rob's heart squeezed into a hard little ball in the middle of his chest. He'd done it again. All he wanted was for Drew to love him the way he loved her, but he kept doing and saying the wrong things. What in the hell was wrong with him, anyway?

"I'm responsible for myself," Drew hissed as soon as they were out of earshot of the groom and exercise boy. "Don't you *ever* make anyone else responsible for my safety again. Do you hear? It isn't fair."

Suddenly, Drew's eyes shimmered with tears. She knuckled them away and sniffed. "I'm so tired of everyone making decisions about what's best for me. First, Momma and Daddy decide to send me away to college, and now you act like I'm an incompetent idiot who can't take care of herself. You all treat me like a baby. If it weren't for Wish, I'd just leave." She kicked the fence post, then stared down at her boots. "I'm *not* a baby. I know exactly what I want, but it seems everyone is dead set against me having it." The anger in her voice was gone now, replaced by resignation and sadness. "It's not as if what I want would hurt anybody."

Rob understood just what she meant. "It's hard, isn't it?" he said. "I'd rather be back at the University of Kentucky working on the literary magazine than ordering supplies and arranging stud dates." Still, if he were, he wouldn't be here now with Drew.

But if her parents got their way, she'd be gone—and along with her, the one thing that made his life here meaningful. "Do you think your folks will really make you go?" he asked. "Trixie told me you had a plan, but she wouldn't tell me what it was." He hesitated for a minute, afraid to call forth her ire once more, then plunged ahead. "Is there anything I can do to help? Maybe I can talk to your parents."

"It's worth a try," Drew said. "If you offered me a job as your secretary or bookkeeper or something, they might be more inclined to listen. I don't think being an exercise boy carries much weight with them. Momma would just point out that I'm not a boy, after all." She grinned at him. "Of course, you wouldn't have to be too specific about your secretary's duties, would you?"

Rob returned her smile, then closed one eye in a solemn and broad wink. "I think I might be able to manage that," he said.

Two hours later Drew had finished exercising her yearlings and headed back home feeling more hopeful about her future than she had in the last three days since graduation. The night she'd been looking forward to throughout those four long years of high school had turned out to be one of the worst of her life.

First, there'd been Momma's terrible revelation; then, as she'd marched into the gymnasium, her eyes red and her nose swollen from crying, she'd spotted Adam sitting right next to Momma and Daddy. She'd thought that he and Victoria had gone back to Philadelphia right after the Derby; she had no idea he was still in Kentucky. She'd been so startled and so horrified—what if he said something about her behavior at the Derby Eve party?—that she tripped on the hem of her long graduation robe and stumbled into Trixie; who pushed against Lucy Claire Thompson, who in turn had stopped dead in her tracks and turned around and glared at Trixie until Trixie had been forced to give Lucy Claire a little shove and whisper loudly, "Get going!"

By this time the titters that had begun when Drew tripped erupted into loud guffaws, and Drew's face burned as red as her eyes. She'd ducked her head, hiding behind the curtain of hair that swung over her cheeks, and stared at Trixie's feet until she finally made it to the front of the gym and sank down into one of the squeaky old folding chairs reserved for the graduates.

Her cheeks flushed now as she remembered the final embarrassment of the evening, and she kicked a small rock, watching as it skittered across the road and into the stone slave fence at the other side. As soon as the ceremony had finished, the graduates formed a receiving line. Drew had been standing between Trixie and Nancy Wilkes when Rob and Adam came through the line with Drew's parents. After the congratulations and hand-shaking were out of the way, Adam smiled at Drew and said, "I heard from Neal that you did quite well at the Derby."

Afraid to look at anyone else, Drew held her breath and stared at Adam, her entire body stiff as a pointer's tail at the sight of a pheasant. "I had a great time," she said finally, hoping her parents wouldn't understand what Adam was talking about. Daddy disapproved vehemently of any form of gambling—probably because of Uncle Andrew, Momma had told her once. Although he hadn't specifically forbidden her to bet at the Derby, he undoubtedly thought that she'd never disobey his unspoken rule.

Adam arched one of his thick dark brows high above his eye and returned Drew's stare. Then his face relaxed, and a hint of a smile sparkled in his green eyes and barely turned up the corners of his mouth. "Neal told me it was uncanny the way you predicted the winners," he said. "He was quite impressed."

Drew's shoulders sagged with relief, and she quickly glanced at her folks. Momma gave her a tight little smile while Daddy continued his conversation with Rob, apparently oblivious to Adam's comment. "Thank Neal for the compliment the next time you see him, will you?" Drew said.

Adam shook her hand then, instead of pulling her into his arms for a big hug and a kiss on the cheek the way he usually did. "I will," he said. "And congratulations. This is a really special moment for me. I wish Scott were here to see it." All traces of his smile had disappeared from his face, and the sadness in his eyes had made tears burn in Drew's.

Afterward she'd realized that Adam had stayed in Kentucky for the sole purpose of attending her graduation— but because of Scott, not because of her. She was still his best friend's little sister, and the only reason he hadn't kissed her that night at graduation was because he'd finally grasped the fact that she wasn't a child any longer.

A bunch of wild daisies and irises by the roadside caught her eye, and Drew stopped to pick them. She was still musing about Adam and graduation night when the familiar sound of a car motor made her heart freeze in her chest. Surely Adam had gone back to Philadelphia by now, and someone else was taking his car out for a spin. She concentrated on the flowers, carefully snapping off the stems of the best of them and gathering them into a huge bouquet for Momma.

The car slowed down and crunched to a halt in the gravel at the side of the road. "Drew!" Adam called. "Need a ride?"

Nine

Drew gaped at Adam, unable to control the sudden pounding of her heart. Her head swam with the noise; surely, it was loud enough for him to hear. Unwilling to trust her voice, she nodded, staring into his intense gray-green eyes.

He leaned across the seat and opened the door for her. "Come on, then," he said. His full lips curved in his familiar half-smile. "I'll take you home—or wherever it is you're going."

She wanted to go with him more than anything in the world—in fact, she'd be glad to go with him *to* anywhere in the world—but she took a deep breath and forced herself to speak calmly. Pining away over a man who was going to marry someone else was starting to seem not only pointless, but pretty stupid as well. Still, her voice croaked a little when she said, "Home. If you're sure it's not too much trouble." She settled herself into the leather seat and arranged her long legs as gracefully as she could, given the small amount of space provided.

"Not a bit—and I'm glad to have your company," he said, pulling the car back onto the roadway. Steering with one hand, he ran the other through his shiny black hair. "Besides, I wanted to apologize."

"Apologize? Whatever for?" Other than for marrying Victoria, she added to herself, reasonably sure that wasn't what he had in mind.

"The remark I made at your graduation. It was thoughtless of me—I had no intention of revealing privileged information." He slowed the car as they bounced into a pothole, then glanced at her, his face serious—not even the slightest hint of that sardonic quirk in his eyebrow.

Drew fiddled with the bouquet of daisies and wild irises in her lap. "It's all right," she said. "Momma and Daddy didn't even notice. They were still too mad at me."

"About your bet?" They reached the dirt lane leading to Ashworth Farm, and Adam steered the car into it, then stopped. He shifted in his seat and looked at Drew. "What happened?"

"Not about the bet," she said. "Although I'd have been in real trouble if they'd found out even half of what I did."

"Two mysteries," Adam said. "Now I'm really curious. Would you think it impolite of me to ask for further clarification?" His smile was warm and genuinely concerned.

"Dreadfully." Drew tried to keep her tone flippant, but in truth she'd always found it impossible to lie to Adam, no matter how innocent or white the lie was. There was something about the way he looked at her that had always made her afraid to fib to him, as if she had to live up to his standards of honesty. It almost didn't matter that he was going to marry someone else; she knew she loved him in a way that didn't make a difference. She'd never be able to betray Adam.

She plucked at one of the daisies, and the petals fluttered onto the floor of the car. "But I'll tell you anyway." She took a deep breath, then recounted the story of her bet, from her decision to claim Secret Wish, to the theft and pawning of the tiara, to putting her money on Rock Man and collecting fifteen hundred dollars. "Rob's going to claim him for me when he races at Dade Park next week. And that's why I can't go to college," she finished.

"Wait a minute," he said. "Go to college? What does that have to do with all of this?"

"That's why Momma and Daddy were so mad at me graduation night. They want me to go to Smith."

Adam's tone was dry. "And I'll bet you told them in that very clear manner of yours that you have no intention of doing so."

Drew nodded. "I yelled at Momma. I *never* yell at Momma—she gets those awful spells when she gets upset sometimes." Tears blurred her vision, then brimmed over onto her cheeks. "She hasn't been well since then, and it's my fault. And if she doesn't change her mind, I'll *have* to go away to school."

While talking with Rob had only brought out her frustration, this time Drew's tears were a release of the guilt and anguish she'd endured for the last three days. Momma had gone directly to bed after graduation, and it was impossible for Drew not to blame herself. When she was little, she'd believed that Momma got sick for the identical reason Drew had thrown fits—to get her way. As she'd gotten older, she'd realized that it wasn't exactly the same. The doctor said Momma's attacks could be caused by exertion or some kinds of blooming plants (not daisies or irises, fortunately) or emotional upsets. It wasn't Momma's fault, or Drew's, if she couldn't breathe after Drew said something that made her mad—it was the asthma.

But that realization didn't make things any easier for Drew. The tears continued to roll down her cheeks, and she couldn't stop them. If Rob's offer to hire her as his secretary didn't work, there wasn't any other way she could see to get out of going to Smith. Not even Trixie's offer to let her stay at Blue Meadow.

"I feel so stupid," she said. "Nancy Wilkes would kill for a chance to go to any college, let alone Smith." She brushed away the tears, but new ones replaced them immediately, glittering on her long black lashes, then streaming down her cheeks.

Adam reached out to her, pulling her into his arms so naturally that it surprised him. "I understand," he said. And to his amazement, he did. Her unhappiness touched him in a way that nothing else had for years. His engagement to Victoria had not brought him happiness or pain—just relief that marriage wasn't something he had to worry about any longer.

A sudden unfamiliar storm of emotion made his arms tighten around Drew, and a horrifying realization struck him like the full force of a hurricane. He'd laughed at Drew's obvious infatuation with him, been flattered and touched by it, but had pretended to himself that he was only concerned with her welfare as a brother might be, nothing more. But she wasn't a child any longer, and his feelings for her definitely weren't brotherly—that much was obvious. Unable to resist the passion that surged through his veins, he lowered his head and pressed his lips against hers.

Her response was immediate. Her hands crept around his neck, pulling him even closer, and her lips parted. She wasn't experienced at kissing, he recognized, but she returned what he gave her with unmistakable desire. For a few minutes, or several, he forgot everything else.

Then, suddenly, he regained control and gently eased away from Drew's embrace. Jesus Christ, what had he unleashed with one kiss? Last month's greeting hadn't counted; he'd been caught unaware and remained oblivious afterward. This was different. Holding her at arm's length, he stared into her eyes, loving the sweep of her long thick lashes against her cheeks when she could no longer meet his gaze. This one kiss acknowledged the love between them in a way neither of them would ever be able to deny again.

Yet he had to. He was engaged, and she was too young to know what loving him the way she did would mean.

Awaking from her afternoon nap, Margaret drew in a blessedly deep breath of the menthol-perfumed air and sighed with relief. Thank God this attack hadn't been as bad as she'd feared. The emotional upheaval surrounding Drew's graduation had brought it on, or so Dr. Miller had guessed, but she felt much better today—well enough, in fact, to socialize with the Carlisles, who were calling later this afternoon.

The grandfather clock in the parlor chimed three times, and she raised herself to a sitting position. They'd be here in an hour, and she still needed to take a sponge bath, pin up her hair, and dress. Slowly, she swung her legs over the side of the bed and stood gingerly, her limbs still weak from five days in bed.

She sat back down and rang the bell on her nightstand. It was going to take all the energy she had to get downstairs—she had none to waste on fetching warm water and combing out her hair. If Drew hadn't kept her promise to be home by two o'clock, Margaret didn't know how she was going to manage. The urge to pout caught her by surprise—she must be recovering if she had the strength to feel petulant. Crankiness was always a good sign in a sick person, her mother had told her.

Margaret smiled despite her increasing irritation when Drew failed to answer her summons. If what Mother said was correct, she was definitely on the mend. Still, she hoped she didn't get caught in one of those interminably long recovery periods where she felt too well to stay in bed all day, yet not well enough to do anything else. The memories of her two-year bout with tuberculosis when Drew was a toddler still filled her with horror. And grief, for missing so much of Drew's childhood. Within a few months of returning home from the sanatorium, she'd had her first asthma attack; she'd become hysterical when she'd started wheezing, thinking the tuberculosis had returned and she was dying, and the doctor said that had made the attack even worse.

Drew had watched the entire incident. Shuddering, Margaret remembered the terror in her daughter's eyes with a clarity other recollections seldom achieved. Drew, too, must have thought her momma was dying and, as children so often did, blamed herself.

Margaret shook her head, as if that would dislodge the memory, then rubbed a fold of her chenille robe between her fingers. She'd had plenty of time these last few days to rethink her insistence on Drew going to Smith. Edward had complied with her wishes only to please her—if Drew were to go to college, his true preference would be for her to stay at home and attend the University of Kentucky at Lexington, just as Scott had done.

And the look on Drew's face after graduation when Margaret had started gasping for air continued to haunt her with its devastating similarity to that awful scene years ago. Once again, Drew blamed herself for Margaret's infirmity.

Finally, Drew's footsteps sounded on the stairs, and Margaret attempted to appear relaxed and cheerful. Despite the love of both of her parents, Drew's childhood hadn't been an easy one, and Margaret had been trying to make it up to her for years. She'd thought Drew would be delighted to attend such a good school, but she realized now she'd been thinking more of herself than of her daughter.

"Momma?" Drew tapped on the door, then stepped into the room. "How are you feeling?"

Margaret smiled at her. "Much better."

She eyed Drew from head to toe. Drew's hair was tucked neatly into a bun at the back of her neck with only a few wayward tendrils making their escape, and she wore a yellow cotton summer frock instead of those awful dungarees. "You look nice," Margaret said. Maybe there was something to this thing with Rob, after all. Drew didn't usually go to so much trouble for a visit with the Carlisles.

"We'd better hurry, Momma," Drew said. "They're going to be here soon."

A half hour later, Margaret surveyed herself in her mirror. Bathing and dressing always boosted her spirits, and Drew had pinned her hair up nicely. She plucked a daisy and an iris from the bouquet Drew had brought her yesterday and quickly pinned them to the collar of her dress, then took Drew's arm and, pausing every two or three steps, walked slowly down the stairs to the parlor.

Rob and Edward rose when Margaret and Drew entered the room. Margaret smiled at Rob and held out her hand. "It's so nice to see you," she said. "But where are Viola and Trixie?"

Rob clasped her hand, then released it. "Actually, Mrs. Ashworth, this is more of a business call than a social call."

"Oh?" Margaret sat down in the overstuffed chair by the window while Drew seated herself on the sofa next to Rob.

"Young Rob here has a proposition you might find interesting, my dear," Edward said.

"Oh?" Margaret said again, looking at each of the three. They looked like co-conspirators, the way they kept throwing quick glances at each other. She lifted an eyebrow and fixed Rob with her most intimidating stare. "I think you'd better tell me, then."

Rob ran his fingers through his sleek light brown hair, then leaned forward, pushing his glasses back up on his nose. "Well," he said, "as you know, I've been running Blue Meadow since my father died last year. Unfortunately, we weren't able to hire someone to help with the

paperwork involved in the managerial duties because—"
He paused, sighed, then held out his hands, palms up.
"Because I didn't know what the heck I was doing—pardon my language, ma'am." His smile lit up his soft blue
eyes.

Margaret returned his smile. She'd always been fond of
Rob Carlisle. Even as a little boy he'd been sweet and
polite, and as he'd grown into manhood, those qualities
had not disappeared as they so often seemed to do in
young men nowadays. He'd make some girl a fine husband. Unlike some other young men of her acquaintance.
She grimaced slightly thinking of that callow Chase
MacKenzie with whom Trixie ran around—so different
from both Adam and Rob. "You're pardoned. You have
my permission to get to the point."

"I find that I need a secretary to keep up with things,
Mrs. Ashworth. And I'd like to hire Drew for that position." Rob's words came out in a rush, as if he were uncomfortable admitting he needed help.

Margaret settled herself against the back of the faded
chintz covered chair, her hands in her lap. Secretarial work
wasn't exactly what she had in mind for Drew, but it was
certainly better than exercising horses, which, despite
Drew's circumspection regarding her daily activities, was
only too readily apparent as her chief occupation when
she wasn't engaged helping Edward in the tobacco fields.
"Just exactly what would be involved?" She had no intention of making this easy for any of them until she was
satisfied that her decision would truly be the best for
Drew.

"I need someone to order supplies, take care of the
payroll, pay the bills, schedule races and services, and do
the bookkeeping. I've been doing it all myself, and I have
to admit that I'm not very good at it." He threw an apologetic look at Drew. "I'm afraid my new secretary will
have a bit of a muddle to contend with at first."

"You've been awfully quiet, Drew," Margaret said. "I'd like to hear what you have to say."

"I want to try, Momma. You know how I feel about going away to college. This way I can stay here and learn something, too." Drew's eagerness suffused her face with a healthy pink glow.

Shaking her head, Margaret lifted her hands in a gesture of defeat. "All right," she said, glancing at Edward in time to see his nod of support. "You win. We'll cancel your enrollment at Smith tomorrow."

Drew jumped up and threw her arms around Margaret. "Oh, thank you, Momma!"

The return of the sparkle in Drew's dark brown eyes and the happy grin on her lips were almost enough for Margaret. *Almost.* She smiled beneficently at her daughter, then at Rob. After all, lots of secretaries married their bosses, didn't they?

Ten

It was about eleven o'clock when Drew, Rob, Trixie, and Chase pulled into Dade Park racetrack in Rob's truck. They'd driven down early the day before, dropped off the horse van at the track, then spent the night at the Vendôme Hotel in Evansville, across the Ohio River from Henderson.

Wedged in next to Rob, Drew bounced on the truck's hard seat as Rob steered it over the rutted dirt road leading to the barns behind the backstretch. She yawned, still tired from the night before when they had all gone dancing until the wee hours. She'd actually had fun—even enjoyed dancing the Charleston with Rob after Chase taught them how all to do it—although she hadn't been able to stop thinking about Adam the whole evening. Every few minutes Chase would mention that "Adam did this" or "Adam said that." Not that it was entirely Chase's fault—during the ten days since Adam had kissed her, he'd been constantly on her mind. After Adam, his face white and tense, had pulled away from her, he'd apologized in a deadly serious manner—not the joking way he usually talked to her, as if she were still a child—and promised it would never happen again. He took her the rest of the way home without a word.

Then she found out from Trixie that he'd gone back to Philadelphia the very next day. Every time she remembered his kiss, her heart raced and butterflies danced in her veins; then she thought of how he'd left without saying goodbye, and a painful spasm pierced her heart with such force she understood why the pictures always showed Cupid with a bow and arrow.

The truck hit a huge pothole, jolting Drew out of her reverie, and Rob slowed it to a stop in front of the Blue Meadow Farm van. They all jumped out and walked along shed row with its hanging pails, rakes, and brooms toward Secret Wish's stall, Chase and Trixie chattering all the way, as usual.

"Dad was so disgusted after the Derby that he's entered Wish in the closest claiming races he can find," Chase said. "He doesn't care if they're one hundred dollars or one thousand—he wants that horse racing for someone else so he doesn't have to think about him or see him again." He pointed out Ben, Wish's groom, standing in front of a stall. "There he is."

Drew strode ahead of the rest. Thank goodness Rob had been wrong—the race Wish was entered in today was a seven hundred and fifty dollar claimer instead of one thousand dollars, and it was only a mile instead of a mile and a quarter

She greeted Ben, then rested her arms atop the stall door, sniffing the familiar odors of sweet hay and horse, underlaid by a pungent greasy smell. Immediately Wish turned toward her and nickered, then nuzzled her hand for his reward.

She didn't disappoint him. She produced two sugar cubes from her pocket and offered them to him, winking at Ben. "How'd he do at the workout this morning?" she asked.

"Not bad, considerin' the heat in them hocks of his," Ben said, wrinkling his dark forehead. "How he run like the devil, I'll never know, but he did." He pointed to the bandages on Wish's rear legs. "I massaged him some with goose grease."

"You mean he might actually have a chance?" Trixie said. She stepped up next to Drew and rubbed Wish between his ears.

He tossed his head up and down, then nudged Drew's hand again. "You greedy old thing," Drew said, laughing. "Or are you telling us you're going to win?"

Imitating Wish, Ben wagged his gray-frizzed head. "He jes' might do it. 'Course, got to consider them legs. Who know how far they carry him?"

"While you give Wish a pep talk," Rob said, "I'll head on over to the track secretary's office to register my claim. Want to come along, Chase?"

Chase shrugged. "Why not? I've never liked the way Dad treated his animals anyway."

"I'll keep Drew company," Trixie said. "Maybe the two of us can sweet talk Wish into giving us a win." She winked at Drew as soon as Rob and Chase got into the truck, then glanced toward Ben, who'd picked up the pail and headed toward the pump for some water.

"Time for a little gossip now that the guys are gone." Trixie grinned at Drew, then giggled. "I've been dying to talk to you, but they haven't left us alone for a second, and I was so tired last night after we got back to our room that I forgot all about it."

"Forgot all about what?" Drew leaned against the stall door, rubbing Wish's neck while she fixed Trixie with a mock-threatening glare.

"Two things I think you'll find just fascinating." Trixie curled a strand of her silky blond hair around her finger.

"Well, are you going to tell me or just tantalize me—or do you want me to guess?" Drew pursed her lips and looked up at the cloudless blue sky for a second. "Let's see—Lucy Claire Thompson got herself pregnant by Reverend Wilkes' son, and Nancy Wilkes ran away with the strong man from the circus that was here last week. Am I close?"

Trixie hooted, and Drew joined her. Of all of their class-
mates, Lucy Claire and Nancy were the prissiest, always
looking down their noses at Drew because they wore new
dresses and turned their homework in on time and never
got in trouble in class for speaking out of turn. Between
them, Lucy Claire and Nancy never had an original
thought or even considered doing anything the least bit
improper, let alone adventurous.

Her laughter fading to giggles, Trixie shook her head.
"Not even close. But I think you'll like it even better.
Chase told me in strictest confidence that Adam and Victoria had a big argument after he got back to Philadelphia." She waggled her eyebrows at Drew.

Drew sucked in a deep breath, then held it. Trixie had
known for years that Drew idolized Adam, but Drew
hadn't told her anything about "The Kiss," as she thought
of it; even though Drew usually shared everything with
Trixie, she knew that she'd never tell anyone about Adam
kissing her as long as Adam and Victoria were together.
To reveal it would be a betrayal of Adam, and she loved
him too much.

Besides, she didn't want anyone else telling her what
to think. As soon as she confided in someone, the whole
incident would become shaded with other interpretations.
She'd considered the matter from as many angles as she
could—that maybe Adam didn't realize what it meant to
her, that it had really meant nothing to him, that he kissed
her to get even with Victoria for something, that he'd been
shell-shocked in France and had moments of confusion
and insanity. She hadn't liked any of those ideas; the one
that kept coming back, running through her head like a
favorite scene from a book or moving picture, was that
he'd finally realized how much he had always loved her.

Trixie's gossip only reinforced her belief. Drew tried to
keep her face blank, as if she couldn't care less what went
on between Adam and Victoria, but her heartbeat quick-

ened. "So," she said, her voice bland despite the warm
surge of hope, "are they calling off the wedding or anything?"

"I don't know. But Chase did tell me that he thought it
was all because of Victoria's jealousy." Trixie rolled her
eyes. "Lordy, that's one stupid female. Can you imagine
Adam the Honorable fooling around with another woman?"

"No, I can't," she said with what she hoped was a non-
chalant shrug. It was pretty easy to sidetrack Trixie as
long as she didn't get it in her head that you didn't want
to talk about something. Then she became as persistent as
a mosquito buzzing in your ear when you were trying to
fall asleep. "You had two things to tell me. What was the
other?"

"You remember Neal?"

"Come on, Trixie. I wasn't that drunk!" Drew laughed.
"Of course I remember him."

"He told Chase he thinks you're swell and he's planning
to drive over to see you this summer when he's visiting
his family in Bardstown." Trixie stretched out her hand
and scratched between Wish's ears, sighing hugely. "Poor
Rob. He certainly didn't choose an easy row to hoe when
he decided to fall in love with you."

"Yep," Drew agreed. "He got one filled with weeds,
didn't he? The worst kind, too—long roots, lots of little
seeds—and stickers, to boot."

Trixie giggled, then the laughter faded from her eyes
as she pointed in the direction of the road. "Here they
come," she said. "I know you're not in love with Rob,
but try not to be too stickery, okay? I may make fun of
him, but he's still my brother—and I'd surely treasure having you for a sister-in-law."

After Rob entered the claim for Secret Wish, which
luckily was the only one registered so he didn't have to

risk shaking for it, the four of them headed back to Evansville for lunch at the Vendôme Hotel, then returned to
Dade Park in time for Wish's race at four o'clock. Rob
found it hard to keep his eyes on the road with Drew
pressed so tightly against his thigh. He kept glancing at
her, then forcing his eyes back to where they were supposed to be in the first place. Last night she'd been flir-
tatious, happy, and warm, but something had happened
this morning after he came back from the track secretary's
office. She'd suddenly become preoccupied and distant.

Owning a racehorse *was* a big responsibility; maybe she
was having second thoughts about her decision to claim
Wish. He turned off onto the racetrack road for the second
time that day. "Everybody ready?" he asked, doing his
best to infuse his voice with enthusiasm.

Chase and Trixie, engaged in their own conversation,
ignored him, but Drew nodded, her head jiggling in time
with the ruts in the road.

"I'm so excited my feet are twitching." She laughed,
pointing at them. "See? I can't make them hold still!"
Sure enough, her long narrow feet seemed to have a life
of their own, tapping an excited rhythm on the truck's
floorboard.

"You look like a little kid who needs to go to the bathroom in the worst way," Rob said. "Do you think you can
hold it until we get there?"

"I surely do hope so. I can't believe the way my stomach is fluttering. I wasn't this jittery before the Derby."

"Well, for all intents, he's your horse now," Rob said.
"You've a right to be nervous." He relaxed a little, glad
that her remoteness was because of Wish, not him. It was
always so hard to know how to treat Drew; if he acted
concerned, she claimed he was being overbearing, but if
he affected nonchalance, she ignored him. Then, suddenly,
for no reason that he could tell, she'd confide in him or

flirt with him or act genuinely fond of him. It was enough to drive a man crazy—which he definitely was for her.

A few minutes later, he'd parked the truck next to the Blue Meadow van and the four of them stopped by Wish's stall for a short visit before the race. Ben stood inside, wiping Wish down with a damp sponge. "Gettin' him ready," Ben said. "It's almos' time to take him on over to the paddock. I's jes' goin' to give him a few sips of water first."

Drew handed Ben the bucket over the stall door, and Wish nickered eagerly, then plunged his nose into the water. Ben allowed him a few swallows before passing the bucket back to Drew. "This here is one sweet horse. I's sure goin' to miss him," Ben said, covering Wish with his green and yellow cooler. "He's got a great big heart, but his legs could sure use a rest. No tellin' what he could do if he wasn't so damn sore."

Smiling at Drew, Rob opened the stall door and stepped aside. "We plan to find out," he said. He nodded at the older black man as he tugged on Wish's lead shank and led him out of the stall. Ben Parker was an excellent groom, and Rob was always looking for good workers. "And if you ever get tired of Ballantrae, give us a holler."

"Thank you, sir." Ben's face wrinkled into a huge grin, and he winked at Chase. "Not that I don't like workin' for your daddy, Mr. Chase, but I might jes' be taking you up on that offer, sir."

"That would be wonderful, Ben!" Her eyes glowing, Drew fell into step beside Ben and Rob. Following behind, Trixie and Chase linked arms, and all of them walked to the saddling shed together.

A lone chestnut tree threw its long afternoon shadow over the paddock, and Willie Williams and the jockey Pete Elliot, in green and yellow Ballantrae silks and with his saddle over his arm, waited for them inside the fence. Rob, Drew, and Trixie joined the small crowd of spectators hanging over the fence while Chase accompanied Ben and Wish inside.

"Are you planning to bet?" Rob asked Drew, folding his arms on top of the fence next to hers. Someone from behind jostled against him, and his elbow pressed against hers. He tensed, afraid she would move away, but she didn't.

"I wasn't planning to, but . . ." Shrugging, Drew smiled up into his eyes. "What the hell." She tucked her arm through his and towed him away from the fence as the paddock judge ordered the riders to mount. "We might as well make the gesture. And who knows—he might even have a chance today."

Rob couldn't keep himself from staring down at her hand on his arm. Drew must have been distracted by her worries about Wish during the drive to Dade Park because she certainly hadn't been distant toward him since they arrived. Cold or hot, warm or tepid—who knew what she'd be running in ten minutes. He'd better enjoy his good luck now.

They each placed five dollars on Secret Wish to win, then joined Trixie and Chase in the clubhouse as the horses reached the starting barrier.

Several minutes later, the field lined up straight behind the web, the elastic barrier swept up, and the yellow flag dropped.

Wish started cleanly, moving to the front at once. Drew grabbed Rob's hand and dragged him to his feet. "Look at him!" she shouted.

Rob stared at the track, but he had a hard time concentrating with Drew squeezing his hand and jumping up and down next to him. Wish led the pack by at least five lengths when they passed the half-mile pole, and by the way the jockey was hauling back on the reins, the horse looked as if he were fighting Pete for his head.

"He's outclassed them all!" Drew yelled.

She was right. A few seconds later Wish passed beneath the finish wire to the roaring applause of the crowd.

Drew stood on tiptoe and kissed Rob on the lips, tears flowing down her cheeks. "He did it!" she said. "He did it!"

Wrapping his arms around her, Rob pulled her close to his chest and reveled in the excited beating of her heart against his. It looked as if Wish might actually have a chance. He hoped he was half as lucky.

Eleven

Leaning against the side of Wish's stall at Blue Meadow, Drew rubbed her aching shoulders while she listened half-heartedly to Rob discuss Wish's progress with Jack Nolan. She already knew what she wanted for Wish—rest, and more rest—so she didn't really care what Jack recommended if it wasn't the same. Besides, she was too exhausted to be patient with either of the men—after helping Rob with the daily secretarial chores, exercising some of the two and three-year-olds, and taking care of Wish, she still had to go home and harvest tobacco until dark.

And she couldn't complain. If she did, Momma and Daddy would just shrug and say, "Well, you can still go to college if you like;" Rob would offer to buy Wish; and Jack would be relieved not to have to deal with a female any longer. She'd rather work from dawn until dusk than give in to any of them.

Jack ran his hand down Wish's right leg. "No swelling, no heat," he said. "I think he's ready to race again. It's already August so we're too late for Saratoga, but we could make Belmont."

"I want to wait," Drew said. She scratched the white star on Wish's forehead. "I'd like to start training him again in September, take it real easy and slow, then race him at Pimlico in May. What I want is several strong showings as a

four-year-old to make up for last year before I retire him
to stud. He's got the same great bloodlines as Man O' War,
and he showed well as a two-year-old before Willie let him
get broken down. A few more wins under his belt is all we
need. I say it's not worth the risk to race him too soon."

Jack exchanged an irritated glance with Rob, then muttered something under his breath about women owners and
pussyfoots. Finally, he shrugged. "You're the boss. But I
still think he's ready. He might lose heart if you wait too
long."

"He's got too much heart to lose any." Drew finger-
combed Wish's silky mane, then patted his gleaming neck.
She smiled at Ben Parker, the groom who'd followed Wish
from Ballantrae to Blue Meadow. "He looks better than
I've ever seen him, Ben," she said.

Then she put her hands on her hips and glared at Jack.
Why couldn't they just treat her as an equal? No matter
what she knew, she always first had to overcome being female. She was tired of cajoling stubborn men when she had
every right to her own opinion. "But still not good enough
to race yet. And I have no intention of discussing it further."

Rob jerked his head toward Drew. "Come on," he said.
"Let's go back to the house."

As soon as they were far enough away from the barn
not to be overheard, he said, "You can't behave toward
Jack Nolan that way. He's one of the best trainers in the
business, and I'm lucky to have him. So are you." He
pushed his glasses back up on his nose and added less
stridently, but still firmly, "And so is Wish."

Drew blinked a couple of times and gaped at Rob. He'd
never used that tone of voice on her before, and she
wasn't quite sure how to react. Usually Rob treated her
diffidently, almost as if he were afraid to be himself for
fear that she wouldn't like him—which seemed a little
strange to her because she hadn't spoken a cross word to
him since he'd claimed Wish for her two months ago. And,

after all, he *was* her boss, so he had every right to tell her what to do—as far as Blue Meadow business went.

But Secret Wish was *her* business. She paid with her labor for his room and board and training fees. She had every right to expect her plans for him to be respected. Elizabeth Daingerfield over at Hinata Stock Farm on Iron Works Pike was a woman, and she managed one of the best-run places in the Bluegrass *and* handled Man O' War for Mr. Riddle as well. Drew would bet no one scolded Miss Daingerfield or pooh-poohed her notions just because she wasn't a man.

Flustered, she opened her mouth to argue with Rob, then changed her mind again. Maybe there was something in what he said, after all. Jack might treat her like a child, but that didn't mean she had to react to his condescension in a childish manner. If she were polite and businesslike, he'd eventually have to see that she knew what she was doing. "You're right," she said finally. "I shouldn't have been so snotty to Jack. Do you think I should apologize?"

It was Rob's turn to gape. "*You*— " His voice squeaked, and he cleared his throat and started again."*You* want to apologize?" His soft lips curved into a big grin.

Drew rolled her eyes skyward and grimaced at him. "I've said that I'm sorry before. Sometimes I do stupid things. Sometimes I say stupid things. Sometimes I say smart things in a stupid way. I've never claimed to be perfect, you know."

His blue eyes twinkled behind the steel-rimmed glasses. "Let's not be too rash, then," he said. "How about discussing the matter over dinner in Lexington on Friday?"

Ten minutes before Rob was due to pick her up for their date, Drew hurriedly sponged off the worst of the dust from a day spent in barns and tobacco fields, threw on the same pink frock she'd worn in Louisville to the

MacKenzie's Derby Eve party, and dragged the brush through her curls. She picked up the bottle of Amour-Amour her mother had given her for graduation from the exact spot she'd put it down that night. Maybe if she gave herself a good, healthy dousing, she'd smell more like a girl than a farmhand—or a horse. But what if it made her sneeze, the way some perfumes did? Of course, with her asthma, Momma had to be careful about perfumes, too, so she'd probably chosen one that wasn't too bad.

Tentatively, she removed the stopper and sniffed it. Nothing happened, except that, unlike graduation night, she actually found the aroma pleasant tonight, so she dabbed it liberally behind her ears, on her wrists, and at the backs of her knees—all the places Momma said you were supposed to put perfume. She hoped Rob liked it. She couldn't suppress a nervous giggle at the thought of actually going out alone with Rob.

She'd never been on a real date before. She'd always been far more interested in horses than in boys until she fell in love with Adam, and then, compared to him, high school boys seemed so pathetically immature she hadn't accepted the few invitations that had come her way. Her rejections, coupled with the rumors about the suspect status of her birth, had been enough to keep the rest from asking.

She pulled on her hose and garters, then slipped her feet into her T-straps. Neither Rob nor Trixie had ever cared a fig about those persistent rumors. "It's not your fault if you're a bastard," Trixie had said once when they were twelve and Drew had started crying on the playground after someone—Lucy Claire, probably—had taunted her. "Anyway I think it sounds kind of romantic and exciting that your mother was in love with your uncle before she married your father." Then Trixie had sniffed and glared at Lucy Claire as she said loudly, "Besides, it's much better to be a bastard than a bitch."

Drew had always liked Trixie before then, but that day they became best friends. Trixie had never been bothered by Drew's family's poverty. Just like Adam.

Adam. Almost two months since "The Kiss" and not a word from him. Trixie hadn't heard any new gossip from Chase, and the real reason for Adam and Victoria's fight, or the outcome of it, still remained a mystery. Sometimes Drew thought she'd imagined the way Adam's lips had felt against hers that day; she'd certainly dreamed of it often enough before then, and since.

Sometimes she wished she could just forget him completely. Loving Adam was never going to do her a bit of good. She had a life to live, and right now Rob was right smack in the middle of it.

Rob. Their date. The clocks in the parlor chimed the half-hour, and she realized she'd been dawdling as usual, so absorbed in her own thoughts that she'd lost track of time. She inspected herself in the mirror, shrugged, and headed downstairs.

They drove into Lexington in Rob's mother's Cadillac with the vast distance of the seat between them. After dinner at the Lafayette, they stopped at Joyland Park on the way back to Paris and danced for almost three hours at the amusement center's dance casino. By then, Rob knew whatever resistance he had left against falling totally in love with Drew was totally gone.

After the band's last song, a moving rendition of "Just a Kiss in the Dark," he kept hold of Drew's hand, tucking it into his elbow as they walked off the dance floor. "You're a swell dancer," he said. "I don't think I've ever danced so much in my entire life."

She laughed and leaned her head briefly on his shoulder. "I had fun, too." She sounded a little surprised.

They walked arm-in-arm back to the car. Rob opened

the passenger door for Drew, and to his delight, she slid over to the middle of the seat.

On the way home she was the one who finally brought up the subject of Secret Wish. "I still think I'm right about not racing him until at least next May," she said. "But from now on I promise to be more polite to Jack when I disagree with him."

"All right," Rob said, too befuddled to do anything but agree with her. All he wanted to do was kiss her again, but this time not in front of hundreds of racing fans. He slowed the Cadillac and turned in at the road to her house, yearning for the courage just to stop the car and pull her into his arms right there.

Instead he continued up the lane, silently reciting lines of poetry he wished he had the nerve to say aloud to her.

She walks in beauty like the night/Of cloudless climes and starry skies;/And all that's best of dark and bright/Meet in her aspect and her eyes.

He couldn't imagine Lord Byron being too timid and afraid to declare his feelings to the woman he loved. Of course, Lord Byron probably never had a woman like Drew for his muse. A wry smile tugged at his lips. Rob didn't know what to expect from her from day to day—or minute to minute. He stopped his car behind Edward's old Model-T and turned off the motor, then sat staring straight ahead with his hands on the wheel for a moment before he turned to look at Drew. "Thank you for accompanying me." He groaned inwardly at how stiff and formal the words sounded, but didn't know what else to say. "May I kiss you good night?"

"Don't be so silly," she said, giggling.

His chest constricted, and he sighed softly. "I'll see you to your door, then."

She laughed, then leaned against him and kissed his cheek. "You're such a goose, Robbie."

He had no idea what she meant, but deciding to take the best possible interpretation, he quickly bent his head and pressed his lips against hers. *I love you, Drew,* he thought as he savored the sensations of her full mouth. The words resonated in his head like a line of great poetry. *I love you, Drew.*

Twelve

December 1926

Drew shivered from both cold and anticipation as she sauntered into the roadhouse on Versailles Pike with Rob, Trixie, and Chase. The place reeked of cigarette smoke and stale grease, but Chase had assured them the speakeasy at the back was one of the best in the area, more than worth the drive from Paris. "I heard they've got a great jazz band playing there for the next couple of weeks before Christmas," he'd said after Rob lodged a protest against taking the girls to a place with such a bad reputation.

"Oh, come on, Robbie," Drew had said. "Don't be a spoilsport." She scooted even closer to him in the back seat of Chase's new car, a shiny black Daimler, and squeezed his hand, then planted a big kiss on his cheek. "You know how I love to dance."

"We can always go to Joyland," Rob said. "It's a lot closer."

"But there's no booze. And we've already finished off Chase's bourbon." Giggling, Trixie turned around and peered into the back seat. "How are you doing back there?"

"As if you needed any more to drink," Rob had mumbled, but everyone had ignored him.

So now here they were at Josephine's. Unimpressed, Drew glanced around the front room. It looked like an ordinary diner—mismatched chairs and tables, dingy oilcloth tablecloths, a long counter with stools at the back wall.

Chase jerked his head toward what appeared to be the kitchen door at the far end of the counter. "Follow me."

Rob grabbed Drew's hand and tucked it through his arm, pulling her close to him. "Stay right with me," he whispered.

Trixie turned around and grinned at them, and Drew rolled her eyes. Now that Drew had officially started seeing Rob, his protectiveness was a joke between them. "I wonder who took care of you for all those years before he came along," Trixie had joked more than once during the last four months.

Most of the time Drew didn't mind it too much. Places like this made her a little uneasy, and it was nice to know that Rob was there. But she hated it when he tried to keep her from having fun because he thought what she wanted to do wasn't "wise."

So what if coming to Josephine's wasn't wise? Wisdom was what you learned after you had lots of experiences, and going to a speakeasy was definitely an experience. Drew intended to have more than her share of adventures, and Rob was just going to have to get used to it if he wanted to be with her. Nevertheless, she tucked her purse tightly under her arm and clutched his hand a little anxiously as they followed Chase through the swinging door, into the kitchen, and down a short flight of stairs to another door.

Chase knocked twice, and the door creaked open. They stepped into a small, dark room heavy with the odors of tobacco smoke, stale perfume, and sweat. The floor was crowded with people sitting at little round tables, and a piano and drum set occupied a raised dais in the front corner. "When does the music start, Jake?" Chase asked the beefy doorman.

" 'Bout fifteen minutes, sir," Jake said, then conducted them to an empty table near the front.

As soon as he left, Drew said, "I hope this place has better booze than the one that Trixie and I sneaked into last year." She wrinkled her nose at the startled look on Rob's face and laughed. "I told you I wasn't perfect a long time ago, didn't I?"

"That you did," Rob said, frowning at Trixie. "But I had no idea you were leading my sister astray, too. Am I correct in understanding that the two of you girls went there unescorted?" Lifting his eyebrows, he eyed Chase.

"They weren't with me," Chase said, shrugging. "Here comes the waiter. What'll you girls have?"

"I like rum," Trixie said.

"Anything but gin is fine with me." Drew made a face and shuddered at the memory of the "gin" at the other speakeasy.

Rob pressed his lips together in a thin line and shook his head.

"Don't be such a stick in the mud." Drew glared at him with annoyance.

Chase ordered a fifth of rum and three bottles of Coca-Cola. "That's the way they drink it in Cuba," he said. "I think you'll like it."

"Bring me a bottle of Coke, too," Rob said. Drew couldn't tell whether he planned to drink it plain or if he'd finally relented and decided to join their fun.

Drew leaned an elbow on the tiny table while they waited for their drinks and the musicians finished setting up. Rob had really been getting on her nerves lately. He always had a reason for not wanting to do whatever she thought sounded like fun: it wasn't proper; it wasn't safe; he was too tired; they had a lot to do tomorrow. He was starting to sound more like a parent than a boyfriend, and she was getting bored with it. When the bottles arrived, she let Chase fill her glass half-way to the top with rum before she motioned him to stop.

She topped the glass with Coke, then drained the whole thing and smiled at Rob as if to dare him to say a word.

He took a swig of his Coca-Cola straight from the bottle and ignored her. "Are you staying in Paris or going back to Philadelphia for Christmas?" he asked Chase.

"We're spending Christmas here," Chase said. "Except for Adam. He and Victoria are celebrating the holidays in Radnor with her family."

Rum and disappointment sizzled in Drew's stomach. She forced herself to smile and say brightly, "So when is Adam getting married?" It would take more than half a glass of rum to make her mention Victoria by name.

"They're planning on June twenty-first." Chase answered Drew's question, but grinned into Trixie's eyes and clinked his glass against hers. "Then they're going on a six-week honeymoon in Europe."

"Lucky dogs," Trixie said, smiling back at Chase.

"Is Adam going to the Derby this year?" Asking about Adam was like pressing on a bruise to see if it still hurt, but Drew couldn't help herself. Besides, the rum was going straight to her head. Whatever passed through her mind spewed instantly out of her mouth.

Chase shrugged. "Victoria doesn't want to. I don't think Adam has decided yet. Too bad if he misses it, though. Ballantrae might have a chance this year—we're nominating Four Star General."

"He's Wish's full brother, isn't he?" Drew asked.

"Yeah." Chase filled her glass with more rum and Coca-Cola. "By Fair Play out of First Star. Father thought Wish had so much promise as a foal that he tried the match again the next year. After all, it's the same nick that produced Man O' War—a Hastings sire and a Rock Sand dam." Chase laughed. "Not that I'm a firm believer in the nick theory. Look at Adam and me. We have the same parents—but we couldn't be more different if one of us were Chinese."

Trixie giggled. "I'll bet Adam never got into trouble when he was a kid."

"You lose, then," Chase said. "And this is my payment." He leaned over and kissed Trixie lightly on the lips. "Adam was constantly in hot water for being so damn stubborn. He'd make up his mind about something, and nothing could drive him to change it—not even the old man. When he decided to join the army and go to France, Mother and Father couldn't talk him out of it. Father even threatened to disinherit him. Adam just laughed and said he might not have to bother." Chase took a long drink from his glass, then set it down with a thud. "And he hasn't changed a goddamn bit. Adam's never wrong. Just ask him."

"I know what you mean." Drew's voice sounded a little slurred, but she didn't care. Talking about Adam was just too painful; she'd be glad when the music started. She raised her glass to take another drink, but Rob grasped her wrist. Rum and cola sloshed over her hand, and she glared at him, a sudden surge of anger at Rob driving out the ache in her heart for Adam. "What the hell are you doing?" She jerked her arm away from him, and the rest of the drink spilled onto the table.

Rob pulled a handkerchief from his pocket and mopped up the dark pool of liquid spreading over the table. "I think you've had enough to drink, Drew."

"What I do is none of your damn business!" Drew jumped up so quickly she knocked over her chair. Her cheeks burning, she grabbed her purse, then wove her way through the crowded room just as the music started.

Jake opened the door for her, and she fled through the kitchen and diner, not even turning around to see if Rob was behind her. She'd rather walk all the way home than spend another minute with him.

Thirteen

"Oh, Lordy," Drew moaned, squinting into the bright light. "Shut those damn curtains, will you, Trixie?" She pushed herself up on one wobbly elbow. "What the hell time is it, anyway?" At least she knew where she was. After all the bourbon and rum she'd drunk last night, that surely was an accomplishment. Of course, she and Trixie had planned that Drew would spend the night at Blue Meadow—they both knew it would be impossible for Drew to sneak in late at her own home, but Trixie's mother went to bed early and slept soundly.

"It's after ten o'clock, you goose. Mom and Rob are going to be home from church any minute." Trixie ran a brush through her blond bob, then sat down on the foot of the bed and peered at Drew. "You look a little green around the gills."

"I *feel* green," Drew said. "I wish I didn't remember last night so clearly. I thought getting drunk was supposed to make you forget things, but it sure doesn't with me. I'm still so mad at Rob I could choke him. Do you think he was being an idiot, or was it just my overcharged imagination?"

Trixie tilted her head and fixed Drew with her bright blue eyes. "He *was* pretty annoying. Chase would never act like that. Sometimes I think Rob forgets that he's not *your* big brother, too. He doesn't mean any harm, though. I know he loves you."

Drew made an effort to control her irritation with Rob. Trixie was probably right. But Rob's love was so overwhelming sometimes, and it often seemed that he didn't really love *her*, but rather some idea of what he thought she was. Whenever she did something that wouldn't fit into a piece of his poetry, his lips grew thin and tight and his voice took on a harsh tone. And every time he acted like that, she wanted to scream at him, "I'm not who you want me to be!" and run away.

Furthermore, she didn't particularly *want* to be a fit subject for anyone's love poem. Not even Adam's. She let her head flop back onto the pillow and closed her eyes. He was getting married on the first day of summer. What used to be her favorite day of the year would now forever be a reminder of her sorrow. Why couldn't he have picked some ordinary day? Her lower lip trembled, and she caught it between her teeth. Adam probably hadn't chosen the day, anyway.

"Drew? Are you all right?" Trixie's voice sounded worried.

Drew opened her eyes and smiled weakly. "Just a little hung over, that's all," she said. She pushed herself up and swung her legs over the side of the bed. "I'll be fine as soon as I have some coffee." She had no idea what she was going to say to Rob, though. Maybe she *had* overreacted—it certainly wouldn't be an unusual occurrence—but he had definitely provoked her into throwing a temper tantrum. If it hadn't been for Chase and Trixie, she'd probably never have gotten back in the car. As it was, she'd refused to sit in the back seat with Rob; and when they'd gotten to Blue Meadow, she'd marched straight upstairs without a word.

Her head throbbing with the memory, she forced herself to stand. Maybe she should apologize to Rob for her outburst—but she'd been damned if she would until after he said he was sorry for being such a jerk.

Ten minutes later, just as she finished dressing, Drew heard the Carlisles' Cadillac pull into the graveled drive. She peered quickly into the mirror. Trixie was right—she did look a little green. She pinched her cheeks to give them some color; then she and Trixie ran downstairs to wait for Rob and his mother in the big, warm kitchen. Trixie started the coffee while Drew eased herself into one of the chairs at the kitchen table.

"I'll have breakfast ready in a jiffy," Vi Carlisle said, bustling into the kitchen. She took off her heavy wool coat and hung, it on a hook by the back door, then grabbed her apron from another hook. She slipped the purple gingham apron over her head, patting her steel gray hair back into place, and tied the sash around her ample waist. "How does pancakes, sausage, and eggs sound?"

"Great, Mom," Rob said. He shrugged out of his brown tweed overcoat and put it on the hook next to his mother's. He sat in the chair across from Drew, throwing a worried glance in her direction.

Drew ignored him. If Rob wanted to be a prig for the rest of his life, that was his problem. She smiled at Vi. "I could eat a horse."

Trixie laughed. "Well, you came to the right place. We've got plenty."

"You're lucky," Drew said. "I wish *we* did."

"Ashworth Farm used to have some good racehorses," Vi said, plucking a handful of eggs from the basket by the sink. "Your daddy sold them all off after young Andrew was killed, though. I remember Hamlet and Macbeth in particular—Andrew was partial to Shakespeare, so all of his horses had names like that. Both of them showed a lot of promise as two-year-olds. Never heard much about them after Edward sold them to some stable up Maryland way." She cracked the eggs into a large bowl, then stirred them with a fork.

Drew's stomach flip-flopped, but whether from Vi's

revelation or the smell of the percolating coffee, she didn't know. No one had ever told her about Uncle Andrew's horses before. She'd known that there used to be thoroughbreds at Ashworth Farm, but she hadn't realized that Uncle Andrew had been so involved in racing.

Actually, though, it wasn't so surprising that she'd never heard about it, since neither Momma nor Daddy hardly ever mentioned Uncle Andrew; whenever his name came up, they usually pushed the conversation toward another topic as quickly as possible. And after Drew had gotten old enough to understand the rumors about Uncle Andrew and her mother, she'd been reluctant to talk about him, too, even though some people thought he might be her real father. Or maybe *because* he might be. There'd been times when she was little that she'd positively hated Andrew, blaming him for her mother's illness and absence, her father's sadness, their poverty, and the names the kids at school called her. Now it seemed that perhaps she could lay the blame for the dearth of racehorses at Ashworth Farm at his door as well. If only she knew enough to figure out why Daddy really didn't want any thoroughbreds on the farm, maybe she could convince him to change his mind after all.

Trixie set a cup of coffee in front of her. "You look like you've got something up your sleeve," she said.

Drew just shrugged and sipped the steaming coffee. "Why do you suppose Daddy sold all of Uncle Andrew's horses, Vi?"

Clearing his throat noisily, Rob frowned at his mother. "That's something I think you should ask your father, Drew," he said before Vi could answer. "I don't think we have the right to speculate about his reasons."

Drew put down the cup of hot coffee before she lost control and pitched it at him. "Maybe I will." She glared at him as Vi placed platters of pancakes, eggs, and sausage on the table between them. Not only had he *not* apologized for being so bossy and overbearing last night, but he actually thought he had the right to keep her from pursuing something that was tremendously important to her just because it offended his sense of propriety.

Seething inside, she ate quickly, refusing to look at Rob. If he thought dating her gave him the right to treat her like this, he had a big surprise coming. She'd turned Neal Rafferty down last summer when he'd asked her out, but maybe she wouldn't if he asked again. Chase had mentioned that he was planning a visit after Christmas.

She glanced across the table at Rob, and the prim set of his mouth as he carefully chewed his sausage irritated her even more. How could she have possibly considered marrying him? Her parents were strict, but even they were more accepting of her than Rob was. She bit back the urge to scream something awful at him, but only because of Trixie and Vi.

Half an hour later, she retrieved her overnight bag from Trixie's room and, still angry, headed toward Rob's office. While she and Trixie had washed the breakfast dishes, she'd brooded about Rob's behavior and ended up even madder. Now she knew exactly what she wanted to say to him. She knocked on the door, then stepped inside.

He looked up from the papers strewn over the top of his desk. "I'm sorry, Drew, but—"

She held up her hand to silence him. "You're not my father," she said. "You *were* my boyfriend. You *were* my boss. You *were* the owner of the farm where I boarded my horse. None of which gives you any right at all to treat me like a child. You are now simply my best friend's big brother."

She spun on her heel and stalked out, banging the door shut behind her. Feeling a little better already, she headed for Secret Wish's stall.

* * *

Drew reined Wish in at the new barn, which wasn't really new but rather the newest of Ashworth Farm's several old barns. Daddy's draft horses and mules occupied a few of the stalls, but most were empty and had been ever since Drew could remember. She patted Wish's neck, then bent forward and whispered to him, "We're home, boy. Now I just have to convince Daddy."

She slid off Wish, led him into the barn, and put him into a stall while she swept out the one next to it. She forked sweet-smelling clean straw onto the floor, then filled the water bucket and feed bin before she guided Wish inside. After removing his tack, she rubbed his forehead and kissed the white star between his eyes. She'd ridden the two miles between Blue Meadow and Ashworth slowly, so he didn't need walking, and she'd groom him later. First, she wanted to talk to her father before she lost her nerve.

She backed out of the stall, but before she got it latched, her father spoke.

"Drew?"

She turned around. He was silhouetted against the wide opening of the barn door, the pale blue winter sky and skeleton branches of the sycamore tree behind him. He frowned at her, his thick white eyebrows forming a single line above his eyes.

"He's mine, Daddy." Her hands suddenly shook, and she straightened her arms and clenched her fists at her side. He *had* to listen to her this time. "And I want to keep him here."

Her father closed his eyes for a long second, then took a deep breath. "You know how I feel about racehorses. We simply can't afford to keep even one."

She itched to ask him if that was the real reason, but she didn't want to jeopardize her position by antagonizing him, so instead she said, "I have the money I've saved from working at Blue Meadow. It'll be enough until Wish starts paying his own way. It won't cost you anything."

He narrowed his eyes and cocked his head. "How could you afford to buy him, then?"

She'd known he'd ask so she'd come up with the answer to that one on the ride over. She'd considered the truth, but rejected it immediately as that would mean admitting that she'd bet on a race. So would claiming that she'd won Wish in a wager with Rob, as Daddy abhorred gambling of any kind. "Rob gave him to me last week. As a sort of early Christmas present."

He nodded, seemingly satisfied. It was Momma who would bring up the question of propriety, but she'd worry about that later. "Well, then, why don't you just keep him at Blue Meadow?" her father asked.

"I can't." She clasped her hands in front of her and stared at them. "We had a fight this morning, and I quit."

"Oh. I see." He nodded slowly. "But what I don't see is how you're going to be able to pay for his keep if you don't have a job."

"I can do it, Daddy. I told you—I have money saved. And I'll get another job if I have to. Wish won't cost you a penny. I promise."

"You'll give him back to Rob if you can't pay for his upkeep?"

"Yes." She wagged her head vigorously, then held her breath.

He sighed loudly, a tiny sad smile lighting his dark brown eyes. "All right, Drew," he said finally. "You win."

Fourteen

April 1927

Drew rummaged through the icebox, finally pulling out last night's ham. She carved off a thin piece, then sliced a couple of pieces of bread and made herself a quick sandwich. Her legs ached after a morning spent inspecting the tobacco seed beds with Daddy, so she eased herself into a chair at the kitchen table and pawed through the day's mail scattered across the yellow and white checked tablecloth.

The sandwich turned sour in her mouth when she spotted the unfamiliar but feminine handwriting on the fancy white envelope on top, and she swallowed the bite quickly. The postmark was Philadelphia. Knowing she wouldn't be able to eat any more of it, she laid the sandwich down and picked up the envelope.

Momma had already opened it. Inside was another white envelope. Drew pulled it out, ripping it in her haste, although she didn't know why she should be in such a hurry. Her heart hammered in her ears, and her whole body felt cold even though it was a pleasantly warm spring day.

She stared at the formal lettering as if her refusal to comprehend what it said made the invitation a joke, a lie. But it didn't work. Somehow the engraved words carved the finality of Adam's marriage on her heart in a way that Chase's news never did. Adam and Victoria's parents requested the presence of Mr. and Mrs. Edward Ashworth and Drew at the wedding of Adam Michael MacKenzie and Victoria Ann Seton, held at 2 o'clock in the afternoon on the first day of summer at the First Presbyterian Church on Windsor Street in Philadelphia, reception to follow at the Hotel Excelsior.

She gasped at the pain knifing through her chest. How could a piece of paper and a few words hurt so much? She still felt Adam's kiss on her lips, recalled the surge of joy and passion when he'd taken her in his arms, but the memory only intensified the grief in her heart. In two months and eleven days, Adam would be lost to her forever.

Tears burned her eyes and streamed down her cheeks. She was kidding herself. Adam was already gone. There'd been a brief moment of hope when he kissed her, but in truth it had disappeared immediately afterward, almost as if it had never really existed.

But it had. She knew it. He'd kissed her as if he loved her. And she'd kissed him back because she loved him.

She dropped the invitation and it fluttered to the floor. Sobs racking her chest, she stared at it for several seconds before running out of the kitchen. She flung open the door and headed for the new barn. She felt like an idiot, but she couldn't help it.

Truly, though, Adam was the idiot. *She'd* never do anything just because everyone else said it was the right thing to do, but he'd always been so responsible, so dutiful, so correct. It was Adam who'd enlisted and gone off to fight in France, Adam who'd taken on his father's workload at the MacKenzie's bank in Philadelphia so old Hugh would have more time for his horses, Adam who gave time and money to charities and good causes. He was so good, so selfless, so perfect.

Perfect, hah! She let herself into Wish's stall, her cheeks still wet with tears. That one kiss gave him away. He wasn't any more perfect than she was—and she didn't even come close. The problem with Adam was that he couldn't admit to himself that he might have made a mistake—and marrying Victoria was the real mistake. Kissing Drew was probably the most honest thing he'd done in years. Laying her cheek against Wish's warm neck, she hugged him tightly against her.

If only Wish could talk. She could tell him everything she was thinking, but sometimes it just wasn't enough. Ever since her fight with Rob, she hadn't seen enough of Trixie, and Drew missed her.

She made up her mind on the spot. Wish needed his daily ride, and she needed to see Trixie. She led him out of his stall and he followed with ears pricked up and tail held high. He'd been in perfect shape for the past month— no heat in his hocks, no problems with his hooves—but she'd decided to wait until the fall classics to race him again. She knew that if he were still at Blue Meadow, both Rob and Jack would be pressuring her to race him in May, just a month away, and Wish would be in intensive training now instead of the easy rides she took him on every day.

But every instinct she had told her Wish still wasn't ready. He'd had such a great start as a two-year-old, but then something had happened about half way through the racing season, and he had never completely recovered. She wanted to give him a second chance. She tacked him up, then led him next to the paddock fence, climbed to the second rung, and boosted herself into the saddle. He deserved every bit of the care and attention he was getting from her, and she was positive he'd have the heart to win again when his legs allowed him to run the way he was meant to, the way he'd run when she'd watched him at his morning workouts at Ballantrae two years ago. Nobody'd ever had to force him to run then.

She squeezed her knees against his sides, and he started off at a fast walk. He might be a thoroughbred and a stallion, but he had one of the sweetest dispositions she'd ever seen. He loved the attention she gave him. Still, she could tell that sometimes he was antsy, especially if they happened to meet another horse and rider when she was exercising him. Then she had to haul back on the reins with all her strength to keep him to the moderate pace she wanted. Her arms ached afterward, but it was a satisfying ache because it meant Wish still had the urge to win.

Half an hour later she slowed Wish to a walk as they entered the lane that led to Blue Meadow. It had been a little under four months since the last time she'd ridden Wish there; and although Trixie came to see her whenever she could, Drew had not spoken to Rob since the day she'd quit and taken Secret Wish home with her.

She dismounted and led Wish to the front door of the Carlisles' home, then knocked loudly. A minute later Rob opened the door. Drew blinked a couple of times. She'd figured that Rob would be working in his office or looking over the stables this time of day. "Oh," she said. "Is Trixie here?"

He shook his head. "She and Mom went to Lexington for the afternoon."

"Oh." She turned to go.

"Drew. Wait a minute." He touched her arm lightly. "I've missed you." He took a deep breath and summoned every ounce of will he possessed. It would be so much easier just to let her go, but the pounding of his heart made it impossible for him to give up. Besides, Trixie had advised him not to go running after Drew but to wait until she came to him. Well, she was here now, even if not precisely to see him, and he'd waited long enough. "Please stay."

Her dark brown eyes narrowed. "Why?"

"Because I want to apologize."

"Why?" She lifted an eyebrow.

"Because I was an ass."

"That's something you just realized today?"

Damn her—he never knew how to respond. Still, he had to try. "I've been trying to understand," he said. "I think I might be getting closer." He stared down at the scuffed wood floor beneath his feet and tried to figure out the best way to put it. Under the best of circumstances, talking to Drew was dangerous. One wrong word now and he might never get another opportunity.

"I was too pushy," he said. "I know that. I don't want another little sister. Trixie is more than enough for me." He tried out a weak smile on her.

To his gratification, she responded with a grin. "That's a start."

"A damn good start if you ask me," he said. "I think I deserve a second chance." When she laughed, he sagged with relief against the doorway. "Does that mean you're willing to give me another try?"

"I've always been willing," she said. "You just never asked."

He clenched his fists at his side and ignored the heavy rock settling in his stomach. "I'm asking now," he said. "How would you like to go to the Derby with Trixie and me next month?"

May 1927

Sipping his third bourbon and branch, Adam surveyed the crowd gathered in his father's suite at the Brown Hotel. Normally he enjoyed Derby Eve parties, but everything was different this year. For one thing, Victoria had decided at the last minute not to come—too many things to do with the wedding just a little more than a month away, she'd said.

For another, there was Drew. Chase had told him she was coming with Trixie and Rob again. It had been almost a year since the last time he'd seen her, and he'd berated himself over and over again for his loss of control that day in his car. Something strange had overcome him, but he'd promised himself it would never happen again. It wasn't fair to either Drew or Victoria. He wasn't an animal ruled by carnal desires and lust; he was a man, an ethical man with a strong sense of right and wrong. And whatever it was that had made him kiss Drew was wrong.

He tipped up his glass for another drink, and the ice cubes clinked. Time for a refill. Usually he wasn't much of a drinker, but tonight he needed something to help diminish his edginess. He was headed toward the bar set up next to the fireplace when Drew and Rob walked into the room.

While the bartender freshened his drink, Adam leaned an elbow on the counter and watched the two of them. Drew wore the same pink dress as last year, but that wasn't surprising given the financial difficulties of Ashworth Farm and the costs involved in supporting a racehorse, not to mention that clothes had never been a priority with her. And, in truth, it didn't matter what she wore; she still looked beautiful in that unconventional way of hers, with her dark eyes sparkling and her thick curly hair cascading over her shoulders. He was glad she hadn't pinned it up in a bun the way she did sometimes.

Rob touched her arm and said something to her; and when she smiled at him in response, her whole face glowed with happiness. Horrified, Adam sucked in his breath with a startled gasp of recognition, realizing that the unsettled feeling in the pit of his stomach was actually jealousy. What the hell was wrong with him? Not only was he already engaged to be married to a stunningly beautiful, intelligent woman, but Drew was much too young—not to mention that she was Scott's little sister and had been like a sister to him since she was a child of seven. He clenched his jaw, grinding his back teeth so hard it hurt.

Fortunately, the arrival of Trixie and Chase gave him time to regain his equanimity. He finished off the last of his drink, procured another refill for himself and a trayful of drinks, and headed off to join them just as they greeted Drew and Rob. After handing out drinks, Adam steered the conversation toward the race tomorrow, just about the only neutral topic he could think of. Since neither Ballantrae nor Blue Meadow had an entry, it was easy to discuss the prospects without offending anyone. He avoided Drew's eyes, concentrating instead with feigned interest on Rob's and Chase's assessments of the Derby entrants.

Finally, after they had debated the merits of the last hopeful, Chase lifted an eyebrow, surveyed the room, and said in a low voice, "Anyone else game to try out the new speakeasy on Sixth and Broadway that Neal told me about? He said they have a swell band and some of the best bootleg booze in Kentucky." Chase grinned and hooked his arm through Trixie's. "In fact, he's probably waiting there for us now."

Drew poked an elbow in Rob's side. "Let's go," she said. She winked broadly at Adam. "Just a bunch of old fogies here."

Rob was silent for a moment, then cleared his throat. "Well, I don't know," he said. "We just got here a little while ago." He jerked his head toward the bar, where a cluster of young men had gathered. "Besides, Curt Hayden just arrived. He was a classmate of mine at U.K., and I'd really like to talk to him."

Drew drained half of her bourbon and water, then forced herself to take a deep breath and smile at Rob. She'd promised herself not to lose her temper with him tonight no matter what he did. "What's the place called?" she asked Chase. "Maybe we can join you later."

"Chateau Fifi," he said. "Fancy French restaurant on

the main floor, speakeasy in the basement. There's an entrance off the alley in the rear. What about you, Adam?"

"I think I'll stick around here a little longer," Adam said. "But enjoy yourselves."

Chase shrugged, and then he and Trixie headed toward the door. "See you later."

Drew fought back her irritation as she watched Chase and Trixie make their escape. Not that she really wanted to go with them—Adam was here, after all—but it was galling to have Rob making her decisions for her once again. If only he'd stop trying to watch out for her all the time. She'd bet that was the real reason he'd turned Chase down, not because he wanted so desperately to talk to some old college chum. She finished off the rest of her drink and set it back on the tray Adam had put down on an end table nearby.

"Let me get you another," Adam said, signaling the waiter circulating the room.

"Thanks." Drew smiled at him, her lips quivering in time to the butterflies flitting about in her stomach. She wasn't sure how to act with Adam. He was just as self-possessed and calm as always, just as friendly, just as *brotherly*. But she couldn't forget that kiss, even if he apparently could.

Her drink arrived, and Rob excused himself. "Will you entertain Drew for me?" he asked Adam. "I haven't talked to Curt since I had to leave school."

"My pleasure," Adam said.

Sipping her drink, Drew stared at him. He sounded as if he really meant it. A daring idea wormed its way into her brain, and her lips curved in a smile as she shifted her gaze to Rob's retreating back. She clinked her glass against Adam's, then tipped up her glass. "I'm going to join Chase and Trixie," she said. "Want to come along?"

Fifteen

"Well," Adam said. "I suppose if I don't, you'll just go by yourself."

Drew couldn't keep herself from grinning at him. "How did you know?"

Shaking his head, he rolled his eyes skyward. "I've learned something in the—what has it been?—eleven years I've known you. It amazes me that Rob doesn't understand yet." He beckoned the waiter back. "Let's have another drink first, though. Besides being free, the liquor here is far better than we'll get at any speakeasy in Louisville."

She narrowed her eyes at him in mock annoyance. "You're just trying to get me so drunk I'll forget about going to that dive over on Sixth Street. Well, I'll warn you now—it's not going to work. I never forget anything." *Including the way you kissed me last year, you idiot.* She studied his face, seeking a reaction to her comment.

A stiffness in his mouth and jaw told her the words had struck home, but the next instant he smiled and the tenseness disappeared. Still, she wasn't disappointed. He'd covered it up quickly, but he *had* reacted. He hadn't forgotten. That was all she needed to know.

"I'm fully aware of that," he said, his tone one of exaggerated ruefulness. "I'll bet you still remember the first time I beat you at checkers instead of letting you win."

She threw back her head and laughed, refusing to let

him get the better of her with his familiar "I'm older and wiser than you" ruse. "I surely do," she said, nodding vigorously. "That was the day when I knew you saw me as a real person, not just a little child. You'd let a child win, but not an equal. It took me a while to understand, but when I did, I realized that it was a compliment."

"Actually, I never thought of it that way at the time," Adam said. "But you might be right." He lifted two drinks from the waiter's tray and handed one of them to Drew.

She clinked her glass against his. "Here's to growing up," she said. "Sometimes I think it's taken me forever."

Adam met her eyes for a long moment before he spoke. "Sometimes I think you've always been grown up," he said softly. Lifting a dark eyebrow, he took a drink of his bourbon and watched her over the top of his glass.

Drew refused to be the first to lower her eyes even though her stomach quivered and her hands shook. Maybe it was only the bourbon, but suddenly she felt lightheaded, and she pinched her lips together to keep from giggling as inanely as Trixie did all the time.

It didn't work. The laughter bubbled up from the depth of her being; and when she couldn't contain it any longer, it rolled out of her mouth in contagious peals. Adam laughed as loudly and as long as she did, but finally they both subsided into broad smiles and an occasional hiccup.

"God, that felt good," Adam said, wiping the tears from his eyes. "I'm not even sure what's so funny, but I haven't laughed like that in years."

"You poor thing." She patted him on the back. "I do it all the time. Especially when Trixie and I are together."

"I'll bet you do."

"Well, I'm ready to get out of here." She set her glass on the table nearby. "Everybody probably thinks we're crazy."

The smile disappeared from Adam's eyes. "What about Rob? Shouldn't you tell him where you're going?"

Drew flicked a hand in the air. "Oh, he already knows. He hates speakeasies, but he won't mind if you're with me." She tilted her head toward Rob, who stood near the bar absorbed in an animated conversation with his friend. "Besides, he's so busy talking about poetry with Curt he'd probably just be annoyed if I interrupted him." In truth, he'd more than likely give her a lecture—which she didn't want to hear right now—or insist on coming along, too, and this was likely the last chance she'd ever get to be alone with Adam. If she didn't find out tonight how he really felt about her, she'd spend the rest of her life wondering.

Adam shrugged. "All right," he said. "Let me get your wrap for you, and we'll go."

"I left it in my room," Drew said. "It's one floor down. We can stop and pick it up on our way."

He tucked her arm though his, then guided her through the crowd. "I'm assuming we'll be back, so let's just take French leave. This party is such a crush I doubt anyone will miss us."

Drew's insides quivered, but whether from the touch of Adam's hand on her arm or the several drinks she'd just consumed she had no idea. Maybe both. She knew that to him it was probably just a casually polite gesture, but even so every pore of her being vibrated with his touch.

A few people smiled and nodded as they wove their way toward the door, but no one detained them. He disengaged his arm from hers to open the door for her, and then they headed down the stairs to the fifth floor.

When they arrived in front of room 515, Drew removed the key from her purse and gave it to Adam, her fingers brushing against his hand. All she wanted him to do was to kiss her one more time—then she'd know for sure if he was really and truly Victoria's. And if he was, she could put him out of her mind and never dream about him again. In a month he'd be married, and she'd never been one to moon around over lost causes.

She stifled a giggle. Not unless, of course, they weren't really lost. Like Wish. Everyone *thought* he was a lost cause, but she *knew* he wasn't. If only it were so easy with Adam.

Smiling at her, he unlocked the door and pushed it open. "After you," he said, returning the key to her, then following her inside.

Drew surveyed the room and grimaced. It was a tiny one this year because Rob had reserved it for Trixie and hadn't been able to get another larger one at such late notice. The double bed occupied most of the floor space, and the rest was littered with open suitcases. The two straightback chairs and the footboard of the white iron bed were draped with articles of clothing. "Sorry for the mess. We got in late, and we were in such a hurry to get to the party neither of us bothered to unpack." She held out her hands and laughed. "I know my coat is here somewhere."

Adam pawed through the pile of clothes on the chair next to him and pulled out a plain gray coat. "Is this it?"

Drew nodded, and he held it out for her. At the same moment that she thrust her arms into the sleeves, the world started spinning and, giggling, she leaned against Adam's chest to brace herself.

His arms tightened around her. She turned her head and looked up into his green eyes, and before either of them had time to think, he bent his head and pressed his lips to hers.

The world kept spinning, but this time she knew it wasn't because she was dizzy. Closing her eyes, she twisted around to face him, then clasped her hands behind his neck and returned his kiss with three years' worth of frustrated passion. If he didn't know how much she loved him now, he never would.

This time he did not back away. Groaning, he covered her face with kisses, then returned again to her mouth, parting her lips with the tip of his tongue. "Oh Jesus, Drew," he murmured. "What am I doing?"

"Don't you mean *we?*" she whispered. She wanted to tell him that she loved him but was afraid to say more. Twice before, Adam had controlled his ardor, then pretended that nothing had happened. She couldn't stand for that to happen tonight. Her lips still tasting his and her arms still twined around his neck, she backed up until her legs touched the bed. She sank onto it, pulling him with her. She wasn't really sure what would happen next, but as long as he kept kissing her as if he couldn't get enough, that was all that mattered.

Because *she* couldn't get enough, either. She pulled his starched dress shirt loose from the waistband of his black trousers and stroked his chest, weaving her fingers through the thick hair, teasing his nipples with her fingertips.

After unbuttoning the bodice of her dress, he matched her caresses with those of his own, then slid her dress off her shoulders and past her hips until it fell to the floor. Suddenly, he cursed under his breath and pulled away from her.

Drew shivered even though she wasn't cold. She opened her eyes and stared at Adam as he gazed down at her, his face tense with passion and his starched white shirt hanging loose and wrinkled beneath his black dinner jacket.

"Christ, you're beautiful," he said, tucking his shirt back in. "Leaving now is the hardest thing I've ever done. I blame myself entirely for what's happened so far, and I apologize." He slurred the words slightly. "I have to—"

"No!" She grasped him around the waist and dragged him back down on top of her. "I won't let you go this time. I love you." Tears filled her eyes and brimmed over, wetting both their cheeks as she kissed him. "I wouldn't care if you were getting married tomorrow—I'd still want you tonight." Then inspiration struck, and she smiled at him through her tears. "Besides, if you won't make love to me tonight, I'll bet Neal Rafferty will."

"Darling Drew." A tiny smile curved the corners of his lips. "Are you trying to blackmail me?"

She shook her head solemnly. "That's a promise, not blackmail. Blackmail is threatening to tell Victoria what you've done so far if you don't stay and finish what you've started."

He lifted a dark eyebrow. "Oh," he said. "Yes, the difference is quite clear. You think I'm more likely to try to protect your reputation than my own." He cupped her chin in his hand, then lowered his head once more to her lips. "And you're absolutely right," he murmured between kisses. "Tomorrow I will hate myself, but tonight I will love you."

He stood and quickly removed his clothing, tossing it onto a nearby chair. Bending over her, he unfastened her bra, then trailed his hand lightly up the inside of her leg until he reached her panties, which he tugged off gently before lying down next to her. Exploring her mouth all the while with his own, he stroked her stomach, then her inner thighs, gradually working his way to her soft, moist folds.

The room whirled around Drew, and she squeezed her eyes shut and lost herself in the delicious sensations pouring through her body. She clung to Adam, her lifeboat in the midst of a surging sea.

Then he became the sea, catching her up in the huge waves of his desire. His body touched her everywhere, and she didn't know if the moans filling her ears were hers or his or, when at last he poured himself into her, the roaring of the sea itself.

Sixteen

July 1927

Wedged between her parents, Drew sat in the front seat of the Model-T, wincing with every jolt. It seemed to her that Daddy hadn't missed a pothole between Ashworth Farm and Blue Meadow, and there were dozens of them. Her back throbbed and her stomach bounced up to her throat every time he hit one, and she was so tired of hearing Momma carry on about how wonderful Rob was that she could just scream. She was bathed in sweat and about as cranky as a water moccasin in the middle of a desert.

She closed her ears to her mother's chatter and counted back the weeks to the Derby on her fingers for at least the hundredth time in the last month. Today was the Fourth of July; the Derby had been a little less than two months ago.

And she hadn't had a period since then.

Hoping that it would start tomorrow was beginning to get difficult, even though her body felt the way it usually did right before—achy abdomen, swollen breasts. The worst thing was that there was no one she could ask, not even Trixie, who'd undoubtedly assume the worst and suspect Rob as the culprit.

Momma mentioned Adam's name as they turned onto the

lane leading to Blue Meadow, and immediately Drew pulled herself out of her thoughts and focused on Momma's words.

"Do you suppose they'll be at the Carlisles' party?" Momma asked. "Vi told me she'd heard that they'd cut their honeymoon short because of Hugh's illness."

The car hit another hole, and Drew almost lost her breakfast. Where had Momma heard that rumor? If Adam and Victoria were at the Carlisles' Fourth of July party, Drew would walk home. The memory of Adam's anger when he'd left her after they'd made love that night in Louisville and his brooding reserve at the Derby the next day still seared her heart. All she'd wanted from him was some small acknowledgment that he still cared. Instead, he'd been cold and formal and distant and polite. He'd looked at her as if he hated her almost as much as he hated himself.

She tried to tell herself she was being unfair, but she was having a hard time convincing herself otherwise. In all likelihood, she figured Adam probably hated and blamed only himself for his own weakness despite his anger with her. He'd always been that way—expecting perfection from himself—but she'd taken the risk anyway. She caught her chapped lower lip between her teeth and chewed on it so hard she tasted blood. But it was hard to be fair when she was probably pregnant with his child, and when he had made no effort at all to contact her since then.

Still, what a mess she'd made of things. She should have known that throwing herself at Adam when he'd had too much to drink and not telling him that she was a virgin would end up the way it did . . .

"Have you heard anything about it, Drew?" Momma's question cut into Drew's thoughts.

Drew stared at Momma blankly for a second. "About Adam, you mean?" She shook her head. "Mr. MacKenzie isn't *that* sick, is he? Wouldn't they take him back to Philadelphia if he were?"

"That would be my guess." Her father pulled the Model-T to the side of the road behind a long string of parked cars. "I don't think we're going to get much closer than this." He looked at Momma, his shaggy gray eyebrows drawn together with concern. "Is this too far away? Would you like me to drop you and Drew off at the front porch before I park the car?"

Momma leaned across Drew and patted Daddy's hand. "I'm feeling fine today," she said. "An easy stroll will be just the thing."

Drew climbed out of the car after her mother, and the three of them walked slowly down the middle of the dirt lane bordered on either side by sparkling white fences and tall elm trees. Beyond the fences, mares grazed on the lush grass while their colts and fillies cavorted nearby. Ordinarily the familiar scene brought Drew pleasure, but today she simply registered its presence as she trudged numbly beside her parents.

She'd even considered pretending to be ill this morning in order to avoid the party, but she didn't have it in her to disappoint Trixie, who was counting on her to help out. And besides, with Wish once again back at Blue Meadow and in training with Jack Nolan for the fall classics, she owed Rob the courtesy of attending Blue Meadow Farm's annual Independence Day barbecue.

Actually, she owed Rob more than courtesy. He'd been nothing but kind to her since the Derby. When he'd asked her where she'd gone to the night of the MacKenzies' party, she just told him that Adam had escorted her back to her room because she'd gotten a sudden awful headache; and all Rob had done was offer her some sympathy. Of course, she'd looked as if she could use some, with her eyes red and puffy from crying. He had no way of knowing she was upset because Adam had gotten angry

when he discovered she was a virgin—and she wouldn't
let him stop. "You're impossible, Drew," Adam had said
while he was putting his clothes back on. "I assumed that
you and Rob had—" He frowned at her. "Why didn't you
tell me?"

"Would you have made love to me if I had?" she asked.
"Probably not."

She just shrugged. "There's your answer."

"Do you mean to tell me that you had this whole epi-
sode planned?" He narrowed his eyes, and what little remained of the softness of love disappeared completely.

She recoiled from the harsh judgment in his eyes, pulling the wrinkled sheet up tightly under her chin. "No,"
she said, "but I doubt if you'll believe that now. I just
wanted to know if you loved me or not. I know it sounds
pretty stupid, but I thought I'd be able to tell by the way
you kissed me."

He'd laughed then, but it was an ugly sound, and a
shudder ran down Drew's spine. Now she knew what Rob
had meant that time when he'd commented that Adam
MacKenzie would be a dangerous enemy. She'd always
seen Adam from the perspectives of adoring child and
infatuated teenager, and he'd spoiled and indulged her
from his lofty position as surrogate older brother. But everything had changed forever since that night. He'd turned
and left without another word, leaving Drew sobbing in
her bed.

And now the worst of it was that she had only herself
to blame for driving him completely away from her. Even
though she preferred to dwell on her own problems, Drew
forced herself to at least pretend to pay attention as
Momma chatted excitedly about the party and the friends
she hoped to see.

Before they reached the circular drive in front of the
house, Rob emerged, waving, from a cluster of people
gathered on the veranda. He loped down the front steps,

his mouth stretched in a happy grin and the sunlight glinting off of his glasses. "I'm so glad you all are here!" he said, shaking Edward's hand and planting a kiss on Margaret's cheek. He smiled into Drew's eyes. "It wouldn't be a party without you."

Thankful that her mother saved her from having to babble something polite and stupid about how glad she was to be there, Drew managed a half-hearted smile in return. Rob was the only person in the world who could help her out of the mess she was in, but she couldn't think of a reasonable way to approach him—despite the fact that he'd been doing a lot of hinting lately about their relationship becoming more serious. There wasn't an easy way to tell the man who loved you that not only did you not love him, but that you were pregnant with another man's child. Yet her only other options were to tell Momma and Daddy or run away.

Rob grabbed her hand as they climbed the steps to the veranda. "I've got something I'd like to show Drew," he said to her parents. "Would you please excuse us?"

Momma and Daddy both smiled. "Run along," Momma said. "Oh, look—the Crosbys and the Norths are here. And there's Vi!" She waved at Rob's mother, then headed across the veranda toward her with Daddy in tow.

"This way." Rob motioned Drew through the front door, then led her into the parlor. His pale face was flushed, and his gray-blue eyes sparkled behind his glasses.

Drew glanced around the parlor. Nothing looked new or different, and they were the only ones inside—everyone else was outside, either on the veranda or the spacious lawn to the side of the house where the long tables were set up and the chef tended his huge pot of burgoo. She lifted an eyebrow and smiled at Rob. "So what do you have to show me?"

He reached into his pocket and brought out a tiny box wrapped in tissue, then held it out to Drew, his hands trembling slightly. Twin red spots flamed on his cheeks, and he stared down at the floor as she took the box from him.

Drew's heart squeezed into a tiny knot of pity. She'd suspected that something like this was going to happen pretty soon, but she'd never have guessed that he would choose such a public occasion. She carefully unwrapped the tissue and opened the box. A thin gold band set with a single diamond lay inside. "It's beautiful," she said. Then she tried to hand it back to him. "But I can't keep it."

He kept his arms at his sides. "I'm asking you to be my wife," he said, his voice shaky and his eyes clouded with pain. He emitted an uncomfortable little chuckle. "I'd recite a romantic poem for you, but my words seem to have fled in terror."

Drew set the ring box down on the table next to her. "You don't understand." She gulped in a huge swallow of air and clenched her fists. "I think I might be pregnant."

The flush left Rob's cheeks, and his face turned the slightly gray color of someone just kicked in the stomach. "How?" he whispered, then blushed again as if realizing how stupid his question was. "I mean, who?"

She shook her head. "I can't tell you. It doesn't matter anyway because I'm never going to let him find out."

He cursed softly under his breath, and a muscle in his jaw twitched. He scooped up the tiny box and paced to the window, where he stood stiffly for several minutes, his back to Drew. Finally, his shoulders slumped and he turned around. "I don't care," he said. His voice was flat, his face expressionless. He removed the ring from the box and held it out to her.

Tilting her head, she squinted at him. "You don't care?" she repeated. "I'm going to have someone else's child and you don't care?"

He tried to speak, but choked. Slowly, he shook his

head. When he regained his voice, it vibrated with anguish. "Of course I care. But what the hell other choice do I have? What choice do *you* have?"

Drew ducked her head and fought back her tears. Rob had always been the most gallant person she'd ever known; and even though she'd vaguely hoped for a miracle like this, she'd certainly never really expected it to happen. "Not much," she said. "My parents would send me away if they found out—if I didn't run away first. But I can't bear the thought of leaving. It's been such a nightmare I can't stand to think about it . . . but I haven't been able to stop."

"This is the only way." He strode quickly toward her and grasped her left hand, then slipped the ring onto her finger. He took a deep breath and exhaled slowly. "I love you, Drew. Will you marry me?"

She hesitated for a long moment before she finally nodded. "All right," she said.

He tried to smile, but his lips quivered and he gave it up. "Let's go tell your parents—and then announce our engagement today."

"Right now?"

"The sooner the better," he said. "Everyone's going to be counting on their fingers when the baby arrives anyway."

Seventeen

Drew had dreamed about going to Saratoga since she was a child, but given her present predicament, the reality wasn't quite as pleasant as the fantasy. It didn't matter that the Grand Union Hotel, where she and Rob and Trixie were staying, was impressive and beautiful, that the air was pine-scented and the weather warm, but not nearly as hot as Kentucky in August, and that the festive atmosphere was exhilarating even though the pace was more relaxed than Derby week in Louisville. It made no difference that the racetrack was lovely, with its long rows of brilliant red geraniums, white clapboard stands, and high pointed cupolas, or that the ladies looked sophisticated and refined and the gentlemen dashing. All she could think about was her queasy stomach, her dread of the Saturday three weeks from now when she and Rob would be married, and her desperate need for enough money to pay Secret Wish's entry fees in the fall classics at Belmont.

Standing outside the tiny pawnbroker's shop tucked away on a back street several blocks from the hotel, she twisted her engagement ring around her finger. A battered trumpet, two accordions, and several boxed sets of cufflinks and studs were haphazardly displayed in the dusty store window. Her ring was all she had with her of any value—she hadn't thought to "borrow" Momma's tiara again before they'd left. She couldn't be without the ring for long—Rob would surely notice that it was missing—so she'd decided to pawn it at the last minute, right before the races she planned to bet on.

She clenched the ring in her hand and stepped into the seedy shop, doing her best to ignore the musty odor that greeted her. It was the only thing that greeted her for several minutes—the proprietor was nowhere to be seen. She tapped her fingers on the glass display case, hummed loudly, and coughed several times.

Finally, the curtain at the back of the shop parted and a cadaverously thin man with a scraggly mustache appeared. "You need something, miss?" he asked in a nasal voice.

Ten minutes later she was back on the sidewalk with thirty dollars in her pocket, no ring on her finger, and a strong urge to vomit. Unless her luck was incredibly good, there was no way she was going to be able to turn thirty dollars into enough money to pay Wish's fees. And this time, she didn't have Neal Rafferty to help her out with the handicapping.

She ran back to the hotel, arriving out of breath just as Rob and Trixie came down the stairs into the elegant lobby. Sticking her left hand in her pocket, she sauntered toward them, forcing herself to breathe normally.

"You're up early this morning," Rob said. He smiled at her and kissed her cheek.

"Yeah," Trixie said. "I didn't even hear you leave."

Even though neither one had asked, Drew felt obligated to explain herself. "I woke up and couldn't go back to sleep, so I decided to go for a walk."

"Well, I'll bet you're hungry, then." Rob's voice held that determinedly cheerful tone he'd affected since they'd announced their engagement at his Fourth of July party.

Drew fought back the spasm of irritation she always felt whenever he talked that way. "I surely am," she said.

She linked her arms with his and Trixie's as they walked into the hotel dining room.

An hour later they were at the racetrack. Drew stuck her nose in the program, mentally ticking off her choices once again. The Travers Midsummer Derby, an important stakes race for three-year-olds, was the fifth race of the day, and the opening lines on a couple of the horses looked pretty good. She'd been listening to the gossip on the hotel's big front veranda, as well as on the backstretch, and she was considering betting all of her money—the thirty dollars she'd gotten from pawning the ring and the twenty she still had left from her winning bet on Rock Man—on Greentree Stable's Saxon. Then again, maybe she should split the bet to spread out the risk a little.

She raised her head and pinched the bridge of her nose. Her head throbbed from the noise and tension. Damn—if only Neal Rafferty were here. Chase said he was the luckiest gambler and the best handicapper he'd ever met, and she'd certainly done well with his advice at the Derby last year.

Sighing, she fanned herself with her program as the horses paraded to the post for the fourth race. As soon as it was over, she excused herself, refusing Trixie and Rob's offer to accompany her.

Her mind still not made up, she wandered among the bookies, each one with his own odds posted on a blackboard. Finally, she stopped at the one with the best odds for Saxon. Thirty to one, and the others had him anywhere from fifteen to one to twenty-three to one. She pushed her way to the front of the group gathered around the bookie, a plump, balding man with twinkling brown eyes, then fumbled in her purse for her money. She pulled the bills out and handed them to him. "Fifty dollars on Saxon to—" She paused, then sucked in a deep breath. What the hell. She might as well go for broke. "To win," she finished.

The bookie scribbled on the chit and handed it to her. "Good luck, miss," he said, smiling.

Her stomach quivering, she nodded at him. It had worked the last time. It *had* to work this time. Wish's career depended on it.

She hurried back to her seat in the stands just as the bugle called the horses to the post parade for the fifth race. Trixie and Rob were already standing, their field glasses pressed against their eyes.

Rob handed his to Drew. "Take a look," he said. "Chance Shot seems a little sore in his front leg. See how he favors the right side?"

Good, Drew thought. She trained the glasses on Saxon. His jockey, George Ellis, wearing scarlet and black silks with white chevrons on each arm, smiled at the crowd, then touched Saxon's neck. The colt tossed his head, his chestnut coat gleaming in the sun like a copper penny. He looked confident and eager to run, with his head held high and his eyes shining.

"I think you're right about Chance Shot," she said, returning the glasses to Rob. "I favor Saxon myself."

He shrugged. "Saxon's a long shot at best. He does look good today, though."

The horses reached the web barrier, but it took the assistant starters several minutes to get the field standing straight and balanced. Saxon was the last to line up.

Immediately, the barrier swept up and the yellow flag dropped. Drew screamed as Saxon tripped, then swerved and almost bumped into one of the other colts. The jockey straightened him out, and by the time they reached the furlong pole, he had fought his way to second place, trailing Brown Bud by three lengths.

"Come on, Saxon!" Drew shouted. "You can do it!" But instead of gaining on Brown Bud, Saxon lost ground as they pounded toward the finish line.

Drew sank onto the bench, her ears buzzing from the

roar of the crowd and a sudden attack of panic. The worst had happened. She'd risked every cent she had, and she'd lost.

Rob smiled at Drew over the top of his menu, pleased that Trixie had gone off with some friends to a casino on the outskirts of town. It wasn't that he approved of her choice of activity—he was just happy that he'd finally gotten a chance to dine alone with Drew.

Drew's lips trembled slightly when she returned his smile, and he wondered once again what had happened to upset her that day. She'd seemed in great spirits, although a bit distracted, when they'd arrived at the racetrack that morning; but by the end of the afternoon, she'd been pale and listless. At the time he'd blamed it on the heat and her pregnancy. Now he wasn't so sure. She looked unhappy rather than ill, and he was never quite sure exactly what to do with an unhappy woman. Sometimes with Drew it was safest just to ignore the symptoms and hope that they went away. Unless, of course, what she wanted was attention.

He sighed and returned to reading the menu. During the easiest of times, Drew was a mystery to him. It was no wonder he was totally mystified now. She kept him so worried about her that he didn't have time to consider how unhappy he was with the whole situation. He loved Drew and he wanted to marry her more than anything in the world; he would do anything to save her from the ignominy of an illegitimate pregnancy; but every time he thought of her making love to another man, his insides burned with jealousy and misery.

With an almost physical effort, he shoved aside the image of Drew and her lover and concentrated on the choices the menu presented him. *Paupiettes de sole* or *tournedos Henri IV*? Or perhaps the *canard à l'orange*?

Frankly, he couldn't care less. Nothing sounded appealing to him right now. "What are you going to have?" he asked Drew. He planned to order the same, no matter what it was. Maybe that would help him understand her, in a mystical William Butler Yeats sort of way. Their bodies, both nourished with the same lamb or pheasant or salmon, might, perhaps, be more in tune; their souls might find harmony.

Drew wrinkled her nose. "What I'd like is a nice big plate of burgoo, or a heap of hoppin' john and black-eyed peas. This stuff is all French to me." She closed her eyes and ran her finger down the menu. "There. I'll have that one."

She handed him the menu, her finger still pointing. He read aloud, *"Tripes à la mode de Caen?* Are you sure?"

She lifted her shoulders. "I'm sure. That sounds wonderful. So romantic."

He almost choked, but didn't have the heart to tell her that she'd just requested the stomach of a cow for dinner. He returned her menu to her, noticing suddenly the absence of her engagement ring when she took it back from him. He spoke before he could consider his words. "What happened to your ring?"

Her face flushed bright pink, but she stared him right in the eyes. "I pawned it," she said. "The same way I pawned my mother's tiara to get the money to claim Wish. Except this time I lost everything on the bet I made."

Before he could think of a response, the waiter arrived to take their orders. Let Drew be hoist on her own canard, he thought, as he ordered the tripe for her and for himself the tournedos. So much for the communing of souls. She asked for it.

He regretted his unkind impulse immediately, for she lowered her head as two thin trails of tears dripped down her cheeks and onto her hands.

"I'm sorry," she said. "I couldn't think of any other way."

"Any other way to do what?"

"To raise the money for Wish's entry fees. I don't have anything left." She sniffed and swiped at the tears with her knuckles.

He took a deep breath and closed his eyes for a few seconds. "You didn't think of asking me? We're going to be married in three weeks, Drew. I'm going to be your husband. Wish's entry fees will be my responsibility."

She picked up the silver salt cellar and studied it closely, seeming to find something fascinating in the whorls and creases. "You mean you'd pay to enter him in the fall races at Belmont?"

He reached across the table and covered her hand with his. If only he could persuade her to trust him, instead of doing everything for herself. "Of course I would. And I will. Wish is ready. More than ready, according to Jack. He's going to vindicate your belief in him, and more."

New tears streamed down Drew's cheeks, and she lifted her free hand to wipe them away. "Thank you," she said finally. Then she added in a small voice, "Will you get my ring back for me?"

He decided to tell the waiter to switch the orders when the food arrived. "Of course, my darling," he said.

Eighteen

It was her wedding day, and all Drew could think about was how badly her feet ached. Even though it was already after nine o'clock in the evening, it was still suffocatingly hot, and her feet were so swollen that her own shoes would have been uncomfortable—and she was wearing Trixie's white satin pumps, which were at least half a size too small. Fortunately, it had been cooler inside the red brick First Presbyterian Church on Pleasant Street, where she and Rob had repeated their vows, so she'd been able to make it through the ceremony without grimacing with pain or fainting from heatstroke.

But now she was standing between Rob and Trixie, her maid of honor, in her parents' front parlor, sweating a small river under her mother's old wedding gown and trying to smile as she greeted their guests. Rob had wanted the reception and wedding supper to take place at Blue Meadow—Drew's new home—and she had been too exhausted and overwhelmed to argue with him, especially since she thought that her parents could ill afford even the most simple affair.

But Momma, who had already been horrified by Drew's stipulation that the marriage take place by the end of August, had protested that it wasn't proper. Momma had looked at Drew speculatively once or twice, but since she hadn't asked the reason for their haste, Drew hadn't told her. There'd be time enough for Momma and Daddy—and everyone else—to figure it out when the baby came three months early.

Drew slipped out of Trixie's horribly tight shoes while she kissed the flushed cheek Lucy Claire Thompson offered her. Even though Momma's white satin gown was entirely too hot for a summer wedding, at least it covered Drew's feet. Sighing with relief, she wriggled her toes.

Lucy Claire smirked at her, then nudged Nancy Wilkes in the side with her elbow. "Who'd have ever thought Drew would be the first one from our class to get married?"

Both girls simpered, and Drew restrained her urge to stick out her tongue at their backs. Instead she exchanged a disgusted look with Trixie as Lucy Claire and Nancy moved to the center of the parlor to chat with the other guests who'd already been through the receiving line.

Drew peered across the room to where her mother greeted the guests as they entered. She'd wanted a small wedding, but Momma had put her foot down about that, too, explaining that she planned to use the money Drew's grandparents had set aside for Drew's education to do everything the right way. So now the line of people stretched out to the front porch.

A sudden stirring in the hallway caught her eye, and she glanced out the parlor window just in time to see Adam and Victoria come up the front walk together. Her heart went numb. There had been no way to avoid inviting them, but she'd hoped when she hadn't seen them at the church that they'd forgotten or missed their train or changed their minds at the last minute.

No such luck. She'd been in such a daze during the ceremony it wasn't any wonder that she hadn't spotted them before. And now in less than ten minutes, she'd be facing Adam for the first time since the Derby a little over three months ago. The realization turned her sweat icy cold, and she shivered.

The butler Momma had hired for the occasion continued to announce the guests in his monotonous baritone, and Drew smiled, shook hands, kissed cheeks, and exchanged meaningless pleasantries in a trance of anxiety. Finally, the butler intoned, "Mr. and Mrs. Adam MacKenzie," and Adam and Victoria stepped into the room.

Adam looked straight at her, and Drew's mouth froze in the phony smile that had been plastered on it for the last half hour. As he and Victoria crossed the room to the receiving line, Adam nodded; and Victoria's lips curved into a smile even more insincere than Drew's.

Adam pumped Rob's hand, then clapped him on the back. "Congratulations, old man," he said, his voice robust. "You've just married one of the two prettiest girls in Bourbon County." He winked at Trixie. "Of course, the other one's your sister, so the new Mrs. Carlisle doesn't have much to worry about."

Rob grinned at him like a love-struck fool. "I'm the luckiest man alive," he said.

Drew wanted to gag. Idiots, both of them—Adam pretending that nothing had ever happened between them, and Rob acting as if he'd just married a lily-white virgin instead of a woman three months pregnant with another man's child. She set her jaw and steeled her nerves, desperately ignoring the tightness in her chest. Well, she'd show them that she could play the game better than either of them.

She linked her arm with Rob's and leaned against him. "Thank you, darling," she said. "I feel exactly the same way." She smiled up at him, then glanced at Adam.

For a second Adam's eyes narrowed, but whether from anger or unhappiness, Drew couldn't tell. She held out her hand to Victoria, who shook it limply; then Drew offered her cheek for Adam to kiss. "I haven't congratulated you on *your* marriage yet," she said after he'd given her a brotherly peck. "Of course, I haven't seen you since—"

Adam cleared his throat. "So where are you going on your honeymoon?"

"I'm afraid it's going to be a working vacation," Rob said. "We're spending the night in Lexington, then leaving the first thing in the morning for New York. Secret Wish is already stabled at Belmont, along with four of my three-year-olds."

Ignoring Victoria's none-too-subtle nudges, Adam raised an eyebrow. "So you're going to race Wish at Belmont. What stakes?"

"The Jockey Club Stakes," Drew said. "He'll have to carry four pounds more than the three-year-olds, but he's ready."

"More than ready," Rob added. "Jack was all for sending him to Saratoga, but Drew declined." He patted Drew's hand to forestall any annoyance on her part. "But Wish is her horse. She makes all the decisions for him."

Adam grinned at him. "You're a wise man, Rob Carlisle."

Drew bit her tongue to keep herself from emitting a very unladylike snort.

"I suppose we should move on and give everyone else a chance to congratulate you. I wish you both great happiness," Adam said. He looked into Drew's eyes, this time without any false heartiness. "Be sure to save a dance for me."

It seemed to Drew that Adam's eyes rested on her frequently during the interminably long supper the caterers served under the canopied platform on the lawn, partly she supposed because she was having a difficult time not looking in his direction. If she'd been capable of ignoring him completely, she'd never have known if he looked her way or not.

But she wasn't. His presence was a magnet that attracted her gaze with a force she couldn't resist—and every time she glanced at him, he was looking at her, a telling tenseness in his jaw belying his joviality. With a shock, she realized he was as unhappy and uncomfortable as she was.

She pushed her roast squab and green beans around her plate and hardened her heart again. Adam was the last person in the world she needed to feel sorry for. He was rich; he was handsome; he was married to a wealthy and beautiful woman he obviously preferred to her. Why should she care if he was miserable or not?

Turning to Rob, she doubled her efforts to ignore Adam and more or less succeeded until the dancing started in the parlor. As soon as all of the obligatory dances had been performed and the band her mother had hired struck up a tango, Adam bowed and requested permission to dance with her from Rob.

"I'm grateful," Rob said. "I've never learned to tango."

Drew trembled when Adam pulled her into his arms, but she was thankful for the hours she and Trixie had spent practicing all the latest dances when they were in high school. At least she didn't have to worry about Adam stepping on her feet, which were still bare despite her mother's disapproving looks. All she had to do was to keep from crying, and that was becoming harder with every second.

And he didn't help at all. Every pore in her body cried out to melt against him, but she forced herself to remain rigid even when he tightened his arm around her back.

They danced in silence for a minute, then Adam said, "I had to come, Drew. I knew it wasn't going to be easy for you—or for me, either—but I felt I owed you an apology."

Drew tipped her head back and stared up at him. "For what?" she hissed. If he tried to take the blame for seducing her, she would walk off and leave him dancing with himself. All she'd ever been upset about was the way he'd treated her afterward.

"My behavior was ungentlemanly all the way around," he said. A muscle twitched in his jaw, and lines etched the sides of his mouth. "But I'm most ashamed of losing my temper with you. I handled your gift to me as a debasement rather than as something that should be considered a great honor, and I want you to know that I'll always remember what happened between us with tenderness."

Drew's mouth dropped open, and she gaped at him in amazement. Without warning, a squeaky giggle erupted from her lips. Lowering her head, she clamped her mouth shut and grated her teeth to keep the hysterical laughter inside.

"I accept your apology," she said finally, when she gained control of her voice again. She kept her eyes riveted on his chest, studying the pearl studs that marched down the front of his white dress shirt. They were the same ones he'd worn the night before the Derby.

She blinked back the tears stinging her eyes. She'd given up all hope on the day Adam wedded Victoria; her own marriage was simply one of necessity. But Adam had done far worse. He'd chosen to deny what he felt for her, and then he'd retreated behind the facade of a gentleman, reducing their passionate lovemaking to a "gift" from her and a "great honor"—and there wasn't a damned thing she could do about it.

Nineteen

Staring down at her feet, Drew followed Rob up the steps to the Blue Meadow box at Belmont. Her pregnancy still made her a little dizzy sometimes, and the last thing she wanted to do was trip and fall down the stairs. The queasiness came and went, but she'd noticed that it got worse when she was upset or excited or nervous about something. And today she was all three.

Upset, because she'd had another fight with Rob that morning about his over-protectiveness. She was fine, she kept telling him. Pregnancy was a normal state. Even a mare could get pregnant and manage to go about her life normally. Wasn't she at least as intelligent and capable as a horse? Then he complained because her language wasn't ladylike. "You want a lady?" she'd finally yelled at him. "You should have married one then."

But right now, it was mainly the excited and nervous part that made her heart beat faster and brought on the dizziness. Secret Wish was racing in the Jockey Club Stakes, his first race since she'd claimed him at Dade Park over a year ago. He was ready to race—and to win, she hoped. His morning workout times since they'd shipped him to New York had been even better than usual. He wanted to run, his exercise boy told her, rubbing his aching arms. Holding him back took every bit of strength he had.

Well, she knew his jockey Earl Sande had what it took. After all, he'd ridden Man O' War, and no one had ever seen Man O' War run flat out—yet he'd set record after record, carrying an amazing amount of weight, and had only one slight injury during his racing career. She trusted Sande to let Wish run well without endangering himself, her chief worry; she'd instructed him not to push Wish, but not to hold him back unnecessarily, either. There'd be other races if Wish didn't do well today, but if he got hurt, he might never run again.

They finally reached the box, and Drew slid into her seat, a little out of breath. She made a show of settling herself and gazing around at the other boxes to hide the effects of her exertion—the last thing she wanted to hear was another solicitous query, accompanied by an "I told you so" look, from Rob. A thick head of graying hair in the box below them caught her eye; and when the owner turned enough so that she could see his profile, she sucked in her breath. It was Neal Rafferty.

"Neal!" she called.

He swiveled around, the look of puzzlement on his face turning to pleasure when he saw her waving at him. "It's Drew," he said, then added, "and Rob." He stood and excused himself from the group in his box, then trotted up the steps to join them. A broad smile lighting his handsome face, he shook Rob's hand. "Congratulations on your marriage," he said. "I was mighty disappointed to hear that you'd married one of the most beautiful girls in Bourbon County." He winked at Drew, then kissed her cheek. "Chase warned me not to tarry too long or you'd be taken."

Drew returned his smile. Neal's good spirits always seemed to brighten hers; his grin and the sparkle in his eyes could surely bring a smile to the lips of the sourest

old maid. And even though she didn't take anything he
said seriously, she enjoyed his compliments nevertheless.
"It's nice to see you again," she said.

He nodded in agreement. "It's been too long. Wasn't
the last time at the Derby?"

"I think it was," Rob said. He sat back down next to
Drew and wished Neal would go away.

But instead Neal settled himself on the other side of
Drew. "You must be pretty excited," he said. "I've been
hearing good things about Secret Wish. Brown Bud did
so much better in the Travers at Saratoga than anyone
expected that he's being touted as the favorite, but my
money is on Wish even though he's carrying four more
pounds. I found a bookie who gave me odds of eleven to
one, and I was more than happy to part temporarily with
my bankroll."

Rob leaned back and folded his arms across his chest.
It was hard not to notice how Drew came alive when Neal
showed up—how she tossed her head so that her dark,
shiny curls danced, how her brown eyes lit up and
gleamed with delight, how quickly she smiled at everything Neal said. "I'm not so sure," he said, drawling.
"Drew here is positive that Wish is going to win it, but
I don't know. The competition is pretty stiff, and Wish
hasn't raced in over a year. There's no telling what he'll
do."

The happiness in Drew's eyes faded at his criticism, and
Rob was immediately contrite that he'd spoiled her pleasure. Perhaps it wasn't Neal who had brought the anima-
tion to her features, but rather Neal's praise of her beloved
Secret Wish. Rob knew how much Drew loved that horse;
to many horse people, himself included, racing horses was
a business, and the horses merely tools of the trade.

But to Drew it was different. She was intelligent, but
she put her heart into it, too. She wanted Wish to win
because she thought it was best for him, not because her

ego demanded that she own a winning horse. That was why she wouldn't allow Jack to race him before he was completely ready. And Rob knew that if Wish had never shown himself completely recovered, Drew would never have raced him.

Rob unfolded his arms and forced himself to smile pleasantly at Neal and Drew. He was being stupid again, he knew. But it was damned hard to marry the woman you loved when she was pregnant with another man's child and wouldn't tell you who the man was. Every man became a suspect, someone who might crook his little finger and off she'd go.

The bugle called the horses to the post for the race preceding the Jockey Club Stakes, and Rob peered through his field glasses as they pranced to the starting barrier.

He was the only one in his box, though, who paid any attention. Drew and Neal chatted about everything under the sun except the race. They paused momentarily while the horses thundered around the track, clapped and yelled perfunctorily when the horse Neal had bet on came in first, then resumed their chatter.

Rob stared at them, suddenly remembering the Derby Eve party at the MacKenzies' suite at the Brown Hotel in Louisville. Chase and Trixie had invited Drew and him to accompany them to a gin and jazz joint and mentioned that Neal was waiting for them there. They'd left, and he'd gone over to talk to Curt; and the next thing he knew Drew was gone. A couple of hours later Neal showed up at the party alone, disheveled, and extremely drunk.

Drew flashed another bright smile at Neal, and Rob ground his teeth. She'd told him the baby was due in late January or early February. It didn't take a genius to figure out that she must have conceived sometime in early May, right around Derby time. It all fit. Still, he doubted that

Neal knew he was going to be a father; for some reason
Drew hadn't wanted him to know.

Rob pushed his glasses back up to the bridge of his
nose with his forefinger and waited for an opening in
Drew and Neal's animated conversation. "By the way," he
said, watching Neal carefully for any sign that might give
him away, "did you know that we're expecting a child?"

Drew narrowed her eyes at him, but Neal's only reaction
was surprise. "Well, that's quick work," Neal said. "Further congratulations are in order." He offered his hand to
Rob.

Trying to appear proud, Rob pumped Neal's hand up
and down.

"And when is this blessed event to occur?" Neal asked.

Before Rob could answer, Drew blurted out, "April or
May."

It seemed to Rob that Neal visibly relaxed at this news.
"You don't look a bit different," Neal said to Drew. "I'd
never have guessed."

Drew's laugh sounded a little uncomfortable to Rob.
"You silly," she said. "No one *looks* pregnant right away."

"Well, I don't know about that. I'd swear that my older
sister blew up like a balloon the very next day. Her husband was home on leave from the army, and when they
went upstairs that night, she was as svelte as a lioness."
He puffed out his cheeks and arched his back. "The next
morning at breakfast I asked her if she'd swallowed a watermelon seed."

Drew rolled her eyes at him. "Oh, you," she said.

Their banter was interrupted by the blast of the bugle
calling the horses to the post for the most important event
of the day, the Jockey Club Stakes Race. Grimly, Rob set
his jaw and pretended to be absorbed in the proceedings
below when he couldn't care less at this moment if Wish
won or not. Actually, that wasn't the exact truth—maybe
if Wish lost, Drew would settle down and behave the way

a wife was supposed to instead of insisting on gallivanting around all over the country and spending more time in the stables than in the kitchen.

The field lined up behind the web barrier with the practiced ease of experienced runners, and a minute later the elastic snapped up and the yellow flag dropped. Rob jumped to his feet with the rest of the crowd when Wish surged ahead of the rest of the pack at the first turn out of the chute. What the hell was Sande thinking of? Rob had told him specifically to hold Wish back until the final stretch; Wish was a sprinter, not a stayer, as his abysmal performance in the Kentucky Derby showed.

"Damn it!" he yelled, then glanced at Drew.

She clapped her hands in ecstasy, seemingly not at all concerned, and her teeth flashed white when she grinned at Neal.

Rob saw why when he turned his attention back to the race. Wish entered the final stretch at least six lengths ahead of the second place horse, Brown Bud; and a second later he flashed across the finish line.

Drew threw her arms around Neal and hugged him, then turned to Rob. "He did it!" she screamed above the roar of the crowd. "I knew he could!"

Rob clenched his fists at his side to keep himself from throwing a punch at Neal. He'd done everything he could to get Wish into the damn race, and then she ignored him during the moment that should have been theirs alone to savor. "Come on," he said. "We'd better get down to the winner's circle." He spun on his heel and headed out of the box. One more second of staring at Neal's smug face, and he knew he'd lose what little control he had left.

Drew sank into the lumpy chair next to the window in their hotel room. What a glorious day it had been—not even the glum expression Rob had worn all day could spoil her happiness. She eased her swollen feet from her shoes and stretched her legs out in front of her. Wriggling her toes, she smiled up at Rob. "I still can't quite believe it," she said. "Fifteen thousand dollars. I can repay everything I owe you and still have some left over."

Rob lifted an eyebrow above his steel-rimmed glasses. "We're married now, Drew," he said. "Or hadn't you noticed? What's mine is yours and what's yours is mine. You don't owe *me* anything for Wish's expenses, and Wish's earnings belong to *us*—to Blue Meadow Farm, actually."

The sarcastic tone of his voice made Drew grind her back teeth in irritation, but she managed to keep her annoyance under control. Her father always said it was best not to get in a pissing match with a skunk, and Rob was certainly in a stinky mood. She shrugged. As long as Wish's upkeep and entry fees got taken care of, she didn't give a hoot where the money came from. "Fine with me."

"Good." His back stiff, Rob paced to the window and stood in front of it, staring out. "I know who the baby's father is," he said without looking at her.

"What?" She gaped at him, but he kept his face turned away.

"I said I know who knocked you up." His voice was harsher this time. "And I don't want you seeing him again."

Her feet suddenly felt frozen, and she pulled them onto the edge of her chair and hugged her knees against her chest. Rob obviously suspected Neal of having seduced her—that explained why he'd been so depressed all day and so cold and distant when Neal had invited them to join him for a celebratory dinner. "But—" She stopped herself mid-denial. Perhaps it was best Rob assume that it *had* been Neal—that way he'd stop trying to guess. And they saw Neal much less often than they did Adam. The one thing she *didn't* want was for her child to grow up with the same rumors that had made her childhood miserable. She would do whatever it took to avoid that.

She rested her chin on her knees. "It doesn't matter who got me pregnant. You knew I was pregnant before you married me, and I told you then that I wasn't going to name any names."

Rob's shoulders slumped, and his back shook. Then he ducked his head and buried his face in his hands. "I'm so sorry, Drew," he said. "But it makes my gut ache to think about you with someone else."

She stood and laid her hand on his shoulder. *"You're* the father of this baby now," she said. "What happened before doesn't matter any more." It wasn't quite the truth yet, but maybe someday it would be.

Twenty

Drew gratefully lowered herself into the chair and then allowed Rob to help her scoot it close to the big dining room table. Her back ached from the long day spent in the kitchen helping out the Carlisles' cook Estelle, but it was well worth it. Momma and Daddy looked so proud and happy, and Vi glowed with pleasure. Rob had fussed at her for doing so much when it was less than two months before the baby came, but she'd wanted to make Momma and Daddy's twentieth anniversary a special occasion.

She bowed her head while Rob said grace. She needed times like this to remind her of everything she had to be thankful for. Her parents were both alive and loved each other and her; her child would have a father; Trixie and Vi were like a sister and mother to her; and Wish had done everything she'd hoped for and then some. Still, even though she tried to pour all the good things in her life into the empty hole left by her loss of Adam, there was never quite enough to fill it completely. Even in the midst of happiness and pleasure, there was always a strange feeling that something was missing.

Rob finished his blessing, and she raised her head as he proposed a toast to her parents.

Rob lifted his glass of apple cider. "To two fine people

who have greatly loved each other through hardship, adversity, and tragedy, as well as through triumph and joy. May you celebrate many more anniversaries, and may I be as fortunate in my marriage as you have in yours." He stared at Drew, his gray-blue eyes serious behind his lenses, before he joined the general clinking of glasses.

Drew's father smiled at her, then at Rob. "Thank you," he said. "Margaret and I appreciate everything you've done. This is certainly one of our moments of joy."

"And triumph, too, dear," Margaret added, winking at Drew. "To see our beautiful daughter as a wife and mother-to-be instead of a jockey is definitely a triumph of our aspirations."

Drew flinched at her mother's words, but refused to take the bait. A *triumph* was hardly what she would call her present situation, but if Momma didn't understand by now that her aspirations for Drew had little to do with Drew's dreams for herself, she never would and there wasn't any point in correcting her notion. Instead of making a comment, Drew simply nodded an acknowledgment, then thanked Estelle when she set the bowl of thyme-scented beef consomme in front of her. She ate silently, listening to the conversations going on around her.

"Well, Drew, you've been awfully quiet. Why don't you tell us what your plans are for Secret Wish next season?" her father asked as the cook removed the soup bowls.

Drew glanced at Rob before she replied. He'd been really touchy about Wish ever since he'd won the Jockey Club Stakes at Belmont. It was almost as if Wish had been an acceptable hobby for her when he was a loser, but now that Wish had done well, Rob no longer wanted her to have anything to do with him.

She thrust out her chin, irritated at herself for tiptoeing around Rob's prejudices and petty jealousies. "I want to run him in the spring races at Pimlico and Belmont, then Aqueduct in July and Saratoga in August." She patted her bulging tummy. "As soon as the baby is born, I'm going to start training him myself. And I have my eye on a promising young filly, too."

Her father nodded, one thick gray eyebrow arched high above his sparkling brown eyes. "I'll just bet you do," he said. Shaking his head, he smiled at Rob. "Well, she's still the same horse-crazy girl. I can see you've got a handful here, Rob."

Rob returned her father's smile, but Drew could see the tenseness in his neck and shoulders, and the annoyance smoldering in his eyes. "I sure do, sir," he said, then turned to Drew. "What filly do you mean? This is the first I've heard about it."

"Kentucky Vixen," Drew said. "I helped break her last winter. She's a beauty—a golden chestnut with four white stockings and almost perfect conformation." She couldn't keep the excitement from her voice, so she avoided looking at Rob. She didn't need his disapproval right now. "She's by Golden Broom by Sweeper II out of Bluebird by Rock Sand. Her daddy came in third in the race Man O' War lost to Upset, and she's got his looks and build, not to mention his speed."

"And the disposition of a polecat," Rob said. "I don't think you ought to go near her, let alone train her." He paused while Estelle brought in the roast beef on a large platter and set it down in front of him. He picked up the carving knife and fork, then narrowed his eyes at Drew. "We'll talk about this later," he said quietly.

Wearily, Drew climbed the stairs to their second floor bedroom. Except for Rob, the evening had been a great success. She'd persuaded Momma to tell about the first time she met Daddy, a story she'd never heard before. "It was at Andrew's graduation from Amherst. Edward was so sophisticated, so mature," Momma had said, "so much more interesting than the college boys I knew. I noticed him even before Andrew introduced us. He was so tall and distinguished-looking. His hair was just starting to turn gray at the temples."

Drew had smiled at her father. "And did you notice her, too, Daddy?"

His brown eyes twinkled. "You bet I did. I spotted that lovely jumble of auburn curls and those bright blue eyes immediately. But I didn't think much about it—after all, I was more than twice her age at the time. Still, I was knocked over when Andrew dragged me over to meet her. I couldn't believe that he knew such a lovely creature and hadn't pursued her himself."

Momma had gotten a strange look on her face when he said that. She'd shrugged, then turned to Trixie and asked her when Chase would be arriving at Ballantrae.

Drew wondered again about what had happened between Momma and Andrew. The memory still seemed to make her mother uncomfortable twenty years later. Drew opened the door to the bedroom, surprised to find Rob already in bed. "I thought you were going to your office to work on the books," she said.

At least that was what she'd hoped he was going to do while she helped the other women clean up the kitchen. If he hadn't, that meant she'd have to do it all herself in the morning. Suppressing a sigh, she changed quickly into her flannel nightgown and slid beside him into the white iron bed. The sheets on her side of the bed were even colder than the frigid air in the room, and she shivered as she pulled the heavy quilt up to her chin.

He closed the notebook he'd been writing in, put it and his pen on the night stand next to him, and turned to face her. "I've made a decision," he said. Deep grooves furrowed his forehead, and he suddenly looked much older, as if he carried the weight of the world on his shoulders.

"Oh," she said, biting back the sarcastic responses

ready to leap from her tongue. She fluffed her pillow, then turned on her side with her back to him and settled her head gently into it while she waited for him to continue.

"Aren't you going to look at me?"

This time she didn't hold back her sigh, but rather exaggerated it as she rolled carefully to face him. "Is this better?"

"You're retiring from the horse business," he said. "I don't want you training either Secret Wish or Kentucky Vixen. That's what I pay Jack Nolan to do. From now on he and I call the shots. You are the owner's wife and nothing more. Do you understand?"

Drew pushed herself up to a sitting position and stared at him. "Just who the hell do you think you are?" she shouted. "Not even my father talks to me that way."

His pale skin flushed bright red. "Shhh," he hissed. "This is our business, not everyone else's."

"I don't give a damn!"

"Please, Drew." The sternness in his voice turned into a conciliatory whine. "Don't make this any harder for me than it already is. I'm not going to change my mind."

The first wave of nausea in months washed over her. He truly did make her sick. "In case you didn't remember, Wish is *my* horse," she said. "What I do with him is *my* business, not yours or Jack's."

"In case *you* didn't remember, it takes money to race a horse. And you have none." The whine disappeared, and the look on his face was dangerously close to a smirk.

Drew eased back down under the quilt and turned her back to him. End of argument. He was absolutely right—she had no money of her own. Wish's earnings from the Jockey Club Stakes had gone straight into the operating fund for Blue Meadow, and she hadn't seen a dime of it. She had no job and, if Rob chose not to give them to her, no rights.

She flicked off her bedside lamp. Somehow she had to

find a way to get some money of her own, money that he couldn't touch. Then they'd see whether he still had the right to make decisions for her or not.

"I'm glad you see it my way." Rob turned his light off, too, then settled himself next to her.

She scooted to the edge of the bed and stiffened her whole body. She would rather fall out of bed than touch him.

Twenty-one

Drew trudged onto the dirt lane leading to Ashworth Farm and walked to the first bend before she stopped to rest again. She tired so easily now that she had this watermelon in her belly to lug around all the time. She smiled briefly, thinking of Neal Rafferty's story about his sister, and thumped on her stomach. The baby was quiet now. Of course, whenever she lay down to rest, the watermelon suddenly turned into an ornery little critter, tumbling around and flopping like a new-caught trout.

She glanced up at the gray sky before continuing. It looked like snow, and it was certainly cold enough. She rewound her muffler around her neck and headed up the lane, her breath a smoky white cloud. She hoped Daddy was home. She hadn't called to tell him she was coming because she knew he would insist on driving to Blue Meadow instead, and she wanted to talk to him alone. What she had planned would never work if Rob found out.

As she approached the house, she veered off to the left toward the tobacco barn. With any luck Daddy would be inside grading the tobacco and getting it ready to take to the warehouse in Paris to sell.

She stepped into the high-ceilinged, drafty building and squinted her eyes in the dim light. Daddy was at the far end. "Hey," she said.

"Drew!" He set aside a big bundle of dried tobacco

leaves and came toward her. "What are you doing here?"
His thick brows were pulled together in concern. "You
shouldn't have walked all the way here in this weather."

She kissed his cheek, then smiled at him. "I'm fine,
and the weather isn't that bad yet. I'll let you drive me
home if you're worried, though."

Shaking his head, her father sighed. "Does Rob know
you're here?"

She rolled her eyes at him. "You know me too well."

"Well, it doesn't take much of a genius to see that
there's some kind of battle going on between you and
Rob." He paused, twining his fingers together and crack-
ing his knuckles. "You know I've never been one for in-
terfering, but is there something I can do to help?"

Tears flooded Drew's eyes, and she sniffed loudly. It
wasn't at all like Daddy to bring up something like this—
he usually let Momma handle everything personal, and
instead of offering to help, Momma always wanted to tell
her what to do. "I didn't think it was quite that apparent."

"Well, you're a pretty high-spirited filly. Frankly, I'd be
more surprised if the two of you didn't have a few problems at the beginning. Most couples do." Tilting his head,
he scratched behind an ear. "Even your mother and I had
our differences."

Drew didn't know what to say. It was as if suddenly,
now that she was married, Daddy thought of her as an
adult. She'd figured it was a long shot, but maybe he
really *would* consider helping her out, after all.

"I made the mistake of reckoning that since she wasn't
much more than a girl and I was a grown man, not to
mention more than twenty years older, my wishes would
naturally take precedence over hers. It didn't take your
mother long to let me know my assumptions weren't the
same as hers." He shook his head and smiled ruefully.
"I'll bet you didn't know your mother was a suffragette,
did you? Well, her ideas about marriage were considerably

different from mine, and she wasted no time in telling me her notions of a 'modern' marriage."

Her mouth hanging open in disbelief, Drew stared at him. It was hard to think of Momma as anything other than frail and frivolous. "So what happened the first time you told Momma to do something she didn't want to do?"

He scratched his chin and smiled. "Well, frankly, it was the other way around. I was going to sell Ashworth Farm to the MacKenzies, but your mother put her foot down. She informed me that marriage was a partnership and that as half-owner of the farm, she didn't want to sell."

"Momma said *that?*" Drew's voice soared into a high-pitched squeak. She'd always thought that Momma wasn't particularly fond of country life. It was almost more surprising to learn that she wanted to stay on the farm than that she spoke her mind about it to Daddy. "Why?" She paused, then frowned at him. "Actually, the real question is, why did you want to sell it?"

The smile faded from his eyes. "It was during a hard time. Your Uncle Andrew had just died, and he left a lot of debts. I couldn't see how I'd ever be able to pay them all off."

Drew had a thousand questions, but, afraid that Daddy would suddenly decide to stop talking, she forced herself to simply nod.

He seemed to read her mind. "I know I've never said much about this before, but I'm sure you've heard from Vi and Rob, if not from Adam. Ashworth Farm was a pretty important horse farm before you were born. But it's a tough business. Some years we barely made enough to feed the horses, and then we had to draw on the savings from the good years."

He pulled out a bench and motioned for Drew to sit, then leaned against the long table used for sorting the tobacco leaves and crossed his legs at the ankles. "But I'm getting off the subject. It was your mother who per-

suaded me to plant more tobacco instead of selling the
farm. She had a small inheritance from her grandfather,
and she insisted that we use it to pay off the most pressing
of the debts and to finance the changeover to a tobacco
farm."

"What would she have done if you hadn't agreed?"

The twinkle came back into her father's eyes. "She
never really issued an ultimatum, but I suspect she'd have
used her money to clear up all of Andrew's debts. I
wanted her to save it for our child—you weren't born
yet—but she claimed that Ashworth Farm was a far better
legacy." He folded his arms against his chest. "I think she
was right."

Nodding in agreement, Drew squirmed to settle herself
more comfortably on the hard bench. It felt strange to see
Momma as a young bride with a mind and money of her
own. "Rob says that since we're married, everything I own
is his and everything he owns is mine. Wouldn't Momma's
money have been yours anyway? Couldn't you have done
what you wanted to with it?"

"Legally, I suppose I could have. But your Momma
expected me to be a different kind of husband, and I loved
and wanted—and respected—her too much to disappoint
her."

Drew's shoulders sagged, and she stared down at the
scuff marks on her heavy brown boots. Her expectations
of Rob didn't seem to have any effect on *his* behavior.
Sighing, she lifted her eyes. "Momma surely was lucky."

"Well." Daddy unfolded his arms and put his hands on
his hips. "You didn't walk all this way in the freezing
cold to hear about all this ancient history. What's on your
mind?"

Drew struggled to keep her voice as matter-of-fact as
possible. The last thing she wanted to sound like was a
whiny little kid after her father had treated her as an equal
for the first time in her life. "I need some money of *my*

own," she said finally. "Rob is holding Secret Wish hostage to make sure I do exactly what he wants."

"What about the purse from the Jockey Club Stakes?" Deep lines furrowed her father's forehead.

"He kept it."

He shook his head slowly back and forth. "Which you probably saw as a call to arms."

"I tried to tell him I didn't think it was fair." No whining, she reminded herself. She took a deep breath, then exhaled, watching her breath form a silvery cloud between them. She tried again. "I want him to treat me the way you treated Momma."

"I didn't learn overnight. And I occasionally backslid." Daddy said. "But your mother was persistent."

"By the time Rob catches on it might be too late for Wish." She blinked to keep back the tears burning her eyes.

Her father slipped his hand between the buttons of his coat and rubbed his chest. "I wish there was some way I could help you out," he said. "It's been a good year, but we have a couple of large payments due in June."

"Could you *loan* me some money? I could pay it back before you need it." It wasn't what she'd hoped for, but perhaps she could make it work. It was certainly better than nothing.

Suddenly she grinned at him. "It would be perfect! How could Rob demand that I give him money that I've *borrowed* from you?"

"Well, that's a ploy worthy of your mother." He laughed. Then his face grew serious. "I'm afraid that I haven't much to spare right now, though. Would a thousand dollars be enough?"

It wouldn't, but she couldn't tell him that. "It would help." Now she only had to figure out how to get the rest of what she needed. Her last experience betting at Saratoga had proved a fiasco, so that was out, but there had to be another way. Everyone was talking about getting rich quick on penny stocks—maybe she should ask Adam.

"I'll have it for you early next week, then," he said. "After I take this load to the warehouse."

Drew pushed herself up off the bench and gave her father a hug. "Thanks, Daddy," she said. "You'll never know how much I appreciate this." A new wave of tears blurred her vision.

Her father knuckled the tears from her cheeks and smiled gently at her. "Oh, I have a pretty good idea," he said.

Drew tucked the stack of crisp new bills deeply into her dress pocket, then leaned back in the kitchen chair and heaved a huge sigh of relief.

"Feel better now?" her father asked, his deep brown eyes smiling at her. He rested his elbows on the scarred oak tabletop.

"Much. At least I'll have enough to nominate Wish and Vixen for some of the better stakes races this coming spring and summer." She rested her hands on her belly, and the baby wriggled so hard her dress rippled. She laughed. "This baby kicks like a little mule."

He joined her laughter. "Well, if it's anything like its parents, it's probably going to be as stubborn as one."

Someone knocked on the front door, and he rose, then clomped across the wood floor and into the front hall. A second later he poked his head back into the kitchen. "Come into the parlor, Drew," he said, winking at her. "We've got company."

Drew pushed herself up and followed him into the hall, a little knot forming in the small portion of her stomach not taken up by the baby. She had a pretty good idea who the guest was, and she didn't really want to see him, especially not now when she looked like an elephant.

"Go on in," he said. "I'm going to let your mother know we have a visitor."

She watched her father climb the stairs, his step sprightlier than usual. Then she straightened her shoulders, lifted her chin, and fortified herself with a deep breath before she strode into the parlor.

Adam stood next to the fireplace, his coat over his arm and his hat in his hand. When he saw Drew, the greeting smile on his lips faltered for a brief second. "Drew! It's so good to see you again." He glanced behind her into the hall. "Chase told me that you and Rob were expecting, but I didn't realize—" His voice trailed off and he held out his free hand to her.

"Let me take your coat and hat," Drew said. "Please, sit down."

He gave them to her, then seated himself in the straight-backed oak rocking chair next to the fireplace while she hung his things on the rack in the entry. Grasping the arms of the chair, he rocked slowly while he gathered his thoughts. When Chase had told him that Drew was pregnant, he'd imagined her to be just a couple of months along; obviously she must have already been with child when she and Rob were married.

Drew's return interrupted his calculations. She settled herself on the sofa. "Are you and Victoria planning to spend Christmas at Ballantrae?" The model of matronly propriety, she folded her hands demurely over what used to be her lap.

"Actually, no," he said. "Victoria didn't accompany me on this trip, and I plan to return to Philadelphia before Christmas." He forced himself to loosen his death grip on the chair's arms. "So—when is the baby due?"

She shrugged, then stared down at her hands. "In May," she said after a long pause. Finally, she raised her head and looked at him, her eyes defiant, almost challenging.

Even if he didn't have the evidence in front of him,

he'd have known instinctively that she wasn't telling the truth. Drew was a terrible liar—he'd always known when she was fibbing as a child because she usually covered her mouth with her hand. She'd become slightly more sophisticated as she got older, but it was still impossible for her to meet his eyes when she told him a lie—or even a half-truth.

Margaret and Edward stepped into the parlor arm-in-arm, so he didn't have time to dwell on Drew's shortcomings or the reasons why she didn't want to be honest with him. He arose and kissed the cheek Margaret offered. "You're looking well," he said.

"It's so nice to see you," Margaret said, seating herself on the sofa next to Drew. "And you're just in time for tea."

"I can't stay that long," Adam said. "I promised Mother I'd be back in time to have tea with her."

He chatted pleasantly with Margaret and Edward for a quarter of an hour or so, carefully avoiding looking at Drew even though her rounded belly attracted his eyes like a giant magnet.

Finally, Drew rose. "I don't mean to be impolite, but I have to get back," she said. "Rob's going to wonder what's become of me." She kissed her parents, then held out her hand to Adam.

Adam stood also. "I must be going, too. I didn't see another car out front. May I give you a ride?"

"Oh, thank you," Margaret said before Drew could answer. "It worries me so much every time she walks all the way over here to see us."

Drew's eyes rolled in exasperation, and she shook her head. "It's only a couple of miles, Momma. And I'm pregnant, not crippled." She shrugged. "Still, if it makes you happy—"

Amid many directions and stipulations from Margaret, Drew and Adam bundled into their coats and hats and mufflers and took their leave. Margaret waved goodbye from the parlor window while Edward followed them out to the sagging front porch. He hugged his daughter goodbye and whispered something in her ear, and Drew giggled and grinned at her father as if he were a conspirator.

As soon as they were settled into his car, Adam turned to Drew. "So, what was that all about?" He started up the car and put it into gear.

Drew lifted an eyebrow, regarding him with a clearly speculative look. "If you had a thousand dollars and needed five thousand, what would *you* do?"

He let out the clutch and steered the car slowly down the lane. "You mean other than robbing a bank—or betting it on a long shot at the Derby?" He shot her a quick grin to let her know he understood more than she thought.

She grimaced as the car bounced into a pothole. "Something just a little safer, please. There's too much at stake this time to risk it on a long shot."

He braked the car at the end of the lane and twisted in his seat to face her. Her belly bulged beneath her heavy coat, and even her face looked swollen, but according to what she'd told him, she was only four months pregnant. He'd never made a study of pregnant women, but she had to be at least six or seven months along, if not further. And there was only one reason why she'd lie to him. Suddenly, he knew with a certainty that couldn't be denied that the baby Drew was carrying was his.

He almost doubled over with the pain of the realization. Whenever he asked Victoria about having a child, she put him off. It was too soon, she said. Maybe next year. He wanted a child, and he was going to have one, but it would never be his. It would belong to Rob Carlisle—just as Drew did. He ground his teeth to keep his face rock solid, cursing himself once again for his weakness that night seven months ago.

But there was nothing he could do about it now—except help Drew multiply her dollars—and the grief his knowledge brought him hardened his heart. "So," he said. "You need to increase your money. You've come to the right man. I won't bore you with the details, but I make my living helping people invest their money."

"What about penny stocks?"

He tilted his head. "Risky," he said. "But not as risky as betting the horses or playing poker. I think I might be able to manage it for you. When do you need the five thousand?"

"Before the first of June." She fumbled beneath her coat, extracted a wad of bills, and handed it to him.

"No problem," he said, pocketing the money. He pulled the car onto the pike, planning how he'd invest it. No penny stocks for Drew. Every cent she gave him would go into good, safe investments in her name—and when June rolled around, she'd get a check for five thousand dollars no matter what. It was the least he could do for his child . . . and its mother.

There wasn't a damned thing he could do for himself.

Twenty-two

March 1928

A folded diaper draped over her shoulder, Drew snuggled her six-week old daughter against her chest. Her heart swelled with joy and adoration as she gently patted the infant's back. Ginnie was such a good baby, everyone said, after they finished exclaiming over her big eyes and her black curls. And it was true. She hardly ever cried, and her funny little smiles and coos kept Drew entranced for hours. She'd never imagined being a mother would be so much fun. In a way, Rob was right; as much as she hated to admit it, she didn't really have the time or energy right now to act as full-time trainer for both Secret Wish and Kentucky Vixen.

Still, she had every intention of overseeing their training and accompanying both of them to Saratoga in August. Ginnie burped, and Drew wiped the white spittle from the corners of the baby's mouth. Ginnie would be six months old, and Drew would just take the baby with her. If Rob didn't want to accompany them—

The kitchen door slammed, and she looked up. Rob stood in the doorway with several envelopes in his hand. "Mail's here," he said, pulling off his boots before striding in his stockinged feet across the freshly mopped floor. He dropped the letters on the kitchen table next to the *Good*

Housekeeping magazine Drew had been reading. "One of them's for you. From Adam."

Drew's hand froze on the baby's back, and her whole body tensed. She hadn't yet told Rob about either her father's loan or her investments. What if Adam said something about the money in his letter? She couldn't let Rob read it.

He dragged out a chair and flopped into it. "Aren't you going to open it?" He extended his arms. "I'll hold the baby."

Drew handed Ginnie to him, then placed the burp rag over his shoulder. "Be careful with her. I just nursed her, and she'll spit up if you bounce her around." Rob still didn't have much experience holding the baby. He'd been angry with Drew before Ginnie was born, and he'd seemed cold and indifferent toward the baby once she arrived, refusing to hold her until she was a month old. Lately, though, he'd warmed up to Ginnie, as if he'd finally realized that the circumstances of her birth weren't her fault.

He nodded and cradled the baby awkwardly against his chest. "I think I can manage."

Her hands trembling slightly, Drew opened the envelope from Adam and removed the single-page letter. Another piece of paper still remained inside, but something stopped her from taking it out, too. She unfolded the paper and read quickly:

Dear Drew,

Congratulations on the birth of your baby. Mother shared the birth announcement with me last week. I hope that you and little Virginia Margaret are doing well.

I have had better luck with your investment than I anticipated and am enclosing a check for your earnings for the last three months just in case you

*would like to put the money to use a little earlier. I
have retained the original amount and reinvested it
for you. Perhaps we will do even better this time.*

*In addition. I would like to be the first to tell you
that Victoria and I are expecting a child in the fall.
I await the birth with great eagerness.*

*Sin-
cerely,*

Adam

Drew refolded the letter slowly, bitter envy souring her
stomach. So Adam was going to have *another* child, Ginnie's half-sister or brother. But Victoria's child would have
Adam's love while *her* child would never really know her
real father. Setting her jaw, she forced herself to remain
calm and dispassionate—not an easy task when she'd
much rather scream, rip the letter into shreds, and burn it
on the kitchen table.

"Well," Rob said. "What did he have to say?"

She gaped at him for a second, then chided herself for
her ungenerous thoughts. Rob had been trying so hard the
last couple of weeks to accept Ginnie. If he could overcome his jealousy, then so could she. She curved her lips
into what she hoped passed for a happy smile. "Adam
and Victoria are going to have a baby. In the fall sometime."

"Gee, that's swell!" Rob grinned, then bent his head
over Ginnie. "You're going to have a little friend," he said
in a squeaky voice.

While Ginnie cooed and waved her fists and Rob
laughed, Drew slid the letter back into the envelope and
surreptitiously peeked at the check. She stifled a gasp. It
was for five thousand dollars!

Quickly she slipped the envelope inside the *Good
Housekeeping* magazine. She was going to have to tell
Rob soon about her plans for Wish and Vixen. Watching

him make silly faces at Ginnie, she hoped her revelation didn't destroy the growing fondness he seemed to have for the baby.

Rob laid Ginnie carefully into the cradle by Drew's side of the bed and covered her with the quilt his mother had made. The baby hadn't fallen asleep after Drew had nursed her the way she usually did, so he'd been rocking her for the last half hour. With any luck, she stay asleep for at least four or five hours. He put his finger to his lips and smiled at Drew when Ginnie's eyes stayed closed.

After he climbed into his side of the bed, he scooted over close to Drew. Ginnie's birth and Drew's stubbornness had made things difficult at first—he'd felt left out and useless, and the baby was a constant reminder of Neal Rafferty. But fortunately Ginnie looked nothing like Neal—she was the image of Drew as an infant, or so Margaret said over and over again. He had found it impossible to harden his heart against the baby, and the original generous impulse that had made him tell Drew he would love her child as his own had been resurrected intact the day two weeks ago when Ginnie smiled at him for the first time.

"Thanks," Drew said. "She really seemed to love having you rock her." She tucked a wayward strand of her curly hair behind her ear and smiled at him, her brown eyes soft with affection. She'd been a lot warmer since Ginnie's birth, as if the abundance of love she felt for her child overflowed to those around her. He'd always known that Drew was capable of great tenderness, and he'd hoped that having a child would soften her hard edges and diffuse her ambitions. He wanted her at home, just for him and their children—a beautiful princess, the object of his devotion, the subject of his poetry.

He put his arm around her shoulder and hugged her

close to him. "I'm so happy," he said. "Ginnie is won-derful."

Drew stiffened, and a strange look passed quickly over her face. "I need to tell you something" She stared down at her hands as she spoke. "I'm happy, too, and I don't want my happiness to spoil yours." She was silent for a long moment, then inhaled deeply and blew her breath out in a lengthy sigh. "Daddy has agreed to lend me the money I need to get Wish and Vixen—and myself—to Saratoga."

Rob couldn't hold back the groan that tore itself from the depths of his belly. "Why, Drew?" Everything had been going so well, and then she destroyed their happiness without a qualm. It had all been an illusion.

"Because Wish is *my* horse, not Blue Meadow's. And I want to buy Vixen, too—I know you're planning to sell her anyway." She spoke urgently and earnestly, as if trying to convince him of the rightness of her cause.

"Isn't Ginnie enough for you? How can you leave her?" Anguish sent his voice soaring, and he jerked his arm off her shoulders.

"I'm going to take her with me. You're welcome to come, too, if you want."

His shoulders sagged, and he tilted his head back against the headboard and closed his eyes. "So what exactly are you telling me?"

"That I need a partner, not an owner or a boss." Her tone was firm but not hostile. She didn't say the words, but he heard the implication—*nor a husband; I will leave you if I have to.*

He couldn't fight both Drew and her father. If Edward had chosen to give Drew financial independence from her husband, then so be it. He tossed aside the covers and climbed out of bed, then grabbed his robe from the hook on the back of the door and thrust his arms into the sleeves.

Drew frowned at him. "Where are you going?"

"Downstairs," he said, and stalked out of their bedroom.

August 1928

Fanning herself with the racing program, Drew leaned forward as the field for the Saratoga Handicap passed below the grandstand on their way to the starting barrier. Secret Wish looked in fine form for the opening day of the Saratoga season, his dark bay coat gleaming in the bright sunlight and his eyes shining and eager as he looked up at the noisy crowd in the stands. Nimba and Valorous, both of them highly touted favorites on the backstretch, appeared equally as eager, their necks arched proudly and their feet dancing.

Drew's stomach squeezed into a hard little ball of nerves. It didn't matter how many times she watched Wish race—there was always the same anxiety. What if he got a bad start? What if he were outclassed? What if he got hurt? So far he'd had a good summer, winning four stakes races at Pimlico and Aqueduct and placing in three others before coming to Saratoga. But there were so many things that could go wrong, even with a jockey as good as Earl Sande in the saddle.

And now that Kentucky Vixen was hers as well, she had twice as many worries, even though things had been going as well for the filly as they were for Wish. Still, she couldn't complain. She was doing what she wanted, and Wish and Vixen were thriving. As was Ginnie, who had turned out to be an excellent little traveler.

The only one who wasn't happy with the situation was Rob. Although Blue Meadow horses raced at Pimlico and Aqueduct as well as Saratoga, he had refused to accompany them—out of spite, Drew figured. Not that it made much difference anymore; after the night she'd announced her plans, he'd moved into his office and she'd been sleeping alone ever since. Vi pretended not to notice, but whenever Drew walked in on a conversation between Vi and Trixie, they abruptly and self-consciously fell silent.

After two months of tension and awkwardness, Drew was glad to escape to the racetrack with Ginnie. Trixie accompanied her as both chaperone and babysitter for Ginnie. If Rob had come along as well, the two of them might have patched things up; but of course Rob's presence would have implied a tolerance for what she was doing, if not an acceptance, and he didn't seem willing to give in even that much. Let the stubborn idiot sleep alone, then!

The horses reached the web barrier, and she wrenched her thoughts back to the present. Thinking about Rob always upset her because she knew the only way to make him happy was to make herself miserable, and that wasn't something she was willing to do.

She grabbed her field glasses, stood up, and peered through them at the starting barrier. The number seven horse, Post Time, reared and backed away every time his jockey brought him close to the web. Wish jerked his head up and down impatiently but Sande, in the new sky blue and yellow silks Drew had designed for her own horses, kept him easily in position nevertheless. Finally, they were all in place, and the barrier shot up.

Wish stumbled, then recovered himself almost immediately. Drew's heart lurched when he rounded the first corner last in a field of twelve. One of her nightmares had come true; she just prayed his misstep hadn't injured him.

But by the beginning of the backstretch, Wish had moved up to the center of the pack; and by the end Sande had jockeyed him to the rail and into second place, right behind Valorous. Drew screamed as the horses thundered around the far turn and onto the homestretch. A quarter of a mile left and Wish was running nose to nose with

Valorous, with the third horse following by several lengths.

Sande reached for the whip, and Wish suddenly bolted forward, as if he'd been waiting for the go-ahead to really run. He surged ahead, crossing the finish line at least a length ahead of Valorous.

Drew clapped and yelled, a little sad that she had no one to share her happiness with. Excusing herself, she worked her way through the crowded row to the aisle, then headed down the stairs to the winner's circle.

Jack Nolan met her at the entrance and pumped her hand up and down. "Except for the start, he ran a damned fine race," he said.

The crowd milling around the circle cleared a path for them, and they stepped inside. Drew patted Wish's neck, and he nuzzled her hand expectantly. "Later," she told him, and he blew out his breath noisily through his nostrils.

Jack bent over and ran his hand down Wish's left foreleg, then wagged his head back and forth at her.

Her heart thumping with anxiety, Drew received the trophy and shook hands with the track officials. She could hardly wait for the short ceremony to be over. Jack wasn't a dramatic person; if he looked worried, something was definitely wrong.

When it was finished, Drew took the reins and led Wish out of the circle. He seemed to be favoring the leg that had concerned Jack. "What is it?" she asked Jack as they headed back to the stables.

"He injured his tendon." Jack's voice was bleak.

"Has it started to fill?" Tears stung Drew's eyes. A bowed tendon meant the end of Wish's racing career.

Jack nodded, his eyes suspiciously shiny. "I'm afraid he's done for," he said, rubbing Wish's neck. "You've just run your last race, old boy."

Twenty-three

Every time he heard Ballantrae Manor's large entry door open, Adam stiffened. He'd been both looking forward to and dreading this evening for the last two months, ever since Chase had declared his intention of announcing his engagement to Trixie at Christmas time. He was pleased his wild younger brother was finally going to settle down, and he thought Trixie was a perfect choice for him; he was happy to be celebrating Christmas at Ballantrae with his family this year; but he didn't relish the idea of conversing with Drew and Rob. If Chase and Trixie had chosen a large formal party, it would have been easier. But instead they'd opted for a small affair with only family and close friends, and that meant there was no possible way for Adam to avoid Drew, especially now that she was going to become his sister-in-law in a few months.

This time his trepidation had a real cause: the butler Philipps announced Mr. and Mrs. Robert Carlisle, and Drew, with a dark-haired baby cradled against her hip, entered the parlor followed by Rob.

His hands clenched at his sides, Adam stood stiffly next to the wing chair where Victoria sat with their three-month-old son Alexander sleeping in her arms and waited while his parents greeted Drew and Rob. When it was his turn, he shook Rob's hand and then kissed Drew on the cheek. As hard as he tried, he couldn't help noticing how wonderful she looked. She was as slender as ever, but no longer in a reed-thin, boyish fashion. Motherhood seemed to have softened the angularity of her features and curved her figure sensously, and the slight tremor in her lower lip almost unnerved him completely.

Guiltily, he forced the memory of making love to Drew from his mind. Victoria had just presented him with a healthy son; he had no business responding to another woman the way he responded to Drew even though he hadn't laid a hand on Victoria in months. Carefully avoiding Drew's eyes, he stepped back and smiled at her little girl. "Hello, Virginia. It's nice to meet you."

"We call her Ginnie," Drew said, her voice flat.

"What a little beauty," he said. "She looks just like you." Except for her green eyes. *His* eyes staring back at him from his daughter's tiny face. His heart ached with a sudden yearning that caught him by surprise. More than anything in the world, he wanted to stretch his arms out and enfold both mother and child in them.

Instead, he turned to Rob. "Congratulations. You must be very proud." He scanned Rob's face for any signs of knowledge but saw with relief nothing there except glowing fondness for the baby, and he wondered once again what Drew had told Rob. Did he think the child was his own?

Rob held out his arms, and Drew placed Ginnie into them. "I am," he said. "And you must be, too." He gestured toward the infant sleeping in Victoria's lap. "Alexander is certainly a handsome lad." He grinned at Adam. "And well behaved, too."

Adam returned Rob's smile with a wry one of his own. "For the moment. But don't be misled—he's capable of creating quite an uproar." The baby boy stirred and whimpered, and Adam held his finger up to his mouth.

It didn't do any good. Two seconds later Alexander was howling furiously, and the senior Mrs. MacKenzie rang for the nurse. A stout middle-aged woman arrived in a whirlwind of efficiency and swept up the screaming baby. "You might as well take the other child, too, Spencer," Victoria said. "I'm sure Drew would be glad to have you watch her."

Drew's shoulders tensed at Victoria's high-handed assumption, but she said nothing as Rob handed Ginnie over to the stern-looking nurse.

Spencer departed with a child on each hip, and Victoria's face relaxed as the howls receded in the distance. "I don't know what I'd do without Spencer," she said.

Drew lifted an eyebrow. "We don't have a nurse."

"Oh." Victoria shrugged. "However do you manage? Of course, Adam's always telling me how capable you are. And you do have Trixie and Viola to help out."

Philipps stepped into the room and announced the arrival of Neal Rafferty, along with Trixie, Chase, and Vi. Drew greeted them, grateful to escape the conversation with Victoria. Neal returned her greeting with a big grin and a kiss on the cheek, and Drew glanced anxiously at Rob, who glowered at her in return. If anything, he'd become even more possessive and domineering since he fell in love with Ginnie. Whatever had made her think that marriage would make things better between them?

A nervous titter fluttered up from Drew's belly to her throat, but she managed to squelch it before it erupted. The situation was so awful it *was* almost funny—but no one else would understand. She was the only one who knew just how horrible it all was—Adam might be suspicious that Ginnie was his child, but she certainly had no intention of verifying it for him; Rob suspected that Neal was Ginnie's father; and the rest of them had no idea that everything wasn't exactly what it seemed on the surface.

* * *

February 1929

The day after the engagement party Drew wrote her first advertisement offering Secret Wish for stud service. She sent it off to the *Blood-Horse* and waited anxiously for replies. By March, only five broodmares were booked, and she was worried even though both Jack Nolan and Rob assured her that it wasn't uncommon for an unproven stud to start out slowly. "As soon as he produces a stakes winner, things will change," Jack said.

But, impatient as always, she stewed and fretted, then pestered Rob to breed at least three of his mares to Wish. He finally agreed to use one of his older, more patient mares as a test mare to train Wish, but he refused to even consider anything more—and Drew was sure the only reason for his obstinacy was his desire to thwart her. The more involved she became in the horse business, the harder he insisted that she stay out of it. The conflict had been bad enough while she was pregnant, but Rob had become even more adamant after Ginnie's birth.

And the saddest part of it all was that Rob didn't really like the business himself. He *needed* her help, but he wouldn't admit it. He had no interest in, or head for, the every day details of managing a horse farm, and he couldn't afford to hire a manager, he claimed. Still, he resisted her offers of help and resented what little she did manage to do. Interference, he called it.

Nowhere did he tolerate her interference less than in matters pertaining to breeding—and nowhere did her involvement mean more to her. Now that Wish could no longer race, her independence—and Kentucky Vixen's future—was tied to his success at stud.

Grimly, she set her mouth and headed for the breeding shed, shivering in the cold early March air. Today was the first of Wish's five bookings for the 1929 season, and the only reason she knew about it was because last night she'd overheard Rob telling Wish's groom Ben Parker to have Wish ready the next morning before the van arrived from Idle Hour Stock Farm. She wanted to see the Idle Hour mare; if Wish didn't cover good mares, he'd be a lot less likely to produce a winner.

And she wanted to watch how Ben handled Wish. He loved the stallion as much as she did, but she wanted to be sure that the handlers protected Wish from injury and avoided forcing him on a mare that wasn't ready and receptive.

Her hands clenched stiffly at her sides, she marched up to Rob just as the Idle Hour van pulled into the lane. "Are you planning to use a teaser?" she asked him. If the broodmare wasn't ready, the horse would take it out on Kirby, the poor old stallion who approached the mare first but was never allowed to complete what he got started. Because Secret Wish was now *her* horse rather than Blue Meadow's, she couldn't just assume that Rob would do things the right way. He didn't care what happened to Wish—he'd made that only too clear.

"What are you doing here?" He glared at her, ignoring her question. "A woman has no business at the breeding shed. Go back to the house."

Drew put her hands on her hips and glared back at him. Two could play the ignoring game. "Are you going to use Kirby?"

The Idle Hour van pulled to a stop in front of the shed, and two men climbed out of the cab. They stared at Drew, eyebrows hovering in the middles of their foreheads.

"Yes." He thrust out his arm and pointed in the direction of the house. "Now go."

"What about a vet? Is Doc Steffens here?"

Rob's lips stretched into a thin smile, which he directed toward the Idle Hour men. "I'll be with you in a minute," he said to them. He grabbed Drew's arm and half-dragged her around to the side of the shed.

"Let go!" She shook herself free. "I have no intention of leaving."

"In that case, I'm going to tell George and Louis they might as well take their mare back to Idle Hour. It's up to you. You leave or they do. I have nothing invested in Wish's success as a stud, but I think you might." Behind his steel-rimmed glasses, his gray-blue eyes were narrow slits glittering with cold anger. "Don't forget that I'm the one doing you a favor."

Just as she opened her mouth to retort, the piercing scream of a stallion split the air, and the Idle Hour mare in the van answered with a shrill whinny. Drew's shoulders sagged. When would she ever learn that it was no use arguing with Rob? If she wanted to see how he handled Secret Wish, she would just have to hide in the loft and watch—and even then, if she didn't like what she saw, what could she do about it? He was right—Wish meant nothing to him, and he was only helping out now because she'd begged him too.

The powerlessness of her situation hit her in the stomach with the force of a fist. As long as Rob was her husband, he would continue to control her life in whatever way he could manage. She'd made enough money on her investments with Adam to repay her father and reinvest another thousand dollars, but it had been months since Adam had written her or sent a check, and there hadn't been a chance to ask him anything when she'd seen him last at Chase and Trixie's engagement party. She had no idea if her money was gone or growing, so she'd been counting on Wish's stud fees to help pay the costs for Kentucky Vixen's spring season.

She spun on her heel and stalked back to the house, her cheeks flaming as she caught the amused glances of the grooms. Rob had won this time because she'd had no other choice. From now on, though, she was going to plan her battles a little more carefully.

Twenty-four

May 1929

Her stomach still quivering with excitement, Drew bounced Ginnie up and down on her knee while they waited for Rob in the lobby of the Brown Hotel. Kentucky Vixen may not have won the Kentucky Derby that afternoon, but she'd come awfully close—just one length behind the winner Clyde Van Dusen, the small chestnut son of Man O' War, and three lengths ahead of Naishapur. Drew's throat still hurt from screaming, and she was sure Rob had bruises on his arm from where she'd clutched him at the end of the race.

Ginnie squealed with delight at a particularly high bounce, and Drew smiled at her daughter. At sixteen months, Ginnie was a little bundle of energy, her mouth and her feet always in motion. Her dark curls had become even thicker and more unruly, and her eyes had gradually lightened from the dark gray of babyhood to the same intense sea green as Adam's.

A fact which she was sure had not escaped his notice. A slight shiver ran down her spine at the thought, and Drew hugged Ginnie against her chest despite the little girl's squirms. Adam had only seen his daughter twice before today—the first time at Chase and Trixie's engagement party and then at their wedding—and both times he hadn't been able to keep his eyes off of her.

Some of the euphoria of Kentucky Vixen's success ebbed away when she remembered her anxiety before the Derby. She and Rob and Ginnie had been settled in their box when the Ballantrae party arrived. Trixie had told her that Adam was coming, but she'd had no idea whether Victoria would be with him or not. It was painful enough seeing Adam when he was by himself, but when he was with Victoria, it was agony for Drew.

She'd caught a glimpse of Adam's shiny dark hair above the crowd as he'd come down the aisle to his box, and her chest had tightened. She deliberately turned away, lifting her field glasses to her eyes and peering through them at the post parade below. When she heard the chorus of greetings from the Ballantrae box, she lowered her glasses and forced her lips into a smile before she looked his way.

He stood next to Victoria, his back straight and chin high; and when he saw her, he didn't return her smile but instead nodded gravely at her. Victoria flashed a brief wave and a smile even phonier than Drew's in the direction of the Blue Meadow box. After shaking hands with Rob over the short railing between the two boxes, Adam chucked Ginnie, who stood on Rob's seat, under the chin and grinned at her. "Hi, there," he said. "I'll bet you don't remember me. Spencer whisked you away two seconds after we met the first time, and the next time you napped through an entire wedding. I'm Uncle Adam."

Ginnie grinned back, her small white teeth gleaming in the sun. "Unk Aman," she said, then giggled, jumped down from Rob's chair, and clutched Drew's leg. "Up, Momma," she said, stretching out her arms.

Glad for the distraction, Drew picked her up and nuzzled her neck, and Adam turned back to speak to his family. Drew had spent the rest of the afternoon paying what she hoped appeared to be rapt attention to the races—even though she didn't register who'd won, let alone any of the lesser details. The only race she completely attended to was the Derby, and she'd escaped immediately afterward, taking Ginnie with her and leaving Rob in their box to socialize with the MacKenzies and the others offering their mixed congratulations and condolences. Just the idea of exchanging pleasantries with Adam while Victoria looked on made her feel queasy. She'd wanted to enjoy the pleasure of Vixen's performance—and the relief of the sizable boost to her income, more than enough to pay Vixen's expenses for the rest of the season—without worrying about Adam or anyone else.

Sure, she was a little disappointed that Vixen hadn't won, but she wasn't really surprised. Fillies were at a disadvantage in the long race so early in the season for three-year-olds; since the first running of the Kentucky Derby in 1875, the only filly to win had been Regret in 1915. For Vixen to place second was a triumph of sorts, as well as a vindication of Drew's belief in her.

Now, in the lobby, she kissed Ginnie's soft cheek and released her from her enveloping hug. Ginnie immediately scrambled to the floor and started to run back toward the stairway that led to the mezzanine.

Drew jumped up and headed toward her just as Adam emerged from behind the white marble pillar at the back of the lobby.

He scooped Ginnie up and carried her kicking and screaming back to her mother. "Did you lose this?" he asked, his face serious but his eyes smiling. "It looks awfully precious to me."

A sudden onslaught of tears burned Drew's eyes, and she ducked her head to hide any telltale sign of them from Adam. "It is," she said. A tiny voice inside her wanted to tell him just how precious Ginnie really should be to him, but the much louder voices of convention and reason protested vigorously. And besides, he obviously suspected that Ginnie was his child anyway, and he hadn't said a word.

She blinked the tears from her eyes and held out her arms to Ginnie. If Adam ever asked, she'd tell him, she decided. But she would never volunteer the truth.

August 1929

Drew and Ginnie traveled with Kentucky Vixen for the rest of the summer, heading north to New York in June for the Belmont Stakes, which Vixen won handily, then to the Jamaica course for the Great American and Tremont Stakes, in which the filly placed first and third respectively. In July Vixen raced at Aqueduct, adding two more first finishes to her stakes record and another thirteen thousand dollars to Drew's bank account. In August Rob joined them at Saratoga with Jack Nolan and two of his horses.

He arrived at the track just in time for the Miller Stakes, the fifth race of the day and one in which Vixen was running. Drew hadn't seen him in over two months, and to her surprise, he appeared drawn and haggard, with dark circles under his eyes. He greeted her distantly but politely, then asked about Ginnie.

"She's at the hotel with Miss Sullivan," Drew said. "I only bring her to the racetrack on special occasions."

"I miss her," Rob said. "The house is so quiet without her."

Drew lifted an eyebrow. It had been several months since the last time Rob had moved out of their bedroom into his office, so his coolness toward her after her absence wasn't too odd. But, still, something about him was different. He didn't look angry and tense anymore—he looked sad, defeated.

"I miss you, too," he said, just as the trumpet sounded for the post parade for the Miller Stakes.

Drew jerked her eyes back toward him. "What?" she asked, her voice a squeak of surprise, which, fortunately, was lost in the noise of the crowd.

"I really miss you," he shouted. "I want you to come back. After Belmont, I mean," he added hurriedly. "After Vixen's last race of the season. I want to try again." Through his glasses, his eyes gleamed with unshed tears. "I know I've done nothing but stand in your way. Sometimes I don't understand why myself. I knew how much Wish meant to you before we were married. Maybe I was jealous. And then there was Ginnie. I just don't know." He lifted his hands, palms up in a gesture of surrender.

Not sure what to say, Drew just stared at him. Why was he bringing this up now? "I'll talk to you after the race," she yelled. She turned her attention back to the track just in time to see the field reach the web barrier. The Miller Stakes didn't have a large purse, but Vixen's performance meant a lot to her. She had no intention of missing any of it just to hear another one of Rob's apologies.

It wasn't that she didn't think he was sincere. Just a glance at his anguished expression told her everything she needed to know about his unhappiness. But he kept doing the same thing over and over again. All she wanted to do was what she'd always wanted to do—own and race thoroughbreds. He'd known that; in fact, he'd even helped make it possible for her before they were married. They'd get along just fine if he'd just leave her alone instead of acting like her father.

And what was even stranger was that her father was her ally now. She'd even overheard him during a visit one evening trying to tell Rob to ease up a bit on the reins. "Drew's headstrong, I know," Daddy had said. "But she'll jump the paddock fence if you don't give her her head once in a while."

Well, Rob was obviously attempting to take Daddy's advice once again, especially now that she was financially independent. Sighing, Drew lifted her field glasses to her eyes. High Strung, the number three horse—well-named, it seemed—was giving the starter some trouble, but Vixen's jockey Frank Coltiletti had eased the filly up to the barrier without any problems. Finally, for a split second the horses were lined up, and the starter gave the signal. The barrier shot up.

From the outside, Vixen rushed to the lead and took the rail by the first turn. Drew held her breath as Blue Larkspur, the Idle Hour colt who'd been touted as a Derby favorite, pulled up beside her in the backstretch. The Miller was a mile and a quarter, still a long race for Vixen—especially when it didn't look like Coltiletti was holding her back.

"Come on, Vixen!" Drew shouted. "Keep going! You can do it!" She clapped so hard her palms stung, then clenched her hands into tight fists as the field, Vixen still ahead by half a length, thundered toward the homestretch.

Suddenly, Blue Larkspur swerved, almost bumping Vixen as they rounded the final corner. The filly broke her stride for a brief second, then recovered, but it was too late. Blue Larkspur crossed the finish line barely a nose ahead of her.

Drew groaned and sat down with a thud. It had been so close, but Blue Larkspur's lunge had thrown Vixen off balance. She frowned and raised the glasses back to her eyes to watch as Coltiletti slowed her gradually. Vixen seemed to be favoring her right foreleg.

"Vixen's hurt," Rob said before she could force herself to acknowledge that something was wrong.

She nodded, her eyes burning from peering through the glasses. He was right. It didn't look good. She stood when

Coltiletti slid off of Vixen's back and peered up into the stands. "I've got to go." She rushed from the box, not even turning around to see if Rob followed.

Her heart thudding in her ears, she ran toward the shed row as soon as she got clear of the crowd. By the time she caught up with Vixen and her groom Mickey, Rob was by her side. One look at Mickey's face told her all she needed to know, and a glance at Vixen's foreleg confirmed it.

"Oh, my God," Drew whispered. It would be a miracle if Vixen ever raced again.

Twenty-five

November 1929

Grinding her teeth to keep from saying something she knew she was going to regret, Drew examined the Blue Meadow ledger over Rob's shoulder. He'd mismanaged the farm for months while he wasn't allowing her to help with the business and while she was traveling with Vixen, and now it turned out he'd invested what little profit there'd been in penny stocks not even worth the paper they were printed on since the stock market crash last week. The bank where they had their meager savings had closed its doors before they could get their money out, so if it wasn't for what was left of Vixen's earnings from last summer—which she'd squirreled away under her mattress mostly out of fear that Rob would take the money away from her if he knew where it was—they'd be broke. And Vixen wouldn't be racing anymore now, either, although her leg had healed enough to breed her. But it would take at least two years before they had anything to show from that, and maybe never.

"We're going to have to sell some of the horses. That's all there is to it." Rob leaned back in his chair and steepled his hands.

Drew wasn't sure why, but his attitude irritated her even more than his ineptitude. Why didn't he just go back to the university and let her run Blue Meadow? He hated it, and she could hardly do worse. And even though they were sharing a bedroom again, the tension between them was like a third person in the room—and just about as inspiring to romance. He looked as miserable as she felt. "Swell," she said, unable to keep the sarcasm out of her voice. " 'Most everyone is in the same fix we are. Who are you planning to sell to? We could probably get more for mules."

The telephone buzzed, and he stared at it for a second as if he had no idea what in the hell it was. Drew grabbed the receiver. "Hello."

"Drew, it's Momma." Her mother's voice sounded thin and flat.

"Momma, are you all right?"

There was a long silence on the other end. "I'm fine," Momma said. "It's your father." She took a deep, shaky breath. "He's had a heart attack."

Drew's breath froze in her lungs. "Daddy?"

Her mother said nothing.

"I'll be right there, Momma," Drew said. She hung up with shaking hands.

"What's wrong now?" Rob frowned at her.

"I have to go. Daddy's had a heart attack." To her amazement, her voice came out normally even though it sounded as if it were far away. The rest of her body felt ice cold and stiff, as if it didn't belong to her anymore.

Rob's demeanor changed instantly. "Oh, Drew, I'm sorry," he said. "I'll drive you."

Drew nodded at him, wishing he'd put his arms around her and just hold her. The shaking in her hands seemed to be spreading to her entire body, and she knew that if he hugged her it would be better.

But instead, Rob gestured toward the door. "Let's go."

She forced her legs to follow him outside into the freezing November air and to the car. Her teeth chattered as she crunched through the crisp fallen leaves that covered the gravel driveway. She opened the car door and climbed in next to him, then pulled the door shut and leaned against it, wrapping her arms around herself. She'd forgotten to put on her coat, but that didn't matter now. Nothing was going to make her warmer. "Hurry," she said.

Rob turned the key in the ignition, and nothing happened. He pumped the gas pedal and tried again. Still nothing. He waited a minute, then attempted to start the car once more. The engine turned over, then died. "It started fine a couple of days ago," he said. "It must be the cold weather."

Drew threw open her door before he had time to try again. "I'm taking Wish," she said over her shoulder as she ran toward the stud barn. "I can't stand to wait."

She flung the barn door open, startling Ben Parker, who was refilling Wish's feed box. "Saddle him," she said.

"But—"

Rob interrupted Ben's protest. "You can't ride him now. Not even the exercise boys ride him anymore. It's too dangerous."

Drew grabbed a saddle and bridle from the tack room and headed toward Wish's stall. "Fine. I'll do it myself."

Ben pulled the tack from her hands. "I don't know what's happenin', but I can see it ain't good," he said. "You're in such a fix, you'll upset that horse, missus."

The tears Drew had been holding back finally streamed down her cheeks. "I have to go home. Daddy's—"

Rob sighed and nodded at Ben. "Go ahead and tack him up," he said. "She's always had a way with Wish. It'll be all right." He turned back to Drew. "I'll follow you over as soon as I can get a vehicle started."

Two minutes later, Ben boosted Drew onto Wish's back. Wish reared, but she brought him under control quickly and turned him toward the lane that led to Ashworth Farm. For the first time in her life, she cared less about her mount than she did about getting where she was going quickly.

Wish swiveled his head and looked quizzically at her, as if he wanted to know where the treat she always brought him was. His eyes were large and shiny, burning with the desire to run, and his nostrils dilated as he breathed in the cold air.

She patted him on the neck. "Sorry, old boy. Just hurry!"

He seemed to understand because she had to pull back on the reins with all her strength to keep him from galloping full out and hurting himself. His bowed tendon had long since healed enough to permit exercise, but allowing Wish his head was out of the question no matter how badly she wanted to get home.

Within minutes they arrived at Ashworth Farm. Dr. Miller's muddy-tired black Oldsmobile was parked in front of the porch. Drew slipped off Wish, led him into the barn, and put him in a stall. She'd send Rob to cool him off as soon as he got there.

After Wish was secured, she ran back to the house, her throat aching from the cold and her cheeks frozen from the tears that had streamed down them during the ride. She trotted up the steps and burst through the door. Her father lay on the couch in the parlor with Dr. Miller and Momma bent over him.

The second they turned their grim faces toward her, Drew knew. "I'm too late," she said. Her heart ached with the hope that she was wrong.

Momma's eyes were glassy with tears as she reached toward Drew and pulled her into her arms. "What are we going to do now?" she said.

For the next few days Drew felt as if she were living in a soft white haze, something like a quiet snowstorm that left her cold and numb, except for brief flashes of jolting pain. She had never realized until her father's funeral how many people in Bourbon County loved and respected him. They all came, from the MacKenzies and the Whitneys and the Bradleys to the tobacco field laborers and hardboots and grooms who lined the street outside the church.

But while she appreciated their affection, it did nothing to lessen her grief; in fact, it actually intensified her guilt. There were so many things she didn't know about Daddy. Even though she was twenty-one, she was still a child whose parents only figured in a peripheral manner in her life, and now she'd never know her father as someone who'd been at the center of his own life. Everything she knew about Daddy had been in relation to her, not him; and the sad presence of so many people she hadn't realized even knew him only made her lack of knowledge more poignant.

Two weeks after the funeral, her mother asked her to meet with her and Sam Harris, their lawyer. "Sam told me it was extremely important," Momma said while they waited for the lawyer in the parlor. "He has Edward's will, and he said there was some other business as well."

It was still hard for Drew to sit quietly in the room where her father had died less than a month before. She stood and walked to the oak mantel, then paced back to the window, parted the old lace curtain, and stared outside. The sky was low and gray, threatening snow. She should have accepted Rob's offer of a ride rather than walking, but she'd wanted the time to herself.

And, besides, she hadn't told him the real reason for the visit to her mother—she wanted to keep her business separate from his. If he were at the meeting, he'd consider it his duty to take care of everything for her, and they'd end up having yet another of their never-ending battles over it.

A soft sigh escaped her lips. Her breath had fogged the window so badly she could no longer see clearly through it, so, shoulders sagging, she let the curtain fall back in place and turned around to face her mother.

Momma was handling Daddy's death even worse than Drew was. The faint lines between her eyebrows had deepened into grooves of pain, and her eyes and skin were dull. Momma had been so strong through everything, holding her slender body upright and taut, her chin high; but as soon as the funeral was over, she'd suffered a severe attack of asthma and collapsed. Drew and Ginnie had stayed with her until she was back on her feet, just two days ago. Even then, it'd been difficult for Drew to leave her by herself, but Momma wouldn't hear of deserting Ashworth Farm, and both her mother and Rob had insisted that Drew's place was at Blue Meadow.

The sound of a car motor and the crunch of tires on the gravel lane sent Drew whirling back toward the window. She wiped off a little patch of condensation and peered out. Mr. Harris' dark green car pulled up in front of the steps. "He's here." She headed toward the door. "I'll show him in."

Several minutes later the three of them were settled around the dining room table, its lace tablecloth now strewn with stacks of legal papers. Momma looked up from the one she'd been studying, her face even grayer than before. "So the essence of the matter is that while Edward has left Ashworth Farm to me, there is nothing left of Ashworth Farm." Her attempt to keep her voice light failed, and she hurriedly stared back down at the papers.

"Well, not exactly," Mr. Harris drawled. He ran his hand back over his bald pate as if he were smoothing his nonexistent hair. "I told Edward the day after the crash that his mortgage had been called due, and he seemed to think that he'd be able to pay. Do you know where he might have been able to come up with that kind of money?"

Momma shook her head slowly. "Edward never discussed business with me. I knew he had to mortgage the farm, but I never knew for how much, or when the money was due."

"Exactly how much are you talking about?" Drew asked Mr. Harris.

"Eight thousand dollars to pay off the mortgage." He rifled through a sheaf of papers, extracted one, and handed it to her. "And the various other notes come to another two thousand dollars."

Drew stared at the note in her hands. Her father's death warrant. Five days after the note had been called in, his heart had given out. Yet he'd never even mentioned it to her. Tears welled up in her eyes, and she blinked furiously to clear her vision.

If only he'd told her what he needed. Now her heart was the one that was breaking. She cleared her throat. "I think I know what he meant." It wasn't the truth, but Momma and Mr. Harris didn't need to know that. She had almost enough left from Vixen's earnings hidden under her mattress to pay off the mortgage, and she would wire Adam first thing in the morning.

Her stomach quivered with anxiety at the thought, but this time it had nothing to do with Adam. What if there was nothing left of her investment?

Twenty-six

Bleary-eyed with exhaustion, Adam leaned back in his upholstered leather desk chair and surveyed the scene of destruction with a tiny wry smile. His once immaculate office was a shambles—files and papers strewn over every available surface, desk and file cabinet drawers half-open, dishes and silverware piled in corners. Since Black Thursday three weeks ago, he'd practically lived in his office, trying every angle he could think of to save the bank from complete and utter ruin.

He closed his eyes and let his head fall forward. He'd thought privately for months that the rampant speculation would end exactly the way it did, even though everyone—from bank presidents to college professors to President Hoover—insisted that the economy was sound. Speculation orgies were always followed by a crash; the Florida real estate boom was the most recent example. The only ones who'd benefited were the Florida farmers who'd sold their land for a tidy profit, then got it back a few years later when the investors ended up defaulting after the "Soothing Tropic Wind" promised in the ads turned into a devastating hurricane.

Unfortunately, Father had been one of the believers in the latest economic boom, approving loan after loan to people whose collateral was now worthless because of powers beyond their control. Now, when depositors in a panic came to withdraw their funds, there was nothing to give them—except Adam's own savings. Which he had done.

And now he had no choice because there was nothing else left. He was going to have to sell the beautiful house he'd bought for Victoria on the Main Line. It was lucky that Father refused to give up Ballantrae. At least they'd have a nice place to live until things improved.

He didn't relish imparting the bad news to Victoria, who considered Kentucky a primitive backwater and always referred to their stays at Ballantrae as "camping out" despite the fact that the mansion was twice as large as their house in Bryn Mawr. She was going to accuse him of using the crash to get what he'd always wanted anyway, since she knew he preferred Paris, Kentucky, to Philadelphia.

A tap on the door brought him out of his ponderings. Heaving a huge sigh, he opened his eyes and sat up straight. "Come in."

His secretary Miss Barlow stepped into the room. "A wire for you, sir. It says 'urgent' on it." She handed him an envelope.

"Everything is urgent these days." He managed a small smile. "Thank you."

As soon as she left, he opened the envelope, grimacing when he saw that it was from Drew. He'd been sad to hear of Edward's death; and although the immensity of his responsibilities at the bank had prevented him from attending the funeral, he'd sent his condolences.

After he read the wire, he berated himself for not having thought of Drew earlier. He should have realized that she'd need money. With the combination of Edward's death, the stock market crash, and the Paris bank failure, anyone to whom Edward owed money would have called in the debt. And if, like so many other people during the last two years—everyone from taxi cab drivers to barbers to grade schoolteachers—Edward had dabbled in the stock market, the situation could be even worse. As it was, all

Drew asked was if the thousand dollars she'd given to him to invest two years ago was still safe, and if so, to please send it as soon as possible.

He stared at the brief message, then tossed it on his desk before he stood up and stretched. It was never easy for him to think about Drew, or Ginnie. He hadn't seen them since the Derby six months ago, and it had taken him several days to regain his equanimity afterward. In fact, he put a lot of effort into *not* thinking about Drew because whenever he did, he always came to the same conclusion—and it wasn't a happy one.

He'd been an idiot.

And Drew had compounded his mistake with an equally large one of her own. It had been only too apparent at the Derby that both of them were miserable in their marriages, and neither Victoria nor Rob seemed particularly happy, either.

He inhaled deeply and straightened his shoulders. He'd never been one to cry over spilt milk. What was done, was done, and now they both had to live with their choices. He'd made his bed; now he had to lie in it. A dry chuckle escaped his lips at his platitudes. He was beginning to sound like Father. God help him now.

Forcing his feelings of despair into retreat, he sat back down in his chair and rummaged through the bottom drawer of his desk for his personal checkbook. Although he'd invested Drew's money in blue chips, even General Electric and Westinghouse stock had plummeted far below what he had bought it for on a margin six months ago, and the margin call had wiped her out completely.

But there was no need for her to know that. He made the check out for one thousand dollars and signed it. He only wished he could afford to give her more.

Quickly, the way Vi had shown her, Drew stirred water into the flour and butter mixture for the pie crust. Although baking wasn't one of Drew's talents, she always did whatever she could to help out, and Vi needed lots of help this Thanksgiving since they could no longer afford household help. Besides, the busier Drew stayed, the less time she had to think about celebrating her first Thanksgiving without her father. Even though Momma and Chase and Trixie would be there, it wouldn't be the same.

The dough formed into a solid lump, and Drew set aside the mixing fork and dusted her hands with flour. It was hard to be thankful this year with Daddy gone and Momma in poor health, but she had at least one thing to be grateful for. She'd received Adam's check two days ago and paid off all the notes, and now Momma owned the farm free and clear.

But the only way the farm would make it was if Drew ran it herself. Momma had no idea what to do; they couldn't afford to hire someone; and if they didn't make enough money to pay the taxes, they'd end up losing it anyway. There was really no other choice.

She gathered the bits of dough left on the side of the bowl into the main lump and patted it into a ball with her hands. As she rolled it out into a large circle on the floured pastry cloth, Rob clomped down the stairs and into the kitchen.

"Coffee made?" He settled himself at the table as if he expected her to wash the flour off her hands and serve him.

"It's on the stove." She jerked her head toward the pot, then carefully lifted the circle of dough onto the pie plate.

Grunting, he pushed himself out of his chair and grabbed a cup from the shelves next to the stove. "Didn't hear you get up this morning." He poured his coffee and sat back down.

"I've been up since four o'clock. I wanted to get the baking out of the way before your mother started in on the turkey." She dumped the bowl of sliced apples tossed with sugar and cinnamon into the bottom crust. Not for the first time, she wondered why being able to have babies obligated her to cook and clean and wash dishes. Rob was certainly capable of learning to bake an apple pie, yet because he was a man, *his* only obligation today was to eat like a pig. And if he did anything at all to help out, he'd act as if he were doing everyone a huge favor.

Actually, he'd do everyone an even bigger favor if he spent more time attending to managing the farm and less time huddled over his poetry notebooks. Yet she'd bet anything that as soon as she mentioned helping her mother run Ashworth Farm, he'd complain that she wouldn't have time to attend to her duties at home. She rolled out another round of dough and settled it on top of the apples, then took a deep breath and faced Rob. She might as well get it over with.

There was no diplomatic way to tell him, so she simply stated her intention and waited for his reaction.

"You can't," he said. "I won't let you."

She shrugged and turned back to the pie. "I will," she muttered. "You can't stop me." She trimmed the edges of the crust, hacking at it more vigorously than necessary. "Mother will lose the farm if I don't."

"Be reasonable, Drew. There aren't enough hours in the day, and we need you here. *I* need you here. Ginnie needs her mother. If you don't care about me, at least think of her." He banged his cup down on the table, and coffee sloshed over the top. "For Christ's sake, think of someone else besides yourself for a change. *I'd* like another child— one of my own flesh and blood. How's that ever going to happen if you're gone most of the time?"

Drew whirled around, clamping her flour-caked hands to her hips and striving to ignore the sudden roar that filled her head. It was early in the morning on Thanksgiving Day; she'd wake everyone in the house if she gave in to her urge to scream at him. She clenched her jaw and said nothing until the thunder in her ears faded to a hollow hum and she knew she could trust herself not to lose control. "If I'd known that you'd resent Ginnie, I'd never have married you," she said, her voice vibrating with intensity. *"You're* the one who should think of someone else besides himself."

She dusted off her hands and resumed crimping the edges of the pie crust while Rob continued lecturing her. There was no point in arguing with him since she had no intention of letting him draw her into a battle this time. They never resolved anything anyway, no matter how much they fought about it. He was as determined to try to make her into his idea of the perfect wife as she was to try to make her own dreams come true, dreams that had nothing to do with baking the best apple pies in Bourbon County.

In fact, she hoped he choked on the damn pie. She slashed air vents in the top crust, then carried the pie to the oven and slid it onto the rack. Still, he was undoubtedly right about one thing—she was going to be awfully busy. Ginnie would not be a problem—Momma loved looking after her, so Drew would take her to the farm with her every day. But it would be hard for her to pay as much attention to the progress of Wish and Vixen as she'd like to. Unless, of course, they were more conveniently stabled at Ashworth Farm.

There was an idea. Deliberately ignoring Rob, she washed the sticky dough from her hands before she untied her apron and stuck it on the peg next to the sink. His voice followed her as she stomped out of the kitchen. She'd arrange to have her horses moved first thing tomorrow morning.

Twenty-seven

December 1929

Adam slowed his Ford Phaeton to a crawl as he turned into the gravel lane leading to Ashworth Farm. As he remembered, the road was pitted with one pothole after another; he couldn't imagine that it had been improved during the last year, not with everything that had happened since then.

He let out a long sigh that seemed to come from somewhere deep in his gut. It had been a year filled with sadness and failure, for both him and Drew personally as well as for the nation in general; and he had a strong sense that nothing would ever be the same again. It was like suddenly growing up and realizing that no matter how hard you tried, you would not be able to do everything you dreamed of. As Father used to lecture, you had to set priorities and make choices, and some dreams simply had to be relegated to the bottom of the list. Endless wonderful possibilities melted into the realities of daily life, and the days melted into each other . . .

He couldn't resist a quick smile at how much his thoughts resembled his father's pompous philosophizing. But this time it didn't apply to just his own life; the entire country was growing up. The last few years had been like an exuberant adolescence; now the nation was ready to enter somber adulthood. Hundreds of thousands of people had finally realized that those who got rich quick could get poor even more quickly—the "anything is possible" innocence of youth had been destroyed almost overnight.

He released another long sigh and straightened his shoulders as he braked the car in front of the Ashworths' house. Ironically, he didn't feel all that bad about losing his job and his house in Bryn Mawr. In some ways, coming back to Kentucky was like coming back to the unspoiled freshness of his childhood. He'd always been happier at Ballantrae, and he'd never really liked the banking business anyway. He swung his long legs out of the car and headed toward the house. If only Victoria felt the same—

"Hey, Adam!"

He stopped at the bottom step and spun back around.

Drew waved from the door of the tobacco barn. She wore baggy brown trousers and a cream-colored sweater, and her hair, except for curly dark tendrils around her face and the nape of her neck, was hidden under a red stocking cap.

Thinking only of how wonderful it would feel to gather her into his arms, he strode toward her; but the sane half of his brain prevailed before he reached her. He held out his hand, then shook hers vigorously when she grasped it. "It's so good to see you again, Drew," he said. "I wanted to tell you how sorry I am about your father. I'm going to miss him."

She dropped his hand and stared down at her feet for a moment. "We all are." When she looked back up at him, tears shimmered in her beautiful brown eyes.

This time he couldn't help himself even though he knew better. He pulled her into his arms and held her against his chest. "I wish I could have been here for the funeral." Somehow holding her seemed justified as long as they were talking of her father's death.

She stepped back from his embrace, and he let his arms

fall to his sides. "Is there anything I can do to help?" he asked.

She shook her head. "You already did. The farm is debt-free—for the time being, anyway—thanks to you." The tears were gone from her eyes, but her face still looked tense and strained.

"I simply returned your capital to you. I wish I could have done more." He tilted his head toward the barn. "What are you doing in there?"

"Grading tobacco. There's a sale at the Paris warehouse next week."

"Oh, really?" He had a lot to learn—he might as well start now. "Would you show me how you do it?"

She wrinkled her nose and narrowed her eyes. "Sure. But why?"

He wasn't quite ready to tell her, and a shrill whinny gave him the excuse he needed not to. "I stopped at Blue Meadow before I came over here, and Rob told me where to find you. He said you'd moved Wish and Vixen here." Rob had also added in a caustic aside that Drew had basically moved back home. He'd appeared so unhappy that Adam hadn't wanted to question him further.

"They're my horses. I got tired of arguing with Rob and Jack about them. Besides, this is where I spend most of my time." She crossed her arms over her chest and shifted back and forth from one foot to the other.

He wanted to ask where Ginnie was while Drew was working so hard, but he could see that it probably wouldn't be wise to inquire while she was clearly on the defensive. Undoubtedly Rob had brought up the same question—unless, of course, he didn't give a damn about Ginnie. After all, why should he? The child wasn't his.

Ginnie is mine. The words vibrated in his head. *Ginnie is my daughter.* With great effort, he forced the thought from his mind. The words could not be spoken aloud, so thinking them was pointless. "Rob mentioned that you were running the farm now."

She jerked her head toward the barn door. "Come on inside. I'll show you what I've been doing." She led the way into the barn, where large stalks of tobacco hung from the rafters. Stacks of leaves were piled on a long table at the far end of the barn.

When they reached the table, she picked up a tobacco leaf and handed it to him. "Tobacco is graded according to where it grows on the stalk and the quality and color of the leaf. This one is called a 'flying'. Flyings grow at the bottom of the stalk." She rubbed the leaf between her fingers. "See how thin and flat it is? Flyings are the most mature leaves, but they're often the most injured and the dirtiest because they grow so low to the ground. They're divided into five classes according to how injured they are—choice, fine, good, fair, and low. Then they're also grouped according to color—buff, tan, green, or mixed."

"I can see I have a lot to learn." Adam smiled at her.

She cocked an eyebrow at him, mystified by his sudden interest in tobacco. "I feel silly telling you all this stuff. Are you sure you're really interested?"

"Absolutely." He picked up a rolled light yellow leaf with a rounded tip from the table. "What do you call this?"

"Leaves like those are called lugs. They grow at the middle of the stalk. That particular leaf is choice buff. See how thin and ripe it is, and how bright the color is?" She frowned up at him. "Just *why* are you interested, if you don't mind me asking?"

He grinned. "I've decided to become a tobacco farmer."

Drew couldn't keep herself from gaping at him. "You've *what?*"

Shrugging, he twirled the tobacco leaf in his hand. "Victoria and Alexander and I are moving to Ballantrae. The bank collapsed, and I sold our house in Bryn Mawr

to pay our depositors. My parents sold their place in Bryn
Mawr, too, but since Father's in poor health, they're buy-
ing a smaller home and staying in Philadelphia. Chase and
I are going to run Ballantrae."

"But what about the horses?" It was hard for her to
grasp what he was saying. The MacKenzies had always
had so much money, but now they were as poor as she
was.

"We're selling most of them as well. Your father was
always right, you know; horse racing is a rich man's
hobby. And we can't afford such an expensive hobby anymore, especially one that involves so much risk. Ballantrae
has to pay for itself." He ran his hand lightly over the
tobacco leaf, then laid it back on the table.

She tilted her head and squinted her eyes at him. He
didn't sound particularly upset about the huge changes
taking place in his life; in fact, he looked happier and
more relaxed than she'd seen him in a long time. But she'd
always thought he loved racing. "You don't mind selling
the horses?"

"I didn't say I was getting rid of *all* of them." He
smiled at her, his eyes not leaving hers. "Even a poor
man deserves a little bit of pleasure. I'm going to keep
First Star and several other of our best broodmares and
the four stallions who've produced the most stakes winners. We'll be producing yearlings for the sales, but we
won't be racing our own stock for a while. And I hope
that the tobacco will pay for everything—and support us,
too."

Drew couldn't help grinning at him. "That's exactly
what I'm hoping," she said. "I'm planning to breed Wish
and Vixen, too—neither of them will ever race again. Except I want to keep their foals. I know it's a gamble, but
I can't help it."

But it wasn't the risk that attracted her; she knew she
wasn't like her Uncle Andrew, from the little she'd heard

about him. It was the horses she loved, and she wasn't willing to give them up. One of the things she'd always loved about Adam was that he felt the same way—unlike his father, who only cared about winning and how being the owner of a Triple Crown winner would enhance his prestige.

What Drew wanted was to breed a horse like Man O' War: an individual who lived to run—and who loved to outrun anything that came near him. Wish had been like that before old Hugh and Willie Nolan had ruined him with too much racing too young. Secret Wish had given his heart and broken down his legs. A horse like that needed an unselfish owner, one who was more interested in the colt's welfare than his own glory.

But if Adam planned to sell his colts and fillies at the yearling sales, he'd never be in the position to provide that kind of protection. She frowned at him. "Won't it be hard for you not to race your own horses?"

His lips quirked into a glum little smile. "It will. But right now I don't really have another choice, except to sell all of them." He hesitated a minute, then winked at her. "Of course, if there should happen to come along a truly great individual—"

Drew nodded knowingly at him. She felt closer to Adam right now than she had in years. This was the way they'd always talked when she was younger, before the strange feelings of growing up had come between them. She'd loved Adam in this special way long before she'd ever thought about kissing him. And more.

"Mommy!" Ginnie's shrill voice reminded her of what that "more" had been.

Their daughter ran into the barn ahead of her grandmother, stopping short when she saw Adam. She ducked her head and ran back to Drew's mother.

"It's all right," Drew said. "You remember Uncle Adam, don't you, Ginnie?" Suddenly afraid to look at Adam, she picked up a tobacco stalk and stripped off several of the leaves.

Pretending to be shy, Ginnie peered from behind Momma's legs. She giggled, then stepped forward. "Wunch is weady," she said.

Momma coughed into her handkerchief before she smiled at Adam. "Would you care to join us?"

"I'd really like that," Adam said.

He glanced at Drew, but carefully avoiding his eyes, Drew held out her arms to Ginnie. "Come give me a big hug, sweetie," she said. Gathering Ginnie in her arms, she headed back toward the house, the moment of communion with Adam and her own childhood gone.

From the time Drew followed Rob into Chase and Trixie's little house—the former residence of the farm manager—on the Ballantrae estate, she'd been uncomfortable. For starters, Adam and Victoria were already there, and it was immediately apparent that Victoria had already indulged in too much of the freely-flowing bootleg liquor.

Then, while Chase took their coats and Trixie kissed their cheeks, Neal Rafferty emerged from the kitchen with a large glass of what looked like champagne in his hand.

Drew felt Rob stiffen next to her when he spotted Neal. "Who invited *him?*" Rob hissed to Trixie.

She giggled and looked at him as if he were crazy. "He's Chase's best friend, and it's New Year's Eve. How could we *not* invite him?"

Drew stuck her elbow in Rob's side and glared at him. Even though she knew why Rob hated Neal, she couldn't tell him how wrong he was. Still, she also couldn't let his hostility toward Neal ruin the evening for everyone else. "Maybe we should leave *now,*" she said, trying vainly to keep the sarcasm from her voice.

Drew was immediately contrite. Trixie had no idea what

was going on, and she didn't deserve any problems tonight. The times were already difficult enough for everyone, no matter what a good face they all put on the situation. Chase had been forced to leave Harvard Law School at the end of the first term because there was no money for his tuition or their expenses in Cambridge after the bank failed.

Now they were living in a little house with cheap furnishings, and Chase worked from dawn until sundown every day to help Adam. "I mean, if you're too tired to be pleasant, perhaps we shouldn't have come."

Trixie giggled again, a little more high-pitched this time. "I didn't know you didn't like Neal," she said to Rob. "He's not bad when you get used to him. Prohibition did to his family what the stock market crash did to the rest of us, but he's managed well in spite of it."

Before Neal reached them, Victoria placed her hand on his arm and stopped him. Neal gave a brief wave in their direction, then joined the group gathered around Victoria and Adam. A moment later, Adam disengaged himself from the circle and made his way through the crowded parlor toward Drew and Rob.

After they exchanged greetings and handshakes, Rob said, "So how are you and Victoria enjoying your new life as permanent residents of Bourbon County?"

Adam's lips quirked up into a wry grin. "It's something I've always wanted, but I'm afraid Victoria is not happy with the situation. She—"

Loud laughter from the group across the room interrupted him. As Drew looked their way to see what was so funny, Victoria threw her arms around Neal's neck and kissed him so solidly on the lips that even Neal seemed stunned.

"Perhaps I spoke too soon," Adam said, his tone dry. "She certainly seems happy enough now." He caught Drew's eye and shrugged. "Then again, I could be wrong.

According to Victoria, I usually am." His words were so quiet not even Rob could hear them over the noise of the party.

Drew stared at him in surprise, then glanced back at Victoria. Something strange was definitely going on between Adam and Victoria, but she couldn't tell for sure whether or not it had anything to do with Neal. She cleared her throat, not sure what to say, horrified by the fierce exultation that swelled her heart.

Twenty-eight

Shivering, Drew lowered herself into the bathtub. The water felt almost too hot because the bathroom at Ashworth Farm was so cold, but nonetheless it was a relief after the long, eventful day. And knowing that she was spending the night with Momma afterward instead of returning to Blue Meadow and Rob made her appreciate the luxury even more. Momma and Ginnie were both already asleep; she could soak as long as she wanted and no one would come knocking on the door.

She stretched out her legs gingerly, then leaned against the back of the tub and closed her eyes. Everything had gone well both with breeding Wish and Vixen and with Ginnie's second birthday party, but she was exhausted anyway. She'd gotten out of bed at five o'clock that morning and left Ginnie with Rob. Then after working on the tobacco seed beds for three hours, she'd helped while Ben Parker, Wish's groom, now promoted to stud groom, and Doc Steffens, the veterinarian, supervised breeding Wish and Vixen. Unfortunately, she couldn't afford to keep a teaser stallion to insure Vixen's readiness, and asking Rob if she could borrow Kirby was out of the question, so Wish had to do all the work himself. It was riskier that way—no one ever knew how a mare was going to behave the first time, and it was possible for a stallion to get severely hurt in the breeding process, even with an experienced broodmare. But Doc Steffens had said it looked good; Vixen was showing a good follicle.

She wiggled her legs in the bathwater, unable to hold back a chuckle at the glum looks on old Ben's and Doc Steffens' faces when they'd realized she intended to be there the entire time. But there wasn't much they could do about it now: she was not only the owner of both horses, but also owner and manager of the farm. Fortunately for all of them, the entire procedure had gone smoothly. Vixen had been a bit feisty at first, but Wish had covered her quickly and efficiently.

With any luck it would take just this one time. The earlier in the season Vixen was bred, the better chances her foal would have during its two-year-old racing season, since all thoroughbred colts and fillies turned one-year-old on January 1, regardless of when they were born. The more mature colts and fillies had a definite advantage, so owners often liked to breed their mares as early as possible.

And that was one of the things that was worrying her. She pushed herself up to a sitting position and grabbed the washcloth from the side of the tub. Wish had had a slow season at stud last year, but by February he'd already had at least a few reservations. There were none so far this year. Business was not picking up the way everyone, from President Hoover on down, kept predicting it would.

She lathered up the cloth with her mother's hard-milled lavender-scented soap and scrubbed her feet, always coarse and dirty now every night from the rough old wool socks and stiff leather workboots she wore. She was working hard and her body felt it, but truly she didn't mind. It helped keep her mind off missing Daddy, and off the constant chafing of her marriage, as well as how much she still yearned for Adam.

And dealing with her heart was even harder now that he had moved his family to Ballantrae and she saw him frequently. There'd been no way she could avoid inviting him and Victoria and Alexander to Ginnie's birthday party that afternoon. She rubbed the washcloth lightly over her legs and underarms, then rinsed it out. Reclining against the back of the tub once more, she laid the cloth over her breasts. At least Victoria hadn't bothered to be neighborly and come along, and Alexander was a delightful baby.

Alexander—Ginnie's half-brother. They both had Adam's intense green eyes, but fortunately Alexander had silky straight blond hair while Ginnie's was dark and curly like Drew's. She reassured herself that she was probably the only one who saw the resemblance, even though Adam always regarded Ginnie with a strangely wistful look.

And the birthday present he'd given Ginnie was really very inappropriate, especially when she knew that he had as little money as she did and was working every bit as hard as she was. She'd bet anything that Victoria had no idea that Adam had bought Ginnie such a lovely hand-carved rocking horse. If Ginnie hadn't fallen so completely in love with it the minute she saw it, Drew would have insisted that Adam take it back, keep it for Alexander.

No one else, though, not even Rob, had seemed to think that Adam's gift was too extravagant. Even Momma probably thought that the MacKenzies still had plenty of money, that they were tightening their belts just a little, like everyone else, but that things were still easier for them than for most.

Well, maybe they were. But Adam had told Drew more than he'd told most of his other friends; she was sure no one else knew that the house he'd sold in Bryn Mawr had not brought him a cent—all the money had gone to pay off debts. And the only reason he'd told her was because she'd asked him why he didn't hire someone to manage the farm for him after he kept showing up and asking her what to do next. He had only been able to keep up the pretense that everything was going fine for so long; fi-

nally he'd just sighed and told her the truth—the Mac-
Kenzies had nothing left but Ballantrae and their wits.
Even his parents had sold their beautiful estate on Sproul
Road and moved into a small home in a less than fash-
ionable neighborhood.

Still, sometimes Drew thought it had to be a lot harder
to go from being filthy rich to dirt poor overnight than it
was to go from pretty damn poor to slightly poorer. In
fact, she and Momma were actually better off now: the
farm was out of debt for the first time in years.

It was too bad Daddy wasn't here to enjoy it. Shivering
a little, she sat up, picked the washcloth off her chest and
wrung it out, then draped it over the faucet. But she was
going to have to work hard to keep them in the black—
and she needed stud dates for Wish, if only enough of
them to help pay Ben's wages and the feed bills.

The bath water was more cool than warm now, so she
pulled the plug, then stood up and wrapped the thin towel
around her. How like Momma to buy expensive soap
when the towels were almost worn out. She resented her
mother's extravagance for a brief second before she
thought about it. Momma didn't have many pleasures in
her life; if she wanted fancy French soaps, Drew would
do whatever it took to buy them for her.

She *had* to figure out some way to sell Wish's services,
especially if things kept going the way they were or got
even worse. Right now she had enough to tide them over
until next year's tobacco sales; what she really needed was
some kind of insurance so that she could afford to keep
both Wish and Vixen *and* provide the best she could for
Momma. She rubbed her body hard with the scruffy towel
until her skin glowed pink. What the hell could she do to
make Wish attractive to potential breeders? Most of them
had no money, either.

That was it! She let the towel fall to the floor and
slipped into her warm flannel nightgown. Maybe if the

other owners didn't have to come up with cash, they might be more interested. What if she offered them Wish's services in return for some kind of trade?

She crossed her arms over her belly and hugged herself as a little shudder of excitement ran down her spine. Everyone loved a bargain, and most thoroughbred owners enjoyed a gamble or they wouldn't be in the business. If she let them breed two of their mares and asked only for the choice of one of the yearling offspring, nobody would lose. The mare's owner would have his foal, and she'd have a colt or filly to sell at the yearling sales. It had to work.

She couldn't stand to think about what would happen if it didn't.

Two weeks later Drew gave a dinner party for her mother's forty-third birthday. Despite Rob's insistence that they have the party at Blue Meadow, Drew gave it at Ashworth Farm because Momma's health had steadily worsened since Daddy's death. She was so weak now that even climbing the stairs to her bed exhausted her, and Drew worried that watching after Ginnie—a sweet, but typically active two-year-old—was becoming too much for her.

The party had gone well, and it had certainly seemed to lift Momma's spirits. Rob and Vi had come, as well as Chase and Trixie and Adam and Alexander. Once again, Victoria had declined to attend, but Drew didn't mind. In fact, it was a lot more pleasant without her. Not even Adam seemed to miss her, and he'd offered no excuse except that she sent her regrets.

Afterward, when it was becoming obvious that Momma was tiring rapidly, everyone, including Rob, said good night and departed. Drew sent her mother off to bed and headed for the kitchen and the piles of dishes. Dinner had not been fancy—she was far more adept at sowing and sorting tobacco and riding a horse than she was at cooking—but not even Rob had complained about the baked ham and sweet potatoes, and Chase had gallantly proclaimed the inevitable apple pie, the only dessert Drew knew how to fix, truly the most delicious he'd ever eaten.

Now, the last dish dried and put away and the kitchen tidy, she hung the dish towel on a knob and yawned hugely, then trudged up the stairs to her bedroom on the second floor. Momma's door at the top of the landing was still open and the light was on, so Drew poked her head inside. As always, the room smelled of Momma's violet cologne and eucalyptus oil. "Good night, Momma," she said. "And happy birthday."

"Thank you, dear." Momma beckoned her to step into the bedroom. "Come here." She patted the bed. "I've got something I want to give you. I've been waiting for you to come upstairs."

Drew sat on the edge of the bed, her fingers tracing the familiar design of the patchwork quilt Daddy's mother had made years ago while Momma retrieved a beaded drawstring bag from under her pillow. She recognized it immediately—it was the old purse from the attic trunk, the one that held Momma's tiara. Even thinking about what might have happened if she'd lost that bet so long ago still made her heart beat faster. How would she ever have explained it to Momma?

Drew took a deep, steadying breath. Well, she'd hadn't lost the bet and she'd returned the tiara to the bag, so there was nothing to worry about now, thank the Lord.

Momma handed her the bag. "Here. This is yours now, to do whatever you want to with it. Save it for Ginnie, sell it . . . pawn it . . ."

Her cheeks hot, Drew jerked her eyes up from examining the bag and its contents, and gaped at her mother.

Momma smiled at her. "Did you think I didn't know?"

"Who told you?" Suddenly, even though she'd been the

one who did wrong, Drew felt betrayed. Only two other people knew her secret—Trixie and Adam.

Momma's face was pale, but her blue eyes twinkled. "No one. Your father and I figured it out ourselves. As Edward always said, the apple doesn't fall too far from the tree. You're every bit as determined as he was, and I astounded everyone in my family by impulsively marrying a man almost twenty-five years my senior and then moving to beyond the pale, as they called it. Then there was your uncle Andrew." She leaned back against her pillow again. "And that brings me to my point—I want you to know the story behind the tiara now that it's yours."

Drew's mortification faded somewhat as she realized her mother was more amused than outraged at her youthful escapade. She was curious to know why her parents had never said anything before, but she was even more interested in hearing about Uncle Andrew. Saying nothing so that she didn't distract her mother, she took the tiara from the bag and held it up to the light. The diamonds and emeralds sparkled with the same intensity she remembered.

Momma closed her eyes for a second. "Andrew gave that to me."

Drew remembered the day she'd shown Momma the photo of herself wearing the tiara when she was a young girl and how Momma had told her about Uncle Andrew's gift. Momma's parents had insisted that she return it to him, but Andrew had refused to take it back. She waited patiently while Momma told her that part of the story again. "Did you ever find out where he got the tiara?" she asked when Momma paused.

"For years I assumed that he'd won it in a game of chance of some kind. He was quite the gambler." Momma reached for Drew's hand and squeezed it. "I know you've been troubled for years by the rumors that Andrew was your father, not Edward." She held up her hand when

Drew started to protest. "You don't need to protect me by pretending it's not true. And you don't need to worry that the rumors *were* true. Edward was most definitely your father. It's true that I was once in love with Andrew—he was handsome, charming, full of high spirits. He was irresistible to me, even though my parents found him much too wild." She chuckled. "Probably *because* my parents found him too wild."

She coughed into the handkerchief always clasped in her hand before she continued. "But *I* was not irresistible to Andrew, even though I knew he wasn't seeing any other girls. And although I was puzzled by his behavior, by his strange lack of ardor, I continued to see him anyway because I enjoyed his company so much, and he invited me to his graduation from Amherst. It was there that I met your father."

Drew wondered what Momma meant by Andrew's "strange lack of ardor," but she hesitated to ask, afraid that Momma would suddenly decide that she'd revealed enough.

"I think I actually fell in love with Edward the moment I saw him." Momma laughed, then coughed again. "I know how silly that sounds, but it was almost as if loving Andrew had prepared me to love Edward, even though Andrew was like air, and Edward was earth. He was Andrew with feet instead of wings, but he was still handsome and charming and full of the same high spirits that I loved in Andrew.

"And then there was Scott. He was ten at the time, and I fell in love with him, too. It never mattered to me that your father was a forty-three year old widower with a son and that I was only twenty." Shaking her head, she smiled at Drew. "Today's my forty-third birthday, and I can't imagine starting over again. Your father was a very brave man."

Hearing Momma talk about Daddy like that made

Drew's eyes shimmer with tears. In her own grief, she'd almost forgotten how tremendously Momma must miss her husband of over twenty years. She took a deep breath and forced herself not to sniff as her mother continued.

"Andrew was delighted when Edward and I told him that we were going to be married. He was much more comfortable thinking of me as a sister." Although no one else could possibly have heard, Momma lowered her voice. "As I'd begun to suspect, Andrew was never really very interested in women romantically."

"Oh." Drew couldn't help herself. So that's what Momma had meant about Andrew's lack of ardor for her.

"So you see, it would have taken a miracle for Andrew to have been your father," Momma said.

Drew nodded, the last tiny bit of doubt completely dispelled. "But what happened to him? Vi told me a little about the day he died, but it still seems like such a mystery."

Momma plucked at the quilt, rearranging it over her legs. "It's still hard for me to talk about." She coughed, then drank from the glass of water on her nightstand. "Still, God knows, keeping these secrets hasn't made me any happier. Edward tried his best to protect Andrew, even after he was dead; and I respected Edward's wishes. But you deserve to know the truth."

"Andrew was a profligate—he gambled and drank to excess. One evening after he and Edward quarreled about Andrew's debts, Andrew saddled up one of the worst-tempered stallions on the farm and rode off." The lines in Momma's face deepened, and she looked sad and far away. "Sometimes I can still hear the hoofbeats drumming away in the quiet of the night."

Drew nodded; she knew the rest. "And Rob's dad found the stallion riderless the next day."

"They organized a search party," Momma said. "Edward found Andrew lying dead beside a stream with his neck broken. That was in June. You were born in August. Your father sold all the horses to help pay off Andrew's debts, but he still had to mortgage the farm."

This time Drew couldn't hold back the tears of grief for an uncle she'd never met, for her father's fortitude, and for the great love between her parents.

Twenty-nine

February 1930

Even though it was still too soon to tell whether or not Vixen was in foal, Drew checked her every morning before she began her long, long day. February was the beginning of ten months of hard work on Bluegrass farms, whether farmers raised horses or tobacco, or both. Tobacco growers continued grading their cured tobacco as well as sowing the seed beds with the incredibly tiny tobacco seeds, while the horse breeders dealt with stud season and training for the spring races.

Although it wasn't necessary for Drew to exercise Wish and Vixen—Ben simply turned them out into their paddocks—Rob could no longer afford two exercise riders at Blue Meadow, so Drew had taken on that chore, too. Every evening she fell into bed wherever she happened to be—either at Blue Meadow or Ashworth Farm—completely exhausted. And the worst thing was, she knew it wasn't going to get any easier; in fact, as soon as the weather warmed up, it would get much, much harder.

Facing Ben over the mare's back, Drew squared her shoulders and lifted her chin. Moaning and groaning wasn't going to make things better. "So far, so good," she said. Only a few more weeks and they'd know for sure if Vixen was carrying Wish's foal. Her stomach fluttered every time she thought, or more accurately, worried about it.

Ben grinned at her, deep lines grooving the sides of his dark, leathery cheeks. "Yes, missus. I'd put my money on it—if I had some." He stroked Vixen's neck. "She's lookin' mighty good."

The sound of a child crying reached Drew's ears, and she frowned. She hoped Ginnie wasn't giving her mother too much trouble this morning. Momma hadn't looked well at breakfast, and her breathing had been wheezy for the last couple of days. Momma said it was nothing, just another reaction to the wood smoke and the cold air, but Drew had been worried anyway. Momma's worst asthma attacks often started just that way.

Ginnie's sobbing continued, becoming even louder. "I'll be right back, Ben," Drew said. "It sounds like Ginnie's outside." Why in the world had Momma let Ginnie play outdoors when the freezing air was the worst trigger of all for her mother's asthma? She strode to the barn door and shoved it open.

As soon as she stepped outside, she spotted Ginnie walking alone up the path toward her, and she ran to the little girl and scooped her up in her arms. Ginnie's wailing gradually subsided to soft hiccups as Drew cradled her against her chest. "What's wrong, sweetie?" Drew asked. "Where's Grandma?"

Rubbing her eyes, Ginnie wriggled in Drew's arms. "GaGa fall down," she said.

Drew's heart beat faster, making a dull thudding noise in her ears. "Where, Ginnie? Where did she fall?"

Ginnie pointed at the house. "There."

Then Momma hadn't taken Ginnie outside to play; the little girl had wandered out on her own after Momma fell down. Drew clasped Ginnie tightly, then ran toward the house with the child clinging to her neck. The front door was standing ajar, and she shouldered it open the rest of the way and stepped inside. "Momma!" she called. "Momma! Are you all right?"

The only sounds were the ticking of the grandfather clock in the parlor and Ginnie's raspy breathing, hoarse from crying. Drew set Ginnie on the floor in front of her and bent down to her daughter's eye level. "Where did Momma fall?" she asked, keeping her voice as calm as she could.

Ginnie pointed toward the kitchen. "There."

Drew grabbed Ginnie's hand and hurried toward the swinging door, then pushed it open. Momma lay on the floor beside the table.

Drew's mouth suddenly tasted bitter, like copper. She dropped Ginnie's hand and rushed to her mother, kneeling beside her. "Oh, Momma, no!" she said, her voice a whisper but her heart screaming.

May 1930

If it hadn't been for Adam, Drew didn't know how she'd have made it through the months following her mother's death. Right after she'd telephoned Dr. Miller, she called Adam, and he was at her side before the doctor arrived. It had never even occurred to her to call Rob; Adam was the one who did that. He'd helped her make the funeral arrangements; he'd taken care of Ginnie whenever Drew needed someone to watch her; he'd even sent several of his farmhands over to tend the tobacco seedbeds when Drew couldn't keep up. Adam became, once again, the older brother who took care of everything, and overwhelmed by her responsibilities, Drew accepted his assistance. Even with his help, there was more than enough to do to keep her mind off her grief.

But, still, despite everything he did, Drew couldn't help feeling terribly alone. She'd never been close to Momma's parents, and Daddy's had died before she was born. Her brother Scott had been dead for almost twelve years now. Even though she was almost twenty-two years old, she still felt orphaned. At night she woke up, her heart beating fast with terror, and tiptoed over to Ginnie's crib just to listen to her daughter breathe.

By Derby weekend, Drew was so exhausted from overwork and lack of sleep that she decided not to accompany Rob to Louisville. Although she hated missing the Derby, there really wasn't any point in spending the money or the time since neither Ashworth Farm nor Blue Meadow had an entry this year, and she was going to be busy transplanting the thousands of tobacco seedlings from the seedbeds into the fields.

She was relieved when Rob didn't waste any energy trying to persuade her to change her mind—perhaps he was just as happy as she was to avoid any possibility of conflict between them for a few days. He'd probably hole up in his hotel room and write poetry while he wasn't at the races, and she'd be able to go over the Blue Meadow books during his absence. Vi had mentioned receiving several unpleasant telephone calls from creditors, and Drew was worried.

Adam had warned her to avoid indebtedness at all costs until the economy recovered, and he wasn't enthusiastic about that happening anytime soon. "The only security you have now is in not owing anybody anything," he'd said when he called her on the telephone a few days ago to invite them all to a Derby Day dinner party at Ballantrae. He was practicing what he preached, he said. To cut back on expenses, not only was he not going to Louisville this year, but the MacKenzies would not be giving their traditional Derby Eve party for the first time in years.

"I wish Rob were as practical as you," she said. "He's going with his mother and Chase and Trixie."

"And those two don't know the meaning of the word."

Adam had laughed. "It looks as if it's going to be a damn small party, then," he'd said. "Victoria has gone to Philadelphia to visit her parents, and Father's still not well enough to travel. Alexander and I are on our own for a couple of weeks."

That Saturday at five o'clock Adam and Drew toasted the Derby, clinking together their tall mint julep glasses. The party had turned out to be even smaller than Drew expected—just Adam and Alexander and Ginnie and herself gathered in the east parlor. The two children played at the far end of the room, where Adam had placed a large toybox and a rocking horse identical to the one he'd given Ginnie for her birthday.

"Ginnie loves her rocking horse," Drew said when her daughter climbed onto Alexander's and started rocking it furiously back and forth. "She's always taking hers for a gallop."

"Reminds me of her mother." Smiling, Adam settled himself on the white sofa facing the fireplace. "When are you planning to give her a real pony?"

"As soon as I can afford one," Drew said. "I only hope she doesn't have to wait until she's twenty before that happens."

"I know what you mean. Unfortunately, though, I'm the only one in my family who really understands that we can no longer satisfy our every whim." Although his tone was light, his voice was edged with bitterness.

It wasn't difficult for Drew to guess at whom his bitterness was aimed. Victoria seemed to be having a hard time adjusting to life in the Bluegrass, or at least that was the way Trixie put it, a mockingly solicitous grin on her face as she cheerfully filled Drew in on her sister-in-law's latest indiscretion. "She bought a diamond cocktail ring last week, and you should have seen Adam's face when he saw it," Trixie had confided to Drew a month ago. "I think she's trying to rile him on purpose, to get back at him for bringing her to Kentucky. Then she drank too many martinis before dinner that night and told him what a failure he was."

Drew had shaken her head in disbelief. "She called Adam a failure?" Her chest had tightened in pain at the dismay she imagined Adam felt. "How could she do that to him?"

Hearing the bitterness in Adam's voice now brought back that same tight feeling to Drew's heart. She wished she could say, "I told you so," to him; she'd always thought Victoria calculating and cruel, and she'd often wondered why Adam couldn't see it, too. But while part of Drew wanted to get back at Adam for choosing Victoria over her, the other part only felt sadness for him. She, too, was not happily married, and she knew the loneliness and anger that he must be feeling.

Even so, she'd given up dreaming about Adam in any kind of romantic way; their marriages were a fact of life that wasn't going to go away. He was a friend; he was a trusted adviser; he could never be anything more ever again. She repeated this litany to herself nightly even while a tiny little voice whispered at the same time, *"He is the father of your child."*

So, although the mean, petty side of her wanted more than anything in the world to ask who Adam meant when he complained about people satisfying their every whim, she restrained herself. "I know what you mean, too," she said instead, and it was the truth. "When I asked Rob how he could possibly afford the expense of the Derby this year, he just shrugged. I'm afraid he's going to dig Blue Meadow into a hole so deep we'll never get out."

Staring at her over the top of his glass, Adam drank his julep. "I've heard rumors that the two best Blue Meadow horses are at Ashworth Farm."

This time it was Drew's laugh that was tinged with acerbity. "First of all, Wish and Vixen are *my* horses, not

Blue Meadow's. But I think the gossip is partly true—in my opinion Rob made some poor choices when he decided to start selling off stock." She took a sip of the sugar-and-mint flavored bourbon, then set the icy glass back on the table next to her chair. "I do have some good news, though. Kentucky Vixen is in foal. I haven't told anybody yet, not even Rob. Secret Wish is going to be a daddy again sometime next January. And several times over again after that. Sixteen breeders decided to take me up on my offer to trade a yearling for servicing two mares."

"Oh, Drew, that's wonderful news!" Adam picked up his glass and held it out to her. "Another toast," he said. "To the success of Ashworth Farm's first foal." He lifted an eyebrow. "Knowing you, you've already decided on a name."

Smiling, Drew tapped her glass against his. "Kentucky Secret," she said. "Whether it's a filly or a colt."

"I like that." His eyes met hers over their mint julep glasses. "And to Ashworth Farm's first Triple Crown winner."

Drew knew she should look away, but she couldn't make herself. And the longer she stared into Adam's eyes, the harder it became to tear hers away. Her heart twisted in a sudden sharp flutter, the same way it always used to whenever she saw Adam.

She lowered her glass and forced her eyes to follow it. "That sounds good to me," she said, keeping her voice as light-hearted as she could. A wave of guilt swept over her. It didn't really matter what she pretended to tell herself; it didn't really matter that each of them was married to someone else. She still loved Adam. She knew it was wrong, but she couldn't do a damn thing about it.

Thirty

September 1930

Every time Drew spent the night with Rob at Blue Meadow, she wondered why she bothered. They always ended up fighting about something. Braiding her hair into a thick plait over the shoulder of her cotton robe, she walked slowly down the hall from the bathroom to their bedroom. Tonight would be different, she promised herself. No matter what he said, she would not let him goad her into arguing with him. "Yes, dear," she'd say with a smile even if she disagreed totally.

But of course that didn't mean that she'd actually have to *do* what he said. He didn't know what she was doing most of the time anyway because he locked himself in his office and wrote his damn poetry, for God's sake. When she reached the bedroom door, she fortified herself with a deep breath before she stepped inside.

Rob was already in bed, sitting with his back propped against several pillows and his poetry notebook in his lap. He glanced up at Drew, then immediately lowered his eyes without greeting her.

Drew suppressed her irritation, barely managing to keep herself from commenting sarcastically about the warmth of his welcome. After all, he was the one who continually badgered her about spending more time with him. Then, when she did, he treated her as if she were invisible. She shrugged off her robe and draped it over the rocking chair next to the window, then slipped into bed beside him.

Still, he kept his eyes on his notepad, even when she sighed deeply, snapped off her bedside lamp, and scooted down under the covers. "Good night," she said, almost relieved that he'd apparently decided to ignore her. At least they wouldn't end up fighting half the night. She turned on her side, her back toward him, and closed her eyes. Exhaustion overcame annoyance, and within seconds her thoughts drifted into strange fuzzy musings . . .

"Drew?"

She twitched, her body jerking back from sleep. "What?" she mumbled.

"We need to talk. About Ginnie."

Stifling a groan, she slowly pushed herself back up to a sitting position. "Is there a problem?"

"I think you need to spend more time with her."

"I couldn't agree more," Drew said, remembering her promise to herself. She would *not* argue with Rob tonight. "I wish I could." She refrained from adding that she might be able to if she didn't have to run both Ashworth Farm *and* Blue Meadow, that if he'd spend more time managing his farm than he did writing poetry, then she *would* be able to see more of Ginnie. "She doesn't seem unhappy, though. She misses Momma, but I know she loves both your mother and Trixie."

"That's not the point. She needs her mother. And I need my wife—here, in my home, in my bed, not out breeding race horses or tending tobacco fields."

Drew's good intentions evaporated. "If I don't do it, who's going to?" She gestured toward the notebook in his lap. "For months, all you've done is write in *that*. You're going to end up losing Blue Meadow, and then what would we do? Eat your goddamn poems?" She clenched her teeth but couldn't hold back the words boiling inside her. "You need a wife. Well, I need a husband. Maybe I could be a wife then. I need someone to carry part of the load, take his share of the responsibilities. I'm tired of doing everything myself and then getting blamed for it."

Even as the accusations came tumbling out, though, she realized she only meant half of what she said. Even if Rob managed the farm competently, she'd still want to raise thoroughbreds herself, she'd still do whatever it took to keep Ashworth Farm. He wanted the kind of wife his mother had been to his father, someone to cook his meals, rear his children, warm his bed, agree with his opinions.

Drew could never be like that. And furthermore, she didn't even *want* to be like that.

His cheeks flushing bright red, Rob knocked his notepad onto the floor where it landed with a loud smack. "I get a hell of a lot more solace from my poetry than I do from you," he said. "I gave up everything that was important to me to come back here and run this godforsaken farm. I hate it, but I do it because it's my duty."

She resisted the urge to roll her eyes. "And therefore it's my job to give up everything important to me in order to do my duty to *you*? Because that's what we're really talking about, isn't it? You don't really give a damn about Ginnie. You know she's happy and well taken care of and that I find time for her here and there during the day." She shook her head so vigorously her thick braid thumped against her shoulders. "You knew what I was like before you married me. You knew what I wanted to do—you even helped me do it." She stared at him, tears burning her eyes, and when she spoke again, her voice was plaintive rather than accusatory. "Why is everything so different now?"

Rob's shoulders sagged. "I don't know," he said. "I thought I loved you the way you were. But I'm not happy."

"I'm not either." The tears in her eyes brimmed over, then trailed down her cheeks.

Rob buried his face in his hands. Seeing Drew's unhappiness was a lot more difficult for him than facing her anger. Finally, he raised his head and looked at her. "I don't think I've ever asked—but what do *you* want?"

Her eyebrows shot up and her eyes widened. "Just what you do, I think. The chance to do what's really important to *me*. A husband who understands and approves of me, who asks for my advice and supports my decisions the way Adam does. I love Ginnie and my horses and my farm and . . ."

Her voice trailed off, and she stared at him with a horrified expression on her face.

Suddenly, for the first time, Rob saw Drew clearly. She had never really loved him; he couldn't remember her ever telling him so, anyway. He had been the one with the fantasy, and he'd cast Drew in the leading role even though she'd never agreed to the part. He'd known for years that Drew adored Adam, but he'd assumed she'd gotten over her childish infatuation years ago.

But the look on her face made it all staggeringly and painfully obvious. Drew was still in love with Adam—the man who in all likelihood was Ginnie's real father. Rob squeezed his eyes shut, seeing Adam's green eyes shining in Ginnie's little face, Adam's black hair haloing Ginnie's head. He'd always suspected that Neal Rafferty was the one who'd gotten Drew pregnant, but there was no Neal at all in Ginnie. He could see that now.

"And you love Adam," he said, finishing her sentence for her. "It was always Adam. I should have known. But I thought you'd outgrown your crush on him." He crossed his arms and hunched over to ease the pain in his gut.

"I thought I had, too. I tried." Drew's soft voice vibrated with the same kind of grief that filled him. "I've been faithful to you. I want you to know that."

"I know," he whispered. "But you love him, not me." He swallowed back the hysteria rising like bile in his throat, then flung off the quilt and stood up. "Jesus, I feel stupid." He paced to the window, parting the curtain and staring out into the black night. "Why did you ever agree to marry me?"

His voice broke, and he took a deep breath to steady himself before he turned back around to face her. He held up his hand to stop her from speaking. "You don't have to answer that. I know why. I knew why then, too. I just hoped that you'd fall in love with me after we were married. I thought I could *make* you love me."

Christ, what a fool he'd been, believing that if only Drew would behave properly, they'd have a perfect marriage. In reality, they had no marriage at all—Drew loved another man, the man who'd fathered her child; for almost a year she hadn't even really lived at Blue Meadow with Rob, but instead just visited him occasionally when she gave in to his demands. He was her husband in name only.

He stared at Drew for a long time, considering his words carefully. "I don't think I can go on like this," he said, finally. "I think—" He paused again, his muscles tightening and his stomach churning.

It was harder than hell to say the words, but the alternative was even more painful. "I think we should get a divorce."

November 1930

For Drew the most difficult part of divorcing Rob was the social aspect, but even that wasn't as bad as she'd thought it would be. Since Momma and Daddy had both died and her grandparents were far away, there was no one close to her to be hurt by her status as a divorced woman—and she was far too busy to care if her social standing suffered.

232 *Lee Hayward*

Social standing, hah! She snorted, parting the lace curtain in the parlor window as Rob's car pulled up to the front porch of her house. She'd learned not to worry about *that* years ago. Being a pariah was nothing new. The only thing that really bothered her was what Ginnie would face once she got old enough to understand.

Fortunately, Rob had agreed to continue acting as Ginnie's father. She let the curtain drop, then headed toward the front door. It was strange the way their anger with each other had dissipated as soon as they admitted how unhappy they were. That night two months ago had been horribly painful, but even then she and Rob had managed to agree that no matter what, Ginnie should not suffer.

And at this point, since it had been so long since they had truly lived together, their divorce proceedings were more of a formality than anything else. Viola and Trixie still cared for Ginnie while Drew worked, and no one except Rob's family knew exactly what was going on.

Before Rob had a chance to knock, she opened the door and motioned him inside, then raised her fingers to her lips. "Ginnie's napping," she said quietly. "I put her down before you called."

"That's all right. If I'd stopped and thought for a second first, I'd have realized that." He removed his hat and coat, and Drew took them from him. "I knew I had to talk to you immediately, though, before I changed my mind." He smiled at her, looking happier than she had seen him in years.

Drew hung Rob's things on the hall tree, then ushered him into the parlor. Unable to contain her curiosity, she asked, "What's up?" before he settled himself on the sofa.

He leaned back and crossed his legs, then rested his arms along the top of the sofa. "I've decided to move back to Lexington and resume my studies at the University."

Drew lowered herself into her favorite rocking chair

next to the fireplace. Eyeing him, she nodded slowly as she warmed her hands in front of the hot fire. "That's swell," she said, unable to keep the sarcasm from her voice. "But what's going to happen to Blue Meadow?"

His smile didn't waver. "How would you like to buy it from me?"

"You're kidding me!" She widened her eyes and stared at him, trying to ignore the sudden excited shiver that ran down her spine. If only she could afford it. Blue Meadow still had a great reputation—not even Rob had been able to ruin that yet. The land was beautiful, and the house was much grander than her farmhouse. And the horses—

She sighed. Although Rob had wonderful stock, right now thoroughbreds were more of a liability than an asset. She wouldn't be able to afford to feed them, let alone pay for the property.

He shook his head. "You don't know me very well, do you? When are you going to learn that I never kid? You were the real reason I came back to run Blue Meadow. Even Dad knew I wasn't cut out for it. He always said he just hoped that Trixie would marry the right man for the job."

She still stared at him, dazed, while her mind whirled with possibilities. "But you can't sell—"

"Oh, yes, I can—if someone will buy it, that is. Mom can either move to Lexington with me or live with Trixie and Chase at Ballantrae—or here with you and Ginnie." His eyes were as gray as the steel rims of his glasses, a sure sign that he was definitely in earnest. "Well, are you interested?"

Drew swallowed, then managed to utter a squeaky "Yes." She nodded vigorously. If Adam could afford to help out financially, maybe they would be able to buy Blue Meadow as partners. Chase could run it, and Vi wouldn't have to move. It seemed like such a perfect solution—if they could only scrape together enough money.

Adam had warned her repeatedly to avoid debt at all costs until the country's economy returned to normal.

"Yes," she said, clearly this time. "I'm interested. Can you give me a few days to work on it?"

"Sure," he said. "But don't take too long. The other interested party is the bank that holds the mortgage."

When the full meaning of his words hit her, Drew gasped. "You wouldn't really default, would you?"

He shrugged. "Unfortunately, I don't have a lot of other options."

Despite the warmth from the fire, her limbs suddenly felt heavy and cold. Rob was putting a brave face on it, but losing his family's farm had to be difficult for him. And he'd turned to her for assistance. Selling Blue Meadow to her was the closest thing he could do to keep it in the family, and she owed it to him to do everything she could to help.

Thirty-one

November 1930

Even though she scolded herself for her fears, it took
Drew two days to build up enough courage to present her
proposal to buy Blue Meadow to Adam. First, she looked
at her own finances from every possible angle to see if
she could manage by herself, but she finally concluded it
was impossible for her to pay off all of Rob's mortgage
and creditors and still have enough left to run the farm.

Bouncing up and down every time she hit one of the
numerous potholes, she practiced what she was going to
say to Adam over and over in her head as she drove to
Ballantrae in her father's old Model-T. As much as she
wanted him to agree, she didn't want him to feel pres-
sured, to feel this was something he *had* to do for her
because of Ginnie. It was obvious that he'd always suspected Ginnie was his daughter, but before there'd been
Rob to consider. Now Adam might think that he owed it
to Drew and Ginnie to buy Blue Meadow.

Drew cursed as the old Ford hit an exceptionally deep
rut and she narrowly missed sideswiping a portion of the
old stone slave fence bordering the pike. And what would
Victoria have to say if Adam agreed? He'd sold the house
she loved in Philadelphia because they'd been short of
money, and the much promised and hoped for improve-

ment in the stock market had not happened yet, even though it was over a year now since Black Tuesday.

Not that Drew particularly cared what Victoria thought. Victoria had made it apparent that she wanted nothing to do with Drew, especially now that Drew's social status was unclear. But Adam's happiness still mattered to Drew, despite everything, and she didn't want to cause any more problems for him than he already had.

Finally, as she turned into the drive leading to Ballantrae Manor, she pushed all the worries out of her head. She was going to ask him, and that was that. It was up to him to say yes or no. The car lurched to a halt in front of the house, and she climbed out, hugging her heavy coat close to her body.

Chase waved at her from the stallion paddock closest to the barn. "Trixie's gone to the doctor in Lexington," he said. "She'll be back later this afternoon."

Drew jogged over to the fence, then leaned against it, watching as Chase finished repairing one of the rails. "How's she feeling?"

"Like an elephant, she says." Chase grinned, shaking his head. "She can't believe she's got two more months to go before the baby comes."

"I know exactly how she feels," Drew said. She wished she had more time to visit with Trixie, but there was always so much to do. She never seemed to stop running, and as soon as she finished one chore, ten more cropped up. "Well, tell her hello for me. I actually came to talk to Adam. Is he around?"

Chase waved toward the stallion barn. "Last I saw him he was mucking out stalls." He laughed. "How the mighty have fallen. He doesn't seem to mind, though. Claims he's happier shoveling manure than counting other people's money."

That sounded exactly like something Adam would say,

Drew decided as she headed toward the barn. He'd always been able to make the best out of any situation.

Except one, but there wasn't a damn thing he could do about that now. Late at night, lying in her bed alone, Drew could almost convince herself that if Adam had it to do over again, he'd never have married Victoria. Drew slid the barn door open and stepped into the dim interior. "Adam?" she called.

"Over here." He stuck his head out of the tack room at the far end of the barn. "Oh, hi, Drew. It's nice to see you." He emerged from the tack room and headed toward her. "How's Vixen doing?"

She smiled at him. Adam was becoming a true Kentucky hardboot, inquiring about a pregnant horse before he asked after his visitor's health. "Doc Steffens says she'll probably deliver sometime in the middle of January. She hasn't had any problems so far, but I'm keeping my fingers crossed."

He winked at her, his green eyes sparkling, and spoke in an exaggerated drawl. "Say, maybe she and Trixie will drop their foals at the same time. Of course, Trixie and Chase won't be able to register their get with the Jockey Club."

Drew laughed at his corny humor. Chase was right; Adam looked more alive here mending tack in his dungarees and flannel shirt than he ever had in a dinner jacket at one of Victoria's soirees. "I doubt very much whether they care," she said. "I know I didn't when Ginnie was born."

The smile left Adam's eyes, as if thinking of Ginnie saddened him. "I know," he said, then paused for a long moment. "I want you to know how sorry I am things turned out the way they did."

He could have been talking about her separation from Rob, but Drew suspected that was not all that he meant. Even so, it was a lot easier to pretend it was. "Thanks."

She clasped her hands behind her back and rocked back on the heels of her boots. "Actually, that's sort of what I came to talk about."

Adam lifted an eyebrow but said nothing.

Her words tumbling out, Drew excitedly told him about Rob's decision to sell Blue Meadow. "He wants me to buy it from him, but I don't have enough capital," she said. "I have some, but I'd have to try to mortgage Ashworth Farm again for the rest, and it's just not worth it to me to risk it."

Adam nodded in agreement. "Definitely not," he said. The smile returned to his eyes. "Would you be willing to buy it with a partner? We finished liquidating the bank's assets, and I ended up with a little more than I anticipated."

"Do you really mean that?" Drew wished she could throw her arms around him and hug him the way she'd done when she was a little girl. People who said Adam was heartless didn't know him the way she did; they mistook his natural reserve and formality for coldness. But he'd seen immediately how hard it was for her to ask him for help.

"Of course I really mean it." He motioned her toward the small office across from the tack room. "In fact, you might be interested in some of the figures I've come up with." He led the way into the tiny room, where he spread three sheets of paper across the scarred up old desk. "First of all, I have to tell you that I already knew Rob was going to try to sell the stud. He told me that he was planning to offer it to you first, since he knew that Chase and Trixie wouldn't be able to afford the mortgage." His eyes twinkled at her. "I couldn't resist listening to your exuberant explanation, though. You look about eight years old when you get excited about something."

Drew put her hands on her hips and pretended to glare at him, but it was impossible for her to be truly irritated when he smiled at her that way. "Thanks a lot." She shifted her gaze to the papers on the desk. "So, what's the bottom line here?"

"First, Chase and Trixie will live on the farm with Vi, and Chase will run the place. Second, we'll sell off at least half of the stock immediately and plant tobacco. Third, Chase and Trixie will work for shares in the farm rather than for wages." He held out his hand. "Are we partners?"

Her hand shaking slightly, Drew grasped his. What a nitwit she was to have spent two days stewing about how to approach Adam. "Partners," she said.

January 1931

A week after Trixie gave birth to her daughter Cecilia, Drew rose at three o'clock in the morning and dressed hurriedly in her warmest clothes—it had snowed a few days ago, then frozen. Doc Steffens had examined Vixen yesterday and told Drew the foal could arrive any time. "The mare's waxing; she breaks out in a sweat while she's eating; and her teats are full and hard. I'd advise leaving her in her stall if you don't want her foaling in the field."

Drew and Ben had taken his advice, and between their myriad duties, one or the other of them checked Vixen every hour during the day, then divided the night into two shifts. Ginnie was spending the nights at Blue Meadow with Chase, Trixie, Vi, and her new baby cousin Cici until Vixen foaled, so at least Drew didn't have to worry about her. She stopped at the bathroom and splashed icy cold water on her face to wake herself completely, then washed her hands in soapy water—just in case.

A few minutes later she stood in the stall with Ben. "How's she looking?" Drew asked, patting Vixen's neck. Glistening with sweat, the mare moved restlessly, trying to turn in the stall.

Ben rubbed his dark hands together, then blew on them. "It's gonna be soon, missus," he said. "I was fixin' to come and get you."

"Is everything ready?" Drew's stomach rolled with excitement, but she forced herself to act calm. Despite Rob's disapproval, she'd helped out a couple of times with the broodmares at Blue Meadow, so she knew what to expect. Of course, the unexpected did happen, and Vixen's first foal was damn special, so she did have a right to a little bit of anxiety—as long as she didn't let it get in the way.

"I was jes' waitin' on you." Ben grinned at her. "Be back in a jiffy." He let himself out of the stall.

"It's all right, girl." Drew rubbed between the mare's ears, but Vixen flinched away from her. "I know how you're feeling." She remembered the night she'd given birth to Ginnie, and how she'd screamed at her mother and the doctor not to touch her. Even the hairs on her head had throbbed with the pain that had consumed her body. "But it's worth it," she reassured the mare. "This is going to be a special baby, I just know it."

Ben returned with a pail of hot water and several towels draped over his arm. "You hold her head while I wash her," he said.

Drew grasped the mare's halter and spoke to her quietly until Ben finished. As soon as she released the halter, Vixen settled herself in the straw, her sides rippling. "She's in good labor now," Drew said, situating herself behind the mare. Two little feet suddenly appeared behind the membrane, and she sighed with relief. The foal was positioned correctly for a normal birth.

Vixen breathed gustily, then her belly tensed with another wave of labor. The tiny hooves broke the membrane, and a minute later Drew saw the tip of the foal's nose. The labor pains continued regularly, and each one revealed more of the foal, a golden chestnut like his mother, with at least two white stockings and the same white star on his forehead as his sire and his granddam, First Star.

A few minutes later the mare gave one last huge heave. The foal's hips slid out, and suddenly it was born. "It's a colt," Drew said, grinning at Ben. "And he's a beauty."

"What're you going to name him, missus?" Ben beamed back at her, then cut and tied the umbilical cord before he grabbed the colt's forelegs and pulled him in front of Vixen.

The mare nuzzled the foal and nickered softly, then began licking away the membrane encasing him.

Drew watched the two of them, happiness warming both her heart and limbs. She'd decided on the foal's name months ago and had already checked the Jockey Club registry to make sure it hadn't been used. "Kentucky Secret," she said. "He's going to be the best of his mother and father. I just know it."

Thirty-two

August 1931

Drew settled herself at Trixie and Vi's kitchen table, then held out her arms for Trixie's baby. "I can't believe she's seven months old already," she said, as Trixie placed the little girl in her lap. "Hi there, Cici. Boy, are you a cutie!" She gathered Ginnie close to her with her free arm. "You used to be this tiny, too," she said to Ginnie, who popped her thumb into her mouth and stared wide-eyed at the baby. "And now you're a big girl, three-and-a-half years old."

Trixie beamed proudly. "She's just starting to crawl."

"Uh-oh." Drew smiled at her. "It's all over now. You're going to be chasing her all over the place."

Cici wiggled and waved her arms.

"See," Drew said. "She wants to get down and take off on her own." She hugged the baby closer to her. "But I'm not going to let you get away already, little one. I don't get to hold you often enough." She bounced Cici on her knee. "I'll just have to make it more interesting for you."

Trixie poured a cup of tea and set it in front of Drew, but out of reach of the baby. "It's hot," she said, sitting down across the table. "Be careful."

Cici waved her arms again, and Drew laughed. "I think I'll put her on the floor before I attempt it." She let out a contented sigh and smiled at Trixie. "Lordy, this feels good. It's been too long."

Trixie nodded, then sipped her tea. "I don't know how you do it, Drew," she said. "You never take any time off. No wonder you're so thin." She patted her hips and giggled. "I'm still a little plump, but I'm so happy it doesn't even matter. Chase says why bother to lose it all when I'm just going to get pregnant again." Shaking her head, she leaned across the table toward Drew. "Would you ever have guessed Chase would be such a good father?"

"Never." Drew winked at her. "He hasn't suggested taking Cici to a speakeasy now that she's almost crawling, has he?"

"He doesn't even go to them himself anymore. We can't afford it, for starters. And he says he doesn't even miss the wild parties we used to go to." Trixie jumped up and scooped her baby out of Drew's lap, then placed the child in the middle of a blanket on the kitchen floor. "Let her entertain herself for a while. Your tea's going to get cold."

Ginnie immediately let go of Drew's leg and squatted on the floor in front of the baby. "I'll play with her, Aunt Trixie," she said. "I like babies."

"Thanks, honey." Trixie propped her elbows on the table and fixed Drew with a serious stare. "Now, tell me how *you* are. Have you seen Rob lately? He drops by all the time, but you know him—he never tells me anything important."

"I'm doing fine." Drew sipped her tea, which was still plenty hot. "Rob visits Ginnie every weekend, but we don't talk much either." She wrinkled her nose in a wry grimace. "Not that we ever did really talk. Mostly Rob lectured me, and I argued with him."

Trixie glanced at the children, then back at Drew. "You know, as much as I love both of you, I have to admit that Rob never seemed right for you. He never really cared much for the horses. And he's always been so serious about everything." She gave a little snort. "I always thought, though, that he might be different with you than he was with me because you weren't his little sister. Doesn't sound like he was."

Drew couldn't keep herself from bursting out laughing. People often thought of Trixie as a lamebrain because she'd been an awful student and she giggled all the time, but the truth was that Trixie usually saw and understood a lot more about things than she let on. "You're exactly right," Drew said when she caught her breath. "I used to argue the same way with Scott when he tried to boss me around. The more he'd try to tell me what to do, the more stubborn I'd get."

Drew started laughing again. "Do you remember that time I jumped on the back of one of old Hugh's stallions and took off galloping? That was because of Scott. Momma had made him take me with him when he went to see Adam, and he left me wandering around the stud barn with strict orders not to touch anything or go anywhere else. So of course when I saw that a groom had saddled up one of the horses and then disappeared to look for an exercise boy, I climbed on." She shook her head, still laughing. "Lord, was I stupid. If it hadn't been for Adam, I might have been killed."

Trixie raised both her eyebrows above her round blue eyes. "I'll bet that's when you first fell in love with him."

"I was only seven!"

Tilting her head, Trixie fixed Drew with a calculating stare. "Are you still in love with him?"

"In love with whom?"

Both Trixie and Drew turned toward the kitchen door at the sound of the deep male voice. Neal Rafferty stood outside the screen door, a grin stretching his generous lips wide and lighting up his golden brown eyes.

Drew sucked in her breath, then held it when she realized the effect his presence had on her. Her heart thumped in her ears, and although she tried to blame it on surprise, she knew that wasn't really the truth. How could she love Adam so much if Neal did this to her every time she saw him?

"Oh, hi Neal." Trixie didn't appear the least bit surprised. "I was wondering when you were going to show up."

Drew narrowed her eyes at Trixie, who ignored her, a mischievous gleam lighting her bright blue eyes.

"Sorry to interrupt such a private conversation." He smiled at Drew. "But now I'm even more sorry I didn't hold my peace for just a few more seconds."

"If you say another word, Neal," Trixie drawled, "I'm surely going to have a hard time talking Drew into having dinner with us tonight."

Neal pinched his lips shut and grinned roguishly at Drew. "In that case, the subject is closed forever."

"What do you say, Drew?" Trixie asked. "Will you stay for dinner?"

Drew drank her tea, now lukewarm, as she pretended to consider Trixie's invitation. She was so tired of doing nothing but working all the time, and although Ginnie was adorable, she often longed for adult companionship. She missed Momma and Daddy so much, and sometimes she was so lonely she even found herself missing her interminable arguments with Rob. Avoiding Neal's eyes, she stared at the two little girls playing happily on the floor.

Finally, she shrugged. He was dangerous, she knew. And too damned attractive. But what did she have to lose? It was just dinner, after all. "Sure," she said. "I'll stay."

Neal pulled his yellow Daimler up in front of Drew's porch. "I'll get Ginnie," he said, opening the back door of the car and carefully lifting out the sleeping child. The last thing he wanted to do was to wake her. If that happened, every inch of progress he'd made with Drew this evening—as well as one of the few remaining bottles of champagne in his parents' cellar—would be wasted.

Eyeing Drew's slim backside as he followed her up the stairs and into the entry with Ginnie in his arms, Neal remembered back to the first time they'd met. Drew had captivated him then every bit as much as she did now, but other things had come up and he'd never gotten around to pursuing her the way he should have. Then, before he had the chance to ask her out, she married Rob Carlisle, and Neal had put her out of his mind—except for whenever he happened to run into her and the sight of her started his blood stirring once again.

"Where do you want me to put Ginnie?" he asked Drew after she shut the front door behind him. He smiled down at the sleeping child, a curly-haired little beauty just like her mother. He wouldn't mind having a daughter of his own just like her some day.

Drew pointed to the stairway. "Her bedroom's upstairs." She led the way, then pushed open the door to a small room wallpapered with pink roses.

Neal laid the child on the bed, then stood back and watched as Drew pulled a sheet up to her chin, tucked her in, and kissed her cheek. "She's certainly a sweet little girl," he whispered.

Drew put her finger to her lips, then tiptoed to the door ahead of him. Once they were safely in the hall, she smiled at him. "She's much nicer when she's asleep than when she's awake and exhausted, and she's not always ready to go to bed when she's tired. Believe me, she can be extremely trying at times." She shrugged as she headed back down the stairs. "But then I look at her when she's sleeping, and I forgive her everything."

Neal nodded but he wasn't really listening. Now that the child was out of the way, he had to find some way to stay for a little while longer. When they reached the bottom of the stairs, he pulled his silver flask from his pocket. "Would you care for a nightcap?"

"I don't think so," Drew said. "I've got so much to do tomorrow—"

"Come on," he said. "It's still early. Surely you have time for just one teeny weeny little sip." He smiled into her eyes. "It's from the little that remains of my family's private stock—smooth as silk, guaranteed not to cause a hangover. Consider it a restorative tonic. Drink enough of it and you'll be able to move mountains."

Shaking her head in amusement, Drew rolled her eyes at him. "I'm sure that's the absolute truth. But—" She stopped herself from uttering a sensible excuse. She didn't have to be practical and wise every minute of the day. In fact, she was getting pretty damn tired of never having any time for fun. "What the hell," she said. "I could use a restorative. Make yourself comfortable in the parlor while I get us a couple of glasses."

"Now you're talking." His light brown eyes sparkling, he saluted her before heading toward the parlor.

Wondering what in the world she was getting herself into, Drew pushed open the kitchen door and grabbed two of her mother's crystal glasses from the cupboard. She and Rob had been legally separated for almost a year now, but neither of them had bothered to start divorce proceedings yet, so technically she was still a married woman.

Which she definitely did not feel like—especially right now. Every nerve in her body was at war; her skin tingled, her hands shook, her heart raced with anticipation and anxiety. And at the same time, she kept asking herself how she could feel that way about Neal when Adam was the man she loved, had always loved. Her feelings for Adam made more difference to her than the technicality of her marriage to Rob, but in truth her love for Adam was pointless, except as an exercise in self-denial—something she'd never been particularly good at.

Adam would never leave Victoria, no matter how miserable he was or how horribly she treated him. He was far too gallant, and he loved his son so completely that he'd never risk anything that might result in losing him.

Finally, she heaved a loud sigh and nudged the swinging door open with her hip. She missed Momma and Daddy with an ache so deep she wondered if it would ever go away; her marriage to Rob had ended in intense disappointment; and she'd long ago given up all hope for happiness with Adam. But despite everything, she still believed she had a life to live.

She carried the glasses into the parlor, turning on her brightest smile for Neal. It would be worth everything if she could forget her heartaches for just one night.

Thirty-three

December 1931

Thinking she heard the crunch of car tires on the graveled drive, Drew turned off the kitchen faucet. She was right, and the motor sounded like Neal's fancy foreign car. Hurriedly, she dried her hands on her apron, untied it and hung it on the hook by the kitchen door, then attempted to pat her unruly curls into place before she rushed to the front door to meet him. She'd just put a reluctant Ginnie down for her nap—at almost four her daughter thought herself too old for something so babyish—and she didn't want Neal's exuberant knocking to wake her.

She had to smile as she opened the door. Neal's courtship during the last five months had been as zealous and enthusiastic as everything else about him; and even though she worried about the possibilities of difficulty with Rob about the divorce, she had to admit she'd been swept away by Neal's attentions. Sometimes she even went so far as to think she was in love with him. She stepped onto the porch just as Neal headed up the steps.

His face lit up when he saw her. "Darling," he said, and handed her a bouquet of shiny green holly branches laden with red berries. "Be careful. They bite." A rueful expression on his handsome face, he opened his hands to reveal several small puncture wounds.

Drew laughed at him. "You goose," she said. "You're

not supposed to rip them from the tree with your bare hands."

"I know that now. But I was a determined man."

"That's certainly the truth." She gestured toward the front door. "We have to be quiet. I just put Ginnie down for her nap."

"Believe me, sweetheart, the last thing I want to do is to wake her." Neal's lips curved into a boyish—and hopeful—grin. He removed the holly from her hand and laid it on the weathered porch swing, then reached over and patted Drew's bottom. "How about visiting the hayloft with me?"

Drew's cheeks grew warm, but she couldn't help returning his grin. Neal was a wonderful lover, ardent and attentive, but sometimes he didn't seem to realize how complicated her life was. Even though he was twenty-six years old and had a degree from Harvard, he had no real job, no one to be responsible for, and he just didn't understand why she couldn't drop everything and go off on crazy adventures with him.

"What if Ginnie wakes up?" she asked. "What if Ben or one of the men grading the tobacco needs me for something? There's plenty enough talk about us already." Her smile faded as she remembered the sudden silences whenever she walked into the market in Paris or the whispers when she attended church. She knew what people were saying—"What can you expect from a bastard? She's just like her Yankee mother and that wild, no-good Andrew Ashworth. It's bad enough she's getting a divorce, but to be carrying on like that before it's even legal!"

And although she knew the gossip about her mother wasn't true and she no longer cared what people thought of her, she worried about Ginnie. In three more years, Ginnie would be starting school, and Drew knew firsthand how much it hurt when the kids on the playground taunted you about your parents. And when Ginnie came crying to her, she wouldn't honestly be able to soothe her by saying none of it was true. Ginnie *was* a bastard, and someday Drew would have to tell her who her real father was. It just wasn't fair for Ginnie to suffer because of Drew's sins.

Shaking his head, Neal pulled her into a tight embrace. "You worry too much. You know Ginnie's a sound sleeper, and why would anyone come looking for you in the hayloft anyway?" He lowered his head to kiss her.

She pushed him away. "Not here. Someone might see." She sounded snappish, she knew, but she couldn't help it.

He tilted her head back and looked into her eyes. "Something's wrong. What happened?"

Sudden tears burned her eyes, and she ducked her head, unable to speak. Her feelings for Neal were still confusing to her. Half of the time she didn't give a damn if the whole world gossiped about them, and the other half she spent trembling with fear that Rob would hear what was being said and decide to make things difficult for her. If he claimed she was an unfit mother, she might lose Ginnie. The possibility filled her with such a surge of hysterical panic that she had a hard time controlling it. In truth, Ginnie was all she had. The farm, Wish and Vixen, Kentucky Secret were all important to her, but she could live without them. She was learning to live without Momma and Daddy, and she'd finally accepted that she would have to live without Adam. But losing Ginnie—and knowing that her own actions led to it—was more than she could stand to think about. Maybe she should just stop seeing Neal.

She shivered, not sure what do. She was more drawn to Neal now than ever; she thought of him all the time, to the point where she even found herself neglecting her duties. Fortunately, the farm was doing well enough and her expenses were so minimal now that she had no debts that she'd been able to afford to hire some help. Still, every time she attempted to put some order and sanity back in her life, Neal's charm lured her in the other direction. She found him impossible to resist because since that day he walked into Trixie's kitchen, she'd felt happier and more alive than she had in years.

But she had to think about Ginnie, too. She'd managed to keep that part of her life normal so far by limiting her time with Neal to whenever Ginnie slept or visited Trixie and Vi, but with the demands Neal had been making lately, that was getting more and more difficult. Crossing her arms tightly against her chest, she shivered again.

"You're freezing standing out here without a coat." Neal took her hand and led her toward the door. "Since you won't go tumble around in the hay with me, how about inviting me inside? I promise to be good."

She let him pull her into the parlor, her mind made up. The words tumbled out before she allowed herself to reconsider. "I can't see you anymore," she said.

Raising his eyebrows, he regarded her for a moment, then slowly lowered himself onto the sofa. "Why not?" His voice was soft, and the mischievous gleam in his eyes was gone. "Did I do something wrong? Have I said something to offend you?"

She shook her head.

"Has Rob said something about us?"

"Not exactly." She crossed the parlor quickly to the fireplace and held her cold hands out toward the flames, her back to Neal.

"But that's it, isn't it?" He sounded relieved. "You're worried about Rob."

"Not about Rob," Drew said. "About Ginnie. I don't want her paying for my mistakes. And I'm so afraid of losing her." She buried her face in her hands, and a second later Neal's arms surrounded her.

"It'll be all right," he said. He lifted her chin with his

finger and gazed into her eyes. "I love you, darling. Will you marry me?"

Drew twisted her face away, then rested her forehead against his chest, her eyes squeezed shut against her tears. "You know I can't," she said. "I'm still married to Rob." Even though her divorce would be final in four months, marriage was something she didn't want to think about right now, not when she was so confused. And she didn't want to tell Neal, but she wasn't so sure that she'd say yes even when she *was* free.

March 1932

Drew waited in the paddock, Kentucky Secret's bridle draped over her arm. She and Ben had started breaking Secret last week, and it was going even more slowly than she had anticipated. She'd managed to get the bridle on his head and fastened around his ears—he hated having them touched and threw temper tantrums the first three days—so today she was going to attempt once again to get him to take the bit. She wasn't looking forward to it. The colt was smart, but stubborn as hell, and he did not like the idea of having that piece of rubber in his mouth.

But it was apparent he wanted to run, and he'd never be able to race unless he allowed himself to be broken. Broken. She hated the word because in truth it didn't at all describe what she was doing. Slowly, gently, with a lot of love and with extreme patience—more than she ever thought she had—she was leading Secret toward cooperation and the acceptance of a rider on his back.

There'd been something special about the golden colt since the morning he was born, and she hadn't been disappointed in him as he'd grown. As a yearling, he more than fulfilled his early promise—high-spirited but not mean, easygoing in his stall but vigorous and energetic in the paddock. She'd known right from the first that he'd fight her every step of the way, but she also knew that her persistence and patience would eventually pay off. Kentucky Secret simply breathed greatness.

Ben, a broad smile creasing his dark cheeks, emerged from the barn with Secret prancing behind him. "He is sure feeling his oats this morning, missus," Ben said.

"So what's new?" Drew said. She shrugged and smiled at Ben. "I guess he doesn't see any point in making it easier for us than it is for him."

"Aw, he'll be all right. Maybe not today or tomorrow, but the day'll come. He's a fine colt, and he knows it." Ben led the colt into the paddock, patting his neck and talking softly to him when they reached Drew. Secret nosed the bridle in Drew's hands, then snorted and tossed his head as if to say he wanted none of it.

"Come on, boy." Drew rubbed his forehead before she slipped the bridle over his ears and fastened it. "This isn't going to be so bad, you'll see." Continuing to murmur to Secret in a soothing voice, she began slipping the bit into his mouth. Finally, it was in all the way, and she let out a soft sigh while she attached the checkpieces to the bit rings. Maybe he'd finally accept it.

Secret champed on the bit until he suddenly seemed to realize that it was firmly fixed and chewing on it wasn't going to make it go away. He stood frozen for a second, then bolted, whipping the lead shank out of Ben's hands and thundering to the far side of the paddock.

Drew hurriedly followed Ben out of the gate, shutting it behind her. Her hands on her hips, she watched from the other side of the paddock fence as the colt reared at the fence, whirled around, and galloped back to the other side, where he stopped and shook his head furiously, trying to spit out the bit.

At that minute, a car sputtered noisily up the drive, setting Secret off once again. He stormed from one end of the paddock to the other, his tail high, his head twisting from side to side. The dilapidated vehicle finally rattled to a stop, and Rob climbed out and waved.

Drew gritted her teeth as he headed toward her, dreading the disparaging comments she was sure he'd make about Secret's behavior and her abilities as a trainer. She'd asked him over and over again to telephone her first and arrange to visit instead of simply dropping by, but he continued to stop in without warning. She was happy that so far he'd never run into Neal; it was bound to happen one of these days, though, and she was looking forward to that even less than she was to having him see how ornery Secret was.

Rob leaned against the fence and watched Secret's antics for a minute. "How's it going?" he asked. "Looks like he's having some fun."

"Yeah. I'm just hoping he doesn't have too much of his great-granddaddy Hastings in him." Although Hastings had been a hell of a runner, Drew worried that his vicious temper and unmanageable spirit had been passed on to Secret.

"Or his granddaddy Fair Play's moodiness. He was one fast colt, but he'd only run when he damn well felt like it." Rob lifted his shoulders in a slight shrug. "Well, good luck. Your colt's certainly a grand looking individual."

Drew blinked, then widened her eyes. Not a single snide comment so far. They hadn't had any major arguments since separating, but Rob usually had something derogatory to say, as if it irritated him that she was doing fine without him. "Thanks," she said. "How are things at the university?"

"I'm graduating in June, but I've decided to apply for graduate school. And I've almost finished my book of poetry." Rob smiled as Secret, still shaking his head and huffing noisily, galloped past them. "He's certainly tenacious, I'll say that for him. What do the rest of Wish's foals look like? I expect you've got a bumper crop from that clever plan you came up with last season."

Drew smiled at him. "Lord, did it ever work. No one had any money, so everybody just jumped at the chance to breed their mares for trade. I've got sixteen new colts and fillies arriving in the next couple of weeks, and I'm planning to take eleven of them to the spring auction at the Kentucky Association. I'm keeping three colts and two fillies—good-looking individuals with lots of promise." She laughed. "I just hope they're a little easier to train than their brother Secret."

He laughed easily with her. "And how's the season going this year?"

"Even busier. I made the same offer again, and the word's gotten around. And Vixen is in foal again to Wish." Tilting her head, she regarded him curiously. He'd been talking to her for fifteen minutes, and she hadn't sensed the least bit of animosity. In fact, he was being downright pleasant. He even looked happy.

Suddenly, she realized why, and the last few remaining grains of guilt in her heart dissolved. Trixie had been hinting about it for the last couple of months, but Drew hadn't really understood what Trixie was getting at. Now she did.

Rob was in love with another woman. He didn't need Drew anymore.

Thirty-four

April 1932

The only things Neal liked better than fast cars were women, gambling, and bourbon—and not necessarily in that order. Bracing his back against the brown leather seat, he pushed the Cord's gas pedal to the floor. The car surged forward like a race horse breaking from the barrier, and he smiled with satisfaction as it roared down the brief straight stretch before the lane leading to Ashworth Farm.

He tapped the brakes, and the Cord responded instantly. Drew was certainly going to be surprised when he pulled up in front of her house in a brand new white Cord L-29. And she was going to be even more surprised when he told her it was hers.

He flipped the steering wheel and turned onto the lane. Of course, he had no intention of telling her he'd spent the last of his inheritance on it. Not that she'd ask, or even wonder, where he got the money. Like everyone else, she assumed he was financially well-off despite the crimp Prohibition had put in his family's business; and while that had never been exactly true, he'd at least been comfortable enough, and lucky enough at gambling before the stock market crash, to be able to give the appearance of wealth.

Sending gravel flying, he sped up the lane, swerving to avoid the potholes. He stopped the car in front of Drew's porch and honked the horn in several short blasts.

She ran out of the barn, her large brown eyes opened wide with surprise and her hair tumbling around her face. Even in worn trousers and one of her father's ragged old sweaters, she was lovely to look at. She smiled and waved when he got out of the car. "Neal! I didn't know it was you."

He motioned her over. "Come here. I've got a surprise for you."

Shaking her head, she trotted down the pathway between the two paddocks at the side of the barn. What now? Neal loved surprising her, and not just with flowers and candy. Once he'd fixed dinner for her and served it in the dining room with candles and champagne; another time he worked half the night sorting tobacco leaves so she could go to Joyland with him and Ginnie.

"Nice car," she said when she reached him. "Is that the surprise?"

He pulled her into his arms and hugged her. "Just a part of it." He released her, keeping one arm around her shoulders and gesturing with the other toward the white car. "So you like it?"

"It's beautiful," she said. "It looks incredibly expensive." Sometimes she wondered where Neal got all his money, but he never talked about it, and he never seemed to run short the way everyone else did nowadays. She assumed that at least part of it—what he spent on the gifts for her and toys for Ginnie, anyway—came from his earnings at the racetrack. But no one, not even expert handicappers like Neal, won all the time.

He shrugged, and his amber eyes took on the same distant, glazed look they had whenever she asked him about his family or anything else he preferred not to discuss. "I ordered it months ago," he said. He stuck his hand in his pocket, pulled out a key, and pressed it into her hand. "It's for you."

Drew stared at the key, then at the car, and finally at

Neal. An embarrassed warmth surged up from her chest to her cheeks, and she opened her mouth to protest, but no words came out. Lordy, she thought, she must look like a dying fish with her mouth wide open and her eyes bulging.

At that instant, Ginnie flew out the front door, yelling, "Uncle Neal! Uncle Neal!" She threw herself into his arms, and he swung her high in the air while she squealed.

Drew finally got her voice back. "No." She held the key out to Neal, but he ignored her. "I can't take it."

Laughing, he set Ginnie back on the ground and turned to Drew. "Of course you can take it. It's my wedding present to you."

Drew's face flamed even hotter, and she jerked her head in Ginnie's direction. Although Neal had asked her to marry him at least once a week since Christmas, neither of them had ever discussed it in front of Ginnie, and Drew just kept telling him that she couldn't even *think* about marriage until her divorce from Rob was final.

Ignoring her again, he opened the car door. "Want to get in and go for a ride?" he asked Ginnie.

The little girl grinned like a monkey and hopped into the driver's seat. "I'll steer," she announced, her green eyes twinkling.

"I'll bet you're a swell driver." Neal closed the door. "Take her out for a short spin. We'll wait here."

Ginnie made loud engine noises and twisted the steering wheel back and forth while Drew and Neal waved at her. "Bye-bye," she shouted, then resumed her motor sounds.

Neal cupped his hand under Drew's elbow and escorted her to the porch. "All right," he said. "She's too busy to bother with us now." He nodded toward the porch swing. "Sit down for a minute."

Drew sank onto the hard slats of the old wood swing. She knew what was coming and she'd been dreading this moment for weeks because she still had no idea what she should say or do. As much as she enjoyed being with Neal, she wasn't sure if what she felt for him was love or just physical attraction. Whatever it was, it was certainly different from her feelings for Rob—which was definitely a good thing.

But on the other hand, it was just as different from the feelings she'd had for Adam for years, which she'd finally decided couldn't be simply infatuation because they'd persisted much too long. Over time, she'd learned to accept Adam's limitations in a way she'd never been able to with Rob.

And she was so afraid that the fun she and Neal had together would go sour if they ever got married. Still, she knew that if it weren't for Adam, she'd marry Neal in a minute; and that worried her.

Because what if she were to blame for ruining her marriage to Rob? What if it had been her fault because she couldn't stop loving Adam? If that were the case, then the same thing would happen if she married Neal.

Neal fell on one knee in front of her and took her hand. "As of today, you're officially a free woman, Drew Ashworth," he said. "Now will you at least think about marrying me?"

She sighed, unable to look away from his eyes. She couldn't stand to be the reason for dulling their impish sparkle. "All right," she said. "I'll consider the possibility."

"That's great!" He jumped up, then pulled her out of the swing and into his arms and danced her around the porch. "Jesus, I love you."

Ginnie honked the horn and flapped her arms excitedly, and they both waved back at her.

"When?" Neal whispered, his mouth against her ear.

He'd been so patient with her that it just didn't seem fair to keep him dangling anymore; and despite her doubts, Drew felt her resistance melting away in the happiness of the moment. "In a few months," she said. "I need time to prepare Ginnie."

"When?" He nuzzled her neck and tightened his arm around her waist. "I'm not letting you go until you give me a date."

Laughing, she tilted her head back and looked up into his eyes. "How about the day after Christmas?"

"Perfect!" He danced her behind the trellis at the far end of the porch so Ginnie couldn't see, then kissed her firmly on the mouth. "In that case, you can consider the Cord an early Christmas present, too."

May 1932

A month later, Drew settled herself against the Cord's leather seat while Neal adjusted the choke and revved the engine. She wasn't looking forward to the trip back home from Louisville. Neal had been in a foul mood ever since Burgoo King had crossed the finish line ahead of Tick On.

He glowered at the dashboard, then rammed the lever into gear. The car backed up with a jolt, and he cursed under his breath.

Drew glanced at him, taking in his stiff shoulders and the rigid line of his mouth. She'd never seen Neal like this before. Usually, nothing seemed to get him down; when things didn't go his way, he just shrugged and smiled and tried another angle. She wasn't sure what to do, but she knew that she sure as hell didn't want to spend the next few hours being jounced all over the car while he drove like a madman.

Still, she waited until they were well out of the city traffic before she opened her mouth. "So," she said, trying to keep her demeanor as casual as possible, "how much did you lose?"

His laugh was short and sharp, almost a bark. "You don't believe in beating around the bush, do you?"

Her heart clenched at the sharpness of his tone, but she forced herself to smile and say lightly, "Sorry. I didn't realize—"

"Forget it." Keeping his eyes focused on the road, he braked for a curve before he glanced at her. The set of his lips softened. "You have every right to ask. I shouldn't have snapped at you."

She let out her breath, and the tightness in her chest eased. Arguing with Neal was a new experience; most of the time they simply laughed away the few differences they had—which was a good thing, considering how bad she was at tiptoeing around dangerous topics. "You didn't actually snap," she said, attempting to laugh. "It was more like a warning growl." She stared at his perfect profile as he concentrated on the road. "I take it that you didn't like my question."

His laugh sounded more sincere this time. "Your question was fine. It was what I was going to have to answer that I didn't like."

"Oh." She said nothing more while he maneuvered the car around a series of sharp turns, but in her mind she tried out a dozen different ways of approaching the same question again. Daddy had always said that a person should never bet more than he could afford to lose; and after Momma's story about Uncle Andrew, she'd understood why Daddy had always been so vehemently opposed to gambling. If Neal had problems, she wanted to know *now*, before she married him. As much as she cared for him, she would never let him jeopardize Ashworth Farm.

Several miles later, she cleared her throat and tried again. "I take it you didn't bet on Burgoo King, then." She paused, then added, "Do you remember the Derby six years ago? You convinced me to bet on Rock Man to show, and Burgoo King's daddy won."

"Bubbling Over was one of the favorites. You'd have risked a lot of money for little gain."

She cocked her head. "Tick On was a favorite today."

"And rules are meant to be broken." Sighing, he slowed the car, pulled over to the side of the road, and cut the engine. "All right," he said, turning to face her. "I bet three thousand dollars on Tick On to win."

Drew couldn't help herself. "Three thousand dollars?" she whispered. She'd bet five dollars on Tick On and felt horrible about losing it, especially when she thought of Daddy's words. She couldn't afford to throw away a dime, but Neal had just thrown away three thousand dollars. It made her sick to her stomach to think of what she could have done for the farm with that kind of money. Right now she was saving every cent she'd earned from the yearling sales to pay for Kentucky Secret's two-year-old racing season next year. With an extra three thousand, she'd be able to afford to race one of her other yearlings, like Witch's Broom, the promising filly from the Broomstick line.

"Three thousand dollars." He sounded resigned, but at least he didn't look angry anymore. He stared down at his lap. *"Your* three thousand dollars."

Struggling for control, she sucked her breath in so hard it hissed in her throat and held it until she was lightheaded before she released it. Her stomach churned with anger and fear, and her voice quavered with disbelief. "You took my money?" Her fingers tingling with numbness, she twisted her skirt in her hands.

"I'm so sorry, darling." He buried his face in his hands until he regained his composure. When he raised his head and looked at her, all of the mischief and anger were gone from his eyes. "My cousin offered to sell me back my family's distillery, and I needed a little more money." He let out a little mirthless chuckle. "He hasn't found medicinal spirits very lucrative, but I'm betting that Prohibition won't last much longer. I figured if I borrowed the money from you and won, I could just replace it and you'd never know. Losing wasn't part of my plan."

So he considered taking the money *borrowing*, not stealing. As much as she wanted to scream accusations at him, she could understand his line of reasoning. After all, she'd used the exact same rationalization when she borrowed her mother's tiara six years ago.

The only difference was that she'd been a scatterbrained seventeen-year-old, not a twenty-six year old man on the verge of becoming a husband and stepfather.

"I'll make it up to you, Drew. I promise." Smiling at her, he chucked her under the chin. "Whew," he said, restarting the car. "Am I ever glad that's over. Thanks for taking it so well."

Still numb with shock, Drew just nodded at him. She had no idea if she was taking it well or not, and she guessed that it might be quite a while before she found out if she could ever trust him again. And how could she possibly marry a man she couldn't trust?

Thirty-five

June 1932

Drew rose after everyone finished the birthday cake and tapped her glass with her spoon. "Before we let Neal open his presents, is anyone interested in taking a look at our yearlings?"

Ginnie immediately clapped her hands in delight, and Cici, in her high chair, joined her by enthusiastically banging her spoon on the tray until Trixie reached over and confiscated the spoon.

"I agree with the kids," Chase said. He picked up his spoon and clanged it a couple of times on his plate, then winked at Alexander, who sat quietly between him and Adam, and handed the four-year-old the spoon. "Want to give it a try, kiddo?"

"Oh, Chase." Trixie giggled. "You're *worse* than the kids."

Adam shook his head at Alexander, then smiled at Drew. "I'd love to see them," he said, standing. "Especially Kentucky Secret and Witch's Broom." He nodded at Alexander. "You may leave the table now."

Chairs scraped against the wood floor of the dining room as everyone stood. Neal pulled back Drew's chair, then squeezed her hand. "Thanks, darling," he said. "It was a swell dinner. And that buttermilk cake was better than my mother's—but don't tell her I said so." Everyone else chimed in their agreement.

Together they all trooped outside, following Drew and Neal to the paddock next to the yearling barn. Drew's stomach fluttered in anticipation and some anxiety. She'd been doing a lot of thinking since Neal had revealed that he'd forged the check for three thousand dollars in order to bet on a sure winner at the Derby. Afterward she'd offered to give him back the Cord to sell, but he'd refused; it was hers, he'd said.

Finally, after she pestered him with question after question, he'd admitted that he was broke, but that he didn't want her to give him anything. He'd been in this situation before, and he'd always managed to get himself back on his feet. This time wouldn't be any different, he'd claimed.

But he was tired of the highs and lows of gambling; once he owned his family's business again, he would no longer have to rely on luck to make his living. He'd been momentarily desperate because he wanted to buy the distillery *before* Prohibition was repealed, not after when it would cost him a lot more. His cousin Tom might be short-sighted, but he wasn't stupid.

The more Neal had told her, the more Drew had become convinced that he needed a fresh start, a way to make the money he needed without having to play the ponies or poker. She'd finally hit on a plan that she hoped he would find acceptable.

Ben was waiting for them with Kentucky Secret when they reached the paddock, and it was obvious that he'd spent a lot of time grooming the colt, whose coat gleamed like molten gold in the June sunshine. Shaking his head, Secret pranced in place, his neck and tail arched proudly and a saddle on his back.

Drew let herself into the paddock. "I just have to show everyone this," she said. Ben boosted her into the saddle, and although Secret tossed his head vigorously, he remained relatively calm.

Adam grinned at her. "I knew you could do it," he said. "And I knew *he* could do it."

Drew slid out of the saddle, then patted Secret on the rump. "It was touch and go for a while there, but he finally figured out that it wasn't so bad."

After Chase and Trixie expressed their admiration of the colt, Ben led him back into the barn and reappeared in a moment with a white-stockinged black filly and a reddish chestnut colt with a white star and blaze.

"These are two of the most promising of Secret Wish's yearlings from other mares." Drew took the filly's lead rope from Ben and led her to the group. "This is Witch's Broom. Her dam is a Broomstick mare who has already given birth to another of Wish's foals and has been bred back to him again."

"She's beautiful!" Trixie said. "And she seems so calm."

"She's got a great bloodline, though," Adam said. "Broomstick sired Regret, and she's the only filly ever to win the Derby."

"She's got a great temperament. Training's been a snap—she's been as cooperative as Secret was reluctant. I'd almost trust her with Ginnie on her back." Drew picked up her daughter and held her up to pet the black filly's neck. "She's like a pet, but she can run like the wind. Our main question is whether or not she'll want to in a race."

Drew returned the filly to Ben, then took the red colt's lead rope. She led him around in a wide circle in front of everyone. "Red Star isn't quite so sweet. He's aggressive and he's fast, though." She smiled at Adam because she knew he'd recognize the colt's pedigree. "His dam's by Star Shoot—she's a half-sister to First Star, Secret Wish's mother."

Drew stopped the colt in front of Neal and then nodded at Ben, who brought Witch's Broom to her. Drew handed both the lead ropes to Neal. "Happy birthday, darling," she said. She hesitated for a moment, forcing herself not to look at Adam because she knew she'd never be able to say the words if she did. "I love you."

Neal's eyebrows lifted, and he stared at the yearlings and then at Drew. "You're giving them to me?" he said with a puzzled frown.

She nodded.

"Why?"

"For the same reason you gave me the Cord. And I'll give you back the car if you won't take them." She spoke quietly to him, her gaze unwavering.

Adam observed their interchange intently. He didn't understand exactly what was going on between the two of them, but it certainly seemed to be more complicated than a simple birthday gift. Indeed, her whole relationship with Neal seemed to be more complex than her marriage to Rob. It had always been obvious to him—after he realized that Ginnie was his child, anyway—that Rob loved Drew, while Drew needed a father for her child. He'd accepted years ago that he'd made a damn big mistake marrying Victoria instead of Drew.

But his excuse was that he'd couldn't help thinking of Drew as a child. A beautiful, impetuous child, the baby sister of his closest friend, the pretty little girl who'd climbed on the back of a stallion and galloped away across the fields. Even after that night in Louisville, which he could never think of without the sharpest pangs of guilt and remorse, he continued to see her as a girl, not a woman old enough for marriage and the responsibilities of motherhood.

Yet a few months later she'd taken on both—and he'd married someone else. Victoria. A woman he'd come to realize he'd never really loved, and one who certainly didn't seem to care much for him after his money and position disappeared. He seldom saw her anymore, and she'd long ago turned her motherly duties over to Spencer and to him. Alexander hardly knew her; he never asked for her, and Trixie and Drew were far more familiar to him than Victoria.

But despite all that, Victoria was still his wife, and he knew his duty even if she didn't. Not only was Drew out of his reach because of Victoria, but she appeared to be truly in love with Neal in a way she'd never been with Rob. And although the best, most altruistic part of him was happy for her happiness, his blacker and baser side— his human nature, he supposed—mourned his lost chance as he watched Drew and Neal together.

Neal handed the yearlings' lead ropes to Adam, then gathered Drew into his arms and kissed her. She melted against his body for a long minute, then leaned back and looked up at his face.

"Well," Neal said. "I'm astounded and overwhelmed. I guess I'm the proud owner of two of the most outstanding individuals in the Bluegrass. Thank you." He beamed at everyone.

Struggling to ignore the sudden bleakness in his heart, Adam forced himself to return Neal's grin. He'd never been a sore loser before.

Then his heart missed a beat when he realized the thought he'd finally put into words. Because it was true, and he'd never admitted it to himself before. He loved Drew, and he'd just lost her forever.

December 1932

Drew pulled the chair up to the kitchen counter. "You can stand on this," she said to Ginnie.

Ginnie clambored onto the chair and peered into the yellow bowl. "Can I have a bite?"

"Sure." Drew handed her the wooden spoon. "Then we'll roll out the rest of the dough." She smiled as Ginnie, with firmly pressed lips and serious eyes, carefully dipped the spoon into the sticky mass of gingerbread cookie dough and pulled out a small piece. It was only two more days until Christmas and three more days until her wedding, and the house was filled with warmth. As the first batch of gingerbread men baked in the oven, the cookies' rich spicy aroma permeated the air. Cedar boughs decorated the parlor and dining room, scenting them with the woodsy, pungent fragrance that always symbolized Christmas to her. Mistletoe from the oak tree in Wish's paddock hung above every lintel, and huge bouquets of holly gathered by Neal—using shears this time instead of his bare hands—filled vases on every table. They'd decorated the tree in the parlor with strands of popcorn and the ornaments her mother had collected over the years.

The thought tightened her chest a little, but she forced herself to let it pass. Christmas without Momma and Daddy was still sad, but she had Ginnie and Neal, and it wouldn't be fair to let her yearnings detract from their joy.

"Umm . . . that was good. Do you want some, Mommy?"

Ginnie's sweet little voice interrupted her thoughts. "I'd love some," Drew said, pinching a piece of dough off the spoon Ginnie held out to her. "I've always thought cookies tasted better raw, don't you?"

The little girl nodded vigorously.

"Now I'll roll some more out, and then we can get to work with the cookie cutters." She gathered the dough into a ball, then patted it into a round on the floured pastry board. "What's your favorite thing about Christmas?" she asked while she pushed the rolling pin over the dough.

"Being a flower girl," Ginnie answered promptly.

Drew laughed. "That's the day after Christmas, you silly goose. What about Santa Claus?"

Before Ginnie could answer, a knock thudded at the kitchen door, and Adam and Trixie stepped inside.

Drew's welcoming smile froze on her face. Trixie was incapable of disguising her feelings, and one look at her face told Drew something was wrong. "What's happened?" she said. "Is Rob all right?"

Trixie attempted to smile, but her eyes glittered with tears. "He's fine." She blinked, then held out her arms to Ginnie. "Hi there, sweetie. Cici really wants to see you. How'd you like to come with me?"

Ginnie stuck out her lower lip and whined, "We're just getting ready to make angels and trees and gingerbread men."

Anxiety stiffened Drew's muscles, but she put her arms around Ginnie and hugged her. "I'll save the dough, honey. It sounds like Cici really misses you." She held her breath, anticipating Ginnie's protests, but none came.

"You promise?" Ginnie squinted at her.

"I promise." Drew lifted Ginnie down from the chair, and she immediately clung to Drew's leg as if she sensed something wasn't right. Gently, Drew released her grip, then kissed her. "It's all right. You can go with Aunt Trixie. We'll finish the cookies when you come back."

A look of relief on her face, Trixie hustled Ginnie out the door, and Drew turned to Adam, who still stood next to the door. "What's up?" she asked, her hands and voice shaking now that she no longer had to pretend everything was fine for Ginnie's sake.

His jaw twitched, and pain darkened his eyes. "Oh, Drew." He grasped her hands in both of his and closed his eyes briefly. "God, I hate this." His voice broke, but he continued. "Neal is gone."

Drew frowned at him. What the hell did he mean? "Gone? He's in Bardstown visiting his family. His cousin has agreed to sell him the distillery."

Adam shook his head. "Jesus, Drew, I'm sorry. There was an accident. An icy curve. He's dead."

Drew felt her mouth open, and she knew she was screaming, but she couldn't hear anything except the roar of her heartbeat in her head. She sagged against Adam, and he caught her in his arms.

Heaving with sobs, she clung to him. "No," she shouted over and over again. "No!"

He held her, his own tears falling on top of her tangled curls. Even if he were free to claim Drew as his own, he'd never wish this kind of pain on her in order to have her for himself. She obviously loved Neal with the same depth of passion he'd only lately discovered in himself.

And if Drew were to suddenly die, he was sure he'd never get over it. The most he could hope for now—maybe ever—was to be her friend; and he knew how badly she was going to need one now.

Thirty-six

June 1933

Sure that she'd heard someone call her name, Drew paused on the stairway leading to Belmont's grandstands and turned around, surveying the crowd below. A waving hand caught her attention, and then she made out Adam's dark head of hair moving toward her. She stepped to the rail to wait for him to catch up.

He joined her a minute later. "I've been looking all over for you," he said.

"I was in the paddock making sure that Secret was going to behave himself."

"I must have missed you, then," he said. "I was just there myself. Do you want to sit together?"

She smiled at him. "Only if you won't take offense if I don't root for Galaxy in the Keene Memorial Stakes."

"I would think it most strange if you did." Cupping her elbow with his hand, he guided her through the throngs heading for the grandstands. "The Keene is Kentucky Secret's first stakes race, isn't it?"

She nodded as they approached her seat in the grandstand—in order to save money, Ashworth Farm had no boxes at any of the major tracks this year. "I plan on picking and choosing his races pretty carefully this year. He's bigger and stronger than Wish was as a two-year-old, but I don't want to take any chances."

"That's a wise move." He waited until she had seated herself, then sat down next to her. "Willie and my father made a big mistake with Wish, in my opinion. He could have done grand things as a three-year-old if he hadn't been broken down by too much racing too soon."

Drew agreed with him, then tried to listen with at least the semblance of attentiveness as he chatted on about the best prospects in his stable. She looked in his eyes, nodded, asked a few questions and offered brief comments, but what she really wanted to know was what was going on between him and Victoria. Instead of "How is First Star's new colt doing?" she wanted to ask, "Why is Victoria living in Philadelphia with her parents?" and "How is Alexander doing? Does he miss his mother?" Most of all, she wanted to know if he'd heard the rumors Trixie had mentioned a couple of weeks ago. Was it true that Victoria was frequently seen in the company of another man?

She had done a lot of thinking—about Adam, about Neal, about herself—in the months since Neal's death. As when her mother and father had died, at first her grief seemed unendurable, but as day after day had gone by and she'd survived each one, she'd learned all over again that her own life was the true center of her existence. As much as she grieved and missed those she loved, she had Ginnie to care for and the farm to run.

And she'd also come to terms with her feelings for Neal. Even though she'd loved him, as her emotions had become less raw and her life had settled back into normalcy—a normalcy which had not existed for her since she'd started seeing him—she'd come to realize that marriage to Neal would not have solved anything for her. In fact, it would in all likelihood have created a whole legion of new problems. Neal was as wrong for her as Rob had been, but she'd been too caught up in his excessive high spirits and her own desires to see the truth.

The conclusion she'd finally come to after rehashing every detail of her life and scolding herself for her obstinancy was that she still loved Adam. Yet, if he were happy and happily married, she'd probably be able to convince herself to forget him, or at least give him up completely.

But he couldn't possibly be pleased with the arrangement between him and Victoria. Because that was all it was—an arrangement, not a marriage. The unfairness of it was a sore spot with Drew. She knew that she and Adam would be happy together; she knew he cared for her, loved her. Even though she'd realized some time ago, just as her parents had always told her, that life wasn't fair, her damn stubborn streak made it impossible for her to give up the notion. Life might not be fair, but it sure as hell *should* be.

Pausing for a moment, Adam looked at her, his eyebrow raised "So," he said, "did you bring any other colts or fillies to Belmont?"

Frowning, Drew hesitated briefly before answering. "Witch's Broom and Red Star," she said. "Neal's horses. They both run tomorrow."

"Oh." The look on Drew's face when she mentioned Neal made Adam wish he hadn't asked. Her pain over Neal's death hurt him doubly: first, he hated for her to feel such sorrow; and second, he hated not being able to do anything about it for her. And he doubted that she'd really begun to recover much—she hadn't given herself a chance, the way she'd immediately thrown herself into a whirlwind of activity.

The trumpet sounded, and the horses began the post parade for the Keene Memorial Stakes. Drew put her field glasses up to her eyes and watched the track for a moment before turning to Adam. "Galaxy looks good."

"Thanks. I've got a soft spot for that colt—I always seem to for First Star's foals. He hasn't broken his maiden yet, but he placed in his first two races. I'm glad I could afford to race him this year." He raised his own glasses and peered at the horses as they lined up behind the starting gate. "Kentucky Secret looks in fine condition, too." He lowered the glasses and held out his hand to her. "Good luck."

She placed her hand in his, and he shook it, then gave it a brief squeeze and released it as the bell clanged and the horses burst out of the gate.

Beside him, Drew jumped up and down, screaming and clapping her hands. He smiled at her enthusiasm; Drew had matured in many ways, but she was still as animated and lively as ever when she watched a horse race.

And she had good reason to be this time. Kentucky Secret had gotten a good start and led the rest of the field by several lengths at the backstretch. Galaxy moved up to challenge the third place colt, and Adam added his encouragement to the general roar as the horses rounded the curve and headed onto the homestretch.

"He's going wire-to-wire!" Drew shrieked, grabbing Adam's arm.

A second later Kentucky Secret crossed the finish line at least two lengths ahead of the E.R. Bradley colt Bazaar, and Galaxy followed the two of them to come in third.

Still jumping up and down, Drew threw her arms around Adam and hugged him. Before he realized what was happening, he lowered his head and kissed her on her lips—and even after he realized it, he couldn't make himself pull away. People swirled around the two of them, but he didn't care. All that mattered was the sweet taste of Drew's lips and the ache deep inside him.

August 1933

The rest of the summer was a blur of train rides and racetracks for Drew. While Ben tended to the horses, she

traveled back to Kentucky whenever she had a break between tracks in order to see Ginnie and oversee the new
man she'd hired to take care of the tobacco fields. Although Witch's Broom and Red Star won their share of
races, Kentucky Secret was clearly the outstanding two-
year-old. Racing at Belmont, Jamaica, and Aqueduct in
New York, he won half a dozen stakes races; and each
time he ran, he carried more weight.

By the time they reached Saratoga, Drew was worried.
Two-year-olds were still growing and therefore more prone
to injury—that was why she'd chosen the races for her
three youngsters so carefully. Then she found out that the
handicapper had assigned Secret to carry one hundred
thirty pounds in the United States Hotel Stakes while Cavalcade, Discovery, and Peace Chance—stakes winners
all—were only carrying one hundred twenty-one pounds.
She briefly considered withdrawing Kentucky Secret, but
decided against doing so when Ben pointed out to her that
the colt hadn't had any problems with the one hundred
twenty-seven pound handicap he'd been given in his last
race. "He's a strong one, missus," Ben had said. "He'll
do fine, you'll see."

Still, she couldn't help feeling anxious when the trumpet sounded the beginning of the post parade for the U.S.
Hotel Stakes. She trained her field glasses on Kentucky
Secret and his jockey Rick Workman, who was clad in
the new sky blue, yellow, and white Ashworth Farm silks,
and stared at them all the way around the far turn and up
the backstretch, watching closely for any signs of problems. Secret seemed as rambunctious as ever, prancing and
straining against the bit as if his heavy load meant nothing
to him. Damn him! He was going to wear himself out
before the race ever got started.

The horses reached the starting gate, and instead of
calming down, Secret became even more fractious, rearing
and refusing to cooperate with Workman.

Finally, the field was lined up, and the gates clanged open. Drew let out her breath in a huge gust of relief as Secret burst forward. As usual, he led the pack—Ben always said that Secret sure did hate looking at other horses' rear ends. Every race he'd won had been from wire to wire.

This one looked to be no exception. Secret was ahead by at least two lengths by the backstretch and appeared to be fighting Workman for his head every step of the way. By the corner he was five lengths ahead of the second place colt, Peace Chance, and it was clear that the jockey was pulling him back with all his strength.

The crowd roared its approval as the field headed into the turn. Secret seemed to falter briefly and there was a collective gasp, but he was back on stride a second later and breezed onto the homestretch still several lengths ahead of the nearest contender.

Drew accepted congratulations from the spectators nearby, then headed down the steps to the winner's circle. When she reached Secret, she put her arm over his neck and laid her cheek against his. "Good boy," she said. She looked up at Workman, who still sat atop the colt. "What happened at the turn?"

"I don't know," he said. "But it didn't feel right. I'd check him out damn careful."

"Thanks." Drew didn't need any more encouragement than that. This was Secret's last race as a two-year-old. He had too good a shot at the Derby to risk any further injury now. As soon as Witch's Broom and Red Star finished their races at Saratoga, they were all going back home to Kentucky. It would be good to see Ginnie and Trixie—and, of course, Adam.

Thirty-seven

Christmas 1933

Drew waved from the front porch as Chase and Trixie, with Cici and Viola in the back seat of their Ford, headed down the driveway. The headlights lit the falling snow-flakes and turned the snow-covered ground and tree branches a lovely golden-silver edged with black shadows. She inhaled the fresh, icy air and shivered, as much from the beauty of the scene as from the cold.

Then she turned to Adam, who stood beside her. "Thanks for offering to stay and help clean up. This is the first time I've ever done a family dinner all by myself. I never realized how much work it was going to be." Letting her shoulders sag with relief, she laughed. "Lordy, am I glad it's over."

"You did a fine job. The ham was excellent, and I've never eaten a better mincemeat pie." Adam held the door open, then followed her inside. "And I'm glad to help. Besides, I'd rather wait until Alexander is so soundly asleep that an earthquake wouldn't awaken him, let alone a bumpy ride home."

"I know exactly what you mean." Holding her finger to her lips, Drew quietly opened the door to the downstairs bedroom where both Ginnie and Alexander were sleeping. The light from the entry softly illuminated the room, and she motioned Adam to join her. Together they gazed at

280 *Lee Hayward*

the two children lying side by side on the bed, an old patchwork quilt covering them.

"God, they look sweet," Adam said. He turned his head and stared directly into Drew's eyes. "Have you ever noticed how much they resemble each other?"

Drew's cheeks flushed, but she didn't look away. It no longer made any sense to pretend that Ginnie wasn't Adam's daughter since she'd done so only for Rob's sake anyway. "And I'm sure you know why. They both have their father's green eyes."

Adam closed the bedroom door, then grasped Drew's arms and gently steered her toward the parlor. "The dishes can wait. Let's talk."

Suddenly, her legs quivered like a newborn foal's, but she managed to make it to the sofa before she collapsed. She shivered, then crossed her arms over her chest. She'd dreamed of this moment so often, and now that it was finally here, she didn't know what to do—or to say.

Adam poked the embers in the fireplace until they turned glowing red before he added another log from the basket. "May I get you a drink?" he asked.

Drew nodded. "Neal's bourbon and some glasses are in the cabinet next to the Christmas tree. He always drank it straight. Said it was a crime to dilute good sipping bourbon with water or ice, not to mention mint and sugar." Even though her smile wavered a bit, she managed to force her lips to hold it anyway. "He wasn't a big mint julep fan." Her words sounded like nervous babble to her ears, but she couldn't help herself.

"I'm not either, except on Derby Day. Straight is fine." He poured two glasses, then handed her one before sitting down on the sofa next to her. He clinked his glass against hers, and a roguish light Drew hadn't seen in years gleamed in his eyes. "Here's to our children."

Her hand shaking slightly, she raised her bourbon to her mouth without taking her eyes from his. She didn't know what to think at this point. What the hell did Adam want? Despite the rumors that kept circulating, he was still married to Victoria, and she knew he'd never ask his wife for a divorce.

"I'm not in love with Victoria," he said "I never have been. But I suspect you know that."

She thudded her glass down on the end table so sharply that the bourbon splashed up to the rim, and a surge of warmth flooded her face again. "What are you talking about? Why did you—"

He held up his hand. "Wait a minute before you bite my head off." He smiled to soften the words. "I *thought* I was in love with her at the time. It didn't take me long to discover that I was wrong, but it was too late by then. Alexander came along, and I love him too much to ever risk losing him."

Drew took a deep breath, and her anger faded. It was hard to stay mad at someone who admitted he was wrong, especially when she understood both his reasoning and his feelings. "I thought I might be able to love Rob, too," she said. "And Ginnie needed a father."

"If I'd known about Ginnie, everything might have been different. But Victoria was already pregnant when I realized—" He covered his eyes briefly with one hand; and after he let his hand fall back into his lap, his face was etched with a deep sadness. "I'm so sorry, Drew. I blame myself for everything."

"That's stupid." The words escaped from Drew's mouth before she realized it, but she had to laugh at the shocked expression on Adam's face. "I seduced you, you idiot. I knew exactly what I was doing. The outcome wasn't quite what I'd hoped or expected, but at least part of the blame is mine. Or maybe it's credit, not blame. In either case, please give me at least part of the responsibility. Otherwise you've reduced my importance in all of this to nothing."

She was gratified by the way his mouth dropped open

and a look of understanding slowly loosened the deep lines in his face. "Jesus, Mary, Joseph," he whispered. "And holy shit. I'm a bigger fool than I realized."

This time it was Drew's turn to gape. And after she finished gaping, she began laughing. And kept laughing. Tears rolled down her cheeks, and still she couldn't stop.

He joined her, adding his deep chuckles to her shrieks of laughter. "We're going to wake the kids," he gasped, covering her mouth with his hand. He pulled her into his arms and held her against his chest until their laughter gradually subsided.

And then when she smiled up at him, his control disappeared. He lowered his head and kissed her, and this time there weren't hundreds of people watching. Her mouth was soft and warm, and he savored the sensation, his entire body tensing with arousal as the kiss consumed him and he lost himself in their passion. He tightened his arms around her, running his hand up her side to her breast.

She melted against him, her lips parting slightly and her breaths coming in quick little gasps. She slid her hand under his sweater and trailed her fingers up and down his back.

"Christ, Drew," he groaned. "I can't stand it." His fingers fumbling in their urgency, he unbuttoned her satin blouse, then slid it off her shoulders, revealing her smooth, white skin and lace edged camisole. She was even lovelier to him now than she'd been six years ago.

They'd made love six years ago. And Drew had gotten pregnant. If that happened tonight, he still wouldn't be able to marry her. The thought froze him, paralyzing his desire in a moment of ice cold reality. Gently, he pulled away from her, closing her blouse over her beautiful bare skin.

She tilted her head and looked up at him, her eyes dark with desire.

"I can't, Drew," he said. "I just can't."

Thirty-eight

April 1933

Adam awoke with a start and sat bolt upright in his bed. He'd dreamed he smelled smoke, and it had frightened him so much he'd awakened immediately. He sniffed the air. Damn! It hadn't been a dream. Something was definitely burning.

Then he heard the shouts and the shrill whinnies. He jumped out of bed, pushed open his bedroom window, and stuck his head out in the wet April night air. His stomach knotted when he saw the red glow surrounding the stud barn.

His hands shaking, he pulled on his trousers and a shirt, then grabbed his boots and ran down the stairs and out the front door.

Nathaniel Jessup, the groom Adam had hired several months ago, emerged from the barn leading Callahan's Choice, Ballantrae's most prized stud. The chestnut stallion reared and almost jerked the lead rope from Nathaniel's hand, but the groom managed to hold on. "Jimmie's inside. He needs help," Nathaniel shouted above the roar of the fire.

Adam shoved his feet into his boots and sprinted toward the barn. He'd hired Jimmie, Nathaniel's nephew, only a week ago; although the lad was eager, he was inexperienced and young, and there were three more stallions inside.

Smoke poured out the open door, and the flames crackled in the dry hay. The stallions still in their stalls screamed and snorted with fear, and Adam's heartbeat thundered in his ears. He ripped the tail off the bottom of his shirt, doused it in the water trough by the barn door, and held it over his mouth and nose before he plunged into the barn.

The heat seared his skin and eyes. Through the fiery haze, he spotted Jimmie yanking at Fly Away's lead. Quickly, Adam tied his shirt tail over the stallion's eyes, and the horse quieted enough to follow Jimmie out of the barn.

In the stall next to Black Rabbit's, Ric Arana reared and whinnied. Adam grasped the bay's halter, then unlatched the stall door and tugged him toward the barn door. A few seconds later, he handed the stallion's lead to Nathaniel. "Get the hoses over here!" he yelled at Jimmie before he headed back into the barn again for the last stallion. Even though it was raining, he knew it wouldn't be nearly enough to put out the fire.

Gasping, choking, his eyes streaming with tears from the smoke, Adam prayed that the barn's roof lasted until he and Sunday Stroll made it out. The calmest of the stallions, the gray pawed the ground and whinnied, his eyes rolling back in fear, but he didn't resist Adam.

"Get these animals out of here! Take them to the yearling barn," Adam shouted, grabbing the hose from Jimmie. "Call the fire truck!" He sprayed himself first to make sure he drowned any embers that the rain hadn't already doused, then aimed the stream of water at the barn door.

"I already called," Nathaniel shouted back. "They're on the—"

The siren interrupted him. "Thanks," Adam said. Then he grinned like a fool. Suddenly, despite the flames and the heat and the smoke and the water streaming down his face, he felt elated, euphoric. The barn roof collapsed in a fury of flames, but it didn't matter. They'd saved the stallions; there was nothing close for the fire to spread to, and the barn could be rebuilt someday, if necessary. Since they'd sold off so much of their stock, there was more than enough room for the four studs.

The small red Paris firetruck arrived with several cars following it, and the volunteer firemen went to work immediately, along with several neighboring farmers and their hired men. Chase was the last to arrive. Adam grinned at him. "Saved the horses!" he shouted over the roar of the fire.

A few minutes later another set of headlights shone on the drive. An old Model-T sputtered to a stop behind the rest of the cars, and Drew got out. Adam handed his hose to Nathaniel and trotted over to her.

She frowned at him. "What the hell are you grinning for? Your barn is burning to the ground!" Then her eyebrows lifted, and she returned his smile, nodding at him. "Oh, I know. The horses are all fine. Thank the Lord." She stepped forward, her arms raised to hug him; then she stopped and let them fall back to her side. Ever since Christmas night, she hadn't been quite sure how to approach Adam. He was as friendly as ever, but he never attempted to touch her. He acted as if their passionate encounter had never happened.

Tonight, though, he caught her up in a giant hug and swung her around in a circle before he set her back down on her feet. "It could have been so bad," he said. "Someone could have been killed, or we might not have been in time to save all four horses. We could have lost them all."

Now Drew found herself returning his grin with the same exuberance. His arms around her had felt so good, so natural that she wanted to step back into the warmth of his embrace.

But propriety stopped her. Seven or eight volunteers and neighbors still surrounded the sizzling remnants of the barn; and despite Victoria's apparent lack of interest in being his wife, Adam was still a married man. Neither of them needed unpleasant rumors further complicating their already confusing lives. The only reasons she was no longer overtly ostracized were because of Adam's friendship and the sympathy engendered by Neal's death. "Do you have any idea what started it?" she asked.

Adam shook his head and drew his slightly singed black eyebrows together. "Faulty wiring, maybe—the stud barn was the first to get electricity. Sometimes mice chew through the wires." He shrugged. "We'll probably never know for sure."

"Well, it looks like they've got it under control." Drew hesitated, not sure what to do next. No one needed her help with the fire, but even though she was getting soaked, she wasn't ready to go back home yet. When she'd dropped Ginnie off at Blue Meadow, Trixie had told her to come back for her daughter in the morning. "No sense waking the poor child twice in one night," she'd said.

"Would you mind doing something for me?" Adam asked. He stared down at his muddy boots, as if asking a favor of her made too uncomfortable to look her in the eyes.

"Of course not." She kept her little tingle of pleasure from showing in her smile. He apparently didn't want her to leave Ballantrae any more than she wanted to go.

"I'll bet the men would like something to drink and a bite to eat, but I—"

"Naturally, you can't fix it yourself. I'd be glad to." She ached to kiss him, but instead hurried off toward the kitchen's back door. A half hour later she emerged carrying a large basket full of sandwiches and leftover pastries.

Beaming at her, Adam took the basket from her hands and carried it to the veranda at the side of the house, where they would be out of the rain. "Do you need help carrying the drinks?" he asked.

After she nodded, he called to the men. "Come on over and grab a bite to eat. We'll be right back."

Together they lugged out a washbasin Drew had filled with bottles of soda, cups, and carafes of tea and coffee. Drew served the tea and Adam the coffee while everyone chatted excitedly, offering their guesses as to the source of the fire. Norman Tucker, the volunteer fire chief, agreed with Adam that the barn's old wiring was the most likely culprit. Finally, after the fire was nothing more than a few embers sizzling in the rain and everything was eaten and drunk, the firetruck headed back down the drive, followed by all the cars except Drew's.

"Let me help clean up," she said, piling the basket into the washbasin.

Adam didn't protest. He grasped the basin's other handle, and they headed back toward the kitchen.

But before they reached the corner, Jimmie ran toward them, waving his hands. "It's First Star," he shouted. "She's going to foal any minute now."

"Just leave this here," Adam said, grabbing Drew's handle and dropping the basin to the ground. "Let's go."

By the time they arrived at First Star's stall in the broodmare barn, the new foal lay on the hay beside its dam. "A perfect little filly," Nathaniel said, his black eyes sparkling in his brown wrinkled face. "She had a real easy time of it."

"It's Fly Away's first. I'd say he didn't do too badly." Adam knelt in the hay and stroked First Star's neck. She nickered softly, then licked her chestnut filly, still wet from the birth membranes. "Good work, old girl," he said. A wide grin lit up his face, and his teeth glowed white against his skin, still streaked with soot and rain.

Drew crouched beside him. "She's a beauty." Inhaling the rich scents of birth, sweat, and hay, she lifted her eyes and smiled into Adam's. "Would you let me name her?"

His laughter was deep and carefree, the same way it had been years ago before the Great War. "I'd be delighted," he said. "What do you want to call her?"

"How about Firefly?"

"Perfect!" Adam leaned back on his heels and looked up at Nathaniel and Jimmie. "I think I can handle it from here." Shaking his head, he checked his watch. "It's almost four o'clock. Why don't you two try to catch a few hours sleep? You deserve it."

"Thanks, boss." Nathaniel edged his way around the mare, then joined Jimmie at the stall door.

"Good night," Adam said. "And thank *you*."

After the barn door rolled shut, Adam grasped Drew's hands in his and pulled her to her feet. "What a night," he said, smiling down into her eyes.

Drew knew that if she didn't look away he was going to kiss her. Yet she couldn't force her eyes to look elsewhere. Adam was more alive, more vibrant than she'd seen him in years—since his marriage to Victoria, in fact. She realized the thought was self-serving and unkind, but she couldn't help believing it was true. The war had changed Adam, but his marriage to Victoria had compounded the damage.

He lowered his head and brushed his lips tentatively against hers, as if testing what her response would be.

Even if she'd wanted to—which she didn't—Drew wouldn't have been able to keep herself from returning Adam's kiss. Over the years she'd trained herself to ignore the sudden quick heartbeats whenever Adam came into a room, whenever he glanced at her with that special smile that she knew was only for her. They'd both been married to other people, and nothing good could possibly come of whatever it was between them that refused to die. At least that was what she'd told herself over and over again.

But tonight she didn't have to. They were alone; she wasn't married, and Victoria was a wife to him in name only. As far as Drew was concerned, Adam deserved whatever happiness he could find. She clasped her hands behind his neck and pulled him closer, answering his kiss with the pent-up passions of years of loving him. It didn't matter that they were both soaked and grimy, their boots caked with mud. It didn't matter that next to them First Star whickered while her filly nursed with soft slurping sounds. The only thing that counted was the taste of Adam's lips and the beat of his heart against hers. She lost herself in the sweet sensations until he pulled his mouth away and stared down at her.

"Jesus, Drew," he said. "I love you. I always have."

Her knees buckled with the shock of his words, words she'd imagined in her dreams for over ten years. He scooped her into his arms, then carried her out of the stall and shouldered open the stall next to First Star's. He set her down on a bale of hay while he spread another bale into a sweet-smelling cushion on the clean floor. "Wait right here," he said, returning a few seconds later with a green and yellow Ballantrae racing robe, which he spread over the hay.

He held out his hand, and she placed hers in it, still not quite believing what was happening to her. Bending one arm behind her back, he pulled her against him, pressing his body against hers while his lips descended and he continued the interrupted kiss. He sank to his knees on the robe, drawing her down with him.

They lay down together on the silky blanket. He slid his hands beneath her rain slicker, then tugged her blouse out of the waistband of her damp wool trousers. "I don't want to stop this time," he said.

"Me neither," she murmured against his lips.

He ran his hand upward over the soft skin of her belly, and Drew shivered. In the stall next to them, First Star stamped her hooves and whinnied softly. "It's all right, girl," he said, as much to Drew as to the mare.

He could tell that Drew understood immediately. "I'm fine," she said, a wicked little grin curving her lips and lighting her beautiful brown eyes. "Don't worry about me." As if to prove her point, she unbuttoned his Levis, fumbling with each button in a way calculated to drive him mad. "I believe in finishing what I start."

He caught the implied criticism, but knew he deserved it. This time it would be different. He raised his hips off the robe and tugged his blue jeans off, followed by his sweater, then gently helped her strip off the rest of her clothing.

Lying beside her, he held her away from himself for a few seconds, reveling in the sight of her lithe body. Tan lines, like those of a field worker, striped her arms and neck, even in early spring. The skin covered by her clothing was so white that her delicate blue veins glimmered in the barn's dim overhead light. Her nipples, still as small as a girl's, perched atop breasts so rounded and perfect he couldn't resist cupping his hands over each one. "You're beautiful," he whispered. And to himself he added, *I will never hurt you again.*

She gathered him close to her, then rolled to her back, pulling him with her. Her dark eyes stared into his without any trace of embarrassment. "I love you, Adam," she said. "And I always have, too. You may not be my only lover, but you were my first, and you'll be my last."

He had no doubt that she spoke the truth even as she guided him deep inside her. He moved slowly at first, as afraid of hurting her as if she were a virginal seventeen year old. But her sensuous response reminded him that Drew was no longer a child. She was a woman, and he loved her as much as she loved him. She moved to his slow rhythm, undulating her hips to match his controlled thrusts, gasping with pleasure as he drove more deeply within her.

She cried out, her whole body shuddering and her fingers twining in his hair; and her pleasure pushed him toward his. When he could wait no longer, he plunged himself to her core with one final thrust and released eight years of yearning in a few unforgettable seconds.

The rustling of the mare and her young foal in the next stall brought him back to his senses, but he had no idea how much later it was until he glanced at his watch. Six o'clock. Nathaniel and Jimmie were usually on the job by six thirty.

Drew's head rested on his shoulder. He gazed at her face, unwilling to disturb her lovely peacefulness. But he had no choice. Outside the sun was preparing to rise.

Suddenly a thought struck him with blinding clarity. For years he'd told himself that he had no choice, that Victoria was his wife, that she would always be his wife.

He knew now, in this moment of happiness and calm, that that wasn't really the truth. He and Drew belonged together. If the rumors were true, and he had no reason to doubt them, Victoria cared for him as little as he cared for her. He'd been more right than he knew when he'd decided things would be different this time for Drew and him.

As soon as everything was set back in order at Ballantrae, he was going on a little trip to Philadelphia.

Thirty-nine

April 1934

His eyes closed, Adam leaned back against the taxi's hard seat. He wasn't looking forward to his visit with Victoria. Even under the best of circumstances their infrequent meetings were tense and strained. And after he spoke his piece today, the circumstances would be a far cry from ideal.

Even so, another part of him anticipated their conversation with great relish. From the first days of their marriage, Victoria had made it clear to him that she valued wealth and prestige above all else; her behavior after he'd been forced to sell their house left no doubt in his mind that the only reason she hadn't asked for a divorce so far was because she hadn't yet found an adequate replacement for him. She would need a man with a respectable name to enhance her social position and one with enough money to afford her extravagances when her father got tired of doing so. From the rumors that came his way occasionally, he gathered that she was looking, but not yet successful.

By the time the taxi driver pulled the cab beneath the portico of the Seton's imposing and pretentious Main Line home on Radcliffe Road, Adam had decided on the approach he was going to take. Because of Drew's vulnerability, it was important to avoid antagonizing Victoria, even though he personally wouldn't mind if she ranted and raved like a madwoman.

But because of Drew, as well as Ginnie and Alexander, the whole situation was extremely touchy. Victoria was notoriously contrary. If she knew how much he wanted a divorce, she'd do everything in her power to make it difficult and unpleasant. He would have to be exceedingly diplomatic, make her think the divorce was her own idea and in her own best interests—and he'd have to insure that Alexander would remain with him. Even though Victoria had thoroughly demonstrated her lack of interest in her son, she would not pass up the chance to use him to hurt Adam if she thought it would benefit her.

He paid the driver and got out of the cab, mentally girding his loins for the battle of wits ahead of him. Indirectness and subterfuge had never been his favorite ploys, but his years as a banker and Victoria's husband had accustomed him to employing them.

He couldn't resist a smile as he thought of the way Drew would undoubtedly handle the situation if it were up to her. He pictured her now, her hands on her hips, her sparkling dark eyes rolling at the sight of the grandiose monstrosity in front of her, the determined set to her chin as she resolutely marched up the steps and pounded on the huge front door with her little fist. "I want to speak to Victoria," she'd demand when the door swung open to reveal the marble-floored foyer. "I'll wait right here."

Then when Victoria appeared, a haughty smile barely turning up the corners of her bee-sting lips, Drew would look her directly in the eyes. "I've come to tell you that I love Adam," Drew would say. "And he loves me."

He was still smiling when the Setons' butler opened the door. "Hello, Thomas." Adam bit his bottom lip to hide his grin. "How are you?"

For a brief instant the English butler's normally impassive features registered shock, but he composed himself quickly. "Why, Mister MacKenzie, sir. What a surprise."

"I've come to see Mrs. MacKenzie. Is she in?"

"I do believe she's on the grounds somewhere, sir. Perhaps at the stables. Would you like me to locate her for you?"

"Please, Thomas, if you don't mind. I'll just wait in the south parlor." Adam stepped into the over-decorated foyer, complete with an eight-foot-tall urn and a chandelier that would have been more at home in a hotel ballroom. Victoria's father had made his money in steel during the early teens and had managed to hang onto it despite the stock market crash, mainly because of his obstinate refusal to contract debt or invest in stocks.

Although Adam respected his father-in-law's business sense, he found the Setons' excesses, well . . . excessive. He hoped it wasn't sour grapes—after all, they led a life no longer available to him.

But he doubted that envy had anything to do with it. He'd been born understated and reserved—at least that was what Mother always told him. "I never know what you're thinking," she'd complained more than once. And she was right. Expressing his feelings openly was as foreign to him as were the gaudily overdone furnishings of Seton House.

"Very good, sir," Thomas said, opening the tall double doors, then standing to one side.

Adam hesitated a moment before entering. "Are Mr. and Mrs. Seton here?" he asked.

"No, sir. They've been in Europe for the last three weeks. I'm expecting them back at the end of May." Thomas inclined his head. "I'll be back shortly, sir."

Adam wandered around the parlor, gazing at the photographs crowding every table top. Finally, after he'd inspected each one and Thomas hadn't yet reappeared, he sat down at the bench in front of the grand piano and picked out the melody line of "Blue Moon." He smiled as he added the bass rhythm. Mother had always thought he should play classical piano, but popular music had interested him a lot more. Furthermore, his teachers hadn't appreciated his attempts to play Mozart by ear.

He'd paused at the chorus, humming the words to himself, when a strange thumping sound from upstairs caught his attention. Perhaps Victoria wasn't at the stables at all. Her parents were gone, and it was unlikely that a maid would be cleaning the bedrooms this time of day. Pushing back the piano bench with the backs of his legs, he stood, then headed toward the double doors.

He poked his head into the foyer. There was no sign of Thomas, so he sprinted up the curved marble stairway to the second floor. Victoria's bedroom was on the right at the end of the hall. She was going to be as surprised as hell to see him. Smiling, he opened her bedroom door.

The smile froze on his face. Victoria lay naked on her mahogany four-poster, a flush-faced, equally naked young man beside her. Adam stared at him a second before he recognized who he was. Stephen Pruitt, the heir to a shipping fortune, with a reputation as a dashing ladies' man. Gossip had paired him with dozens of rich, beautiful young women over the last few years. If Victoria planned on snaring him, she had her work cut out for her.

Adam replaced his smile with a grimace that he hoped looked like agony and rage. "I think it's time we talked about a divorce, Victoria," he said. "Don't you?"

May 1934

Reserving a box for Ashworth Farm at Churchill Downs had been an extravagance, but it was one Drew felt she deserved. After all, Kentucky Secret, Ashworth Farm's first stakes winner as well as first Derby nominee, was racing in the Derby, and Witch's Broom had run in the third race of the day, taking second place.

She leaned forward, craning her neck to get a view of the Ballantrae box. It was empty. Trixie hadn't come this year because of Cici and money problems; and although Drew had spotted Chase in the box earlier that afternoon, he was probably off placing a bet or talking to Willie Williams, the Ballantrae trainer.

Her shoulders sagged, and she slumped against the back of her seat, blinking her eyes to ward off the disappointed tears lurking there. Adam had left for Philadelphia the day after his barn had burned, sending her a one sentence note—"See you at the Derby"—and a single red rose. She'd had no idea then what he was up to, and she hadn't heard from him since. Drew had quizzed Trixie relentlessly every day, but not even Trixie knew what was happening. All they could figure out was that something important was going on in Philadelphia, and that Adam wished whatever it was to remain his own personal business.

It had been a little over two weeks ago since that early morning when they'd made love in the stall next to First Star's, and only the red rose Adam had sent gave Drew any hope that she wasn't going to have to live through the same kind of grief and pain she'd felt on Derby Day seven years ago.

But her hope had died a little more each day as the rose wilted, the red petals gradually turning black and the blossom drooping on the slender stem. And when she'd found the petals scattered next to her bottle of Amour-Amour on the white dresser scarf her mother had embroidered for her, she'd cried uncontrollably for at least half an hour. Then she forced herself to attend to the multitude of tasks that had to be completed before she could leave for Louisville. As long as she kept herself busy, it didn't hurt so bad.

Until she lay alone at night in her bed. Then there was nothing to do except think about Adam. He'd told her he loved her that night; surely he hadn't gone back to Philadelphia to try to patch things up with Victoria. And she couldn't believe that he would ask his wife for a divorce because he loved another woman, not only because she couldn't picture Adam going back on his vow, but also because he knew as well as she did that Victoria would never agree to do anything that wouldn't be to her benefit or profit. Perhaps he'd just gone to see his parents—but why the mystery, then?

The trumpet sounded, calling the horses to the post parade for the last race before the Derby. Drew wiped away the tears on her cheeks before she peered at the Ballantrae box again. Chase was back now, but still no Adam.

Then there was a light tap on her shoulder. She started, jerking her head around; and her heart contracted with a sharp jolt of pain.

Adam stood at the entrance to the Ashworth Farm box with his hands behind his back and a soft smile lighting his sea green eyes. "Hello, Drew," he said. "May I sit with you?" From behind his back, he pulled out a huge bunch of red roses, one larger even than the bouquet presented to the Derby winner's owner, and laid it in her lap.

Drew's throat squeezed shut on her words, and all she could manage was a nod of assent as she stared up at him.

Adam settled himself next to her, then leaned forward and waved at Chase, who gaped at the two of them. Smiling, Adam turned back to Drew just as the gates opened and the horses surged onto the track.

Swallowing back her tears, Drew made no pretense of watching the race. She caressed the dark red rosebuds, burying her nose in the midst of them and inhaling the rich, spicy fragrance. All around her people screamed and clapped, but she hardly heard them. She wanted so badly to look at Adam, but raw terror froze her muscles. For all she knew, the roses could be a goodbye gift.

When the race was over and the crowd quieter, Adam lifted her chin with a knuckle and pulled her face toward his. "I love you, Drew," he whispered.

Widening her eyes and staring at him, Drew suddenly went limp. Such a huge rush of tears blurred her vision that she couldn't keep them back, and they flowed unhindered down her cheeks.

Adam wiped them away as he smiled into her eyes. "I'm so sorry I couldn't let you know what was going on, but I simply couldn't risk it. Too much was at stake."

"At stake?" Mystified, Drew tilted her head and frowned. What the hell was he talking about? He couldn't possibly mean—

"Our happiness," Adam said. "We've both waited too long, and I didn't want anything to come between us ever again."

Suddenly, a smile quirked her lips, and she couldn't resist rolling her eyes at him. "You mean like that damn wife of yours?"

He hooted with laughter, and the people in the boxes next to them regarded them curiously. Then before he could finish his explanation, the band struck up the opening chords of "My Old Kentucky Home." He leaned over, took the roses from her lap and placed them on the empty chair next to her, and grasping her hand, pulled her to her feet as everyone around them stood for the song and the Derby post parade.

Aghast, Drew realized she'd completely forgotten to visit the paddock while Kentucky Secret was being saddled. In fact, during the last fifteen minutes before the most important race of her life, she'd been totally oblivious to everything except her own tumultuous emotions and Adam.

To make amends for her lapse, she riveted her attention on Kentucky Secret as he emerged from the tunnel and strutted onto the track. His golden chestnut coat gleaming in the May sunshine, he pranced uneasily despite the jockey's tight hold on the reins. Drew was confident that Frank Coltiletti knew how to handle the rambunctious colt, but even he seemed to be having a few problems today. Coltiletti took another wrap in Secret's reins as the big colt skittered sideways.

As soon as Secret was back under control, Drew turned her attention to the rest of the field while they paraded onto the track. Brookmeade Stable's Cavalcade, paired with Time Clock, was the favorite entry, followed by Kentucky Secret, and then Colonel Bradley's Bazaar. All of them shone with good health and vigor, and while their jockeys cantered them toward the starting gate, Drew found herself clutching Adam's hand so tightly than her own ached.

She loosened her hold and smiled apologetically up at him. "Sorry," she mouthed at him.

Flexing his fingers, he shrugged and returned her smile, then suddenly jerked his head toward the track.

Drew swiveled her head back around, and she sucked in her breath with a hiss. Kentucky Secret had bolted, and he swept up the track, his mane flying and his tail held straight out behind him. Coltiletti stood in the stirrup irons, hauling back on the reins, as the crowd roared.

Secret slowed, turning his head, ears pricked forward, toward the stands. He seemed to regard the crowd curiously for a second, then resumed cantering peacefully toward the gate.

For a minute it looked as if Coltiletti was going to have a hard time loading the colt, but Secret calmed down quickly. Drew's breath whistled out between her clenched teeth. Lord, that colt would give her a heart attack yet. Before she had time to regain her equanimity, the bells clanged and the gates clattered open.

The horses jumped onto the track. Almost immediately, Kentucky Secret swerved to his right, and Drew screamed her protest, holding her field glasses to her eyes with one hand. Her colt was behind a wall of horses with no clear way out, and Coltiletti looked off balance in the saddle.

Quickly, though, the jockey regained control, his whip in his hand. He moved Kentucky Secret to the rail and held him there through the first turn. Then Coltiletti moved the chestnut colt to the outside on the backstretch, passing more than half of the fourteen horse field.

Screaming until her throat ached, Drew held Adam's hand in a death grip while Kentucky Secret moved through the pack. When they reached the seven-sixteenths pole, still running outside, he came abreast of the leaders. By the time they reached the final turn, Discovery led the field into the stretch, followed closely by Cavalcade and Kentucky Secret.

On the stretch, both Cavalcade and Kentucky Secret made their moves at the same time, and Secret clipped Cavalcade's heels as they passed Discovery. Drew gasped as her colt stumbled, his head whipping forward almost to the ground. For an excruciating second, she thought he was going to fall to his knees until he miraculously regained his balance.

It had been only a split second mistake, but it was enough. Cavalcade passed under the wire barely a nose in front of Kentucky Secret. Drew's knees gave out, and she sank back into her chair while the thunder of the crowd gradually faded. Kentucky Secret had come in second. Even if he won both the Preakness and the Belmont, he wouldn't win the Triple Crown. Tears of disappointment streamed down her face.

Adam knelt in front of her, clasping both her hands in his and staring earnestly into her eyes. "I'm so sorry, Drew. The colt had some bad luck out there." He kissed her hands, then her wet cheeks. "I love you, you know."

Drew's mind cleared. Suddenly, what was truly important stood out over everything else. Adam loved her. The bouquet of roses he'd given her today meant far more than an entire blanket of roses draped over a Kentucky Derby winner. Secret's loss was a disappointment, of course, but he would very likely win other races for her. And even if he didn't, he might do as well at stud as his sire, Secret Wish. And if that didn't happen, there would still be other colts, other fillies.

But she'd known since she was a child that no one could ever take the place of Adam in her life. "I love you, too," she said, attempting to push her quivering lips into a smile for him.

"In that case," Adam said, his heart showing in his eyes for the first time since she'd met him, "when I'm a free man—" He held up a hand to silence her. "Victoria has very generously agreed to divorce me." The irony in his voice didn't escape her.

He cleared his throat and began again. "What I want to ask is, Drew, will you marry me?" This time there was no irony, only heart-rending sincerity.

Drew laughed through her tears. "That's been my secret wish all along, you fool," she said. "I've wondered for years when you were finally going to figure it out."

Taylor-made Romance from Zebra Books

WHISPERED KISSES   (0-8217-3830-5, $4.99/$5.99)
Beautiful Texas heiress Laura Leigh Webster never imagined
that her biggest worry on her African safari would be the handsome Jace Elliot, her tour guide. Laura's guardian, Lord Chad-
wick Hamilton, warns her of Jace's dangerous past; she simply
cannot resist the lure of his strong arms and the passion of his
Whispered Kisses.

KISS OF THE NIGHT WIND   (0-8217-5279-0, $5.99/$6.99)
Carrie Sue Strover thought she was leaving trouble behind her
when she deserted her brother's outlaw gang to live her life as
schoolmarm Carolyn Starns. On her journey, her stagecoach
was attacked and she was rescued by handsome T.J. Rogue. T.J.
plots to have Carrie lead him to her brother's cohorts who mur-
dered his family. T.J., however, soon succumbs to the beautiful
runaway's charms and loving caresses.

FORTUNE'S FLAMES   (0-8217-3825-9, $4.99/$5.99)
Impatient to begin her journey back home to New Orleans,
beautiful Maren James was furious when Captain Hawk delayed
the voyage by searching for stowaways. Impatience gave way
to uncontrollable desire once the handsome captain searched
her cabin. He was looking for illegal passengers; what he found
was wild passion with a woman he knew was unlike all those
he had known before!

PASSIONS WILD AND FREE   (0-8217-5275-8, $5.99/$6.99)
After seeing her family and home destroyed by the cruel and
hateful Epson gang, Randee Hollis swore revenge. She knew
she found the perfect man to help her—gunslinger Marsh
Logan. Not only strong and brave, Marsh had the ebony hair
and light blue eyes to make Randee forget her hate and seek
the love and passion that only he could give her.

*Available wherever paperbacks are sold, or order direct from the
Publisher. Send cover price plus 50¢ per copy for mailing and
handling to Penguin USA, P.O. Box 999, c/o Dept. 17109,
Bergenfield, NJ 07621. Residents of New York and Tennessee
must include sales tax. DO NOT SEND CASH.*

JANE KIDDER'S EXCITING
WELLESLEY BROTHERS SERIES

MAIL ORDER TEMPTRESS   (3863, $4.25)
Kirsten Lundgren traveled all the way to Minnesota to be a
mail order bride, but when Eric Wellesley wrapped her in his
virile embrace, her hopes for security soon turned to dreams
of passion!

PASSION'S SONG   (4174, $4.25)
When beautiful opera singer Elizabeth Ashford agreed to care
for widower Adam Wellesley's four children, she never
dreamed she'd fall in love with the little devils—and with their
handsome father as well!

PASSION'S CAPTIVE   (4341, $4.50)
To prevent her from hanging, Union captain Stuart Wellesley
offered to marry feisty Confederate spy Claire Boudreau. Little
did he realize he was in for a different kind of war after the
wedding!

PASSION'S BARGAIN   (4539, $4.50)
When she was sold into an unwanted marriage by her father,
Megan Taylor took matters into her own hands and black-
mailed Geoffrey Wellesley into becoming her husband instead.
But Meg soon found that marriage to the handsome, wealthy
timber baron was far more than she had bargained for!

*Available wherever paperbacks are sold, or order direct from the
Publisher. Send cover price plus 50¢ per copy for mailing and
handling to Penguin USA, P.O. Box 999, c/o Dept. 17109,
Bergenfield, NJ 07621. Residents of New York and Tennessee
must include sales tax. DO NOT SEND CASH.*